GOOD NEIGHBORS

GOOD NEIGHBORS

A NOVEL

SARAH LANGAN

THORNDIKE PRESS
A part of Gale, a Cengage Company

Thorndike Press, a part of Gale, a Cengage Company.

ALL RIGHTS RESERVED ₁/2022
Thorndike Press® Large Print Basic.
The text of this Large Print edition is unabridged.
Other aspects of the book may vary from the original edition.
Set in 16 pt. Plantin.

LIBRARY OF CONGRESS CIP DATA ON FILE.
CATALOGUING IN PUBLICATION FOR THIS BOOK
IS AVAILABLE FROM THE LIBRARY OF CONGRESS.

ISBN-13: 978-1-4328-8796-4 (hardcover alk. paper)

Published in 2021 by arrangement with Atria Books, a Division of Simon & Schuster, Inc.

Printed in Mexico
Print Number: 01   Print Year: 2021

For Clem

For Clem

FROM *BELIEVING WHAT YOU SEE: UNTANGLING THE MAPLE STREET MURDERS,* BY ELLIS HAVERICK, HOFSTRA UNIVERSITY PRESS, © 2043

Fifteen years after the fact, our preoccupation with Maple Street seems quaint. The details aren't especially gory. The number of casualties holds no candle to the Wall Street Blood Bath, or the Amazon Bombings in Seattle. What happened was horrific, but no worse than any calamity we now hear about five days a week.

Why, then, is it a national obsession? Why do people dress like its key players on Halloween? The Broadway show, *The Wildes vs. Maple Street,* has run for more than a decade. During this immersive theater experience, the audience is asked to choose sides in a reenactment, arguing to the literal death* over who was at fault, and who was innocent. Every year, another media outlet reinvents the facts of what happened on that hot August day; the

---

* It's role-play theater, the outcomes dependent upon how the game is played.

7

murderous fever that spread across an American neighborhood. Some blame the heat wave, the first of its kind. Some blame the sinkhole in the collapsed park nearby. Still others blame suburbia itself.

My theory is this: Maple Street has stuck with us because no one has adequately resolved the mystery. It's a nightmare in plain sight. We ask ourselves how an upstanding community could conspire toward the murder of an entire family, and we can make no sense of it.

But what if we've overlooked the most obvious explanation? What if the accusations lodged against the Wilde family were true? In other words, what if they had it coming?

THE STRANGERS
July 4, 2027

Map of Maple Street as of July 4, 2027
*116 Wilde Family
*118 Schroeder Family

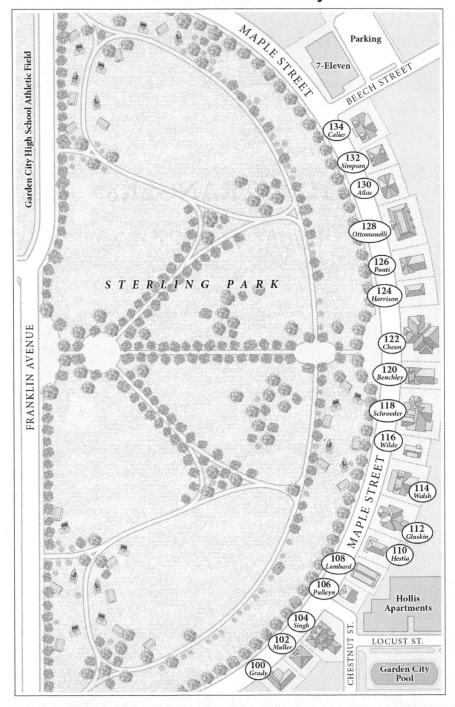

122 The Cheons — Christina (44), Michael (42), Madison (10)

124 The Harrisons — Timothy (46), Jane (45), Adam (16), Dave (14)

126 The Pontis — Steven (52), Jill (48), Marco (20), Richard (16)

128 The Ottomanellis — Dominick (44), Linda (44), Mark (12), Michael (12)

130 The Atlases — Bethany (37), Fred (30)

132 The Simpsons — Daniel (33), Ellis (33), Kaylee (2), Michelle (2), Lauren (2)

134 The Caliers — Louis (49), Eva (42), Hugo (24), Anais (22)

TOTAL: 72 People

116 Maple Street

Sunday, July 4

"Is it a party? Arc we invited?" Larry Wilde asked.

They weren't invited. Gertie Wilde knew this, but she didn't want to admit it. So she watched the crowd out her window, counted all the people there.

Gertie and her family had moved to 116 Maple Street about a year before. They'd bought the place, a fixer-upper, for cheap. They'd meant to renovate. To reshingle the roof and put in new gutters, tear up the deep-pile carpet and nail down bamboo. At the very least, they'd planned to seed grass across the patchwork lawn. But stuff happens. Or doesn't happen.

The inside of 116 Maple Street was haphazard, too. As a kid, you might have visited this sort of home on a playdate and intuited the mess as happy, but also chaotic. You had a great time when you slept over. You never worried about the stuff you had to bother with at home: making your bed, hanging your wet towel, carrying your dishes to the sink. Still, you wanted to go home pretty soon after, because even with the laughter, all that mess started to make you nervous. You got the feeling that the management was in over its head.

Maple Street was a tight-knit, crescent-shaped block that bordered a six-acre park. The people there dressed for work in business casual. They drove practical cars to practical jobs. They were always in a rush, even if it was just to the grocery store or church. They didn't seem to worry as much about their mortgages. If their parents were sick, or their marriages weren't happy, they didn't mention it. They channeled those unsettled feelings, like everything else, into their kids.

They talked about extracurriculars and sports; which teachers at the local, blue-ribbon public school were brilliant miracle workers, and which ones *lacked training via the social-emotional connection*. They were obsessed with college. Harvard, in particular.

The Wildes were different. With their finances out of sorts, Gertie and Arlo didn't have the bandwidth to obsess over their kids, and even if they'd had the time and mental

14

space, no one had ever taught them about *creative learning* and *emotional intelligence*, *healthy discipline* and *consistent boundaries*. They wouldn't have known where to begin.

The kids, Julia and Larry, made fart sounds in public, and also farted in public. Julia was fast. Their first month on the block, she stole her dad's cigarettes and taught the neighborhood Rat Pack how to French exhale. Larry was *quirky*. He didn't make eye contact and had a flat affect. When he thought the other kids weren't looking, he stuck his hands down his pants.

The Wildes knew that they'd been breaking tacit rules ever since arriving on Maple Street. But they didn't know *which* rules. For instance, Arlo was a former rocker who smoked late-night Parliaments off his front porch. He didn't know that in the suburbs, you only smoke in your backyard, especially if you have tattoos and no childhood friends to vouch for you. Otherwise, you look angry, puffing all alone and on display. You vibe violent.

Then there was Gertie. Before she met Arlo at the Atlantic City Convention Center, where he'd played lead guitar for the in-house band, she'd won thirty-two regional beauty pageants. Like a living Barbie doll, she still conducted herself with that same

15

pageant training: phony smiles, over-bright eyes, stock answers to questions that begged for honesty. The neighbors who'd tried to befriend her had mostly given up, under the misapprehension that there wasn't anybody home under all that blond. Worse, nobody'd ever told Gertie that mom cleavage isn't cool. She didn't know that when she wore her halter tops, painted gold chain-necklaces dangling between her breasts, she might as well have been waving a great banner to the other wives that read: INSECURE FLOOZY WHO WANTS TO STEAL YOUR HUSBAND AND MAKE YOUR KIDS ASHAMED YOU'RE NOT A 5'10", BLOND VIKING WITH PERFECT SKIN.

That summer of the sinkhole was the hottest on record. Because the center of Long Island was as concave as a red blood cell, there wasn't any mitigating wind. Just mosquitoes and crickets and living, singing things. The smell was saltwater sifted through too-ripe begonias.

The Wilde family had just finished dinner (cheese toast washed down with fizzy water; Trader Joe's frozen cherries for dessert). They'd heard the sounds of people, but hadn't noticed anything special until the notes of a Nirvana song carried through their windows.

I'm not like them, but I can pretend.

"Is it a party? Are we invited?" eight-year-old Larry asked. He lifted Robot Boy from his lap. Nobody was allowed to call it a doll or he got embarrassed.

Gertie hoisted herself to the window and pulled back the thin curtains. She was twenty-four weeks pregnant, so everything she did took a few seconds extra, especially in this heat.

It was seven o'clock exactly, and everybody out there seemed to have gotten the same memo, because they were carrying quinoa salad in Tupperware, or chips and salsa, or a sixer of artisanal beer. Gertie quick-counted: the Caliers-Lombards-Simpsons-Gradys-Gluskins-Mullers-Cheons-Harrisons-Singhs–Kaurs-Pulleyns-Walshes-Hestias-Schroeders-Benchleys-Ottomanellis-Atlases-and-Pontis. Every house on Maple Street was accounted for, except for 116. The Wilde house.

"If it was a party, Rhea Schroeder would have told me," Gertie muttered.

Twelve-year-old Julia Wilde lifted a single blond eyebrow. She wasn't pretty like her mom, and had decided early to contrast this by being funny. "Loooooks like a party. Smellllls like a party . . ."

Arlo poked his head next to Gertie's and

17

together they leaned. He was wearing just a Hanes T-shirt and cutoff Levi's, his sleeve-inked arms exposed. On the left: Franken-stein's Monster and Bride. On the right: the Wolf Man and the Mummy.

Gertie was bad at reaching out. At asking. But he was a warm person who'd always in-tuited when she needed to be reassured. He kissed the top of her head. "Fun," he said. "Should we go?"

"I'm game for a second dinner," she an-swered. "Guppy's growing bones today, I think."

"I don't understand. How is this not a party?" Larry called from behind.

"Sounnnnds like a party," Julia said.

It *was* a party, Gertie finally admitted. So why hadn't anybody posted about it on the Maple Street web group? Was Rhea Schroe-der mad at her? It was true they'd fallen out of contact lately, but that was because Gertie was exhausted most nights. This third baby was heck on her body. And Rhea's summer course load was full, plus she had those four kids. It had to be an accident that she hadn't been invited! Rhea would never intention-ally do her wrong.

She should have expected a Fourth of July party! She should have asked around. For all she knew, the neighbors had come up with the idea only this morning. There hadn't been time to post about it. Besides, you don't need a written invitation to a block party . . .

Do you?

Just then, Queen Bee Rhea Schroeder passed by their window. She was overdressed in a fancy Eileen Fisher linen pantsuit; white and stainless.

"Rhea!" Gertie called through the open window, her voice stage-loud, reverberating all through the street and into the giant park. "Hi, sweetie! How are you?" Then she waved. Big and pageant-winning.

Rhea looked straight into Gertie's window — into Gertie's eyes. The attachment between them felt wrong. Like a plug connected to a faulty socket, sparks flying. For just a moment, Gertie was terrified.

Rhea turned. "Dom? Steve? Did someone bring chicken or do I need to make a Whole Foods run?" Her voice faded as she walked deeper into the park.

"That was weird," Arlo said.

"She's spacey. Smart people are like that. She probably didn't see me," Gertie answered.

"Needs to get her eyes checked," Arlo joked.

"She sucks chocolate balls. So does her whole family. They're ball suckers," Julia said.

19

Gertie turned, hands resting on her full belly like a shelf. "That's terrible to say, Julia. We're lucky that people like the Schroeders even talk to us. Rhea's a college professor! You're not giving little Shelly a hard time, are you? She's too sensitive for that."

"Sensitive? She's a crazy bitch!" Julia cried.

"Don't say that!" Gertie cried back. "The window's open. They'll hear!"

Julia hung her head, revealing strong shoulders mottled with pubescent acne eruptions. "Sorry."

"That's better," Arlo said. "We can't be fighting with the All-Americans. You gotta be nice to these people. Make it work. For your own good."

"Totally," Gertie said. "Should we see what the fuss is all about?"

"No. It's too hot. Larry and I'd rather sit in the basement and eat paint like sad, neglected babies," Julia answered. Her normally curly-wild ponytail had gone limp.

"Lead paint tastes sweet! That's why babies eat it!" Larry announced.

"Paint's not really your option two here," Arlo answered as Gertie started for the kitchen, where she grabbed a half-eaten bag of Ruffles potato chips to offer the crowd. Then he leaned over the table, his voice soft. It wasn't threatening, but it wasn't *not*

20

threatening. "There's no option two. Get the fuck up and slap on some smiles."

"So, should we go?" Gertie asked.

"'Course!" Arlo answered, his voice soft and nice now that Gertie was back. He opened the front door. The Wilde parents took the lead, then the kids, who followed closely. Maybe it was coincidence, and maybe it wasn't. But a few feet out, someone switched the music to a song in a minor key. It was "Kennedys in the River," Arlo's number-eighteen Billboard hit single from 2012.

Don't know what love is.
Don't think it matters.
I got sixty dollars.
And a dream that won't shatter.

Arlo blushed. Hearing his own music was a complicated thing. His family knew this. As a result, Larry and Julia walked slower, like their feet had short shackles between them. Gertie held a smile tight as a zipper. One step after the other, they arrived at Sterling Park.

Sai Singh and Nikita Kaur glanced up from the barbeque. OxyContin-addled Iraq War veteran Peter Benchley ran his fingers along the tender edges of his residual limbs. The gang of kids, self-named the Rat

Pack, stopped jumping on the big trampoline someone had wheeled to the center of the park. Shouting something too distant to hear, Shelly Schroeder pointed straight at Julia.

The vibe wasn't hostile. After all her pageant training, Gertie was good at reading a room and she knew that. But something had changed since the last barbeque, on Memorial Day, because the vibe wasn't welcoming, either.

She tried to catch Rhea's eye but Rhea was busy talking to Linda Ottomanelli. There were people everywhere, any of whom she could have approached, but during her time on Maple Street, Gertie'd only ever felt comfortable with Rhea.

You're heavy under me
and above.
Crying in cemeteries
like it's love.

Arlo's song kept going. Shoulders hunched, the Wildes played captive to a low-class history they couldn't hide from:

I see my dad in you
all sweat and junk.
Baby, run away with me.
We'll shake these blues.

22

At last, Fred Atlas and his sickly wife, Bethany, picked their slow way through the crowd to greet them. "Dude! You made it!" Fred called as he clapped Arlo on the back. Then they went in for the bro hug. Bethany offered Gertie a winsome smile, her body brittle as a straw man's. The Atlases' dog, a rescue German shepherd named Ralph, nudged the whole group of them, trying to keep them safe and in the pack.

"You're the fijizzle, Fred. You, too, Bethany," Arlo answered. Then he and Fred took orders and went to the drinks table.

Over by the kids, Dave Harrison disconnected from the Rat Pack. He slid off the trampoline and jogged to Julia and Larry, handing each a sparkler. They lit them and Julia wrote *shart* in the air while Larry made circles.

"Can I have a burger?" Gertie asked Linda Ottomanelli. On the table were mini American flags on toothpicks, which people had stabbed into their sesame seed buns.

Linda took a second, eyes focused on the burgers, even though it was clear she'd heard. Gertie waited, still and tall. Wondered if she should have worn a shawl over her low-cut dress. But pregnancy was the only time her boobs got to be D cups. It was fun to show them off.

"Cheese or plain?" Linda asked at last.

"Plain? You're such a trooper to cook in this heat."

"I can't help it. I love making people happy. I'm just that kind of person. It could be a hundred and fifty degrees and I'd still do this. It's my nature. I'm too nice."

"I noticed that about you," Gertie offered, which wasn't true. She'd never noticed much of anything about Linda Ottomanelli, except that she was the kind of woman who wore a fanny pack to the grocery store and who got her politics from the social network. She got the rest of her opinions from Rhea Schroeder, whose word she treated like gospel.

Linda sighed like a martyr. "You must be hungry. I was always hungry when I was pregnant. I mean, I was carrying twins! But maybe you're not hungry, because you're so skinny. I hate you for being so skinny! How are you so skinny? You're like an alien!"

Gertie bit into the burger. Juice ran down her chin and then her cleavage. "I'm just medium skinny if you don't count the baby. I used to be really skinny, but it's too hard. You can't eat bread."

Linda's grin flickered.

"One time, I cut out carbs and dairy together, plus I did high-intensity interval training. You could do that if you wanted. I still have some of the books."

"Thanks," Linda said.

Over by the trampoline, Julia and Larry started jumping with the rest of the Rat Pack kids, and at the drinks table, Arlo was telling a story to a whole bunch of guys. Something about the clerk at the 7-Eleven who made everybody late for their trains because he was so bad at making change. "I just gave up. I said, 'Take it, ya rich bastard!'" Arlo drawled, then popped his Parliament Light into the corner of his mouth and made an air fist. His voice was louder than everybody else's, and they were standing back to get away from the smoke, even Fred.

Pretty soon, everybody was laughing from that first beer or wine, and clapping, and retelling some story from work, or what cute and mischievous thing their kids had done in their kindergarten class that had left the teacher flabbergasted. The Gradys, Mullers, Pulleyns, and Gluskins were planning a trip to Montauk. Margie and Sally Walsh were explaining how Subarus aren't really lesbian cars; they're just practical. The Ponti men compared biceps size. They were in ripping spirits, having come straight from the town baseball league's end-of-year keg party.

Food and second rounds began. The heat

stayed thick. At last, Gertie summoned her courage. She found Rhea Schroeder by her famous German potato salad. The secret ingredient came by way of her mother-in-law from Munich: Miracle Whip.

"Hi," Gertie said. "I saw you before but I don't think you saw me. So, hi again!"

Rhea frowned. She'd been doing that a lot lately. Probably, she was stressed out. Between the four kids and the full-time job, who wouldn't be?

"Has it really been since the spring? I miss our talks." Gertie willed her eyes to meet Rhea's. "Want to come over next week? Arlo'll make his pesto chicken. I know how you like that."

Rhea seemed to consider, but then: "I'm so busy at work. They can't spare me. I'm practically holding up the entire English Department. Plus, I've been planning things like this. Barbeques. I really don't have a second."

Gertie stepped closer, which wasn't her nature — she liked a wide swath of personal space. But for the sake of this new life she and Arlo were trying so hard to make work, for the sake of her friendship with this smart, funny woman, she pushed past her comfort zone. Her voice quivered. "Did I do something? I know you plan these things. I'm sure it was an accident, that you didn't invite us?"

Rhea affected surprise. "Accident? No accident at all!" Then she walked, white linen swishing over heels just high enough to keep the grass from staining.

With rod-straight posture and a cement smile, Gertie watched her disappear into the crowd. The party continued. And it was stupid. Pregnancy hormones. But she had to trace her index fingers along her under-eyes to keep the mascara from running.

That's when it happened.

The music cut to static. The earth rocked. Linda's red-checked picnic table with all those burgers started to shake. Gertie felt the vibrations from her feet to her teeth.

Early fireworks? . . . Earthquake? . . . *Shooter?*

There wasn't time to find out. Gertie did a quick take of the park; met Arlo's eyes. They fast-walked to the kids from opposite directions. Like magnets, the four snapped together.

"Street?" Gertie asked.

"Home!" Arlo shouted.

They hoofed it, running along the thick clovers and dandelions, past the trampoline and hem of pudding stone that bordered the park. With her pregnancy and bad feet, Gertie brought up the rear.

She didn't see the sinkhole as it opened.

Only watched later, from the footage people captured with their phones. What she noticed most was how hungry it seemed. The picnic table and all those burgers fell inside. The barbeque followed. Ralph the German shepherd got away from Fred and Bethany, banking the sinkhole's lips as they swelled.

A surprised *yelp,* and Ralph was gone.

By the time Gertie looked back, the hole had reached an uneasy peace with Maple Street. It had stopped growing, leaving just the people. Some had run, some had stayed frozen. Some had even hastened toward that widening gyre, their instincts all messed up.

And then there was Rhea Schroeder. In the stillness, she didn't turn to her family, whom she'd deftly rescued and corralled to the far side of the sinkhole. She didn't pet their hair or check in with her spouse like so many others did. She didn't cry or gawk or take out her phone. No.

She looked straight at Gertie, and bared her teeth.

Between them, a gritty smoke rose up. It carried with it the chemical scent of something unearthed.

SLIP 'N SLIDE

July 5–9

Map of Maple Street as of July 5, 2027
*116 Wilde Family
*118 Schroeder Family

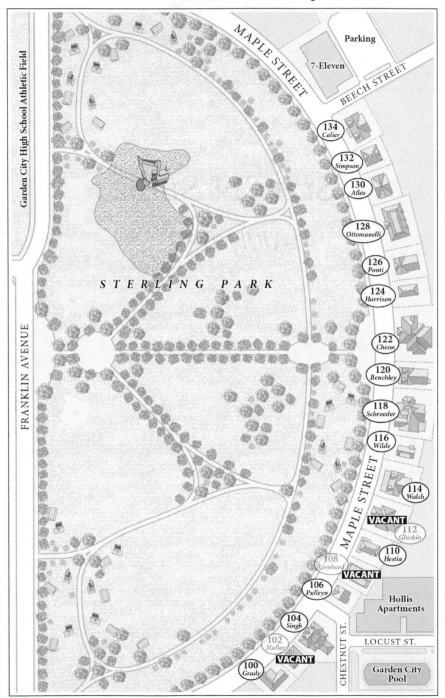

Index Of Maple Street's Permanent Residents As Of July 5, 2027

100 The Gradys — Lenora (47), Mike (45), Kipp (11), Larry (10)

102 VACANT

104 The Singhs-Kaurs — Sai (47), Nikita (36), Pranav (16), Michelle (14), Sam (13), Sarah (9), John (7)

106 The Pulleyns — Brenda (38), Dan (37), Wallace (8), Roger (6)

108 VACANT

110 The Hestias — Rich (51), Cat (48), Helen (17), Lainee (14)

112 VACANT

114 The Walshes — Sally (49), Margie (46), Charlie (13)

116 The Wildes — Arlo (39), Gertie (31), Julia (12), Larry (8)

118 The Schroeders — Fritz (62), Rhea (53), FJ (19), Shelly (13), Ella (9)

120 The Benchleys — Robert (78), Kate (74), Peter (39)

122 The Cheons — Christina (44), Michael (42), Madison (10)

124 The Harrisons — Timothy (46), Jane (45), Adam (16), Dave (14)

126 The Pontis — Steven (52), Jill (48), Marco (20), Richard (16)

128 The Ottomanellis — Dominick (44), Linda (44), Mark (12), Michael (12)

130 The Atlases — Bethany (37), Fred (30)

132 The Simpsons — Daniel (33), Ellis (33), Kaylee (2), Michelle (2), Lauren (2)

134 The Caliers — Louis (49), Eva (42), Hugo (24), Anais (22)

TOTAL: 60 PEOPLE

From *Newsday*, July 5, 2027, page 1

MAPLE STREET SINKHOLE

LONG ISLAND'S DEEPEST spontaneous sink-hole appeared yesterday, this time in Garden City's Sterling Park during holiday festivities. A German shepherd plummeted inside the 180-foot-deep fissure and has not yet been re-covered. No other injuries were reported.

This is the third sinkhole event on Long Island in as many years. Experts warn that more are expected. According to Hofstra University geology professor Tom Brymer, "The causes for sinkholes include the continued use of old water mains, excessive depletion of the lowest water table, and increasing periods of flooding and extreme heat." (See diagram, page 31.)

In conjunction with the New York Department of Agriculture (NYDOA), the New York Environmental Protection Agency (NYEPA) announced yesterday that Long Island's aquifers have not been affected. Residents may continue to drink tap water.

The NYDOA has closed Sterling Park and its adjoining streets to nonresidential traffic during an excavation and fill, which will begin July 7 and is slated to run through July 18. The nearby Garden City Pool will also be closed. For more on the sinkhole, see pages 2–11.

FROM "THE LOST CHILDREN OF MAPLE STREET," BY MARK REALMUTO, *THE NEW YORKER,* OCTOBER 19, 2037

It's difficult to imagine that Gertie Wilde and Rhea Schroeder were ever friends. It's even more ludicrous to think that the friendship would turn so bitter as to result in homicide.

Connolly and Schiff posited in their seminal work on mob mentality, *The Human Tide,* that Rhea took pity on the Wilde family. She wanted to help them fit in. But a closer look belies that theory. When the Cheon, Simpson, and Atlas families moved to Maple Street during the five years prior, Rhea did not attempt the same kinds of friendships. Though she welcomed the families with baskets of chocolate and perfume, by their own accounts, she was cold. "I think she was intimidated," Christina Cheon admitted. "I'm a doctor. She didn't like the competition for *most accomplished woman on the block.*" Ellis Simpson added, "Everybody from around here had family to help them out. That's why you moved to the suburbs. Free babysitting. I mean, it definitely wasn't for the culture. But the Wildes were alone. I think that's why Rhea plugged into Gertie. Bullies seek the vulnerable. You know what else bullies do? They trick people who don't know any better into believing they're important."

It's entirely possible, then, that Rhea had it out for Gertie from the start.

118 Maple Street

Friday, July 9

"It's a hairbrush night," Rhea Schroeder called up the stairs to her daughter Shelly. "Don't forget to use extra conditioner. I hate that look on your face when I hit a knot."

She waited at the landing. Heard rustling up there. She had four kids. Three still lived at home. She had a husband, too, only she rarely saw him. It's unnatural, being the sole grown-up in a house for twenty-plus years. You talk to yourself. You spin.

"You hear me?"

"Yup!" Shelly bellowed back down. "I HEAR you!"

Rhea sat back down at her dining room table. She tried to focus her attention on the Remedial English Composition papers she was supposed to grade. The one on top argued that the release of volcanic ash was the cheapest and smartest solution to global warming. *Plus, you'd get all those gorgeous sunsets!* Because she taught college, a lot of

Maple Street thought she had a glamorous job. These people were wrong. She did not correct them, but they were absolutely, 100 percent wrong.

Rhea pushed the papers away. Sipped from the first glass of Malbec she'd poured for the night, got up, and scanned the mess out her window.

She couldn't see the sinkhole. It was in the middle of the park, less than a half mile away. But she could see the traffic cones surrounding it, and the trucks full of fill sand, ready to dump. Though work crews had laid down plywood to cover the six-foot-square gape, a viscous slurry had surfaced, caking its edges. The slurry was a fossil fuel called bitumen, found in deep pockets all over Long Island. It threaded outward in slender seams and was mostly contained within the park, but in places had reached under the sidewalks, bubbling up on neighbors' lawns. There was a scientific explanation, something about polarity and metal content. Global warming and cooked earth. She couldn't remember exactly, but the factors that made the sinkhole had also galvanized Long Island's bitumen to coalesce in this one spot.

All that to say, Sterling Park looked like an oozing wound.

They never did find the German shepherd. Their theory was that a strong current in the freshwater aquifer down there had carried him away. They'd likened it to falling through ice in a frozen pond, and trying to swim your way back to the opening.

He could be anywhere. Even below her feet. Funny to think.

This evening, the crescent was especially quiet. Several families had left town for vacations or to get away from the candy apple fumes. Those who remained, if they were home at all, stayed inside.

Just then, pretty Gertie Wilde emerged from 116's garage. She carried a haphazardly coiled garden hose, its extra slack spilling down like herniated intestines. Gertie's big hair was coiffed, her metallic silver eye shadow so glistening that Rhea could see it from a hundred feet away. She stopped when she got to the front yard, hose in hand.

Rhea's pulse jogged.

Gertie peered inside Rhea's house, right where Rhea was standing. She seemed frightened and small out there, like a kid holding a broken toy, and suddenly, Rhea understood — Gertie had no outdoor spigot to which to attach her hose. She needed to borrow. But because of the way Rhea had acted at the Fourth of July barbeque, she was afraid to ask.

A thrill rose in Rhea's chest.

Margie Walsh screwed it up. She came out from the house on the other side of Gertie's and walked fast to meet her. Waves and smiles. Rhea didn't hear the small talk, but she saw their laughter. Polite at first, and then relaxed. They hooked the hose, then unrolled a plastic yellow bundle, running it the length of the Walsh and Wilde lawns. Water gushed and sprayed. A Slip 'N Slide. With the temperature lingering at 108 degrees, its water emerged like an oasis in a desert.

Pretty soon, Margie's and Gertie's kids came out. Fearless Julia Wilde gave herself ten feet of running buildup, then threw herself against the plastic and slid all the way down until she landed on grass. Charlie Walsh followed. Each took a few turns before they could convince rigid Larry. At last, he did it, too. But Larry, uncoordinated and holding Robot Boy, didn't build enough momentum. Only slid halfway.

The lawn got torn up. The kids got covered in mud and then hosed themselves off and started over. Tar from the sinkhole stuck to their clothes and skin like Dalmatian motley.

Now that the seal was broken, all of Maple Street opened up and shook loose. The rest of the Rat Pack and some of their parents streamed out. Laughter turned to screams of delight as even the grown-ups joined in.

Rhea watched through her window. The laughter and screams were loud enough that muffled versions of them permeated the glass.

Gertie didn't know any better. With her central air-conditioning broken, she'd probably gotten used to that slightly sweet chemical scent. The rest of them were stir-crazy. Figured, if a pregnant woman was willing to take the risk, the rest of them were pansies not to go out, too.

But anybody who watches decent science fiction knows that the EPA isn't perfect. The stuff her neighbors were rolling around in tonight might glue their lungs with emphysema twenty years from now. Even her husband, Fritz, who never had an opinion about anything domestic, had announced that if the hole didn't get filled like it was supposed to, they ought to pack the family into a short-term rental. He'd crinkled his nose that very first night it happened, grudging fear in his eyes, and said, "When it smells like this in the lab, we turn on the ventilation hoods and leave the room."

Rhea ought to warn these people. She was obliged, for their safety. But if she did that, they'd think she was a killjoy. They'd think it had to do with Gertie.

She played the conversation out in her head. She'd go out to 116, trespassing on Gertie's property, and urge them to go home. To take hot showers with strong soap. They'd put down their beers, nod in earnest agreement, wait for her to go away, and then start having fun again. Probably, they wouldn't say anything mean about her once she was gone. Not openly. But she knew the people of Maple Street. They'd chuckle.

She backed away from her window.

Returned to her papers. Sipped a little more Malbec as she reviewed the next assignment in the pile, which was written in 7-point, Old English font. It was about how the last stolen election had proven that democracy didn't work. *We needed to move into Fascism, only without the Nazis,* the student argued. She took out her red pen. Wrote, *What???? Nazis = Fascism; they're like chocolate and peanut butter!*

Between the papers, the people outside, her husband at work, and even her children upstairs, Rhea felt very alone right then. Misunderstood and too smart for this world. All the while, Slip 'N Slide laughter surrounded the house. It pushed against the stone and wood and glass. She wished she could let it in.

Like so many people who find themselves on the far side of middle age, Rhea Schroeder had not expected her life to turn out this way. She'd grown up only a few miles away in Suffolk County, the daughter of a court officer. Her mom died young, of breast cancer, and her dad had been the strong, silent type. He'd loved her enough for two parents. They'd shared an obsession with science fiction, and what she remembered most about him was the hours they'd spent on the couch together, watching everything from *The Day of the Triffids* to the poor man's *2001 — The Black Hole.*

As a kid, friends hadn't come easily for Rhea, but school had. She'd been the first in her family to graduate college — SUNY Old Westbury. Her first job out had been retail at the mall, like everyone else. Through connections, her dad got her into the officer's academy. Too many personalities. Too much phys ed. She didn't want to be a cop. She dropped out, floundered for a while, then stopped her dad one night before he headed down to tinker in his workroom. Told him about this PhD program in Seattle. People expressed themselves through imperceptible signs, she'd explained. She wanted to translate them. She wanted to solve the puzzle of what made people tick. Her dad was understanding. Hugged her and said he'd been selfish, suggesting detective work on Long Island because it was close. He hadn't wanted to lose her.

She'd been sad to leave him on his lonesome. But excited, too. Her life became her own. Five years later, the University of Washington awarded her a PhD in literature, with a focus in semiotics. Then they hired her, tenure track. The work was great. The students were great. The teachers were great. It was the happiest she'd ever been.

But then she got a phone call. Her dad died suddenly, of a disease she'd never imagined. Would never have suspected. In the shock of it, her work downslid. Her sadness felt impossibly heavy, a physical accumulation that she couldn't expunge. A knotty weight inside her that she came to think of as *the murk.*

Before her dad died, she'd never felt the need for other people. Never understood the phoniness of passing notes with fellow third-grade girls, or the high school version of it: trading clothes. Who were they kidding with all that desperate posturing?

Those friendships weren't real. In adulthood, the women her own age had seemed so alien, with their bad jobs and insecurity. She'd stayed away from them, afraid low self-esteem was contagious.

But after her dad, she'd had nobody to call on Sundays and remote-watch *Solaris* with. Nobody to visit over holidays, or shoot clay pigeons with at the Calverton Shooting Range. They'd had something easy and perfect between them. A stillness, into which no words had ever been necessary.

Seeking relief from her empty apartment, the blank page that was meant to be a book based on her dissertation, she started taking her students out for coffees and beers after class. Their cheerful passion distracted her. Made time pass a little easier.

By the next semester, she was starting to feel like herself again. Waking up wasn't as scary, because the memory of his passage didn't suddenly grab her like undertow at an ocean. She was starting to actually become friends with her students and the faculty, too. The murk lifted.

That's when the accident happened. A totally unforeseen, random event. Through no fault of her own, she wound up with a sprained knee. To this day, it ached in bad weather. The other person got hurt even worse. An accusation was lodged. False, but damning nonetheless. Rhea got demoted, which, in academia, is the same as being fired. And that was that. A stellar career, destroyed.

Her life got even emptier. No more coffees. No more beers. School and home and school and home. She felt bad about the accident. It was a terrible mistake that her mind wanted badly to undo.

That's when fate stepped in. Fritz Schroeder, a German chemistry PhD ten years her senior, moved into her apartment complex. He knocked, asking if she knew how to use the cheap convection ovens provided in each kitchen. Wearing a pink polo shirt with the collar pulled up, his khakis stained at the knees with brown chemical from the lab, he'd looked lonely. Helpless. Something about him was broken.

"Let's look it up!" she'd said, because at the time, she hadn't known how to use an oven, either.

A boyfriend hadn't been a part of her plan. She'd always pictured her future as an empty room, clean and bright; filled only with ideas and the long-distance adoration of colleagues. She hadn't imagined sharing her time with anyone but her dad. Not when she had so much important work to do.

46

But plans change. Careers crash and burn. She'd been so lost. Then along came Fritz: a brain in a box with occasional human urges. Unobtrusive but breathing. The perfect choice.

As a person, he had peccadilloes. He needed his shoes to be arranged in specific directions, and he couldn't stand tags in his shirts, and he had an earwax buildup problem, except he hated the sensation of Q-tips, so he used steamed washcloths. He ate whatever random items he found in her cabinets, including tuna out of the can with his fingers. It grossed her out so much that she learned to cook. When she bought clothes for herself, she bought new khakis and tagless shirts for him, too. It's nice to do things for other people, especially when they return the favor with wide-eyed gratitude. Besides, she'd had plenty of peccadilloes of her own. She'd just been better at hiding them.

About a year into dating, Fritz accepted a high-paying job formulating perfumes at the BeachCo Laboratories in Suffolk County. Sugary-smelling stuff with names like *Raspberry Seduction* and *French Silk* for the low-end Duane Reade market. She'd suggested marriage, even though she'd known that it wasn't right between them. They weren't close in an emotional way. Didn't confide in each other or talk about their upbringings. For instance, he had no idea about *The Black Hole,* or *the murk,* or the accident that had ruined her career.

Still, one evening he took her to the top of the Space Needle. Led her to the edge. "Even around people, I always feel separate," he'd explained without looking her in the eyes. "I'm lonely with you, too."

Her gag reflex had triggered. Was he dumping her? Didn't he know that without him, she had nothing? She'd seen him standing there, looking scared, and it had taken a great effort of self-control not to shove him right off the ledge.

He took the small, princess-cut ring out of his pocket. "But you take care of me. No one's ever done that. I'm a limited person. I think this is the best it will get," he'd said. "And I do love you."

"You know?" she'd answered with total surprise. "I think I love you, too." By then, tourists were watching, clapping. So they'd kissed.

The wedding was at the justice of the peace. No honeymoon. Just a flight to Long Island. She never got around to unpacking the box that contained the pieces of her unfinished book, because by then, she'd been pregnant with Gretchen.

In her pre-Fritz life, she'd debated abstruse theory with Ivy League geniuses. Now, she spent her days on Maple Street, alone with babies. These babies often cried. Sometimes she didn't know why. She didn't speak baby. It got hard. All that stuff she'd always thought was stupid, destructive female fantasia — stuff like friends and hugging and hot sex — she found herself watching *Terminator* and *Starman* and *The Abyss*, wishing she had it. Wondering what was wrong with her, that she didn't.

Fritz spent the time building his career. He only showed up on weekends and when his family visited from Munich. When he and Rhea were together, they cheered soccer games and dropped kids at the mall and paid bills in perfect agreement; partners who know each other like the lines of their own hands. But it was all surface. No laughs, no confidences, no companionship.

It was so lonely.

The first ten years, she cried a lot. But she kept it a secret, a hidden shame, because she was sure that her lackluster marriage was evidence of her own inadequacy. If she confessed her loneliness to Fritz, he'd know the truth: that she was messed up. He'd divorce her. His lawyer would unearth the accident. Everyone would know why she'd been fired from U-Dub. All of Maple Street. They'd look at her and see right through her. They'd know everything. Unthinkable.

And so, she dried her eyes. She buried her loneliness so deeply that she lost the knowledge of it. She stopped seeing it.

The following decade, she transformed herself into everything a suburban wife and mother ought to be. She organized all the block parties and made it her business to befriend every new addition to Maple Street with a basket of chocolate goodies and Fritz's newest perfume. She volunteered at the kids' schools and raised funds for iPads and art teachers. She resolved arguments and reported bullies. She sent out annual family Christmas cards with the Schroeders in matching sweaters, adopted class crayfish, and stayed up late most nights with her daughters, because one of them invariably had a crisis.

She worried about Gretchen's perfectionism, and Fritz Jr.'s shyness that he used to medicate with food and now he medicated with other things. About Shelly's instability, and Ella's stutter, which had since resolved. Four kids is a lot. But she did it well. She raised them popular and healthy and smart. Teachers complimented her. So did neighbors. She dressed like she was supposed to, in Eileen Fisher, and she cooked nutritious foods, and she kept her figure acceptably trim. She looked the part until she felt the part. Until she *was* the part.

Once her youngest started grammar school, she picked up work as an adjunct professor, teaching English Composition at Nassau Community College — the only job she'd been able to get after the stain on her record.

Mostly, these things were enough. But occasionally, the murk unfurled. She'd spy her reflection in a mirror when she was alone, mid-argument with an imaginary enemy (and there was always some jerk she was mad at), or else brushing Shelly's hair, and think: *Who is that angry woman?*

It frightened her.

When her oldest left for Cornell University last year, she'd taken it hard. She'd been happy for Gretchen, but her brilliant future had made Rhea's seem that much more dim. What was left, once all the kids were gone away, and she was left with a thirty-year-old dissertation and Fritz Sr., Captain Earwax Extraordinaire? She'd wanted to break her life, just to escape it. Drive her car into the Atlantic Ocean. Take a dump on her boss's desk. Straddle her clueless husband, who'd never once taken her dancing, and shout: *Who cleans their ears with a washcloth? It's disgusting!* She'd wanted to fashion a sling-shot and make a target range of Maple Street, just to set herself free of these small, stupid people and their small, stupid worlds.

It would have happened. She'd been close to breaking, to losing everything. But just like when Fritz moved into her apartment complex: fate intervened. The Wildes moved next door. Rhea couldn't explain what happened the day she first saw Gertie, except that it was magic. Another outsider. A beautiful misfit. Gertie'd been so impressed by Rhea. *You're so smart and warm,* she'd said the first day they'd met. *You're such a success.* Rhea'd known then, that if there was anyone on Maple Street to whom she could reveal her true feelings, it was this naïf. One way or another, Gertie Wilde would be her salvation.

Rhea had courted Gertie with dinner invitations, park barbeques, and introductions to neighbors. Made their children play together, so that the Rat Pack accepted the new kids on the block. It wasn't easy to turn local sentiment in Gertie's favor. The woman's house wasn't ever clean or neat. A pinworm outbreak coincided with their arrival, which couldn't have been a coincidence. The whole block was itching for weeks.

Worse, her foulmouthed kids ran wild.

Larry was a hypersensitive nutbar who carried a doll and walked in circles. Then there was Julia. When they first moved in, she stole a pack of Parliaments from her dad and showed the rest of the kids how to smoke. When her parents caught her, they made her go with them door to door, explaining what had happened to all the Rat Pack parents. Rhea had felt sorry for crying, confused Julia. Why make a kid go through all that? A simple e-mail authored by Gertie stating the facts of the event would have sufficed — if that!

It's never a good idea to admit guilt in the suburbs. It's too concrete. You say the words *I'm sorry,* and people hold on to it and don't let go. It's far better to pave over with vagaries. Obfuscate guilt wherever it exists.

The sight of all the Wildes in their doorways had added more melodrama than necessary. The neighbors, feeling the social pressure to react, to prove their fitness as parents, matched that melodrama. Dumb Linda took her twins to the doctor to check for lung damage. The Hestias wondered if they should report the Wildes to Child Protective Services. The Walshes enrolled Charlie in a health course called *Our Bodies: Our Responsibility.* Cat Hestia had stood in that doorway and cried, explaining that

53

she wasn't mad at Julia, just disappointed. Because she'd hoped this day would never come. Toxic cigarettes! They have arsenic!

None of them seemed to understand that this had nothing to do with smoking. Julia had stolen those cigarettes to win the Rat Pack over. A bid toward friendship. She'd misjudged her audience. This wasn't deep Brooklyn. Cool for these kids meant gifted programs and Suzuki lessons. The only people who smoked Parliaments anymore were ex-cons, hookers, and apparently, the new neighbors in 116. What she'd misapprehended, and what the Wilde parents had also missed, was that it wasn't the health hazards that bothered the people of Maple Street. If that were the case, they wouldn't be Slip 'N Sliding right now. It was the fact that smoking is so totally low class.

Despite all that, Rhea had stuck by Gertie Wilde until, one by one, the rest of Maple Street capitulated. It was nice, doing something for someone else, especially someone as beautiful as Gertie. There's a kind of reflective glow, when you have a friend like that. When you stand close, you can see yourself in their perfect eyes.

At least once a month, they'd drunk wine on Rhea's enclosed porch, cracking jokes about poop, the *wacky stuff kids say!*, and helpless husbands whose moods turn crabby unless they get their weekly blow-ies. This latter part, Rhea just pretended. She accepted Fritz's infrequent appeals for missionary-style sex, but even in their dating days, their mouths had rarely played a part, not even to kiss.

Rhea's attentions were rewarded. Eventually, Gertie let down her guard. Tears in her eyes, voice low, she'd confessed the thing that haunted her most: *The first, I was just thirteen. He ran the pageant and my stepmom said I had to, so I could win rent money. He told me he loved me after, but I knew it wasn't true. After that, I never said no. I kept thinking every time was a new chance to make the first time right. I'd turn it around and make one of them love me. Be nice to me and take care of me. So I wouldn't have to live with my stepmom. But that never happened. Not until Arlo. I'm so grateful to him.*

When she finished her confession, Gertie'd visibly deflated, her burden lightened. Rhea had understood then why people need friends. They need to be seen and known, and accepted nonetheless. Oh, how she'd craved that unburdening. How she'd feared it, too.

They built so much trust between them that one night, amidst the distant catcalls of children gone savage, Rhea took a sloppy risk, and told her own truth: *Fritz boom booms me. It hurts and I've never once liked it . . . Do you like it? I never expected this to be my life. Did you expect this, Gertie? Do you like it? I can tell that you don't. I wanted to be your friend from the second I saw you. I'm not beautiful like you, but I'm special on the inside. I know about black holes. I can tell you want to run away. I do, too. We can give each other courage . . . Shelly can't keep her hair neat. It goads me. I'd like to talk about it with you, because I know you like Shelly. I know you like me. I know you won't judge. Sometimes I imagine I'm a giant. I squeeze my whole family into pulp. I wish them dead just so I can be free. I can't leave them. I'm their mother. I'm not allowed to leave them. So I hate them. Isn't that awful? God, aren't I a monster?*

She stopped talking once she'd noticed Gertie's teary-eyed horror. "Don't talk like that. You'll break your own house."

There'd been more words after that. Pleasantries and a changed subject. Rhea didn't remember. The event compressed into murk and sank down inside her, a smeared oblivion of rage.

Soon after that night, Gertie announced her pregnancy. The doctor told her she had to stop drinking front-porch Malbec, so they hung out a lot less. She got busier with work and the kids and she'd played it off like coincidence, but Rhea had known the truth: she'd shown her true self, and Gertie wanted no part of it.

Retaliation was necessary. Rhea stopped waving at Gertie when she saw her, stopped returning her texts. When that didn't make her feel any better, when oblivious Gertie didn't even *notice* her coldness at the Memorial Day barbeque, she bit harder. She told people about Arlo's heroin problem. How that was the reason for the tattoos covering both his arms. He was trying to hide the scars. She told about Gertie and all those men. Practically a hooker. She told everything, to anybody who'd listen.

The more she told those stories, the more the past kaleidoscoped. She reevaluated every interaction she'd ever had with Gertie and her family, every judgment she'd ever cast.

For instance, Arlo yelled. His voice boomed. You could see Larry, who was sound-sensitive, shrink inside himself when that happened. But Arlo never checked himself. He just kept shouting, like he didn't care that he was hurting his own kid. What was even more alarming, Gertie had all kinds of rules. Unless it was baking hot, Julia couldn't wear short sleeves and shorts to-gether because they revealed too much skin. No bikinis, ever. If she changed clothes on playdates, she had to do it in the bathroom. She couldn't walk to the bus stop by herself, or even with Shelly. A grown-up had to ac-company. Why was she so nervous? What did she know about sexual threats on Maple Street that no one else knew?

In other words, why was Larry always jerk-ing himself?

Here's a story: One time, Rhea, Fritz, and the kids were at the Wildes' for dinner. It was its usual mess. Greasy dishes and thumbprints on the wineglasses. So Rhea'd washed while Arlo had cut vegetables, and Gertie had poached eggs. Even Fritz had helped out; for maybe the first time ever, he'd set the table. Until then, she'd never have guessed he knew how!

They'd all had so much fun and felt so close. On their way out the door, saying their good-byes, Arlo had leaned into Rhea, hug-ging her a beat too long. "Thanks for being so good to Gertie," he'd said, and then he'd kissed her cheek but gotten the corner of her lips, too. Dazed, she'd looked to Gertie to see if her friend was jealous, only Gertie'd acted like it was nothing.

At the time, Rhea'd felt flattered. But later

she'd wondered: Had Arlo been hitting on her? And if a wife can ignore something like that, what else can she ignore?

She'd related her observations to Linda Ottomanelli, who, most likely, had spread it around to the rest of the neighbors. And then, last week, she'd been planning the barbeque, and she'd known that if Gertie and her family showed up, that the neighbors might ask questions, compare stories. If Gertie found out about the rumors Rhea had spread, she might get mad enough to retaliate. Spill beans she had no business spilling. So she'd eliminated the problem, and excluded the Wildes.

The exclusion didn't feel cruel. It felt like self-preservation. And if the murk had unfurled again, more rage-filled than ever, at least she'd found the proper target against whom to direct it.

F, Rhea wrote along the top of the final paper. It argued that heroin should be legal, since it would garner more tax revenue to fight the immigrant crisis.

"Mom?" a voice asked. Thirteen-year-old Shelly stood in the kitchen, just at the edge of Rhea's alcove office, calling in. No one but Rhea was allowed in here. It was her solitary place.

"Yeah?" Rhea asked.

"Can I go outside with the Rat Pack?" Shelly was wearing her hair in a long braid down her back that ended at her hips. The edges were snarled. Even with a bottle of conditioner, tonight's brushing session would be a long one. "They've got this yellow thing. They're sliding on it."

"It's a Slip 'N Slide. They're from my day. I think they stopped making them 'cause kids crash and get paralyzed," Rhea answered.

"Oh. Can I go? I won't get paralyzed."

"You'll get cancer, which is worse. You know why that sinkhole happened? Because people like the Wildes don't pay taxes."

Shelly mumbled something under her breath. Presumably it was contrary. The girl was a disturbing cocktail of meekness and fury, uneven since birth, in ways that kept Rhea awake nights with worry.

"Your trouble is that you sympathize with everybody. But not everybody deserves it. Now help me out and set the table," Rhea said as she made a pile of her papers and set them aside.

Shelly's eyes got full. "She was my best friend."

"We've been through this. It's not Julia. It's her parents."

"You should trust me, Mom."

60

"I do trust you. I don't trust them. I've told you this. I don't like repeating it. I don't ever want you in that house, especially not sleeping over. Gertie and Arlo are strange. I don't like the way he looks at me. Do you understand what I'm saying?"

"Yeah. I know. You said. But he looks at me normal."

"He doesn't," Rhea said, which did not feel like a lie. More like a perceptive extrapolation. "He's got his eye on you. You're just too young to understand it. Do you promise you'll keep away?"

Shelly nodded, blushing softly.

Rhea set her papers aside and retrieved the Crock-Pot dinner she'd made. Shelly set the table: plates, utensils, and glasses. When both were finished, Rhea leaned down and held her daughter's slender shoulders, kissed her graceful neck.

Of all her children, Shelly was Rhea's greatest burden and her greatest gift. The child could be impossibly sweet, volunteering for the first flu shot of the season so her little sister could see that they didn't hurt. She cried at the sight of homeless people. She could also be terrible, hitting Ella hard enough to bruise, mouthing off to teachers, screaming loud enough to hurt Rhea's ears. She tended to fixate on Rhea's moods, twinning her own to them in ways that were both flattering and alarming. Though she was the brightest Schroeder child by far, Rhea had recently concluded that she would go to community college, and then live at home after graduating, too. People with her kind of fragility needed a strong foundation from which to grow. It would be Rhea's privilege to scaffold this child. To keep her close until she was strong enough to stand on her own.

"Forget the Slip 'N Slide. I'll take you and Ella to Adventureland tomorrow. All day if you want."

"Please let go of me," Shelly said.

So Rhea did. She walked into the hall and called up the stairs. "FJ! Ella! Dinner's ready!"

FJ came down first. He'd be starting at Hofstra University as a freshman in the fall. He was lean and muscular and so quiet that the family often forgot he was present. He'd been a submarine man all summer, surfacing at the house in the early hours, sleeping until noon. He was popular in school. Every night was another graduation party. But he managed to keep up his preseason lacrosse practice, so she figured: Why cramp his style?

Outside, the Rat Pack still skidded across the yellow plastic Slip 'N Slide. Everybody was eating ice pops, laughing hard, covered in tarry muck. It did look fun, she admitted. Rhea drew the curtains, so her own kids wouldn't feel excluded.

Nine-year-old Ella came down last. Like Rhea, she had hazel eyes, close-together features, and a habit of frowning when surprised or happy. "Sorry. I was reading!" Ella said. "Nicholas and Smike just ran away and I had to know what happens to Fanny. She's my favorite."

"Brilliant!" Rhea pronounced. "Harvard. I'm sure of it."

"I read that book," Shelly said. "Smike is an outcast. O-U-T-C-A-S-T. It's very sad. What did he have, Mom? Cerebral palsy?"

"Don't spoil it for your sister," Rhea answered. "And don't phony. You Netflixed the miniseries. The day you read a chapter book to the end is the day I have a stroke."

"Shelly watches *Buffy*. It's all she does is watch *Buffy the Vampire Slayer* on her screen in bed at night," Ella volunteered as she scooped half the stewed beef from the tureen. "She loves Angel the vampire like he's Dave Harrison and she makes me play Dawn and it's so lame!"

Shelly looked down at her plate. "I do *not* love Dave Harrison, and I *did* read *Nicholas Nickleby*."

If the family heard Shelly, none responded. The sounds were forks and spoons, rattling plates, water glasses lifted and replaced. Pretty soon, dinner was done. Rhea drained another glass of wine, her second, which was her limit on weekdays. FJ got up without asking. He seemed preoccupied by something. Probably a girlfriend. He was always having high drama with some girlfriend.

"Magic words," Rhea said.

"Can I go?"

"You may be excused."

"Can I go, too?" Ella asked.

Rhea nodded. "PJs, brushed teeth, and two more chapters."

"I'll do a book report. You'll love it so much! Because I'm a genius!" Ella cried, all enthusiastic sincerity, then bounced toward the stairs.

Last, it was just Shelly and Rhea. Rhea eyed her empty glass. With the heat this high, even the central air-conditioning couldn't combat it, and she'd lost her appetite. She poured just a little more, letting the sweetness sizzle on her tongue, then fade as a means of making it last. Shelly watched. Noticed, in ways the others never did.

"Mom?"

"Yup?"

"I'm out. Of tampons."

"There's nothing in Gretchen's old room?"

Shelly tugged on her loose navy blue skirt, which Rhea could now see was damp in the crotch. It was on the fabric of the chair she'd been sitting on, too. Red against tan. "It happened just now. I just realized. I'm sorry," she said.

Rhea sighed. Who doesn't know when they have their period? Things like this only happened to Shelly, which was why she feared the child would have a nervous breakdown, a kind of psychological aneurysm, before adolescence finished with her.

Tears rolled down Shelly's cheeks to the bib of her blue shirt. Her shame was in extreme excess, and this worried Rhea, too. "I'm so sorry. I don't know what's wrong with me."

"Calm down. Take a shower while I clean up. I'll brush your hair first, then I'll be ready to drive to the store. Does that work for you?"

Shelly clutched her mother's wrist. "Do you think we could take a break? For tonight? And not brush my hair?"

"You know what happens when we do that. Boomerang. It's ten times worse tomorrow. Just put in lots of conditioner. I'll make it as painless as I can."

After Shelly left, Rhea cleaned the kitchen

and turned the laundry. She could still see Maple Street out there. Imaginary conversations played. These were directed at the dumb neighbors, who were going to give their kids cancer, and at pregnant Gertie, who'd proven to be the worst kind of friend. And then at Fritz. And then at every rando in fragile Shelly's future, who might one day threaten her or make her feel bad, and then at her jealous accuser, who'd ruined her career, and finally, back at Gertie. Her face made expressions as if inhabited by ghosts.

At last, she started up the stairs.

Fritz Jr.'s door was shut. She knocked. He opened a crack. She could see an open bottle of Heineken on his night table. She handed him his uniform, cleaned, for practice. "You're going out tonight?"

"Yeah."

"Be smart. Don't drive."

"Okay."

"Promise."

He smiled small, his only way of smiling, sweet kid. "I will."

The next door belonged to Ella. It was open, the girl sleeping atop her bed in her street clothes, *Nicholas Nickleby* open on her chest. Rhea took off her shoes for her, but even with the air-conditioning, the heat was such that she didn't bother with a blanket.

Last, Shelly. Lost in thought, she broke her own rule and opened the door without knocking.

Shelly was standing in the center of the room, wet from her shower, big towel tightly cinched. Her taut body was precious as a colt's, with big feet and hands and eyes, the rest not yet grown in. She was perfect, and loved perfectly. And if she seemed *off* sometimes, too dark and too sad for a rational person her age, it wasn't Rhea's fault.

"Mom?"

Something gritty and inscrutable unfurled inside Rhea Schroeder. A thing that had piled over the years, growing too large to control, too heavy to jettison. A murky monster. Holding the brush, she walked inside and shut the door.

THIS ACCIDENT
July 10

Map of Maple Street as of July 10
*116 Wilde Family
*118 Schroeder Family

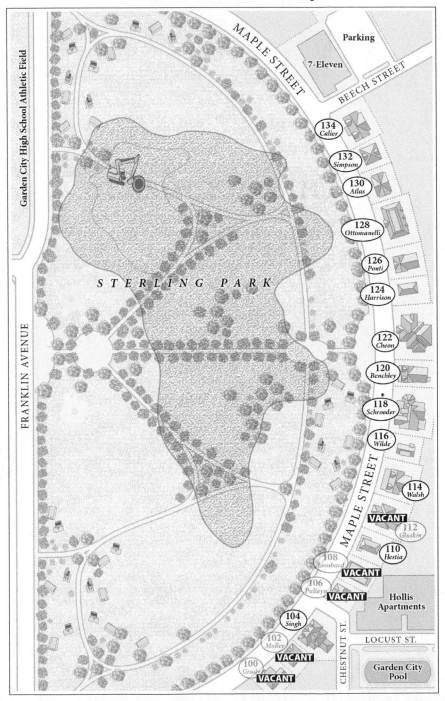

Index of Maple Street's permanent residents as of July 10, 2027

100 VACANT

102 VACANT

104 The Singhs-Kaurs — Sai (47), Nikita (36), Pranav (16), Michelle (14), Sam (13), Sarah (9), John (7)

106 VACANT

108 VACANT

110 The Hestias — Rich (51), Cat (48), Helen (17), Lainee (14)

112 VACANT

114 The Walshes — Sally (49), Margie (46), Charlie (13)

116 The Wildes — Arlo (39), Gertie (31), Julia (12), Larry (8)

118 The Schroeders — Fritz (62), Rhea (53), FJ (19), Shelly (13), Ella (9)

120 The Benchleys — Robert (78), Kate (74), Peter (39)

122 The Cheons — Christina (44), Michael (42), Madison (10)

124 The Harrisons — Timothy (46), Jane (45), Adam (16), Dave (14)

126 The Pontis — Steven (52), Jill (48), Marco (20), Richard (16)

128 The Ottomanellis — Dominick (44), Linda (44), Mark (12), Michael (12)
130 The Atlases — Bethany (37), Fred (30)
132 The Simpsons — Daniel (33), Ellis (33), Kaylee (2), Michelle (2), Lauren (2)
134 The Caliers — Louis (49), Eva (42), Hugo (24), Anais (22)

TOTAL: 52 People

From the University of Washington's faculty personnel file for Rhea Schroeder (née Munsen):

On February 12 of 2005, the accuser, Aileen Bloom (English Literature PhD candidate, 2008), claims that Associate Professor of Literature Rhea Munsen invited students of her graduate seminar, The Internet as Reverse Panopticon, for after-class snacks at the Hungarian Pastry Shop, a local hangout. As Dr. Munsen is a popular professor, the entire class arrived, whereupon they resumed the heated philosophical debate they'd been having in class. A truce was reached, but Ms. Bloom continued to argue with Dr. Munsen. The rest of the group approached the counter for pastries. Ms. Bloom then excused herself to the ladies' room.

Soon thereafter, Dr. Munsen followed Ms. Bloom to the ladies' room, whereupon she kicked in the locked stall door . . .

Maple Street Group Chat

July 5, 2027, 2:05 p.m. RheaSchroeder@smarty pants.com: Hey, guys. Anyone having reception issues with Verizon? I can't get a connection and I'm supposed to post grades tonight! ☺☺☺☺☺☹☹☹☹☹

July 5, 2027, 2:31 p.m. BTomato@gmail.com: Same here and I'm Sprint. Took me half an hour just to post this! ☺☹☹☹☹

July 5, 2027, 3:14 p.m. RheaSchroeder@smarty pants.com: Okay — I left the block and am getting a better signal. Verizon says it's the sinkhole. Lots of people have called. ☺☺☺☺☺ ☺☺☺☺

July 5, 2027, 3:21 p.m. Swish@mac.com: My cable's out, too. AT&T. ☹

July 5, 2027, 8:16 p.m. FATlast@sgghlaw .com: Check this press release put out by Hofstra: *Bitumen reported to interfere with satellite signals. . . .* No point calling your provider. It'll work again when the hole gets filled. ☺☺☺☹☹☹

July 6, 2027, 3:30 a.m. RheaSchroeder@smarty pants.com: WTH? They're telling us it's safe but there's something in the air that's strong enough to interfere with satellite relay? Pretty sure that's a vague description of radiation. Guys, stay inside. Windows closed. Lots of showers. Please! ☺☺☺☺☺☺☺☹☹☹

July 6, 2027, 8:04 a.m. Lottomanelli@captain .com: Rhea's right. I'm getting other people's phone calls when I do connect. It's weird. I didn't know cells could have crossed signals. ☹ ☹

July 6, 2027, 3:58 p.m. Jponti@gmail.com: How are we supposed to communicate? Sheets out windows? ☺☺☺☺☺☺☺☺☺☺☺☺☹

July 6, 2027, 4:15 p.m. JHarrrison@littledoves .org: It's getting worse. Had to post this from Little Doves School. Sprint says to just wait. So inconvenient!!!!!!!! ☹ ☹

July 7, 2027, 10:49 a.m. NKaur@hushedpuppy .com: Is this normal?

July 8, 2027, 3:16 a.m. RheaSchroeder@smarty pants.com: Nikita — no! It's not normal. Never happened here before. ☹☹☹☹

July 9, 2027, 10:02 a.m. GWilde@Century21. com: Hi guys! Rhea! You work so hard! I miss you! I miss all of you! So glad we sorta caught up at the BBQ! 😊 😊 😊 Just wanna let ya'll know about an open house I'm showing Saturday mourning at 1425 Savile Row, Glen Head, which is souper pretty to visit. Thought ya'll could like to take a trip away from this heat! 😊 😠 😠

July 9, 2027, 1:03 p.m. RheaSchroeder@smart-ypants.com: Please remember — this is a community site. No advertising! 😊 😊 😊 😊 😊 😊 😊 😊 😊 😠 😠 😠 😠 😠 😠 😠 😠 😠 😠

116 Maple Street

Saturday, July 10

"Triple digits for the twentieth day in a row. That's got to be some kind of record!" a static-riddled NPR host announced. Since the sinkhole, everything was static. "What's gonna happen next? Is it gonna rain frogs?" the host asked. Then she started talking about all the global warming refugees dying at the border. It was all so depressing that Gertie Wilde bellied up between the kids eating Froot Loops at the breakfast bar and switched *off*.

"I've got an open house in Glen Head. While I'm gone, I want you guys to go out and get some fresh air." She pointed at the trampoline on the Ottomanelli lawn, where all the kids were jumping. "Look. The Rat Pack's up and at 'em."

Julia didn't look. "Those nerds? Their parents won't let them go outside until the hole's filled."

"I guess last night we started something, 'cause there they are, Jules."

"It's too hot for outside," Julia answered as she stretched, still without looking. Her legs went one way, her arms the other, while her back arched. She was wearing Arlo's Hawaiian shirt that brushed the tops of her knees. Not exactly street wear, but the loose fabric would keep the heat rash away. Larry was the real problem. He was wearing green shorts and a green turtleneck, because it was the only green top he owned. He'd decided that green was organic, and would make him a real boy instead of an "aspy cyborg."

"I'm serious. Get your shoes on and brush your teeth," Gertie said. "I don't want you screaming like banshees, waking your dad as soon as I'm gone."

"Can I eat avocados for dinner? Are they expensive?" Larry asked.

"What?" Gertie asked.

"OMG, you are *so* weird. It's because they're green, isn't it?" Julia asked.

"He's not weird. Don't say that."

"Sor-ry, Lar-ry," Julia answered in singsong. "You're sooo not weird." Even this early in the morning, her curls were damp with sweat. "Why can't we wake Dad? He could take us to Jones Beach. That's outside."

"He's exhausted, Jules. Plus there's some kind of algae bloom. The beaches're closed," Gertie answered. "I left the Slip 'N Slide out

78

front and Margie Walsh said you can attach a hose to her house anytime. It'll be better than sitting in here getting baked. Which reminds me, you're not to play near the sink-hole. And you're to keep your eye on Larry."

"Why don't *you* take Larry?"

"You're talking about me like I'm not here," Larry said.

Holding her belly, which felt way too heavy for twenty-five weeks, Gertie faced the both of them. "Enough! Get your flip-flops and sun block! Now!"

"But they're mean!" Julia cried.

"You played with 'em last night. They're perfectly nice kids. Better than anybody from East New York, for sure."

"They were nice 'cause you bribed 'em with ice pops. Besides, Shelly wasn't there. It's Shelly that counts. The rest of 'em follow."

"Well, what did you do to Shelly?"

"Nothing!"

"So there's nothing to worry about!" Gertie announced as she squeezed her baby-bloated feet into a pair of black, size-ten Payless pumps. She tried her best not to notice the condition of the house: a pigsty decorated with puckered, home-stitched drapes and creaky estate-sale furniture.

"Fine, you dictator," Julia said.

"Good," Gertie answered.

Afraid he'd get teased, Larry left Robot Boy behind. The three of them headed for the front door. Once out, Gertie got into her dented red Passat. Larry and Julia made their way toward the Rat Pack.

Windows down, engine idling, Gertie watched.

The more Julia walked, the more she hunched. By the time she got halfway to the trampoline, even her head and pimpled neck hung heavy. "Wanna play on my Slip 'N Slide?" she called to the pile of kids.

Shelly Schroeder stopped jumping. Her hair was braided intricately, about ten of them all down her back. It had to have taken hours for her mother to set. "When's your mom gonna get that crappo car fixed? It looks like it's made outta clay," she hollered.

Gertie stiffened. Replayed the words, to be sure she'd heard them right. How could such viciousness have come from sweet Shelly Schroeder? This was a girl who'd set Gertie's table for dinner without asking, who used to watch the *Robot Boy* show with Larry when nobody else'd had the patience. A girl who squirmed at *Animals* on *National Geographic* on the TV because she hated to see the otters get hurt. What had gotten into her?

Julia stole a glance back at Gertie. She

80

and Larry looked so flummoxed and out of place. *Help me,* Julia's expression pleaded.

Gertie rolled down her passenger-side window and leaned, but the seat belt caught her belly and held her. She used the time to try to think of something to say.

What was going on here?

The last time Gertie'd spent a serious chunk of time with Rhea had been back in April. Rhea drank too much wine and didn't eat enough pesto that night. Gertie'd done the opposite because she'd just found out she was pregnant. The two of them wound up on the front porch, Rhea in tears, mumbling gibberish. For her own good, Gertie'd cut her short. Called it a night. They'd still been friendly the next morning. Waving and texting and such. No overt hostility. She couldn't imagine Rhea held a grudge over something so small.

But then, what was the problem? Why all this attitude?

It had taken all her courage to approach Rhea on the Fourth of July. She'd felt like a beggar with that half-eaten bag of Ruffles, crashing a party right in front of her own house. *Was it an accident that we weren't invited?* she'd asked straight-out.

Of course! I'm so sorry! she'd honestly expected Rhea to answer. *We forgot and used an*

81

old chat chain! Then they'd laugh and catch up like old times, because suburban college professors aren't supposed to be petty. They don't invent problems and instigate pointless fights. They're bigger than that, aren't they?

No accident, Rhea'd said. Then she'd grinned this stark, toothy grin, and Gertie'd been totally gutted. It had hurt to see that kind of grin, because she'd known what it meant. She'd seen it before, on her crazy stepmom, Cheerie, who'd kept Prozac in the Vegas-era Elvis sugar jar, and she'd seen it on fellow pageant contestants, right before they Vaselined somebody's wig, and she'd seen it on the handsy judges whom Cheerie had liked so much. *Hunters* grinned like that.

Instead of letting her walk away, Gertie could have followed Rhea that day. Challenged her. But in all her time dealing with hunters, she'd learned a very serious golden rule: never confront. It doesn't make them stop. It just whets their appetite, like blood in the water.

No accident.

Gertie hadn't wanted to believe that Rhea was a hunter. Even after Rhea'd walked away, Gertie'd tried hard to pretend that they were still great friends. Rhea was distracted, or playing a joke, or heck, had a brain tumor.

When the sinkhole opened, she'd figured

it would put the entire neighborhood on a reset. A real and serious thing had happened, rendering everything before it inconsequential. Rhea couldn't still be mad after something like that! Probably, she hadn't been mad to begin with. Gertie was just paranoid. You see enough bad guys in your life, and you start to imagine them. You forget that the world is mostly good.

That's the story she'd told herself, anyway.

But, watching Shelly Schroeder spew vitriol at Julia on that trampoline, the truth came hurtling back. Rhea hadn't been making a joke, and she hadn't been confused. She'd been intentionally cruel on the Fourth of July. She'd turned on Gertie, even though they'd shared and confided so much. And now, her daughter Shelly, the leader of the neighborhood Rat Pack, was being cruel to Julia on purpose. Why was this happening? Gertie didn't know. All she knew was that she felt bad. And something deeper than bad: She felt scared. Full-on panic.

Stuck in her seat belt, Gertie noticed then that all the kids were looking at her. Julia and Larry and the Rat Pack, and even Shelly from up high. They seemed somber. Overwhelmed by their own emotions the way all kids get overwhelmed when their thoughts are too big for their bodies. *I'm the grown-up here. I should say something,* she thought. But she didn't have the words. Had never had the words in moments of confrontation like this. And so, feeling frightened and awful and heartsick, avoiding Julia's eyes, Gertie punched the gas.

Gertie's car pulled out. Julia watched it go. Just like that time with the Parliament Lights, her mom had offered her up like a sacrifice. A shield to take the blame. And now the kids knew that no one had her back. They could do anything they wanted.

The Rat Pack's eyes were on her, boring through. She didn't know why they'd started hating her. Only that Shelly had spear-headed it. Shelly, who'd been her best friend since practically day one. They used to prank Dave Harrison, pretending to be sexy Russian hookers. He figured it out, but let them keep doing it because it was so funny. Especially Shelly's spelling: *Chello! I want the rubles for the intercourse!? Jes?* They used to stay up nights, talking about God and death and their dreams. Shelly wanted to be a doc-tor with a practice on Boylston Street, wher-ever that was. Julia didn't know her dream yet. Regarding sex, Shelly wanted to wait until college. Julia thought it was okay to do before, but she didn't know how it would work, because she hadn't had her period yet and didn't know how anybody was supposed to find a vagina amidst all that skin down there. Out of boredom one day, they'd discovered that it felt super good to straddle the arms of soft chairs. They also both liked sugar and lemon on their pancakes, not syrup.

They'd been inseparable. Spent practically a whole school year together. And then spring came. Sleepovers ended. Julia's texts suddenly went unanswered. Shelly wasn't ever home when Julia stopped by. One time in June, when Julia'd tried to join the Rat Pack in the park, they'd all run away from her. She'd waited, hoping it was a game. They must have sneaked behind the houses to avoid her, because pretty soon, she heard them all playing *Deathcraft* in the Ottomanellis' den.

After that, it was over. Shelly pointed and called *Loser* when she saw Julia. Everybody went along with it. If she caught Dave Harrison or Charlie Walsh on their own, they might give her a wave, but otherwise, nothing.

The most upsetting part wasn't getting dumped. It was the way Shelly turned evil. She used to be this really nice person who could read people easy as tarot cards. It was a kind of superpower. Julia'd be thinking about Larry, or about the possibility that the world was going to end before she ever even had the chance to vote. There'd be famine and war and girls would get bought and sold like sandwiches. She'd be all worried about stuff like that, and Shelly'd *feel* it. *Relax,* she'd say. And then, as a joke, *We'll always have Maple Street.* In the old days, she'd defended kids like Larry. Told the whole school bus that if anybody imitated him, she'd reach down their mouths and pull out their stomachs. Back then, she'd only used her powers for the forces of good.

It was different now. She ruled the Rat Pack with an iron fist. Once, Julia heard her screaming at them out her window. She'd yelled so much her face turned red. The freaky part: it looked the same as crying. The older kids had walked away, but Lainee Hestia and Sam Singh had stuck around for it, covering their ears and balling themselves small. It's wrong to do that; to go after the weak.

Julia never told her parents what happened. She was afraid that if she did, her mom would ask uptight Rhea about it, and Rhea'd know exactly what to say: Julia's not good enough at spelling. She doesn't take seat belts seriously. Remember how she smoked? She's a bad influence. And then Gertie would go crazy. She'd love Julia even less than she already did.

Julia wanted to run home right now. Hide in the hot kitchen with Larry until her dad woke, like she'd been doing all summer. But there was a breeze out here. The trampoline looked fun. A Slip 'N Slide would be even better. Bathing suits and cold water. Laughter and ice pops. She had a right to those things, even if she wasn't good or pretty or going someplace important like the rest of them. Even if she was just Julia.

All eyes were on her. She didn't know what else to do. She stood her ground.

"How much does your mom's car cost? Think I can buy it for a Snickers?" Shelly asked from the center of the trampoline. The rest of the Rat Pack sat on the edges or else stood just outside.

"It's a car. It's doesn't have to be pretty. It just has to work," Julia answered. "I don't know why you're so mean. I never did anything to you."

"I'm not mean. You're just a loser. And losers aren't allowed," Shelly answered. She was wearing a Free People plaid linen jumpsuit and matching long-sleeve linen blouse underneath, Free People socks, probably even day-of-the-week Free People underpants, too. For the heat, it was a lot of clothes.

"That's not even your trampoline. It's the Markles's," Julia said, tugging on her Hawaiian shirt.

"So?" Shelly asked as she started to bounce. She looked angrier than usual, which was saying something. Her elaborately braided hair rippled in dyssynchronous arcs like each one was alive. The kids sitting around her bobbed like buoys.

"So, you guys wouldn't even be allowed out here if it wasn't for my mom's Slip 'N Slide. She's the one who chilled your uptight parents out," Julia called out across the Ottomanellis' perfectly green lawn.

"We're still not allowed. Shelly sneaked so I sneaked," little Ella announced.

"Shut up," Shelly answered as she started jumping: *Plat! Plat! Plat!* It echoed, that sound, and reminded Julia of all the stuff kids around here bragged about, like memberships to the town pool, season ski-lift tickets, and buttered popcorn with M&M's mixed in at the movies. That trampoline was money.

"Go home!" Shelly shouted from the air. "The whole reason we have that stupid sinkhole is because your parents don't pay taxes!"

"Just go home," one of the Ottomanelli twins added. She thought it was Michael, the mean one, until the other one added, "No food line feet allowed, you dirty Wildes!" So, probably, that one was Michael. They were dressed in identical Islanders jerseys, only today Michael wore glasses and Mark had on blue-tinted contacts. Nobody in the Rat Pack could tell them apart, so they just got called Markle.

"Go home!" Lainee Hestia chimed, which hurt the most, because Lainee was a total weenie. We're talking dressing-up-like-Rey-from-*Star-Wars*-for-class-photos, bringing-a-light-saber-to-field-trips, owning-over-a-hundred-action-figure-erasers—level weeniedom.

"I'm not on your property. My parents bought our house and it's ours and I have a right to stand on this sidewalk like anybody else," Julia said.

Shelly jumped harder. The springs screamed. Sound-sensitive Larry covered his ears. The kids sitting around the edges — the Markles, Ella Schroeder, and Lainee Hestia — maneuvered toward the platform's edge and clung to its circular rail while the rest of the Rat Pack — Sam Singh, Dave Harrison, and Charlie Walsh — huddled with wary expressions a few yards away.

Plat! Shelly hit the tramp, then flew back up again: "GO! AWAY!" *Plat!* She landed. Then up again, her jumpsuit big as a sail: "GO AWAY!" Her voice was high-pitched and happy and sad all rolled into one.

Plat!

Up again. Julia saw something bright and red and wrong between Shelly's spread legs. "GO!"

Plat!

"THE FUCK!"

Plat!

"AWAY!"

Plat!

Shelly came down hard that last time, catapulting her little sister right out of the trampoline. Ella landed on her hands and knees. "I'm telling!" she wailed.

"Don't you dare —" Shelly started.

"— I'm telling Mom you came out here even though you're not allowed and you made me come, too, and now I'm hurt and she'll be so mad at you!" Ella screeched with fake tears.

Shelly's chest puffed out. So did the veins on her neck. Between her spread legs was a thin red stain. Julia looked away because it was too embarrassing. Maybe that was why no one else pointed it out, either.

"Why is Shelly bad now, Julia?" Larry

asked without whispering or even lowering his voice. His green turtleneck was tight, his face blotchy red from heat.

Shelly shined her fury in Larry's direction, and vented it. "Aspy," she hissed.

Larry squinted, which was his way of showing hurt feelings.

"My mom said he's gonna get kicked out of normal school," said Shelly. "He's draining all the resources."

"I'm leaving school?" Larry asked.

"Call him Robot Brother. That's his nickname. And he's not aspy. He just hates you, because you super-suck a bag'a dead dicks," Julia said.

Shelly flipped off the tramp and ran, stopping just short of knocking Julia down. Tiny veins throbbed across her eyes like blood mites. "Face or body?"

"Shelly, stop," Dave Harrison called.

"The eight of us took a vote," Shelly answered without taking her eyes off Julia. "We all agreed. Nobody talks to the Wildes . . . So, which is it, Julia?" she asked, like they were strangers. Like they'd never promised during sleepovers, while their drunk moms had guzzled wine on the porch under fake tiki torches, that they'd be best friends forever.

"Our air-conditioning's gone to shit," Julia

panted. "We have to be out here. I don't want to fight and I don't want to be in a place nobody wants me but it's too hot. Whatever your problem is, get over it." She pointed at the deflated yellow mat on her dried-up lawn. "We could all Slip 'N Slide. You could, too, Shelly. Plus my mom went grocery shopping and there's Eggo pancakes."

Shelly's frown eased.

"We won't tell your mom. She'll never even know you came outside," Julia said. "It's totally early. She's sleeping for another hour at least." *Hungover,* Julia meant, but she didn't say it.

Shelly let out a long sigh, and Julia knew she was winning. *Please, please, please let this turn out okay,* she silently prayed. *Let Shelly act like a human being again, and let the neighborhood kids not tease anymore, and let the Slip 'N Slide be awesome, so I can have just ONE GOOD DAY.*

But then Larry opened his big mouth. "Shelly can't be on our Slip 'N Slide, Julia. Robot Boy says no bullies in school."

Shelly spun. In three strides, she was toe to toe with Larry. "Face or body?"

Larry's eyes engaged a point just over Shelly's left shoulder. "You are a bad person," he said in monotone and without contractions, which meant he was terrified.

"Okay, I'll pick for you," Shelly answered as she flicked her index finger at his nose, then his small chest, then his nose, and back to his chest again, singsonging: *"My-mother-punched-your-mother-right-in-the-nose . . .*

"What-color-was-the-blood?" Shelly continued, nose-chest-nose-chest. It was so weird. What thirteen-year-old plays *It*? All the other kids watched. Except for the mean Markle, their faces registered discomfort.

"R-E-D spells red and you are it!" Shelly finished, pointing at Larry's nose. Then she smiled. "Face! I'll break your nose."

Rocking, Larry reached into his pants and yanked his willie. Which meant he was about a breath away from a full-on meltdown — the kind that lasted for hours, and ruined all the weeks of progress and energy Julia had put into him, trying to get him normal.

Shelly grinned, teeth bright and fancy black hair shining.

Stuff went out of focus for Julia. She stopped hearing the morning heat-song of the cicadas, and the soft, uncomfortable shuffles of the rest of the Rat Pack. She bent low and rammed, headfirst, into Shelly's skinny belly.

"Uumph!" both girls cried.

Julia's neck made a *crack!* It hurt so much

it felt like it was broken, and when she stood right again, her throat swelled.

Shelly staggered. Tears of pain welled in her giant blue eyes. "You slut! You don't hit me! Nobody *ever* hits me!"

"You don't touch other people's brothers," Julia rasped through her hurt throat. "Every dumb fuck with a brain cell knows that in East New York. He's mine to beat up, not yours."

By now the rest of the Rat Pack had surrounded them.

"Girl fight! Girl fight!" the Markles chanted.

Charlie Walsh, Sam Singh, and Dave Harrison were watching, too. Larry stayed where he'd been, rocking and afraid. But at least he'd taken his hand out of his pants.

"Stop," Julia panted. But Shelly didn't stop. She came at Julia, grabbing her shoulders in front, shoving a foot behind, and trip-pushing her down. Then she straddled her. Julia wriggled but couldn't get out from under. Shelly's fist slammed down, smashing Julia's cheekbone so hard she saw white sparks.

"You do it with your daddy. You're his ghetto girlfriend!" Shelly screamed.

Another meaty *punch!* Julia jolted to swelling, impossible pain. "Help!" she begged.

At last, Dave Harrison broke away from the group. He wrapped his arms around Shelly's waist. Chubby Charlie got her by the arms. They held her while Julia scrambled out from underneath.

Stronger than both boys put together, Shelly broke away. She was crying and screaming, and even laughing. "He looks at me!" she shouted, the red plainly visible now. It etched a fibrous, marker-like caterpillar along the loose linen seam of her crotch. "I know because at sleepovers, he was always looking at me!"

"Time-out," Julia rasped, staggering. "You're lying. It's too far."

Shelly charged.

Julia only had a second, and for true, she was scared another blow from Shelly would break her neck. "Perfect hair. Perfect Free People. But you're all messed up inside. Your period's bleeding through," she croaked in a whisper you had to listen for to hear.

The words sank in. Shelly's fists unclenched. Julia kept going, saying all the bad thoughts she'd never voiced. All the things you think when you're alone and you're mad, and you fantasize about telling somebody off. The things you'll never really say, because they're way too mean.

"My dad doesn't look at anybody but my

mom. You're just jealous because I have a dad. Yours is just some ghost who sleeps in your house. Your mom treats you like you're crippled. She doesn't hear and she doesn't see. You're not a person to her. Just a doll she dresses up and shows off. You could be made of maggots on the inside and she wouldn't care so long as your hair's brushed."

Shelly paled. Her under-eyes, by contrast, got more purple.

"Shelly, what is that? Are you hurt again?" Ella asked, pointing at Shelly's low-slung linen jumpsuit. The stain. Now that Julia had named it, everyone could see it for what it was.

"It's her crimson tide," a Markle answered.

Shelly's mouth wrenched open as if to gag, but no sound came out. It was a grisly thing to see, like invisible fingers were strangling her. Then, croaking words, soft and hideous: "It's not a period. Your daddy did me."

"Liar," Julia answered, mad and shaking and sick to her stomach, because she'd never been in a fight so mean. *So low.*

To hide the red, Shelly fanned her hands in front of her, and then behind. And then one hand in front and the other behind. But her jumpsuit hung too loose. You could still see.

Someone laughed. And then somebody

else. And then even Shelly's own sister Ella was laughing. The laughter got louder. It wasn't fun-laughing. It was scared, pressure-release-laughing, like the soulless sound a filled balloon makes when you let it go and it zings across a room. The whole Rat Pack, in hysterics. Everybody but the Wilde kids, who were horrified.

FROM *INTERVIEWS FROM THE EDGE:*
A MAPLE STREET STORY,
BY MAGGIE FITZSIMMONS,
SOMA INSTITUTE PRESS, © 2036

"It started long before that child fell down the sinkhole . . . The Wildes were strange. I never liked them. No one did, except for Rhea. Which is ironic." — Jill Ponti, Sterling Park

Sterling Park

The Rat Pack's laughter sagged. They watched as Shelly, fanning her linen jumper's backside with her hands, disappeared into her house. After that, it was just the Markles still laughing, plus Lainee Hestia, who matched her titters to theirs, trying to make sure she stayed on the inside of the joke.

"She's hurt?" Ella Schroeder asked.

The Markles heard that and got quiet. Lainee emitted one last, humorless shriek.

"It's a period. No big deal," Dave said.

"Does she need a doctor?" Ella whispered. She was built small like her mom, and even though she was upset, her squint expressed anger. She had resting rage face.

"It's okay. She's okay. It's normal," Julia answered. Her throat hurting, her voice was just a sandpaper whisper.

Ella started crying. She ran for 118 Maple Street. She didn't shut the front door behind her after she got inside. It stayed wide, offering a full view of the Schroeder hallway. Clean wood floors, a secretary with mail neatly stacked, an indigo and orange Persian rug.

Julia expected a grown-up or big sibling to come out. *What the hell? You don't laugh at someone's period! they'd shout. What's wrong with you?* She felt she deserved to be yelled at. They all did, no matter what Shelly had done.

The rest of them must have felt the same way, because the Rat Pack stood very still. Seconds passed. A full minute. No one came out of Shelly's house. Somehow, that was worse.

Sam Singh broke the pause. "I didn't do anything!" he hollered, then jogged back toward 104 Maple Street, where he lived. Lainee Hestia wandered away next, slow and seemingly oblivious. By the time she was at her house, she was softly humming the *Star Wars* theme. The Markles climbed back on their trampoline. "She's gonna pay for this," Michael Ottomanelli threatened while inspecting the tiny red speck of blood that had, at some point, stained the mesh. "It's gonna be a huge dry-cleaning bill," Mark added.

Julia stayed. The heat made beads of sweat

along her brow. She stood on one foot, then the other, looking into that silent, open house. She'd never been in a real fight with anybody but her brother before. Never hit someone or gotten hit. Where do you go after something like that happens? Who do you become?

Dave Harrison and Charlie Walsh were the last to go. They looked her up and down. She'd worn her dad's Hawaiian shirt because she thought it made her look grown up. But maybe it just looked like she couldn't afford clothes.

"It's head games all summer with her," Dave Harrison said. "I can't take it another second."

"We're going to a place Shelly can't follow," Charlie Walsh said. "Exploratory mission. Wanna come?"

"Me?" Julia asked.

"You," said Charlie Walsh, with his bowl haircut and chubby cheeks. When she first moved here, he'd told everybody that he had a crush on her. It hadn't felt like a real crush. He hadn't known her well enough. As girls go, she'd been the only option, given Dave liked Shelly, and Lainee was . . . Lainee.

"Where?" Julia asked.

"The sinkhole. Shelly's mom would kill her."

"Is it safe? Should we go?"

Charlie extended his hand. She took it. Held it a little longer than she needed to, because it made her feel calm. "I don't care if it's an asbestos mine, long as it's away from Shelly," he said.

They started walking. She waved to Larry and he followed. Pretty soon, it was four astride. It felt good to get away from Shelly's open house, so still and watching, if houses can watch. Accusing, too, if houses can accuse.

"Don't feel bad. She had it coming. We're all sick of her," Charlie said.

"Nobody has that coming," Julia answered.

"She did," Dave said. He seemed especially sad, as though he were betraying Shelly by saying this.

They stopped at the curb. It felt momentous. Larry traversed it first. Then they were all on the grass, headed into the place they weren't allowed, to get away from a girl who'd turned mean, and from themselves, too.

Into Sterling Park.

As they walked, shoulders touched. Arms swung and caught hands and let go again. Cicadas screamed and gnats swarmed. But not the birds. She hadn't heard birds in a while. The ground got sticky the closer they got. It was strange, but she had the feeling that something out there was watching them. Listening and waiting.

Dave stopped short at the orange traffic cone barrier.

The hole.

It was covered by a giant two-inch-thick wood slab with the rough dimensions of a small bedroom. Beside it was a John Deere truck-bulldozer-kind-of-thing that read COMPACT EXCAVATOR in massive yellow letters across its green side. The crane's retracted hook had come loose from its industrial-sized clip, so that it swung in tiny arcs just over the slab.

"My dad's got this get-rich-quick scheme," Dave said as he walked past the cones and touched the wood. "He thinks the oil companies'll buy us out and frack."

"Bitumen's worthless," Charlie answered. "Even if they do want it, they'll just declare imminent domain. No way we're gonna get rich when some lawyer can steal it."

"What's eminent domain?" Julia asked. She was holding her throat. That made it easier to talk.

"Imminent," Charlie corrected.

Dave unsheathed this sly, super cute grin. "Sam Singh thinks the sinkhole ate his cat."

Julia chuckled.

"Since when?" Charlie asked.

"Fluffy!" Dave called in an old-lady voice, hands cupped to his face. "Oh, Fluffy!"

Julia let go of a real laugh, which felt good even though her throat stung. "Sam's so nice . . ."

"He's dumb as rocks," Dave finished. "He said he let Fluffy out last night and she never came back. She's probably lost with that dog — the one that belongs to the bald chemo lady."

"You mean Mrs. Atlas," Julia said. "She has big eyes."

"Yeah."

They got quiet for a second, thinking about skinny, big-eyed Bethany Atlas, who came out sometimes, a scarf over her head, and walked ever-so-slowly up and down the park for exercise. She wore this brave and terrifying smile.

"Thing is," Dave said, "Sam's onto something. 'Cause there's no squirrels or birds around."

"You think it's eating animals?" Julia asked. She tapped her toe against the slab's firm edge.

"A sinkhole can't eat pets," Charlie said. He looked pissed at the very notion of this, like it went against his religion. Charlie was *that* guy. A guy who's already thirty years old and waiting for his shoe size to catch up. "It's just a hole. They're finding them all over the country, because of the heat. We're lucky it's just bitumen. Some of 'em are bringing up landfill garbage."

"Naw. It's more than a hole," Dave said.

Julia didn't look right at him, because Dave Harrison was maybe the coolest fourteen-year-old she'd ever met. He never followed. He always did exactly what he wanted. "So, what is it?" she asked.

Dave nodded. Shook his head. Nodded. Finally shrugged.

"Okay," Julia croaked through her sore throat. "Here are the Maple Street sinkhole rules."

"You're a clown," Dave said.

"Rule number one," Julia continued as she laid her hand across the slab. It felt soft and too warm, like chemicals from below had mixed with the sun's heat and cooked it. "This wood doesn't look strong enough and we should stay off, especially Larry."

"The government does everything bad," Charlie said. "They used cheap wood."

Dave stood, walked across to the center, where the whole thing bowed and smoke plumed out from the knothole there. Julia covered her nose. It had a sweet, wrong odor that burned, like candy apple coating melting and hardening in your throat. Dave stayed for a five-count, then walked slowly back.

"That was a bad decision," Charlie said. "You could have died."

"You talk like your moms," Dave answered.

"No I don't!" Charlie answered.

"You're like their mouth puppet," Dave said.

"Well, you're conceited," Charlie answered.

Dave grinned. "I'm the most popular guy in my grade. That's not conceited."

"It's like he doesn't know what *conceited* means," Julia said.

"I've had three girlfriends this year. Which is more than any of you've had your whole lives. I know everything and you know nothing."

"Every girl you go out with is horrible," Charlie said.

"They're hot!" Dave said. He did this — talked about girls like you could scoop them all together into a pile. That was one of the reasons Shelly had always turned him down. She hadn't wanted to be a scoop of girlfriend. Julia thought she'd be okay with being a scoop. At least, if it was Dave Harrison, she'd be okay with it.

"Define *hot,*" Charlie said.

"Nobody cares what the girl looks like.

You don't *fuck the face,*" Julia said. She was trying to be funny and mature like a woman of the world, and only realized she'd gone too far after she said it.

Charlie and Dave exchanged funny looks. "What does *fuck a face* mean?" Larry asked.

"Sorry," Julia said.

"What's *fuck a face*?" Larry repeated.

"Nothing," Julia said. She needed something to do with her hands, so she pulled Larry's turtleneck over his head and handed it to him. He'd sweat it clean through, and his chest was a moth print of red heat splotches.

Dave smirked that gorgeous smirk. "You're sexist, Julia."

"Whatever, Mr. Hot Girlfriend Man. Let me write that down," she said. "I'll add it to the eighty million other rules for Maple Street that suck ALL THE JOY."

"Put it in black Sharpie. 'Julia Wilde is sexist.'"

"Rubber and glue, dude!"

"Lamest. Comeback. Ever."

Julia started laughing. "No, that was."

Dave opened his mouth like he was going to say something mean. "Aw, you're just so . . ."

Ghetto, Julia knew he was going to say. He pretended to be laughing too hard to finish, but she knew he was afraid to hurt her feelings. He was treating her differently from Charlie, like she was fragile.

"GHETTO!" she shouted.

Dave locked eyes with her, totally delighted. Then, falling over, holding their guts, they were all three laughing. The sound echoed through the empty park, banishing the tension. It made them feel normal again. It made them forget how strange Shelly had acted, and how strange this hole was, too. The holes popping up all over the country, dredging buried things.

Feeling *not lonely* for the first time in weeks, Julia was so bursting with cheer that she kissed Larry's cheek. He stayed still, eyes open and looking straight ahead, which was how she knew he liked it. Or, at least, he didn't mind it.

"What's *fuck a face*?" he asked one last time, which made everybody laugh even more.

"Don't worry. You'll never be that guy," Dave said. "You might want to be that guy, but it'll never happen." Then he flopped, pressing his legs straight up against the edge of the slab and sitting square into the bitumen muck. Charlie did the same. Julia tugged on Larry's crazy green shorts and had him sit, too. The oil was more solid than she'd have guessed, and not as sticky.

The closer you got to it, the less smeary the colors, and the more it looked like your own, skewed reflection in blue and black and red.

All four lined up in a row, their feet kicking the side of the slab, digging at the sludge underneath. They felt brave, like explorers, doing what they weren't supposed to do, proving they were stronger and smarter than the grown-ups thought.

One day they'd run the world. They'd do a better job.

"Rule number two for sinkhole survival," Julia started.

"Clown!" Dave cried out in a fake sneeze.

"Forget rule number two. Dave ate number two. Like, literally, he ate poop. Rule number three," Julia interrupted. "As you can see from the freaky-ass sludge, there's our dead ancestors down there. This is their puke. Don't believe the hype; the birds didn't fly away and your pets aren't hiding, they got eaten by great-grandma Loretta."

"It's primordial stew, like from *Star Trek*," Charlie answered, blushing. It surprised her that he was playing along. She'd thought he was too literal for that.

"*Star Trek*'s for suckers!" Dave cried.

"You guys!" Julia said. "Doesn't a little part of you wanna rip off this wood and ride down the hole on the crane?"

"So, go ahead," Dave said.

"You go!"

Dave slapped her with some snot from a vein of bitumen running out from the hole. Charlie slapped Dave. Julia slapped them both. Larry joined in. Then they were all slapping each other.

The playing felt good, and she reminded herself to enjoy the moment. Soon, Charlie and Dave would go inside to air-conditioning or coding lessons or tutoring. The day would get even hotter. She and Larry would wait for their dad to wake up. But he'd be tired. They wouldn't go anyplace or do anything. They'd just sit by the fan, chewing ice.

The kids on this block always had places to be and vacations to take. They never worried that their clothes were someone else's hand-me-downs, bought from the thrift store on Hempstead Turnpike. Most of them were proud of their houses. They had their own rooms, and those rooms were decorated with real furniture. When you asked them what they wanted to be when they grew up, they knew the answer.

What was it like to be pretty? To have nice things?

"My dad's got this friend from his old band who lives in California. Writes music for TV. I wish I lived there," Julia said.

"We'd miss you," Charlie said.

"Yeah, but in California, nobody'd be mad at me," Julia answered. Her eyes teared up. She let them dry in the air instead of wiping them. "People wouldn't turn on me."

"Is Shelly crazy?" Charlie asked. His chin and cheeks and clothes were marked with sand oil, like the rest of them. Only Larry had stayed clean. "Bleeding . . . Saying that stuff about your dad."

"I don't know," Julia answered. "But it's not true about my dad. She made it up."

"She's messed up," Dave said. "Your dad's famous. He's probably the only dad around here who could get pussy wherever. He doesn't need to get it on Maple Street."

"Gross?"

"Shelly hit you," Larry said. "It's not okay."

Julia squeezed Larry's hand to let him know she was okay. He squeezed back, to let her know something, too.

"Why would she say those things?" Charlie asked.

"Do you think it's true?" Julia asked. "Because it's not."

"No," Charlie answered. "It's just, I've known her since kindergarten. She's been mean, but it's usually for a reason. Have you ever been to her house? Everything's so perfect. It's like you can't move inside of the perfection. Like the air's glass, and just trying to walk around gets you cut into pieces."

Julia let that sink in. She'd felt uneasy in 118, but had never thought to articulate it. If you moved something, you had to put it back exactly. Junk food wasn't allowed because you might get fat. There was this bowl of ribbon candy that matched the green couch, but you couldn't ever eat the candy, and you couldn't sit on the couch, just like you couldn't use the hand towels in the bathroom. It was all too pretty to use. "What's wrong with perfect?"

"It's a lie. There is no perfect," Charlie said.

"How is it a lie?" Julia asked.

Dave blew a long raspberry. "Eeeeemo. Shit's tough all around. My parents divided our house with a Sharpie because they're too cheap to pay for a divorce. That's way worse than pseudo-perfect. You see me going psycho killer?"

"Why does she hate you?" Charlie asked Julia.

"Does she? Hate me?" Julia asked back. "Did she tell you that?" Even though it was obvious, it felt bad to say out loud.

"What's she got against you, is what Charlie's asking," Dave said, frowning at Charlie, who blushed.

"I don't know," Julia answered. She'd wondered a lot about this, hadn't been able to come up with anything that made sense. "She's spoiled. Her mom does everything. My parents spoiled her, too. Like, my mom would always make her whatever meal she wanted even if she had to go to the Trader Joe's for it, and my dad would always play harmonica with her. He didn't do that when it was just me . . . She got whatever she wanted. People bow down because of her mom. I really liked her, but honestly, I just think she got bored. It was fun to pretend to be a nice person and be my best friend and now it's fun to act horrible and rip me a new one. What did she tell you guys?"

"Nothing," Charlie said. "I didn't mean to say anything wrong. I just wondered."

". . . Is it true that you guys took a vote not to hang out with me anymore?" she asked.

"Shelly did," Dave answered. "Not us."

Julia looked away so they didn't see the depth of her relief.

"I don't like talking about her," Dave said, his eyes squinting. "It makes me mad. She sucks the oxygen."

"Fine by me," Julia answered. Then she grinned, to let them all know she was okay. "Rule number nineteen! It's a primordial stew apocalypse down there!"

"Borg," Charlie said. "Resistance is futile."

Julia giggled. "Sucker! Our parents are down there."

"Doing what?" Charlie asked.

Julia shook her head. "Worrying about the wrong things. It's all they know how to do."

Dave kicked the board. "I really do wish they were down there. I'd have the house to myself."

Julia pictured her Beauty Queen mother down at the bottom of that hole, pregnant and sweating and wringing her nervous hands. *Square your shoulders! Smile! Go put on a bra so nobody can see your business. If a grown man ever talks to you, just scream. They got no business talking to you. Are you getting along with the neighbors? Don't make yourself unpleasant, Julia! These people are so important! . . . Did you bring Larry? Don't you know he's your responsibility?*

She pictured her dad down there, too. Playing sad songs and walking slow and sad like every day he woke up as *Julia and Larry's father* instead of as a rock star was a disappointment.

"Let's throw 'em down. Then we'll take over. We'll run the world."

"I like my parents!" Charlie cried.

"I like mine, too," Julia answered. "But they still suck."

114

That was when the only tranquility they'd forged that summer broke.

Shelly and the rest of the Rat Pack came howling back.

116 Maple Street

Arlo Wilde's phone chimed a wake-up. The tune was Bernard Herrmann's shower scene music from *Psycho,* and it seeped into his dream, in which Gertie gave birth to a kitten. The kitten had these huge, cute eyes, so Gertie and the kids were ecstatic. He'd known something was wrong, but he hadn't wanted to upset them.

Then the *Psycho* music, and he was like: *Seriously, guys, that baby is a cat.*

He slapped off his phone and got up. The room was dark, all shades drawn. The sluggish window air conditioner whined loud and sad. It was no competition for this heat wave: his skin was wet with sweat. He stepped over and also *on* the humidity-damp towels and assorted feminine garbage like lipstick and Spanx that Gertie had tossed on their floor. She had many good qualities, but cleanliness was not one of them.

"Julia? Larry?" he called a couple of times

after splashing some of the swell from his booze-puffed face.

Wearing just tiger-striped boxer briefs Gertie had gotten for him as a joke, he checked the kids' rooms first. Julia's: like mother, like daughter, it was a clothing bomb, peppered with plates whose unrecognizable crumbs had congealed. Larry's room: perfectly organized, and without a personal item on display, save a Robot Boy doll, which he was still trying to convince them was not actually a doll, but a tool. Like superheroes have utility belts and Iron Man has a vibranium heart, Larry had his Robot Boy. What Larry didn't know was that they all preferred he had a doll; it made him more like a normal kid.

"Anybody home?" Arlo called once he got into the hall again.

Crickets.

On the ground floor, he found the note taped to the refrigerator.

AW-at 8br Open House in Fancy-Schmancy-ville. Say a prayer somebody shows up to buy the monster. Sent the kids outside so you can sleep your drunk off. PS: You smell like a brewery, and you fart like one, too. Maybe brush a tooth next time.
*   -Gert (your saint wife)*

"Oh, she's funny now!" he mumbled, then poured himself a glass of watered-down Trader Joe's brand orange juice concentrate. It eddied the corners of his mouth as he glugged. He carried the glass to the window and spotted his kids. They were sitting around a trampoline with some of the Rat Pack. The weird Ottomanelli twins (Mack? Mason? Mooson?) poured what looked like a gallon container of Clorox bleach over the top.

"Okay. You're fine," he muttered.

He went back up, found his phone, and got a patchy connection. Left a voicemail for Fred Atlas, the guy who lived in Maple Street 130. "Fred! Let's do a movie night. Malverne's showing *The Conversation*. Gert says she'll bring the kids to your place and keep Bee company . . . I know you got shit going on, but it's good to get out. You can't say no to Hackman."

After that, he popped on his analog radio. Reception was terrible since the hole, so streaming didn't work. All he got was live local access, in which two talking heads argued about the looming stock market crash.

He picked up all the clothes. Wiped down the bathroom sink. Got a new load of laundry going, and folded what was in the dryer. Left the piles in front of the kids' bedrooms.

He'd grown up keeping house for both his divorced parents. It came second nature.

In the kitchen, he collected the cereal-crusted dishes. Slugged some more juice, then decided on something better, and stuck his entire head inside the freezer door. Ice made white steam as he reached his shoulders in, too.

He wasn't usually so hung over. Most bartenders at Arlo's regular downtown joints knew his special drink — the Mermaid Avenue: ginger ale, rocks, and club soda with a twist, made to look like a vodka tonic. Most bartenders. But not all of them. Last night Oscar Heep, head office manager for Bankers Collective, had insisted on a hole-in-the-wall Irish pub on Pearl Street called The Full Shilling. Arlo wound up matching the red-nosed alkie beer for beer. Five rounds passed as slow and excruciating as an etherless tonsillectomy on the Western Front.

"Sing a few bars of 'Kennedys in the River' for me!" the sot cried as soon as he found out who Arlo used to be.

So Arlo sang. More than a few bars. But not that song. The other song. His favorite. "Wasted." The whole three-minute-and-forty-second shebang.

The Full Shilling patrons had watched. Once they'd realized that they were in the presence of Wild Arlo Wilde, chart-topping, *Rolling Stone*–sanctified lead singer of Fred Savage's Revenge, they'd swayed.

I can still see it.
Bet you can't.
On your coffee table
next to the lamp.
Saturday morning,
watching Super Friends.
Ming zaps Batman, Robin runs.
Blackened spoons on the floor.
I use them to eat stolen Apple Jacks.
Irene knocks. You nod.
It doesn't mean "come in."

I can still see it.
Bet you can't.
The brown couch
and shut windows.
The girl you told me to call Mom.
The places I looked out
through a broken window
and didn't know were better.

Sad and drunk, he'd been thinking about his pop, and everything else that had gone wrong in his life, when he finished that first refrain. So he'd pulled out his Hohner 64, and punched it home:

Firestar blasts Iceman
the first time I get high.
And I'm nine years old.
Nostalgic for something
that never happened.

The twentysomething yuppie bankers in thousand-dollar suits, and the Irish bartenders with put-on brogues, and even Oscar had clapped. Arlo'd been tight by then, lights spinning, sound reverberating in all the wrong ways, like the walls were acute angles, closing in. "I keep my soul in there, you fucks," he'd mumbled, not that anyone had heard. Not, frankly, that it had meant anything, other than that he'd been feeling sorry for himself.

"Sing 'Kennedys in the River'!" they'd shouted, at first in noisy bursts and then all together at a quarter-beat, *"Ri-ver! Ri-ver! Ri-ver!"*

Arlo closed his eyes through the chanting and he pretended he was back at that old dive on Orchard Street, right before the band got signed. When the whole world had seemed like something small and easy to conquer, and the guitar in his hand had been his ticket out.

Then he gave them what they wanted, and sang "Kennedys in the River."

The night ended when Oscar refused to sign on the dotted line for a new fleet of printing suites, even at the deep discount Arlo offered. "We tightened our belts this year, so I can't. But I think you're sexy. You've got that rugged thing going for you. Maybe we could get together sometime, when it's not about work?"

Arlo handed the prick his business card, shook his clammy hand, and said, "You told me you needed new printers. I'm a salesman. I sell printers. That's what I do to put food on the table for my family. My wife's knocked up and I'm late on my mortgage. When you want to buy some fucking printers, you let me know."

He waited an hour at Penn Station with the rest of the late-night punks and sad-sack businessmen for the 3:06 a.m. train to Garden City, then walked the mile home from his stop, listening to the echo of his footsteps on eerily empty suburban streets.

Less than five hours later, Arlo jammed his shoulder inside the open door of his freezer, rubbed his face against a cheap Western Beef frozen steak, and thought about how nice it would be to have a win. He didn't want to go back in time. He wasn't that same guy, and he didn't think it would be all that fun anymore, staying out with the band, shooting white gold up his arms in Horseshoe Bar's grimy toilet room, eating runny eggs, staggering along Avenue D.

No, he didn't want to run away. He just wanted a decent commission, or a pat on the back from his regional sales director, who didn't seem to notice that he'd never called in sick or missed a meeting. He wanted his music agent at Gersh to get back to him about the new demo he'd sent. Mostly, he wanted somebody to notice how hard all this had been, and that he'd done it, nonetheless.

None of these things would happen for Arlo Wilde. Not today, at least. Today, the children of Maple Street were skittering over the surface of something dangerous. One of them was about to fall in.

Sterling Park

A rational person would have stayed home. Hidden in her room until Monday, when her mom drove her to coding camp or Girl Empowerment Engineering Club or whatever. A rational kid would have waited until the period thing blew over.

It became clear to Julia Wilde right then, that her former *best friend forever* Shelly Schroeder wasn't rational.

Even from an acre out, Julia could see that Shelly's intense line of vision was fixed on just one target. She ran at top speed, dirt and sand oil kicking up all around. She tripped once, but even then, her eyes stayed on Julia.

"We should run," Charlie said.

They didn't run. Shelly halved the distance. Quartered it. She looked wrong.

"What happened to her?" Dave asked.

Shelly was really close now, and they could see what she'd done. Her hair was gone. It looked like she'd hacked off each braid near the scalp, because the black that remained had unwound in thick, uneven tufts.

"Whoa," Julia said.

Without slowing down, Shelly burst between Julia and Larry, who were holding hands. Then she was standing on the giant wood slab. Right in the center, her feet over the knothole.

"What the hell's wrong with you?" Dave Harrison shouted.

She didn't look at him, only at Julia. Her face was a mask of scrunched fury. It was scary, like the real Shelly, the Shelly who'd been her friend, didn't live inside her anymore. "Bck! Bck! Bck!" she hollered, wrists tucked under her armpits so that her elbows appeared like the tips of hollow wings. "You came all the way out and you didn't even walk the plank. You're all chicken — I knew it!"

"Get off," Charlie said. "It'll fall."

Still glaring at Julia, Shelly grinned through clenched teeth. Talked through those clenched teeth, too. "I'm the bravest."

"Fuck this," Dave Harrison said. He leaped for the compact excavator's hook and caught it with both hands. He swung, ramming Shelly right in the boobs with the soles of his flip-flops, then dropping almost clear to the

125

other side. But he still landed on wood, and that wood made a disquieting groan.

"Go home, Shelly," he announced as he walked to safety.

Shelly stayed on the board, legs akimbo. She'd changed into a clean, pink skort so there wasn't any blood to see. Looking only at Julia, like everyone else was furniture, she announced, "You and me. We fight right here. To the death."

"You're crazy," Julia said.

"Bck-bck-bck!" Shelly rage-shrieked.

"What is this, first grade?" Julia asked.

Julia pressed her toes up against the edge. Warm wood vibrated through the soles of her flip-flops, like a dryer set to low. It really did feel like something was down there. Something alive.

"This is my Rat Pack. Take the aspy and go back to Brooklyn. Lock him in a loony bin where he belongs."

Julia didn't look to see Larry's reaction. She knew he'd be grabbing for himself, maybe walking in a circle. He didn't cry when people teased him. It happened too often. At school, on the bus, at the grocery store — there weren't enough tears. Instead, he retreated. His eyes went dim and faraway, and they stayed faraway even after the teasing was done. Every time that happened, she felt like she'd lost a piece of him that she'd never get back. She'd once explained this to Shelly, that it was her job to keep him whole and alive, only she didn't know how. She was so afraid of failing. The one thing that made her special in her family was protecting him.

"I heard for a fact that the school shrink diagnosed him mentally retarded," Shelly said. "Imbecile level, which is better than idiot but worse than moron."

Julia charged the slab. *Crrrrck!* The wood creaked under their combined weight and she didn't care right then if she fell. All she wanted to do was slap that dirty, toothy grin off Shelly's mouth. "Don't you dare talk shit about my brother. I'll fight you anytime."

"You dumbasses need to get off. It's gonna break," Dave called from the edge.

Hearing that, Shelly bent low, then sprang, tucking her legs like the slab was a trampoline. As soon as she landed, the knothole split an inch on either side:

Crrrck!

"Stop!" Dave shouted, angry as spit. "Seriously, Shelly. You wanna die, go ahead. Don't take Julia with you."

By now Ella, Sam, the Markles, and Lainee had arrived. They'd surrounded the sinkhole on every side.

"You shouldn't do that, Shelly!" Ella called. "Mom says —"

Shelly started laughing, only no sound came out. Her whole body convulsed. Without all that hair, there wasn't anything to soften her features. Her big eyes looked like they'd receded into their sockets; her cheekbones and jaw jutted, sharp and too defined. She was the thirty-year-old version of herself that had lived a hard, bitter life. She jumped again, high and hard.

Crrrraaakk!

The slab bowed, tearing even more. Julia crouched down. She'd forgotten about her anger. All she wanted was off this damn slab. *Please, God. Please, please, please don't let me fall in. Don't let the hole get me . . .*

The slab got still. The Rat Pack got quiet. Everything slowed, so the only sound was the angry cicada heat-song.

"Stop," Julia said, low and loud, even though her throat still hurt. She was in the center, afraid to stand. Worried any movement at all would send them both tumbling down.

"Ask nice," Shelly answered.

"Crawl off, Julia. Leave her!" Charlie called.

"Stick your hands through!" the Markles heckled like brainless stereo speakers.

128

"Please, Shelly. I'm asking nice. Stop jumping," Julia said.

Shelly walked off the slab. It cricked and moaned with every step. "Julia's a chicken and a loser, but we all knew that when we voted not to hang out with her."

Still crouched, Julia gathered her courage, trying to decide whether to stand and walk off, or to be smart and crawl.

"My mom's throwing another barbeque once the hole is closed. To celebrate. Everybody except Julia can come," Shelly said. "Julia has to admit she's a lying hypocrite. Then we can all be friends again, and I'll stop holding it against her, that her family is a buncha sluts and criminals and crazies. So are you gonna say you're sorry, Julia?"

"I don't even like barbeques," Dave said.

"Stick your hand inside!" Michael cried.

"Stick it! Stick it!" Mark added in exactly the same voice.

Julia knew the smart thing to do, what her parents and brother would *want* her to do: crawl off this stupid slab before it broke open, apologize, and move on with this hot, shitty day.

But it was one thing to avoid her friend-turned-enemy; it was another to buckle under her. She didn't want Larry to see that. He'd think it made Shelly right, that he didn't deserve decent treatment. If she apologized, Dave Harrison and Charlie Walsh might still act nice, but they'd think less of her. She wouldn't be an equal anymore. The rest of these kids weren't strong personalities. They'd internalize the pecking order, that she could be treated badly without repercussion, that she and Larry were the lowest people on the block.

She'd been on good behavior for a long time. Trying to fit in like her parents wanted even though she had crazy curly hair and her accent was Brooklyn, but not the gentrified kind. Even though her clothes weren't as nice and she didn't care as much about school. Even though everybody here had met practically at birth, she'd tried to find a place for herself and for Larry. When that stopped working, she hadn't gone on the offensive. She'd just taken Larry and hidden out in her house. She'd been cool about it. But this was past her limit. No way she was going to say she was sorry. Not after everything Shelly had said and done. Julia did the only thing she could think to do. The bravest and craziest possible thing. She plunged her fist through the knothole.

"Gee, Shelly. That's funny. Were you scared? Because it feels just fine to me," she called as she wiggled her fingers down there, inside the hole.

The Markles hooted. Charlie held Larry by the shoulders so he didn't follow Julia, which it looked like he was trying to do. Julia reached deeper. Maybe because of her weight on the slab, vibrations rattled the metal rivets, making a high-pitched ringing.

Sound-sensitive Larry covered his ears.

Everybody was watching. Julia plunged her arm in all the way up to her shoulder, her ear against the warm, oil-greasy wood.

"You're so stupid. I was kidding," Shelly said. Except her voice was 100 percent awe.

"Real, live, human flesh! Come and get it!" Julia said. Her arm itched with a chemical kind of heat, and she felt the displaced air of something else's movement. Her fingertips trilled with the sensation of something living and breathing that was very close. *Her hand wasn't alone.* She should have been worried, but she wasn't, because everybody looked terrified, and impressed, and spellbound. For once, these Maple Street All-Americans were in awe of ghetto Julia Wilde.

"Oh no!" She rolled her eyes and drummed her legs against the wobbly slab. "Help! It's got me!" she cried.

"Get off!" everybody was shouting, but she didn't care. This was fun. This was real. Now that she'd done this, nobody had the right to tease her or Larry. Not ever again.

Then: The air against her hands got hotter and wetter. It blew like breath. The entire slab rattled, screws singing with vibration. Something lunged. She yanked back. Not in time. The pain was strangely clean. She screamed for real. Her hand tore free. Steaming fumes shot up through the knothole as she fell back and rolled off.

"It bit me!" Julia cried, except her voice didn't come. She'd inhaled some of the fumes. Her lungs were hot; burning! She didn't feel the warm blood running down her wrist, or even the pain. Just this adrenaline sense of something clean and thoroughly done to both sides of her palm. A bite that had met in the bony middle.

— *CRACK!* —

Something punched the slab from underneath. The wood went convex.

"It's alive!" Sam shouted. "Holy cow! It's alive!"

The Markles jogged a few feet away. So did Ella.

Larry made this terrible sound, this mewl, his hands over his ears.

CRAAAACK!

The whole slab popped, spitting out its

anchors and wrenching free from its sonorous rivets.

Sam started running back toward the houses, then Ella and the Markles. Dave's expression registered unease at the sight of Julia's hand. He weaved on his feet like he was going to faint. You couldn't see her wounds for all the blood. "I'll get help," he said, staggering back. Then he was running, too.

Only Larry and practical Charlie stayed. "Are you okay? What can I do?" Charlie sputtered. "That definitely needs stitches, plus tetanus shots and maybe rabies. You have health insurance, right? It's okay if we call an ambulance, right?"

"Go away," Shelly rasped. "It's never gonna happen. She thinks you're a sphincter."

Julia's hand was gummy. Her breath short. By the time she had the presence of mind to speak, Charlie had backed up. "I'll get help," he called, soft and nearly inaudible.

"Get up," Shelly said once he was out of earshot. "That hole's still barfing steam all over us. I can't stand it."

Julia shook her head and pointed at her chest, which was burning.

"Come on!" She pulled Julia by the upper arms and made her stand, then walked with her, step by step.

Julia looked ahead and behind. She couldn't see Larry. Was he near the hole again? Had he gone with the rest of the kids? She couldn't catch her breath! She pulled her hand from the cradle of her chest to look at it. She could see puncture wounds, two on each side. Fangs. *Was she infected?* she wondered crazily. *Would she turn zombie?*

She lost her center of gravity and sank down, feeling faint. "Go," Julia coughed out. "Just get Larry. I'll be fine."

"Larry's gone already, like we should be."

"I can't move, Shelly."

"I'll get in trouble if you die," Shelly answered as she dragged Julia along the tar-sticky grass. "Come on!"

Julia helped, using one arm to scoot. Pretty soon they were forty feet out. She'd left a trail of blood, which worried her. Because maybe the thing down there had caught her scent.

Shelly got down and scooted alongside Julia.

"Move!"

Julia went faster. She could breathe a little deeper. She knew she was supposed to hate Shelly, and mostly, she did. But being alone with her felt comfortable. It felt like something missing, suddenly returned.

"You're such a liar, Jules," Shelly said

as they scooted. But her voice was much warmer than before, like she was thinking the same thing.

Fifty feet, maybe more. A safer distance. Julia took a deep breath, and a little more air got through. Her rational mind returned. It had to be an animal down there. A scared dog on some ledge, trapped and trying to break out. Ralph the German shepherd had bit her . . . right?

"What are you talking about? I don't lie," Julia said.

Shelly stopped scooting. Red veins skittered across her pupils. Those tufts of black hair were now slicked to her bony scalp with sweat. "You never told your parents that I wanted to live with you. You lied."

"I did so ask them."

"Bull."

Was Larry ahead of her? He had to be. She wanted to call for him but her breath and throat, her *everything* hurt too much. "Lady, I need stitches and Larry's AWOL. I can't deal with your drama right now."

"You think you're so tough. Brooklyn girl from New Lots Avenue. You don't know anything."

"I know you've been badmouthing my whole family."

"It's not badmouthing if it's true."

"It's not! Larry's smart. You know that. And my dad? Come on! He'd never do that to you."

Shelly didn't bother denying it. With the Rat Pack gone, there wasn't anybody left to perform for. She squeezed her hands, then squeezed her forearms. She left pale marks against the pink.

"Why'd you even want to live with me?" Julia pushed. "You told Lainee Hestia my house is a pigsty. You're just flexing. I'm not one of your Maple Street followers."

She put her head between her knees and talked from there, soft this time, like the real Shelly. "You said we were like family. Best friends forever."

"We were. And then you fucked me over. Every time I tried to hang out with the Rat Pack you made it a shit show. You said those things about Larry. You know how hard I've been working to make him normal. How could you do that?"

She ran her fingers through her hair. Seemed alarmed that there wasn't much. "It was a joke. You Wildes've never been able to take a joke."

"You hurt him. He trusted you."

Shelly let out a breath. Felt for her hair again. Her hands seemed lost. "She's gonna be so mad," she mumbled.

"What?"

Head bowed, hands reaching, Shelly kept feeling for her hair. It was all patchwork — some cut close to the scalp, some farther away. "I wasn't asking just to flex. I told you it was bad. I shouldn't've needed proof. You were supposed to be my friend. You said you believed me."

Julia looked ahead. The Rat Pack had slowed down but was still running. Everything felt foreign and unsettled, like this whole town was on Mars. "I believed you. I mean, you're sensitive. You have a lot of feelings. I always believed your feelings."

"Then why didn't you help me?"

"I mean, I get it. Your mom and the red wine and Ella's annoying. Everything at your house is about nice clothes and Harvard. You can't eat with a plate on your stomach and even if you could, the sofas are like rocks. I get it. But my house is hard, too. They put on a show when you were around. It's not like, if you moved in with me, your life would suddenly get better."

"How do you know?"

"My parents can't handle things. My mom goes to la-la land. She shuts off like a robot. You saw her drive away this morning. If I ask her about it tonight, she'll fuck me over. Won't even say she's sorry. She'll just pretend it never happened. My dad's a phony. I push him. Like I don't do what he tells me or I climb all over the couch with dirty shoes. And I'm not allowed, but he doesn't say anything. He gets so mad he grits his teeth. He curses and walks away. Sometimes he yells. I can tell he wants to hit me. But he doesn't. I can't explain, but it makes me feel sorry for him . . . I didn't ask either of them because it's impossible. They'd never let you live with us. Even asking, my mom would tell your mom, and then it'd be a big thing. I'd get in trouble for stirring the pot. I'm always the one who gets in trouble. Your mom protects you. Nobody has my back."

Shelly pulled strands of her short hair, like she was trying to make it stretch. "I get in trouble."

"I never see anybody raise their voice at you, Shells. Your mom treats you like a glass princess. You don't even have to take care of Ella. I don't get why you'd want to leave that to live with me."

Shelly burst into tears. "You're wrong. She'll kill me for this. She loves my hair."

Julia touched her shoulder and she collapsed, crumpling into her arms. Alarmed, wondering if this was a trick, Julia held her. But then Shelly was sobbing. The sound of her old friend's pain was too much, so Julia hugged back, sticky with grime, keeping her bleeding hand at a distance, so as not to stain.

"It was too long before. This is better," she crooned.

"I see myself doing these bitchy things," Shelly said, her voice muffled by Julia's shoulder. "I can't stop. It's like a . . . a monster inside me that I can't control."

Julia breathed Shelly in — that strange smell of someone who's nothing like your family. They eat different foods and they use different detergents. She felt herself crying, too. She'd missed this. You turn twelve, and suddenly it's not cool to hug. The best you can get is sitting extra close during carpool or sharing a blanket while playing *Deathcraft*.

"Why didn't you do a tampon?" Julia asked. "You know the Markles and your sister are gonna tell everybody."

Shelly looked ahead, at the neatly lined houses along the crescent. "I ran out. She was too boozy to drive. I was going to just put a bunch of toilet paper or something, but I forgot . . ." Her mouth screwed up and she looked at her knees. "That's not even true. I saw it was bleeding and I didn't care. Last night was so bad. It took so long for those braids. I woke up and *couldn't* be home. I

139

knew the blood would happen and you'd all see and I didn't care."

"Oh . . ." Julia didn't know what to say to that. It didn't make sense. Periods are mortifying. They're giant, blood-soaked pads of shame. Julia spent at least ten minutes a day checking to see if her first had come, making sure there was no way, if it ever happened, that it would show. Nobody *wants* to get caught with a period. "Brooke Leonardis had it happen in school and nobody even talked about it. Sienna Muller saw it all over her lunch chair. You weren't that bad. It's deniable. I'll deny it with you. We can just act like the people who say it are mental."

"You don't get it."

"How do you mean?"

She was still looking at her knees, tufts of hair sticking up. "It's like I see my life from far away. The real me's stuck, and the rest of me, it's just this body that walks and talks and screams at people. The real me's dying."

Julia felt her eyes go hot. She remembered how much she used to love Shelly. Right now, in this moment, she still loved her. "Please don't talk like that."

Shelly sniffled. "I think about a razor. I keep this Pain Box that has my proof. It's got all the evidence. I'd leave a note on top."

140

Julia blanched. Proof? What kind of proof? "Don't talk about razors," she said.

Shelly's voice got low and steady as a wishful incantation. "It'd say: *You made me do this. Now I'm dead just to get away from you. I hope you're happy.*"

Julia tried to be brave. To be firm, because maybe Shelly needed firm. "Stop it. You're being a drama queen. You'll make yourself sick."

Shelly's jaw opened like she was going to gag and her eyes got wide, and Julia could almost see a terrible nothing inside her, wasting and strangling, eating her up from the inside out. She dry-cried, no sound and no tears.

Julia took her friend in her arms. Squeezed as hard as she could.

"Stop. It hurts."

Alarm. A jolt of a thousand volts. Julia loosened.

"No one wants to hear it," Shelly said. "If I told them, they wouldn't believe. You were my best friend and I couldn't tell you anything. You still don't want to know. How can Miss PTA be anything except perfect? I'm the one they don't like. I'm the one who's mean. Unstable. There's nobody to back me up. Even my family, they don't see it. Or if they do, they pretend not to. I just, I'm all broken and nobody else is broken. Nobody else is in this."

The words jumped and bounced, and Julia kept trying to fit them together differently, so they'd tell a kinder story. But there wasn't one. "What's happening to you?" Julia asked.

Shelly's lips trembled. "She's *killing* me," she whispered.

"She?" Julia asked.

"Her," Shelly answered.

Tears burned Julia's eyes and she stanched them, trying as hard as she could to be strong. If this was true, it was bigger than too many rules. Bigger than getting yelled at or not being allowed on playdates unless you got straight As. It was even bigger than getting slapped around when you didn't deserve it. It was marrow deep.

"Your mom," Julia said.

Shelly's voice broke. "Don't tell anyone."

Julia looked across the hot, empty park, and the hole behind them, which kept getting bigger. Nothing made sense. Nothing was how it was supposed to be because the world was upside down. All the grown-ups were kids, and the kids were on their own, and maybe that's how it had been all along.

"Show me your hurt," Julia said. "I have to see."

Shelly's eyes watered. "You won't think of me the same."

"That's not true. I know you exactly. We played Truth or Dare a thousand times. I know you."

Shelly leaned forward and slid her shirt up her back. Her skin wasn't pale but bruised yellow. Every part was marked by pinprick bruises aligned into oval shapes. Most were in a state of healing — just blended shadows. There were four recent ones. Bright red with trapped blood, like the hickey Dave Harrison had given her last year behind the 7-Eleven as a joke but not a joke.

Julia touched the center one very gently. Index and middle finger, tracing a soft line down Shelly's spine. Shelly eased at Julia's touch. She sighed out. Happy, almost.

Shelly let her expensive Free People shirt fall back down. "I wanted this special French twist. You know, with braids all around. For my thirteenth birthday party." Shelly looked to Julia. "September? Was it that long ago?"

Julia didn't know how she was supposed to answer. "That's your birthday. Yeah."

Shelly seemed confused on a deep, unsettled level. "I think that was the first time. I *think* so. She did it as a joke because she was so frustrated and we both laughed. And then she did it again and it wasn't funny . . .

Sometimes I forget. I go someplace else when it happens," Shelly said, her voice soft, like it was night and they were alone in Julia's room, in sleeping bags. "It's never outside where a bathing suit goes . . . When I see myself in the mirror it's a surprise. It's so crazy and so secret that I think I did it to myself. Maybe I turned thirteen and something happened that made me split personality or schizophrenic. I know I'm not right. But they're too high up my back. There's no way I did it to myself. That's half the reason I started taking the pictures. So I can be sure it's real."

A memory returned to Julia, and it made her weary. She felt as old as Shelly looked with that cropped hair and sunken eyes. "Do you remember that time we were rehearsing at your house?"

"When?" Shelly asked.

"When we did the Billie Eilish for the talent show. Your mom didn't know I was in your room. She opened the door. Like, slammed it open. And it was so weird, because I'd just heard her talking on the phone downstairs and she'd been laughing. But she looked so mad all of a sudden. And then she saw me and it was gone. Like it had never happened. She was smiling."

Shelly didn't say anything.

"It was so crazy. I thought she was going to murder us, and then she was asking if I wanted a strawberry smoothie. I didn't know what to think. It was unreal. I thought I'd imagined it. Do you remember?" Julia asked.

Shelly shook her head. Without hair, her neck looked long and vulnerable, like a sea creature out of its shell. "No. But she does that sometimes, when people aren't looking. People who aren't me . . . I wanted to tell you. I kept thinking you knew. I thought because we spent so much time, it was like osmosis and you knew. That's why you and your family were always so nice to me. You were trying to make up for it."

Julia tried not to cry, but Shelly's bruise had been like any other skin, to the touch. It seemed wrong that it hadn't been like fire. "I didn't know. I'm sorry."

Shelly winced. "It's okay. I think I just wanted to imagine that you knew, so I wouldn't have to do something about it. I could pretend the whole world was in on it. Especially Maple Street. But then she said I couldn't hang out with you anymore, and if you were with the Rat Pack, I couldn't hang out with them. And I knew."

"Why did she do that?" Julia asked. "Is it because I stole those cigarettes?"

Shelly smiled dark. "It wasn't the smoking. She was afraid I'd tell you. That's how I knew for sure it was real. The whole world isn't in on it. Not even the whole block. It's just her, and it's real."

"But now you did tell me." Julia's voice broke, even though she wanted it to be kind, strong, an affirmation.

"Yeah." Shelly tried to smile again; failed. Her eyes were so sunken that it startled Julia.

"What do we do?" Julia asked.

Shelly shook her head. "I don't want her to get in trouble. I love her. And sometimes, when she does it, it almost feels like it's because she loves me most. It's a thing we share. But it's not right. I know it isn't."

"Can you tell your dad?"

"He's invisible. Like you said. He's a ghost." Shelly bit her lip. Swiped the sweat from her brow that was trickling down into her eyes. ". . . What about your parents?"

Julia thought about that. Felt sad to admit the truth of it. "No. They don't always know what to do. We could tell Ms. Lopez, but she won't be back at school until September. This can't wait. I think we have to go to the cops."

Shelly went to smooth her hair again. Her hands came back disappointed. She looked at Julia's with longing. "She'll get in so much trouble. I don't want that."

"She won't," Julia said. "That only happens in the ghetto. Here, they'll just make her stop."

"What if they don't believe me? What if they tell my mom I'm a troublemaker and then she hates me forever?"

"I don't think cops do that," Julia said. "Look at your back. Nobody would call you a liar."

"You don't understand. I'll have no one without her."

"You'll have me. If it goes bad, we'll run away. We won't come back until it's safe," Julia said.

"You'd do that?"

A calm settled over Julia. A kind of steel she'd never imagined she possessed. "I'm in this. Now that you told me, I'm part of it. I can't do nothing. I can't let *you* do nothing. You said it yourself. You'll die if you stay. I believe that. I can see it happening already. I won't let you die."

Eyes welling with tears, a kind of peace settled over Shelly, and she nodded. "Okay."

They hugged. "I got blood on you. I'm sorry," Julia said.

"S'okay." She pointed at a speck on Julia's Hawaiian shirt. "I got blood on you, too."

"We're blood sisters."

"Blood sisters," Shelly echoed. She

147

chuckled for the first time Julia could remember. The sound broke her heart and then healed it, changing it forever.

While the girls reconnected, the Rat Park had been doing their part. They'd run the half mile at first, but in the heat, eventually walked, except for Sam Singh, the athlete. When they arrived, they'd rushed into houses, stirred parents still sleeping or working or pouring ice into coffee for breakfast. Eventually, parents were informed. An ambulance was called. The block became lively, like morning birds. Those without tweens still heard the shouts along the houses, the panting and the warning and the general milieu of unease. They came out to see. Some came running.

The Pontis, the Hestias, the Ottomanellis, the Walshes, and Jane Harrison all made haste, wearing house robes and flip-flops. Jane carried a Krispy Kreme Doughnuts mug that she dropped along the way. Arlo Wilde was still nursing his hangover when he heard the commotion. He didn't stop to dress. He saw the frightened Rat Pack out his window, pointing into the park. He saw the crowd heading there. Something urgent was happening. Something bad. He scanned the faces, looking for Julia and Larry. Couldn't find them. And then he saw what looked like his own Hawaiian shirt and a tangle of blond by the sinkhole. In tiger-striped boxer briefs and nothing else, Arlo got out and ran.

Fifteen minutes into their talk, the girls had been so preoccupied that they hadn't noticed the adults headed their way. Julia spotted them first. Their pace was swift. Rhea Schroeder had the lead. She looked stark and small and devastatingly normal.

It felt like life-and-death. Like the only possible option. Because if they waited, Julia might lose courage. She might let herself be convinced that this wasn't as serious as it seemed. She might tell her parents, who would conceal and make excuses, because underplaying was all they knew how to do when it came to the people of Maple Street. And Shelly would lose faith, too. She'd shrink into herself while the monster grew meaner and angrier. The Shelly that Julia loved would die.

"Shelly!" Rhea Schroeder screamed.

Shelly's eyes widened at the sound of her mother's voice. She grabbed at her shorn hair with an expression of pure fear.

"Now!" Julia cried. "We can't let them catch us!"

Shelly lurched up and started running in the direction of the sinkhole and beyond, to

149

the police station far away. Legs and arms fully pumping, Julia joined. They ran together in the summer heat while bewildered adults gave chase.

Julia looked behind. Saw her dad back there. Half clad in silly boxer briefs and nothing else, he was faster than the rest, overtaking them one by one. The adults wore concerned expressions. Love and fear and disappointment blended, like it always did with them. She heard the insect heat-song, felt the sticky grass, the burn in her chest, saw the alien-seeming buildings beyond the park. It was hard to keep up with Shelly. Her face clenched tight, her eyes nearly closed, she looked possessed.

Once they got out of the park, they'd take side roads and cut through yards to avoid detection. Julia imagined arriving at the police department, panting and sweating. They'd try to find the right person to talk to. But they'd choose wrong and Shelly's mom and dad would wind up in jail for child abuse instead of at some nice therapist's office. Her family would get broken apart and no one would be able to pay the mortgage on 118 Maple Street. Or maybe she and Shelly would get caught before they ever made it to the cops. Dragged into the back of some Maple Street parent's car and afterward,

Shelly would get a beating so bad it killed her spirit.

Doubt crept: What if they needed the adults and not the police? What if this plan was dumb?

Rhea screamed again, angrier this time. "Shelly! Come back here NOW!"

Like a spooked horse, Shelly pulled ahead of Julia, running blind and straight for the slab — the shortest distance between the park and the road. She pounded wood. It cracked with every step and she didn't stop. She didn't seem to know she was running on it.

Julia stopped short, afraid the added weight would bring them both down. In the cab of the excavator was Larry, watching out the window. He'd probably gotten scared and hidden there. Now he poked his hands out and squinted, that perspective game kids play, as if trying somehow to catch her.

Shelly's steps made hollow *bangs!* The rivets sang, loud and dissonant. The entire slab groaned toward the mouth of the hole like a board game folding in half.

"Shelly!" Julia shouted. But she didn't seem to hear. She was stuck in the fold the wood made, unable to climb high enough to get out. She flailed, an animal trapped in a snare.

Cold settled over Julia. She pictured herself flying through the air and rescuing Shelly. She willed the wood to hold, as if life were wishes.

The folded wood cradled Shelly as she struggled to stand. She didn't look for Julia or shout for help. She didn't seem to know where she was or what was happening. She pushed hard with her hands, unfolding the board, but it was too heavy. She let go and it all slammed back.

Oh, God, no, Julia thought.

CRRRRAAAAAAAAAAAAAAAACCCCK!

The entire slab collapsed. It was there, and then it wasn't.

Julia looked over, just as Arlo arrived at her side, the first adult to reach them. He took her by the shoulders and pulled her back. Together, they saw.

Shelly Schroeder fell. For a moment, it seemed as if the broken slab would hold her. A magic, midair cradle. But no. She plunged through the center, even as she reached for its muddy, useless edges. Down, down, down, into the murk.

152

BRICK

July 11–July 25

Map of Maple Street as of July 15, 2027
*116 Wilde Family
*118 Schroeder Family

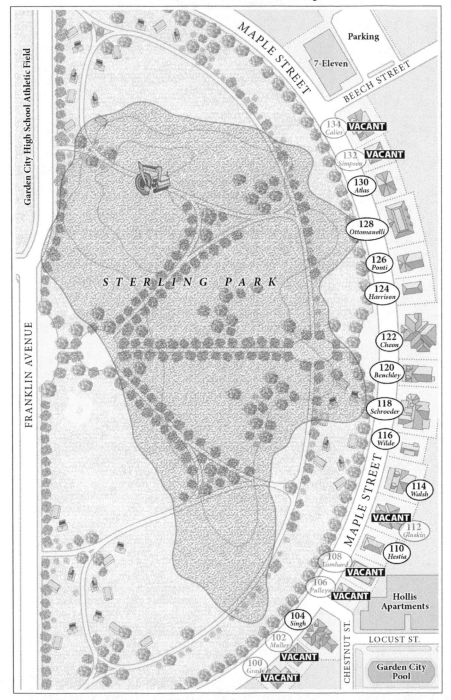

Index of Maple Street's permanent residents as of July 15, 2027

100 VACANT

102 VACANT

104 The Singhs-Kaurs — Sai (47), Nikita (36), Pranav (16), Michelle (14), Sam (13), Sarah (9), John (7)

106 VACANT

108 VACANT

110 The Hestias — Rich (51), Cat (48), Helen (17), Lainee (14)

112 VACANT

114 The Walshes — Sally (49), Margie (46), Charlie (13)

116 The Wildes — Arlo (39), Gertie (31), Julia (12), Larry (8)

118 The Schroeders — Fritz (62), Rhea (53), FJ (19), Ella (9)

120 The Benchleys — Robert (78), Kate (74), Peter (39)

122 The Cheons — Christina (44), Michael (42), Madison (10)

124 The Harrisons — Timothy (46), Jane (45), Adam (16), Dave (14)

126 The Pontis — Steven (52), Jill (48), Marco (20), Richard (16)

128 The Ottomanellis — Dominick (44), Linda (44), Mark (12), Michael (12)
130 The Atlases — Bethany (37), Fred (30)
132 VACANT
134 VACANT

TOTAL: 42 People

A local thirteen-year-old fell through the Sterling Park sinkhole Saturday morning. Rescue teams were immediately called to the scene. Says Kirsten Brandt, spokesperson for the Nassau County Office of Emergency Management, "We're looking and we're going to keep looking. That's all I have for you right now."

The Maple Street sinkhole is about 180 feet deep, penetrating Long Island's water table. Hofstra University geology professor Tom Brymer says, "The complication with this kind of thing is that the underlying aquifers extend through the length of Long Island. If she hit her head or anything like that, it's very possible that she traveled."

Authorities at the Garden City zoning office, which had the Maple Street sinkhole scheduled for sand fill beginning today, have postponed the work until the child, whose name has not yet been released, is found.

A spokesperson at the EPA reiterated today that the air remains safe. In addition to the bitumen seen upswelling throughout the area, it is believed that the sinkhole's high metal content is interfering with radio and satellite reception.

From the TMZ website, December 6, 2014:

Arlo Wilde of Fred Savage's Revenge was taken into custody last night for attacking his manager and father, Hawshawn Wilde. He is charged with felony assault and battery. Hawshawn is in critical condition at New York–Presbyterian Hospital. The Wilde men have a notoriously rocky relationship, first reported here, when Arlo sued his father for back wages.

It's a fall from grace for Arlo, who won a Best New Artist Grammy last year. Sources say that as part of his plea agreement, Arlo plans to enter rehab for heroin addiction.

Click for mug shots!

From *Believing What You See: Untangling the Maple Street Murders*, by Ellis Haverick, Hofstra University Press, © 2043

Investigators have researched Rhea Schroeder's past exhaustively. We all know about the event at the Hungarian Pastry Shop. Franklin and others have tethered this incident to the subsequent Maple Street Murders. But that connection is tenuous at best.

We've not looked as much at Gertie Wilde, whom we might argue arrived at Maple Street with the most troubled history of all. Gertie's parents were drug abusers. She was shuffled through the foster system until her father's wife, Cheerie Maupin, agreed to keep her. Cheerie was problematic. She freely admits to having loaned Gertie out to men. It's not so surprising, then, that Gertie would have missed all the signs of sexual abuse. It's equally possible that she did recognize them, but chose to cover for her husband. Potentially, she even participated.

Maple Street

July 11–21

The search for Shelly Schroeder began at the moment of her fall, when parents and children shouted her name down the mouth of the hole: *Shelly Schroeder! Shelly Schroeder! Where are you?* It continued through the day, when police sectioned off the periphery and rescue workers attached to thick ropes belayed down. Oil-slick footprints tracked a reflective sheen all over the park until no grass was left. The day turned to night and into the next day without sign of life. The weekend passed. The oil and bitumen spread to the street.

As if fed, the hole grew. A gaping, excavated wound.

The media picked up the story, and quickly, blogs and streams unleashed news of the missing child, lost down a hole. "I can't understand it," Rhea told NBC's local affiliate, and Maple Street watched on static-filled screens, her bereavement seeming worse, somehow, when pixelated in their living rooms. "She knew she wasn't allowed out there. It doesn't make any sense."

Shelly Schroeder! Shelly Schroeder! Where are you?

Two more families left the block, for a total of seven gone. Those who remained felt the burden to represent. To support this lost child and her family. They doubled down, canceling trips to the beach, forgoing summer museum nights in the city. They stayed on Maple Street like sentries, as if Shelly, and the horrible sinkhole itself, belonged to them.

Never comfortable with uncertainty, the people of Maple Street struggled for explanations. They reviewed the events of that morning with their children, and they contrived reasons among one another, their voices respectfully soft. Why *had* Shelly been out there? Whose idea had it been?

They met at their curbs when hauling garbage, or on one another's front porches. In the shadow of that ominous and active hole, their chitchat degenerated. The things they'd been worried about, the deep-down disquiets about their parents' health and their children's futures and their jobs and this falling-apart world, began to erupt.

Margie Walsh carped to Cat Hestia and Nikita Kaur about the state of things. About women's rights and that poor girl in Buffalo who'd been beaten to death by fraternity brothers. She scratched invisible itches along her fingers when she spoke, her querulous voice uplifted. "Don't you even care?" Margie asked a surprised Cat Hestia, then narrowed her gaze to Nikita Kaur. "I suppose you'd have us all in those ridiculous burkas if you could."

Nikita, whose mom had taught astrophysics at the Indian Institute of Space Science and Technology at Trivandrum, India, was at a loss for words. Cat Hestia changed the conversation, fast, but Nikita stayed stuck on it, her body rooted, her face flushed. "Sikhs don't wear burkas," she said, even as Margie kept talking, tears in her eyes, about how unfair it is for girls in college. They go out into the world expecting adventure, and the patriarchy eats them.

Linda Ottomanelli fretted over her boys, following them from room to room as if, without her, they'd disappear. Jane Harrison wondered if she ought to educate the students at her preschool about sinkhole preparedness. Fred Atlas continued his morning jogs despite the heat. He had so much to run from. Sick Bethany watched from her shut window, looking out. To her, the hole was an especially terrifying thing.

More than anything, the Ponti men feared impotence. And so, they had a frank discussion. They felt it was their obligation to say out loud what no one else would admit: the child was dead. There was nothing to do but help those who'd loved her most. Fritz Sr. seemed ill-equipped for the task, so they inducted Dominick Ottomanelli and Sai Singh into their club. Like heroes, these men devised all variety of scenario in which to protect the Schroeder women from having to see Shelly's body, once it was finally raised.

A week passed. Rescue crews descended with less urgency. Engineers inserted hydraulic pistons and shields to prevent the hole from collapsing, and their ropes stretched deeper and farther as they dove into surprisingly cold water. When they climbed back out in black wet suits like spacemen, their hands were always empty.

Ten days missing. The heat wave continued, straining the power company past its limits. Brownouts turned to blackouts, making the people of Maple Street glisten. Trapped on that crescent, their thoughts circled and distilled into the simplest expression of worry.

Shelly Schroeder, Shelly Schroeder. Where are you?

They thought her name in a constant loop and it didn't just mean Shelly. It meant hope and life and death and community. It meant the future and the steady ground beneath their feet. It meant their validation and their justification. It meant their fear and their joy. It meant everything.

The girl became mythic and tragic, and they thought they'd found her on a Wednesday evening, drifted a quarter mile along an underwater stream. They felt the kinetic energy, heard the sirens, the calls through bullhorns. They stumbled out through front and back doors, even Peter Benchley in his wheelchair. They circled the hole's lip just as darkness set, and they bore witness as people in a community are supposed to do.

Shelly Schroeder, Shelly Schroeder.

First emerged three men in wet suits. They rolled out, apparatus weighing their hinds, flashlights bleaching the dark. These handed their ropes to another set of men, who attached them to a winding crank where more men turned the wheel. The rescue crew peeled off their second skins with solemnity. The crank got stuck. The men crawled to the hole and leaned on flattened bellies. They freed a black zipped bag and hoisted it to the bitumen-rich surface.

"Back away. It's not her," the lead crew-man shouted. But they knew this couldn't be true. It had to be her. The bag was too big to be anything else. They gathered, the news crews among them. Dominick Ottomanelli, Sai Singh, and the Ponti men pushed to the front. Using their bodies as barricades, they protected the Schroeders from the sight.

Pushed to the back, the Schroeders' only son, FJ, found Larry Wilde alone. In his nervousness, Larry had tucked Robot Boy inside his green shorts. FJ approached with such slow, heavy steps that it seemed his body was a weeping sponge.

"Freak. Should have been you."

While the Ottomanelli children and the entire Harrison family heard this cruelty, none corrected. They would later bristle at the memory, thinking they should have.

"It's not her," one of the men in thick neoprene announced. "Go home."

But Rhea wouldn't be stopped. What else could it be? She charged through the Ponti men to get to the body, her family following, and unzipped the bag.

They could all see what was inside: a German shepherd. His long pelt was slick with sand oil. His paws were bloody, nails missing from trying to smash his way free. Most unnerving, the cocktail of chemicals and cold had kept him perfectly preserved. A fossil of exactly the thing he had been eleven days before, trapped in time.

Fritz Schroeder looked away. Ella Schroeder began to cry. It was unclear whether her tears were relief or exhaustion. Then, Rhea. It wasn't simply the corpse that unnerved her. It was its perfect preservation. She imagined Shelly, discovered this way. Her raw body exposed for all to witness. Rhea staggered, hands flapping, unable, somehow, to understand what she was seeing: the wet fur, the pink tongue, the open, rolled-back eyes.

She faced the crowd, expression beseeching, and wailed, sonorous as an echo through a great canyon. It shuddered across the crescent and down the hole, too. Those who heard were unmoored by its upwind. Unsettled, not just in space, but in their very identities. They watched this woman, but did not come to her. There was so much space around her, unfilled.

Shelly Schroeder. Shelly Schroeder.
What happened to you?

Rhea's mad, witless focus took root in just one person: Gertie Wilde. Still screaming, she staggered in Gertie's direction. How apt this unity, they thought. The mother of the living child and the mother of the missing one, taking solace. What a perfect convergence from which healing could begin.

But instead of holding Rhea, Gertie flinched. "I'm so sorry," Gertie muttered. "But at least . . ."

Slap!

Rhea open-handed Gertie across the face. The sound was final. Cathartic, rendering the terrible unknown of these last horrible eleven days into something concrete. (*Shelly Schroeder! Shelly Schroeder!*)

It took a second before the blood. Rhea's large diamond, turned inward, had snagged a piece of Gertie's perfect cheek.

"Jesus Christ! Get the fuck away from my wife!" Arlo barked.

Gertie braced his tattooed arm and held him back. "It's okay," she mewed, her voice small and childlike. Disturbingly reminiscent of baby talk.

Shaking with violent intent, Arlo took a beat to calm down. Too long.

Linda Ottomanelli came to Rhea's side. She clutched Rhea's hand. "You need to go," she told Arlo and, by association, the entire Wilde brood.

The Wildes hunched, self-conscious and shamed. None came to their rescue. None could summon the correct words. And so, they slinked back to 116 with their children, shutting their door behind them.

Except for Peter Benchley, who rolled back home in disgust, the rest of the neighbors remained. Though they intended only to pay witness, their presence issued validation to Rhea's slap. They chatted with the rescue crew and consoled the Schroeders and offered licorice to sick Bethany, who gagged at the sight of her dog being zipped and packed as evidence. They remained until their own disquiet calmed. Because it was Rhea they stayed with, and because they were empathetic people, it was Rhea's side that they saw. What harm did a simple slap do Gertie, the woman whose children had survived?

Really, it was Arlo who'd scared them more. He'd seemed so angry. So quietly violent. Even Gertie had shrunk in fear beside him.

Shelly Schroeder.

What happened to you?

That night, the neighbors ruminated over the events of the day. They remembered that terrible wail, punctuated by a shocking slap, like an arrow pointing blame. They recalled the shortened, most repeatable version of what Gertie had said: *I'm so sorry.* They remembered Arlo, shaking with disproportionate rage.

*SHELLY SCHROEDER! SHELLY SCHROE-
DER! SHELLY SCHROEDER!*

In the dark, unsettled quiet, they would know that there was something deeper to this story, something as yet unrevealed: *Sorry for what?*

Directed against the wrong person, violence assumes a will of its own. It wants to continue to hurt that person, as if to right the wrong, as if, in some way, to provoke violence in kind, thereby coercing its own legitimacy.

After all the neighbors went home that night; after Fred Atlas put his sick wife, Bethany, to bed and headed to the Wildes to check in and say, *What happened out there was absurd,* but was told, *Thanks anyway. Nobody's much in the mood for a visit* by Arlo, who'd felt betrayed that his only real friend on Maple Street had not spoken out; after the Ponti men, Sai Singh, and Dominick Ottomanelli conferenced about how they might better have handled the situation, and good thing it hadn't been Shelly, but it was a dry run upon which they could improve; after Peter Benchley conducted his mirror therapy, then took an extra Oxy to calm his hurting, phantom legs; after Fritz Schroeder muttered something quick and polite about a new scent he was working on, then took the Mercedes out of Maple Street; after screens tuned to static because it was better than nothing were shut down, and every remaining family was tucked in its own fold; after the rescue crew at last gave up, covering the hole with new and thicker wood, hammered by wide and deep rivets, sealing it off for the first time since Shelly had fallen inside, and going home. Long after all these things, Rhea Schroeder's murk bubbled up.

Grief was not an emotion Rhea cared to entertain. It was a cockroach that waited until she turned out the lights, scampered in the dark.

In the light, she was all about blame.

Shelly's fall had been an accident, but accidents have causes. The flimsy slab over a mammoth hole was negligent. She could sue the police department. The sinkhole by rights ought to have been filled long ago. She could sue the town. And why had the children been out there to begin with? Whose bad judgment had they followed? She still remembered the expression on Shelly's face as she'd run from the crowd of chasing adults. She'd seemed so spooked.

Was it possible she'd been running from someone? Might her house contain a clue?

She searched the basement first. She passed

the pile of bricks in the laundry room, which had once made up the front walk. She opened the closet full of empty wine bottles, added two more. Fruit flies buzzed, laying eggs in the wet slurry at the glassy bottoms.

Nothing.

She stalked the kitchen, slammed dirty plates into the sink where they broke like sand dollars. She tore down the toile drapes because they were ugly. Tacky. Twenty years old. Up the stairs, to her bedroom that she hated, which she shared with a man she only then realized she couldn't stand. A man who wasn't home. Because when important things happened, Fritz Schroeder was never *there*.

"Stay in your rooms!" she shouted along the hall. Doors shut quietly, no hands visible, as if dispossessed of authors.

She opened cabinets and closets in Shelly's room, flinging out all that belonged to her bright, sensitive daughter. The pretty red winter coat; the homemade snow globe with a Sculpey snowman inside; the black knoll of shed braids sawed away with dull safety scissors; the horsehair brush, the goddamned brush.

She stripped the sheets so they floated, pregnant with old ghosts of the child who'd once slept beneath them. She turned the mattress. She shook every book, unleashing ticket stubs and class notes passed between schoolgirls, emblazoned with hearts, and even one from a boy — Dave Harrison — asking if she'd sneak out to meet him at midnight at 7-Eleven.

Shelly.

The bottom drawer of Shelly's desk was locked. She used a hammer to smash it open. Inside was nothing. An emptiness. She yanked out the drawer, and then all the other drawers. She overturned the entire desk. Something that was stuck to the back tore away. A tin lockbox. Written across green-and-pink-snowflake-patterned masking tape it read: *Pain Box.*

She yanked. Couldn't open it without the key. So she tapped it with the hammer. The frame bent. She stopped. There might be something fragile in there. Something just like Shelly. She took it, along with the other evidence, back down to the main floor. She hid the Pain Box in her office.

Then she slammed the brush and cut hair in the sink and poured lighter fluid all over, along with the broken dishes beneath. She hoisted the stepping stool and ripped out the ceiling fire alarm as it sounded, tearing batteries loose from their holsters. She poured more lighter fluid until the blaze

172

was deep blue at its roots, the hair perfect, protein-scented kindling. She poured until the bristles turned to ash and the polyure-thane melted and the compressed wood went to char. She did this until the sink itself was ruined.

A proper mess. Stinking and flamboyant. The char was the center, blue and orange and red flaming out, like entering a black hole. She followed with her eyes and with her mind, a kind of unburdening. She was spiriting Shelly to the safety of the other side, a game with time itself.

All the while, she thought: *Someone else was to blame for all that was happening. She had not done this.*

Thursday, July 22

Shelly Schroeder. Shelly Schroeder.
What happened to you?
For the people of Maple Street, the scream and the slap that followed stayed fresh in their minds. *I'm sorry,* they remembered. *Sorry for what?*
A bright girl. Brittle, too, with rough, bully edges — in a family that large, there's bound to be one of them. The people of Maple Street agreed she wasn't a black sheep. She came from too good a family for that. Rhea paid too much attention, helped too much with homework, rallied too much for the PTA. Fritz was too well respected, devoted in his quiet way to supporting his family. No, this was just a phase Shelly would have outgrown by high school, all the more resilient for having expunged it from her system.
Shelly Schroeder. Shelly Schroeder. Did you have a secret?

Nikita Kaur asked her son Sam to repeat every detail of the story, one more time.

He remembered something new: comments Shelly had made about Arlo Wilde. Nikita asked him to repeat these. She had her husband, Sai, listen. Sai, knowing that his son was both eager to please and easy to influence, said it was probably nothing. Still, Nikita had Sam repeat it to Cat Hestia, and then the Ponti men, who reacted with shocked outrage. *It's outlandish,* Sally Walsh said, though when she went home and relayed the story to her wife, Margie, they agreed that it added up. Even if Julia's story was true, and they'd been racing each other to the far edge of the park, Shelly was far too smart to use a dangerous slab for a shortcut. What if Julia was lying, to protect someone? Perhaps something had *driven* those girls. Perhaps . . . they'd been running from Arlo.

The Hestias asked their daughter Lainee, who corroborated and also embellished Sam's story. Lainee wasn't malicious, just immature. Sheltered her whole life, she lacked the ability to extrapolate that her story might get Arlo Wilde into serious trouble.

Mrs. Jane Harrison asked Dave to corroborate: *Did Shelly tell you kids that Arlo Wilde was bothering her?* Mouth agape in disappointment (how could his mother make

175

such a reckless suggestion?), Dave said: *It was a crazy lie Shelly made up like she always used to make things up, because she was batshit.* Then he ran away to punch some pillows, not because he was mad at his mom — she'd done so much dumb stuff that his fists would fall off if he punched something every time that happened — but because he'd talked about Shelly in the past tense. And he owed it to Shelly, his first kiss, and the only one he'd ever kept a secret, to believe until the end.

At last, Nikita forced Sam to repeat the story to Linda Ottomanelli. By this time, Sam had become reluctant. He did so haltingly, with tears.

Upon hearing this news, Linda Ottomanelli took it upon herself. She was obliged, as Rhea's best friend (and a little threatened, that it was Nikita who'd unearthed this inside poop). She decided to distill this hurtful hearsay — *this gossip* — and locate the truth. She went to the Roosevelt Field mall and bought the latest PlayStation. Promised the boys they could have it, so long as they tried their best to remember. Then she asked them the same question she'd asked a dozen times before, only this time, she gave them Sam Singh and Lainee Hestia's version first. Then she asked: *What happened?*

176

The boys corroborated the story. But because they had a cruel streak, they added something, too. *She said he'd done it to her, Mark said. I think that morning. That's why she was bleeding. It wasn't period. I think that's why she was so mad. Yeah, Michael added. She called him a rapist. She was screaming all about how he raped her. She was scared he was gonna come after her.*

Weeping with fear and confusion and sadness and even gratitude that her own children seemed healthy and unscathed (or was it possible they'd been tainted, too?), Linda rewarded them with the game system, then walked straight to Rhea's house, breathless and terrified and feeling just a little bit of the German word that means delight in the tragedy of another.

Rhea thought about Shelly's body, which still might be found. She thought about the dog, perfectly preserved. She listened to Linda's story; let it sink and fill her, like crawling along the bottom of a wine-dark sea, and opening wide.

Fourteen days into the search, representatives from the police department rang the Schroeder bell. Heads heavy, they informed Rhea (Fritz was at work) that they'd been unable to pass a final tidal tunnel; the last possible place that Shelly's body might be. They'd need several days to shore it before they could resume their search, and even then, the tunnel might be too narrow to traverse. They would have to send for small divers trained specifically for such tasks. Unless Shelly's body had gotten into the sewer system, this was the last place she could have drifted.

In situations like this, the waiting tended to be more excruciating than the answer. They believed that Rhea ought to schedule a memorial service. It was time to stop hoping.

Slowly, because her knee had been acting up, Rhea came forward. Shook hands and thanked them for coming. She'd already prepared a list of funeral directors, blown up a seventh-grade class photo. It wasn't that she'd hoped for this. Not that. But she'd prepared.

Maple Street watched this interaction through their windows. They witnessed, so she would not have to go through it alone.

Saturday, July 24

Sheened in sweat, the people of Maple Street sat up. They bathed and powdered and perfumed and then sweat through, their skin a fragrant crust. They dressed in black. They put out dark suits and muted dresses for their children. The Walshes came out early. After that, the Hestias, then the Pontis: Steven, Jill, Marco, and Richard. Quarrelsome Tim and Jane Harrison demanded that their children choose which parent to ride with. Elder brother Adam picked his mother. Younger Dave opted out. He stayed in his hot box of a bedroom, wishing the PlayStation's connection worked, so he could lose himself into *Deathcraft,* and forget this whole, terrible thing. The divided house, of course. Not Shelly, whose death was still too raw for him to believe.

The Atlases did not attend, as Bethany had spent the night throwing up. The Singh-Kaur family departed in their Honda

Pilot, each kid bopping in headphones to music on separate screens. Peter Benchley didn't go, but watched from his attic perch. Dominick and Linda Ottomanelli knocked on 118's front door, and the Schroeder and Ottomanelli families collected on the porch. The adults, having seen too many movies, wore sunglasses and knocked back shots of whiskey. Then they headed for their cars, so they could caravan.

They passed the Wilde house on their way. FJ picked up a quartz rock, two inches thick. The cloudy white kind that only sparkles when broken. He threw with a strong running back's arm. It ricocheted against the front door and landed back at his feet.

Everyone stayed still for a moment. Shocked.

"Don't be stupid," Rhea said at last. "It's broad daylight."

The front door opened. Pregnant Gertie stood inside the screen, Arlo beside her.

Rhea picked up that same rock. Wiped away the dirt and bitumen, and put it in her purse like an idea that needed warming to hatch.

The Wildes watched the last car leave for Shelly's memorial service. Excluded, again. And now somehow blamed. "Let's do it here," Arlo said, thinking of the life his pop had lived, and all the funerals they'd had for his street friends. Not the church kind or the coffin kind — the junkie kind. "Everybody get something important — something that means what you feel about Shelly. Bring it back to me."

Nobody moved.

"Just get something that reminds you of her, that you wouldn't mind parting from."

First Larry left for the stairs, then Julia. Gertie stayed. He acted braver than he felt and kissed her hard; slapped her ass. A firm and just-the-right-side-of-sexy tap. "Git! Git yer special thing!"

They reconvened back in the hall. "Okay," Arlo said as he opened his Montecristo cigar box. It smelled sweet. "I'll go first." He placed his Hohner 64 in the box. He was sorry to part with it — it had been a gift from Danny Lasson back when the band had been solid. But it was also the harmonica he'd always lent to Shelly on sleepovers. The last song he, Julia, and Shelly had worked on had been "Werewolves of London."

Next went Larry.

"Are you sure?" Gertie asked. "You won't get it back."

Larry nodded. "She was bad sometimes but she shouldn't be alone . . ." He dropped his Robot Boy, which he'd washed with Trader Joe's shampoo, into the box.

Gertie followed. She unclasped her pearl pendant. Her stepmother, Cheerie (*Call me Cherry, honey!*), had kept all her crowns and trophies, so except for her wedding ring, it was the only piece of real jewelry she owned. She'd planned to give it to Julia one day. "You don't think it's wasteful?" she asked Arlo as she held it over the box.

"No," he answered.

Gertie clutched the pearl tight. One last squeeze. Then she let go. After so many years of working to acquire the pieces of their life that surrounded them, it felt good to surrender a *thing*.

Everybody looked down. These items were such pretty offerings, their intent so personal and specific, that they were no longer sorry to miss Shelly's service. She'd slept over at their house scores of times. They'd only known her via this crescent, and for them, this was the better place to honor her.

At last, they turned to Julia, whose hands were empty. The right was still tender, blue stitches half dissolved. A dog, the emergency room doctor had told them, without any doubt.

"I don't have anything important," Julia said. "I wish it was me in that sinkhole."

"I don't," Larry said.

Julia's face crumbled. "It's my fault. I could've saved her!"

"You couldn't," Gertie said.

"I could!"

Arlo smiled bittersweet — impressed by the depth of his daughter's empathy, sorry she'd had to plumb it this way. "It was an accident."

"You don't understand! She wanted to live with us. She begged me!"

"Oh, Julia," Gertie said. "Why would she want that?"

"She wasn't happy."

"Well, her mom wouldn't have gone along with that."

"How do you know?"

"Sweetie. I know she's been acting out, but Rhea's a good mom. All those kids are college bound."

"She's sneaky mean."

"Lots of people are mean," Arlo said.

Julia was still crying. "God meant to get me, but he got her by accident. He was trying to punish me for being a bad friend."

"That makes no sense," Gertie said.

"It's true."

"It's not," Arlo said. "It's a story you're telling yourself."

Julia looked at them all, and took it in.

Understood that she'd spoken this fear with the hope of being contradicted. No, it wasn't her fault Shelly had died. This was not God's wrath. Still, she felt responsible.

"She hurt her."

"Who?" Arlo asked.

"Her mom. We weren't really racing. We were running away. That's why she fell. She was so scared her mom would murder her for cutting her hair that she wasn't looking where she was going."

The memory of that last, drunken conversation Gertie'd had with Rhea turned over right then. It flipped like a rock, insects slithering beneath. "Don't say that! It's a very serious accusation!"

"You take everybody's side but mine," Julia said. Her voice went flat. Too calm.

"Don't attack me! All I do is think about you," Gertie said. "We moved here for you."

"You never have my back. That's why I didn't come to you. But it's real. Shelly took pictures of what her mom did. Evidence. In her Pain Box."

"Rhea doesn't seem like the type," Arlo said.

"She's a college professor!" Gertie said.

"So?" Julia asked.

"So, Shelly was sensitive. Girls like that invent stories. It feels real but it's not. The pain's coming from someplace else. A problem within."

"I saw Mrs. Schroeder hit you. She hits."

Gertie touched her cut cheek, the humiliating memory of that slap fresh again. "But that's extreme stress. God forbid if you were hurt, I'd go a little crazy, too."

"You make excuses for people here. It's like you're scared of them."

"You're not making any sense to me, Julia. This is out of left field. I always —"

"What was this fucking Pain Box?" Arlo interrupted, his voice raised.

"It was real. I know because I saw. She showed me. I couldn't hug her too tight. It hurt her. And if you think about it, that's why she never let anybody hug her."

Gertie winced. Wiped the overfill of water from under her eyes. "You're sure she didn't do it to herself?" she asked.

Julia looked down.

"Then you can't —"

"Stop it!" Larry cried.

"Honey, I'm just trying to understand," Gertie said.

"No!" Larry cried. "Stop calling her a liar."

"I'm not!" Gertie said. "You're tag-teaming me!"

"Julia!" Arlo shouted. Everybody got quiet.

Julia sniffled. Shook. Hid her face to hide the tears. "Do you believe this shit you're telling us to be true?" Arlo asked.

Julia nodded, crying hard like you do when you've been yelled at, face hidden.

Gertie looked out the window, to the empty crescent. She followed the eddies of oil to the hole with her eyes. They reflected the sun; a smeared rainbow humbled by gravity to the earth, made of blue and black and red.

"And your instincts tell you this. You trust those instincts," Arlo said, voice modulated now.

Julia nodded. "Her mom hurt her when no one else was around. She hid it from me. She kept it a secret because she thought it was something to be embarrassed about. But she couldn't take it anymore. Her mom got meaner. So she told." Then she pressed her hands to the small of her back and worked upward between her shoulder blades. "She didn't do it to herself. She couldn't have reached."

Gertie kept her eyes on the hole. She felt them wet. Felt her whole self break apart. "Rhea did keep Shelly close, didn't she? Never gave her an inch of herself. Cheerie used to keep me close."

Arlo's voice was thick, his body tense. "Let's not talk about Cheerie."

"No," she said. "Nobody wants to hear about Cheerie . . . I think . . . I think it's true. I think she tried to tell me once. Rhea. But I didn't understand."

Julia burst into tears. "She was my friend. I loved her and now she's dead."

"I know," Gertie said.

Julia came to Gertie. Gertie held her off. She'd never been a hugger, especially not in moments of panic. But Julia wouldn't be denied. She pushed Gertie's arms aside, rested against her breast. Gertie held her, heart beating fast, thoughts broken and flying.

"If I'd known," Arlo whispered. His tenseness had resolved into something softer and more honest.

"We could have helped her," Julia muttered.

"Maybe. But an accident happened," Arlo said. "She fell. Not even her mom did that."

"She loved you," Gertie said. "And you loved her."

Julia's expression balled tight, tears still falling. "There wasn't anybody I liked talking to more, when she wasn't being mean. We didn't even have to talk. We just knew each other. But she was hiding something inside. She was hurting. And what if she wakes up down there, all alone? What if she thinks I abandoned her?"

"It's not your fault," they all said, together,

even Larry. "It's not your fault," they repeated.

She slackened like a drugged calf, resting her head on Gertie's breast. Larry petted her frizzy hair. With his skinny, monster-tattooed arms, Arlo leaned down and encircled his family, trying but not quite able to encompass the entirety of them.

Very softly, Julia said, "One day I'll save kids. All the kids."

Yes, they said, and they knew she meant it. They knew, when she grew up, that this would happen because of Shelly. *Of course you will.*

In the end, Julia asked that her hair be cut short just like Shelly had done. They did this, and braided the eighteen wild, curly inches with elastic ponytail holders, then added this to the cigar box. Each hammered a nail into one of the box's corners to close it. Then they showered and dressed in their summer best. Not black, but pretty florals for the girls, the Hawaiian shirt for Arlo (cleaned now of blood), and Larry's typical green. They discussed the backyard, but knew where they'd eventually agree upon.

They walked out of their house and into Sterling Park. They passed the orange cones and tape. The crew, having stopped coming on weekends, were all gone. A new, thicker slab covered the hole. They knelt at the edge. Arlo pried loose six rivets to lift a corner.

Sweet fumes wafted up. Together, they dropped the box down. It fell for so long they didn't hear the *splash* of its landing.

Arlo hammered each rivet back into place. Tested, to make sure the slab was solid again. They walked back home feeling lighter. Julia picked some hydrangeas from a bush in Sterling Park and tied them with a leaf. Gertie pulled a pen from her purse and wrote a note on her Century 21 business card:

Thinking of you.
— The Wildes

They deposited this on the Schroeders' front porch. Then they walked to their house, ready to recover from so much.

They slept deep and dreamless that night, the kids in bed with the grown-ups, and everyone tucked close. In the morning, there was coffee and sugar cereal and extra harmonicas. There was the optimism of a new day. But then their front bell rang. They opened the door to the police.

Sunday, July 25

Two detectives, a black-and-white cop car parked out front. Gertie assumed they were partners, but who knows how these things worked? They wore plain clothes and showed their badges. They actually handed them over, so Gertie and Arlo could read every word.

The first was an older Black woman named Denise Hudson, the other a younger red-haired Asian man named Gennet. Both had sweat through their business-casual work shirts. They informed Arlo and Gertie they were wanted at the police station. Now.

Neither detective offered a smile, not even to the children.

This was not Gertie's first clue that something was wrong, but it was the most startling one.

"Sure! We'll go now!" Arlo said, nervous and high-pitched. After deliberation with Gertie and also with the detectives, they headed over to Fred and Bethany's house.

Though Bethany lay on the couch with pillows piled along her sides and behind her back (her eyes rimmed with what looked like smeared, dark blue eyeliner, but was in fact her actual complexion), the Atlases agreed to watch the kids.

"Oh, you sweethearts," Bethany cooed. "Fred? Do we have milk for them? Go get some milk!" She winced when she craned her neck to look at the children, pained from just that small movement. "Darlings? Why don't you bring that deck of cards over here? I'll teach you rummy."

Arlo gave Fred a sorry shrug. "I owe you big."

Fred, looking exhausted, squeezed Arlo's shoulder. They'd missed the last two movie nights — life had gotten in the way. "It makes her happy," Fred said. Then he raised his voice loud enough for the detectives outside to hear: "Call me if it gets serious. I know people at the DA."

Arlo and Gertie took the Passat. They followed the cop car to the Garden City police station.

Inside, they walked past reception and through a deep atrium with open desks to the back, where they were ushered into a small, closed-off room, folding chairs surrounding a long table. Gertie and Arlo took one side, Detectives Hudson and Gennet took the other, deploying an old-fashioned tape recorder in the middle. The table was pale wood under polyurethane — school desk material. It was clean, save for pen smears. Hudson and Gennet had replaced their muted suit jackets, both of which were ill-fitting, and Gertie now understood why: the room was over-air-conditioned. Both Gertie and Arlo shivered.

"Rhea Schroeder reported a crime last night," Hudson explained.

Gertie squeezed the table. Despite the chill, her palms left a sweaty trail.

"Crime?" Arlo asked. His voice remained overly cheerful. His sales voice. In it, Gertie could hear fear, and worse than that, ignorance. The kind of ignorance that waits out its trial at Rikers, because free lawyers don't mean shit.

"She claims her daughter was raped on the morning of the fall."

Gertie froze. Her conscious mind refused to conceive of where this was going. But the deeper part, the part that had survived the pageant circuit and all those cutthroats, that part understood exactly.

"Witnesses testified that she'd been bleeding," Hudson continued. "She'd also cut her hair."

Gertie wanted to say something, but nothing came out.

"Mrs. Schroeder believes she cut her hair due to post-traumatic stress. She was running away from you when she was pushed down the hole by your children, who were likewise traumatized, and trying to conceal their father's crime." Hudson looked them in the eye the entire time, betraying no emotion. Gennet scribbled notes.

Gertie started. "Running away?"

"Crime?" Arlo asked. His voice lost that personable quality and took on something like a growl.

"She believes you raped Shelly Schroeder, and this action directly resulted in her death."

Arlo leaned forward, looked Gennet, then Hudson in the eyes. "I did not do that."

"That's insane," Gertie said. "It's not even possible."

"Why isn't it possible?" Hudson asked. She wore a mask of indifference, but emotion boiled underneath. She gripped the table with her hands, so tight it made her fingernails white.

"Because he's not a hunter. I've known hunters my whole life and he's not. He'd never do that —"

"I work in the city," Arlo interrupted. "I

didn't get home that night until around four in the morning, when I crashed into bed. With Gertie."

"That's right!" Gertie cried.

Arlo stretched his arms in their direction. Their eyes roamed along his monster tattoos. "There's probably still footage of me at Penn Station around two-thirty a.m. If not there, then the newsstand — I got a Coke and popcorn for the ride. So you can check that. You can check my getting off the train around three-fifteen."

Gennet scribbled. Hudson didn't take her eyes away.

"And what about the morning? Was Mrs. Wilde with you then?"

"I was showing a house. In Glen Head. But he never gets up before ten if he can help it."

"Yeah, by the time I rolled out of bed, the kids were out playing. There might be footage there, too. The Cheons have a camera, I think. Dunno if it works since the sinkhole. Everything out on the block gets static."

Hudson's voice got scary soft. "You're certain that you were never alone with Shelly Schroeder within the twenty-four hours of her death?"

"I swear."

"He wasn't," Gertie said. Relief flooded

her system. Proof. You can't argue with proof.

"Were you *ever* alone with her?"

"Probably."

"You can't say for sure."

"I don't remember, specifically."

"Do we need a lawyer?" Gertie asked.

Gennet stayed looking at his notebook.

"If we can clear this up, you won't need a lawyer," Hudson answered.

"Oh," Gertie said.

"Now, were you ever alone with any of the other children in the neighborhood?" Hudson asked.

"No offense, but this is pretty scary. I think we need a lawyer," Arlo answered.

"You're not under arrest, sir," Hudson said.

"Can we leave?" Gertie asked.

"Anytime," Hudson answered. She moved back from the table, as if ready to walk out. "But we'd prefer you cleared this up."

"Let me make a phone call," Arlo said.

"You won't need one if we clear this up."

"He's gonna make a phone call," Gertie said.

Hudson nodded, as if she'd expected this answer all along. As if they'd have to be fools to do anything else.

They excused themselves and went into

195

the waiting room. Arlo called Fred Atlas, but the connection had too much static. They couldn't hear each other. He searched his contacts, looking for anyone important. He found coworkers and some old Brooklyn friends, none of whom knew any lawyers. He broke into a cold sweat and scrolled to Danny Lasson's number. Danny'd been drums for Fred Savage's Revenge, was now writing jingles in LA. He might know someone. But it was entirely possible that Danny hated him, for having broken up the band. Not possible. Probable.

"Do you know anyone important?" Arlo asked.

Gertie let out a hollow laugh. "Rhea's about it."

Arlo and Gertie were gone by the time Maple Street woke to a new day, Shelly Schroeder's memorial service behind them. The mercury in their thermometers climbed past any temperature they'd ever before seen. Their air conditioners were no use. By ten that morning, the senior Benchleys had to catch a bus several blocks away to the local cooling center. That candy apple scent from the sinkhole cooked like chemicals in an oven. It permeated the air and the dirt and their clothing.

It appeared that the Wildes weren't home. But they remembered that Gertie had made an offer weeks ago. The Slip 'N Slide was for everyone's benefit. Carte blanche.

The people of Maple Street had no qualm with Gertie or her children, they reasoned. Their problem was only with Arlo. The day was swelteringly hot. With the pool closed, they longingly gazed at the yellow Slip 'N Slide. Some of the kids begged.

It was Cat Hestia who gave in, connecting the Walshes' hose to the Wildes' Slip 'N Slide, and unrolling it. Except for the Schroeder kids, who were in no mood for play, the Rat Pack got on their bathing suits. They slid across the Walshes' lawn. They were somber at first, but pretty soon, they were howling with joy. They were joined by older siblings and even some adults. Like a rebirth in tar sands and dirt, even the adults went sliding.

In the light of day, amid yellow plastic and happy, communal laughter, the accusation against Arlo seemed outrageous. They decided that they were glad to be using the Slip 'N Slide. It was a way of including the Wildes, even in their absence. It was a way of moving the line just slightly away from Rhea's side of things, and all the ugliness that it had always been her nature to spread.

When the Wildes returned from wherever they were at, the neighbors would speak to them. They would ask them directly about the accusations Shelly had reportedly lodged. They would allow Arlo the chance to defend himself.

When a brown Chevy sedan pulled in to the crescent, they took note. A man in a clean, unwilted three-piece suit approached, knocking door to door. Those parents not already there returned to their houses to answer. *Yes, they said, we saw Arlo Wilde in just boxers, chasing Shelly that morning. Yes, his own kids were running away from him, too . . . Yes, they said, our children heard Shelly tell them in no uncertain terms: Arlo raped her, possibly that very morning.*

At this, a detective named Bianchi asked to speak with their children, and so, one by one, they called them away from the Walsh lawn. Only, their children were filthy with tar. It covered their hands and cheeks and hair. They appeared anonymous and indistinguishable.

Standing in thresholds, dripping Slip 'N Slide water and sand oil, these children corroborated: Lainee Hestia, Sam Singh, the Ottomanelli twins, and to his chagrin, Charlie Walsh: *Yes,* Charlie said. *She said that stuff. But she lied a lot.* Dave Harrison glared, not

198

at the detective, but at his mother, without answering, until Jane Harrison announced that maybe Bianchi ought to come back, as clearly her son had a fever.

After each interview, feeling strange and hypocritical (If it was true that Arlo had done wrong, why were they letting their children play on his Slip 'N Slide? And if it wasn't true, why were they corroborating a false narrative?), they cleaned off and kept their children home. At last, the Slip 'N Slide was empty, water streaming along yellow plastic. Looking out their windows, they saw what they'd neglected: propelled by the force of its water, and lacking a handler, the yellow plastic had careened across the Walsh lawn and gotten stuck against the common privets that divided the Wildes from the Schroeders.

Cat Hestia, who'd plugged the hose in to begin with, had left for her silent meditation class by then. The Walsh family was gone, too, having scheduled a lobster dinner at Waterzooi. The water kept spraying, none wanting now to turn it off. All thinking it was someone else's job. They didn't dare go near that tainted Wilde house right in front of Detective Bianchi, who would see them. They didn't want to get caught pulling the yellow plastic from the shrubbery just as the

Wildes returned from wherever they'd been, either. The family might get the wrong idea. Arlo might shout. Or worse.

As Detective Bianchi was leaving, Peter Benchley rolled out his door and stopped the man. They spoke for nearly half an hour. Maple Street was surprised — hadn't known Peter was capable of that level of interaction. This haunted them. What if, all this time that he'd been watching, he'd been *seeing*, too?

I'll swear to it in court, Linda Ottomanelli heard him say. *There's no way Arlo Wilde hurt that girl. Not that day, anyway. Probably not any day.*

Bianchi left.

The water kept running, flooding the Wildes' side lawn and reaching into the Schroeders'. Linda Ottomanelli and Rhea Schroeder sat drinking red wine on Rhea's porch, but the rest stayed inside their houses with their doors shut.

At last, Rhea stood. She made a big deal of it, arms wide as if to say: *It's always me, isn't it? The buck stops here.* She cut through the Wilde lawn, to the Walsh house, and turned off the hose. Petite and walking with what they noticed was just the hint of a limp, she dragged the Slip 'N Slide toward her porch to allow the Wildes' lawn to dry. The rest

200

of Maple Street felt silly, that they had not done this.

They felt ashamed.

While Gertie and Arlo were waiting on the police department front steps, Fred Atlas walked to an outgoing connection and called them back. Arlo explained the problem. Fred told him to sit tight. He had a criminal attorney friend by the name of Nick Sloss, who'd meet him there.

"I can't believe this is happening," Arlo said.

Silence on the other end for a good few seconds. Arlo waited, shorn of pride. "I think you'd better believe it," Fred said.

When they returned, it was explained to the Wildes that because Arlo was the suspect, and Gertie was not, they needed to be placed in different rooms while they waited. This seemed specious — like a divide-and-conquer plan of attack. But they felt that arguing would make it seem like they had secrets to protect — a story they needed to get straight. And in truth, the nature of the accusation was so shocking that they weren't thinking straight.

Gennet led Gertie to a new room, shut the door behind him, and sat next to her instead of opposite. "Are you absolutely certain this accusation is false?" He had a kinder demeanor than Hudson. She felt empathy from him, even though his expression, too, was an emotionless mask.

"It's a sickness. You'd be helping him if you told me the truth," Gennet said.

"Have you met Rhea?" she asked. "Her son threw a rock at our house. This" — she pointed at the fresh scab on her cheek — "this is from her ring. She slapped me. She blames me for what happened to Shelly, I think. Because my kids lived . . . Or, I don't know. I can't pretend to understand how she thinks."

Gennet took a photo of her scab. "Did anyone see her slap you?"

"Sure. The whole crescent. Ask any of them."

Gennet wrote this down.

"I should tell you something," Gertie said, her voice lowered. "I'm not an eye-for-an-eye person. Bitter just makes more bitter. It's toxic. Every book says so. So that's not why I'm saying this, but you tell me you're doing your job and you want to find out the truth, and I think you're being honest with me, so I should tell you."

Gennet looked up from his notes. He had freckles across the bridge of his nose. His wedding band was an old-fashioned claddagh, heart pointed down. She pictured him meeting his wife at Croxley's Ale House in New Hyde Park after work, noshing the all-you-can-eat wings. He looked the type.

"Rhea's the one who hurt that child. This is her guilt talking."

"What makes you say that?"

"She told me once, that she was unhappy. That she wanted to cause her family hurt. That Shelly galled her. Something about her hair. She hated brushing it. And Julia, my daughter, she told me. She saw the bruises. Said there was evidence Shelly was keeping. Pictures."

Gennet kept writing. His pen-to-paper made a soft, reassuring sound.

"Where's the evidence?"

"Her room, I'll bet? But I don't know. My daughter said she kept it in something called a Pain Box."

"What's the evidence?"

"Julia said it hurt her to be hugged."

They sat like that, in quiet. Gertie stopped shaking enough to pour herself a glass of water. She let that sink in again: it had hurt Shelly to be hugged. She wondered where Shelly was right then, and if anything had comforted her, at the end.

"People from your kind of background cope with a lot of stresses."

"My background?"

"You were raised by a Cheerie Maupin in Atlantic City. She had a rap sheet for fraud. You never finished high school. Your husband's got a rap sheet, too."

"That was before I knew him," Gertie answered. "It was just drugs. He never hurt anyone. He's not that guy anymore."

"But he did hurt someone." Gennet slid a glossy sheet of paper in Gertie's direction. It was a photo of a skinny old man with a broken nose. Black hair and tall and reedy. Holes in a dingy white T-shirt. "He broke this man's nose."

"That's his dad. His dad doesn't count," Gertie answered. Her face felt hot.

"But you said he never hurt anyone. Is there anyone else he hurt, that you don't think counts?"

Gertie understood then that there wasn't any winning over that was going to happen here. She'd been right to tell him about Rhea, but that didn't make him sympathetic to her cause. They weren't now best friends. This wasn't a pageant, she wasn't sixteen, and no wide, dimpled smile was going to charm him. This realization, or maybe just the baby due in thirteen weeks, and all its hormones, caused her to break down.

"Do you need a tissue?"

Gertie opened her purse. "I have my own."

She blew her nose. "People cry under stress. Stop writing. It's normal to cry."

"Mrs. Schroeder was very thorough. She gave an exhaustive statement. She claimed that Shelly slept over your house at least a dozen times."

Gertie sniffled.

"But your daughter, Julia, never slept over at the Schroeders'."

"Rhea's very particular. You know — only one slice of French toast, then everybody's got to clean their plates and read Shakespeare. Julia had a hard time with that. Shelly, too. They liked to goof around . . . Why am I getting interrogated? After what I just told you about Rhea, you're not even calling somebody to look for that evidence?"

"What about Julia? The detectives on the scene told me your daughter cut her hair short like Shelly Schroeder's. Why is that?"

Gertie held her belly. Guppy kicked, stimulated by the cold water. "I'm tired of this. I don't know what you want me to say."

"We're told your son behaves inappropriately. Self-fondling. You understand that's a symptom. If we find proof of something untoward, you'll be charged as an accessory. They'll both be removed from your home right now. Today."

"But I'm not lying," she said.

Gennet wrote something else down in his book. "Let's go over it all again," he said.

"No," she answered.

Gennet got up, walked out, returned with three slices of pizza and a Coke, plus a beige cotton cardigan he must have borrowed from a coworker.

"Can we go over it one more time?" he asked.

Gertie bit into the pizza. She was starved. "I bet you go to Croxley's for wings. You do, don't you? I'll bet when this all gets cleared up I'll see you there, and you'll feel bad. You'll say sorry, and you'll buy my husband a beer."

A blush warmed his freckled cheeks. "I really hope so."

Hudson, clearly the tougher detective, joined Arlo in his room. She smiled warmly when she sat down beside him, and she was a good actress, because that smile reached her eyes.

"I have to do this," she said. "I'm inclined to believe you. But this has to be thorough, for your sake."

"Okay."

"Mrs. Schroeder seems over-the-top. We all thought so."

"I guess. Her kid died. Maybe she's not in her right mind."

"Exactly. I mean, come on. What, like you kissed Shelly on the cheek one time, right?"

"Nope."

"Want a Coke?"

"Nope."

"You look pretty rough. You grab a little hair of the dog that bit you this morning?"

"Nope."

"But you were drinking the morning Shelly fell, is that right? Witnesses said they could smell it."

"Don't recall."

"Can we test your blood?"

"Nope."

"Your daughter, Julia, cut all her hair off this morning. Why do you think a twelve-year-old girl would do something like that?"

Arlo flinched. He didn't like this woman using his daughter's name.

"They said when Shelly fell, you were chasing her. Both of them. You weren't dressed except for a pair of . . ." She looked through her notes. "Tiger-striped briefs. One witness saw an erection. Can you tell me what had you so aroused?"

A terrible red blush rose from his neck all the way to his scalp. An erection? Who could imagine such a thing, let alone say it out loud? "Nope."

"Do you know why Shelly Schroeder cut her hair?"

"Nope."

"This lawyer thing, is it necessary? I'm starting to feel like you don't want to cooperate. That's not the impression you want to give, is it?"

Despite the cold, a bead of Arlo's sweat dripped to the table. It was possible that telling his story for a seventh time would, in some way, help his cause, but he doubted it. "Nope."

"So tell me what's going on. Why are you here?"

"I dunno."

Detective Hudson stood. At last, her mask of calm cracked. She didn't look angry and she didn't look warm. She just looked finished. Like she'd done her diligence, and could move on to the next thing.

They were both left alone for another couple of hours, awaiting a lawyer who never showed up. Or had the police detained him? Were they allowed to do that?

Gertie broke down and cried for the second time.

Once something is said out loud, you can't help but wonder if it's true. If you've got kids, it's your job to imagine the worst possible outcome, be it hot coffee near a baby, or slippery rocks at the beach . . . What if her messed-up history had blinded her to an obvious threat? What if Arlo *had* done harm? She thought about that, and she thought about the kids, Larry and Julia. Was there a reason Larry touched himself when nervous? They'd had him tested. It wasn't autism or anything on the spectrum. It wasn't low intelligence. He actually had a genius IQ and they'd told her that some especially smart kids develop social skills at a slower rate. Every expert said he'd grow out of it. Some kids develop unevenly. He was just weird, because some kids are weird.

But what if something untoward had been done to him?

Gertie'd been through so much, abused so often as a kid, that her perspective might be warped. What if it was like all the books said? She'd reproduced her own childhood without knowing it, because damaged people seek more damage?

And what of Julia? She'd accused Gertie just today of never being on her side. What had she meant by that? Was it possible that Arlo had gotten to both Julia and Shelly at some sleepover? That this had bound them, making their friendship deeper and more turbulent? It would explain their secrecy and closeness, and then the abrupt end to all that.

Were these accusations real?

She thought about herself as a girl. How scared she'd been. How she'd believed everything was her responsibility and fault. She'd never spoken unless spoken to, and even then, only ever told people what they'd wanted to hear. And she'd been good at knowing what people wanted to hear. Her life had depended on it. Larry wasn't like that. If he got mad, you knew it. He had no problem defending himself, and given all the teasing, his self-esteem had held up pretty okay, too. Same with Julia. Together, any rooms those two walked into, they owned. You can't have strong, happy kids if the people who are supposed to love them most are betraying them. It's not possible.

And Arlo. Was he a hunter? Anyone could see that he had a temper. But in the years she'd known him, he'd never lost control. Gertie had come closer to spanking Julia, to grabbing Larry by the arm and forcing him out the door to get where they needed to be on time. Arlo hollered and threatened, sure. But he never hit.

The real question here: Was Arlo squirrely for little kids? Their own sex life was straightforward. Nothing experimental. But that was her fault. She had scars. It had to be her on top — the way she'd never done it with any of the men before. To make it new and her own. But so vanilla, had he gone outside for fulfillment?

He fit the profile. A cowed man, ill-used by his dad in ways that are too dark for the movies. It had made him soft and unsure. Overly agreeable in the presence of strong personalities until he felt cornered, and then he barked. But those dark feelings have to go somewhere.

Maybe they'd gone into the children.

Her heart was beating too fast. She held the table because things got swimmy. Breathed slow and imagined the smell of chocolate chip cookies until she wasn't dizzy anymore. She came to a decision then. She had to stop thinking about this. It was making her crazy. Even if Arlo was guilty, she still had to get out of here and back to her kids.

She wiped her eyes, then Googled a practical question: "Can police detain lawyers?" But the internet was blocked in the room. So she stared at her phone, and then it occurred to her to get the hell up. The door was unlocked. No one stopped her. She went outside and under the sun, where it was warm and she stopped shivering.

"Can police detain lawyers?" she asked her

phone. The answer from the hive mind was a resounding *no*. Next, she looked up the thing she was *really* worried about: "What happens to kids when parents go into police custody?" Foster care, it turned out. As soon as tonight, any kinds of people could be alone with Julia and Larry. Doing whatever they pleased to them.

She stared at her phone, wishing she had someone to call for help. But she didn't. Her whole life was Arlo.

On Arlo's end, the time passed even more slowly. What do you do when falsely accused of the worst possible crime? He felt the camera on him, aware that his room was under surveillance. He thought back, trying to remember a time he'd been alone with the child — Shelly Schroeder. Had he ever walked in on the girls when changing? Was that illegal? Had he ever walked around with his shirt off? Was that wrong? What if the newspapers found out? They loved scandals about has-beens. Front-page news. Internet trolls would barrage every interoffice e-mail address they could find. He'd be fired within the hour. And what of Julia and Larry? How would he explain this to them? Would doubt creep, smearing his relationships, so that no one ever trusted him again?

Eventually, Arlo realized that he, too, could go outside. He smoked three Parliament Lights and called Fred. After a time, Fred called back, explaining that the lawyer was stuck in traffic. After sixty minutes, Arlo called again. Phone tag. This time, Fred seemed concerned, and said he'd check things out. On his way back, Arlo stopped in the room where Gertie was sitting. Realized it was stupid they weren't together.

He didn't come to her like he ordinarily would have. He just stood there, stiff and uncomfortable, because maybe someone was watching this reunion. Judging it. Maybe Gertie was upset. After what she'd been through in her own childhood, doubt had crept. She no longer loved him.

He sat one chair away from her. She didn't ask him to move closer, but she did pass a slice of cold pizza and half a Coke.

At two hours, they went outside and called Fred again. Tag. He called back and told them that Sloss had already arrived at the police station, spoken with the police, discovered that Arlo was a "high-profile" former celebrity, and decided to leave without informing anyone, including Fred. He didn't want his name associated with a pedophile.

It could ruin his career. Fred was calling around, looking for someone else.

"Will it hurt your career to help me out like this?" Arlo asked.

"It's fine," Fred answered, too quickly.

"You do believe me, don't you?"

"I don't know," Fred answered. "I know you've been good to me and my wife. Listen, I was hoping I could get this cleared up for you. A lawyer would put it all on record. But at this point, your kids are starting to get upset. Just come home."

They found Hudson and Gennet in the wide main room, at a pair of open desks. Another man in a more expensive suit was with them. He looked like he'd just come out of court, and for a moment, they both fantasized that he was the lawyer Fred had sent, returned at last.

"Detective Bianchi," he said. "I'm supervising this case." He shook their hands. Firm shake, but not jerk firm.

"My wife's ready to drop," Arlo said. "I'm taking her home. As soon as I find a lawyer, I'm happy to come back and answer all your questions."

"Give us just a second," Bianchi answered as he took both detectives aside. Words were spoken. It lasted twenty more minutes.

Arlo found a chair for Gertie and had her sit. She noticed him fidgeting, getting annoyed. "Don't blow your top," she whispered.

Bianchi returned. "You're on surveillance at Penn Station the night before the incident. And we have a witness who places you in your home for the subsequent duration."

Gertie burst into gasping tears. Arlo and the detectives surrounded her.

"It's the hormones," she muttered. Arlo rubbed her back. "Don't touch me!" she said.

Arlo let go. "Give her space," he said, and they all backed up.

"I'm sorry to put you through all this, ma'am," Gennet said. "Can I get you more pizza?"

"Don't look at me crying," Gertie answered, which she knew sounded nuts. "I don't want you to see me cry."

Except for Arlo, they averted their eyes. She pulled herself together.

"Who was the witness that vouched for me?" Arlo asked.

"Somebody called Peter Benchley," Bianchi answered. "A veteran. He witnessed Shelly's actual fall, from his window. He says she fell because something had been punching up, making the wood weak, and that checks. Forensics matched the dog to the teeth marks on your daughter's hand.

"Benchley says he was up all night. Insomnia. He says you didn't come out until it was already going down."

Arlo let out a sigh. "Well, that's good. I'm glad he was watching."

"You can go. We'll be in touch," Bianchi said.

Clear-eyed now, Gertie fidgeted with her cardigan, handed it back. "How did you know to ask Peter Benchley?"

"I was on Maple Street. Rhea Schroeder named a great many witnesses. I went door to door," Bianchi answered.

"To the whole block?" Gertie asked. "You asked the whole block about Arlo? What did you ask?"

"I spoke with the witnesses Mrs. Schroeder named. Mr. Benchley came forward on his own. So did your Atlas friends. But the Atlases hadn't seen anything. These are the questions I asked," Bianchi said. "It's protocol: Can you corroborate the witnesses' story? Do you have any new or unreported information about the incident? Has the suspect been behaving strangely? Have you ever seen him acting strangely around the child in question?"

"Oh shit," Arlo mumbled.

216

"I don't understand. I told you about Shelly. That there's evidence of abuse. If you're so interested in finding the truth, why aren't you at that house right now? Why aren't you asking the neighbors about Rhea?" Gertie asked.

Gennet spoke at last. "We're getting full, conclusive statements regarding all parties. There's not enough evidence for a warrant. But I have passed the information along."

"It would be a lot easier if we found the body," Bianchi resumed. "Most rape cases in this age category show bruising and vaginal scarring. If we find the accusation against you specious, you can always sue. Probably not in your best interest. It's smartest to just forget about today. But I can give you the full report so you know. You're entitled to that."

They stood nervously, waiting for the receptionist behind the intake desk to print the report. The office was surprisingly empty. Just a few plainclothes police worked at their desks, leaving another twenty desks empty.

Gertie's knees were weak. "I don't think I want to know what that report says."

But the receptionist was done by then. She handed the report to Arlo. Witnesses included Rhea Schroeder; Ella Schroeder; Nikita Kaur; Sam Singh; Linda, Dominick,

Mark, and Michael Ottomanelli; Lainee Hestia; Steven Ponti; and Margie Walsh. The list of witnesses in Arlo's defense was much shorter: Peter Benchley.

Gertie and Arlo got into their Passat. Halfway to Maple Street, he pulled over. Gertie opened the door and vomited.

Shaken, they got back in and continued home. They'd only been gone for a day, but in that time, their whole world had changed.

Sunday night on Maple Street. Cars were parked in driveways, dining room curtains opened for late-day dinner light. But they weren't playing on the trampoline or barbequing burgers, like they ordinarily would have done on a weekend evening. No, they were inside, looking out. Gertie could see faces peeking from windows. Weirdest and most unsettling of all, they'd set up the Slip 'N Slide. It looked like they'd only recently, hastily, turned off the water and scattered. The Wildes' entire side lawn was ruined. Just mud and viscous oil. Not a blade left of grass.

No one waved at the Wildes as they parked and started down the sidewalk. They didn't walk away from their windows, either. They watched.

When the Wildes retrieved their children

from Fred and Bethany Atlas, they expressed their deep gratitude and stanched their tears. Fred said he was still looking for a lawyer. It was tricky. People don't like to be associated with that kind of accusation, and when they do, they charge a lot. Arlo should be prepared for photographers. This could leak to the tabloids.

"If we're detained again, could you take the kids? Otherwise, I'm worried it's foster care," Gertie asked.

"Sure!" Bethany called from the couch. "We love them so much!"

Fred walked them to the door, his voice lowered. The kids walked ahead down the lawn. "She's back in the hospital tomorrow," he whispered. "I'll be at work or with her. They say we'll know right away if it works. This targeted gene therapy. A week or a month, they say."

Arlo and Gertie stayed frozen on the stoop.

"I want to help you," Fred said. "But . . ."

Arlo walked back up the steps. Clapped his friend on the back, and when he saw that was welcome, he hugged him. Fred shook with quiet crying. Arlo held him. The distraction from his own burden was a relief. "I didn't even tell you I'm sorry about your dog. I'm sorry about your dog, Fred . . . You take care of your wife. Don't worry about another fucking thing."

"We're here if you need us, Fred," Gertie said. "Anything. Both of you. I swear to God, I mean that."

After Fred shut the door, they caught up to their kids. Julia squeezed her dad, hard. Larry took both their hands and walked between them, the way he liked to do when he was scared. Seeing her good, kind children in full flesh, a certainty came to Gertie Wilde: her husband was innocent.

Her relief was great, and so was her fury. She hated Rhea Schroeder more than she'd hated anyone in her life.

Rhea was sitting out front with Linda Ottomanelli and a glass of red wine, the half-filled bottle between them. She was still wearing yesterday's black linen suit. Bitumen stretched out from the hole now in thick seams. It crossed under the sidewalk pavement and up again, daubing the yards.

"Gert," Arlo barked in warning.

Gertie walked up 118's wide, well-kempt slate. Rhea and Linda raised their eyes. Gertie's speed increased. She stood before them. Linda looked away. Rhea did not. Between them was the note the Wildes had written, only someone had added to it and drawn over the words with the kind of red pen teachers use to grade papers:

MURDERING RAPING
~~*Thinking of you.*~~
FUCK
— *The Wildes*

There's this thing that happens to people who've grown up with violence. It changes their hardwiring. They're just slightly a different species, built more for survival than for social networking. They don't react to threats like regular civilians. They do extremes. They're too docile over small things but they go apeshit over the big stuff. In other words, they're prone to violence.

Gertie approached Rhea now, when a shrewd person would have walked away, licked wounds, and if she was crafty, mounted a covert counterattack. But a switch inside Gertie had flipped. There wasn't any going back.

"Fuck you, Rhea Schroeder. You beat that child and we both know it," Gertie shouted. "I should have called the cops on you months ago."

Linda gasped.

Gertie reared. With an awkwardly slow launch, she punched the concavity between

Rhea's chest and her shoulder. At first, Rhea did not fall back. The impact wasn't great enough. But after a second, she pretended that it was, and slumped.

The people of Maple Street saw this. The adults and the teenagers and the Rat Pack children, even Julia and Larry.

Gertie didn't wait for retaliation. She walked around the Schroeder house and yanked the Slip 'N Slide that was drying there, dragging it back to her own house. Her pretty dress that she'd worn for Shelly's homespun funeral got mucked with dirt and oil. She stomped into her house, a public tantrum, leaving Julia and Larry and Arlo behind.

Back at the stoop, Rhea Schroeder followed Gertie with her eyes.

Once the neighbors witnessed Gertie's act of violence, the impartial line they'd been trying to balance sprang firmly back to Rhea Schroeder's side. Rhea had taken the blame for something that was entirely their fault. They felt responsible. It was true that she had a gossiping tongue, but in her kindness to every one of them, and in her inclusion of the terrible Wilde family for so long, she'd proven that she was a good person. The people of Maple Street owed her their loyalty.

They converged that night. They came outside to escape the stifling heat, and inevitably found themselves at the hole. Here, they discussed. This had happened: a child had died and even the police knew it wasn't an accident. There was blame. A cancer was growing on Maple Street.

Linda Ottomanelli, who had considered herself Rhea's best friend until Gertie Wilde moved in, was the first to suggest a brick. She hoped to get back into Rhea's good graces. Supporting his wife, who'd been down lately, Dominick refined the idea. And then the Ponti men, plus the Hestias, who wanted to be of use, added their thoughts on how best to execute such a plan. Margie Walsh felt it should happen soon. Tonight.

"What do you think, Rhea?" Linda asked.

Rhea shook her head in sadness. "I can't believe it's come to this," she said. "But I don't see any other way."

Consent given, the inchoate scheme took form, and so many contributed to its birth that none felt wholly responsible. They were passengers, riding the momentum of something greater than themselves.

They waited until long after lights went out. They wore dark clothing. As if they'd gotten the idea from their children's Slip 'N Slide games that afternoon, some ducked down. When they came back up, their faces were smeared with oil.

As levity or as a scare tactic or something in the vague in-between, twenty-year-old Marco Ponti turned on his phone.

Monday, July 26

There are certain prisons from which other people can provide no solace. Gertie and Arlo fell asleep with white space between them, each tucked into small bundles on opposite sides of their bed. Staticky music played. It entered the cracks of 116 Maple Street. Gertie heard it first. She shook Arlo by the Elsa Lanchester–tattooed shoulder. "Listen."

Arlo jackknifed.

"Somebody's playing 'Wasted.'"

Arlo pulled the blinds. "There's someone out there. Wait. More than one, I think. It's hard to see. They're all . . . They did something to their faces."

Something crashed against the window nearest Gertie.

The creaking air conditioner fell out the window, she guessed. Or maybe it was the old computer that they'd turned into a fish tank. She jolted, struggling, but couldn't sit upright. Her belly felt like it had been punched by an industrial stapler to the mattress.

Was it the music? The heat? Why was she stuck?

"Arlo! Where are you?" she pleaded. Music played louder. The part where he's watching cartoons the first time he gets high. "Arlo! Why won't you answer?"

The lights came on. Skinny Arlo was standing over her, all four tattoos bright and animate against his pale, needle-scarred arms.

"The kids! You need to go check —" Gertie started, but her voice sounded muddy to her own ears.

"Give me," Arlo said, taking the phone from her bedside table, kissing her cheek and the side of her lip gentle and quick.

"Why am I . . . ?"

She saw then that the window was broken, and the floor beneath it spilled with shattered glass. She followed an imaginary trajectory across the room. Through the window, up toward the bright white ceiling, and then back down, over the bed.

"It's my wife. I need an ambulance. 116 Maple Street. Can you hear me? Are you getting this?" Arlo looked at the phone. "They got my wife!" he shouted at it, then dialed all over.

By now the kids had woken. They stood in the doorway, Larry in just underpants even though he was too old.

"You're 'kay, babies. We're all 'kay," Gertie croaked as blood surged, sealing her nightgown to her belly.

SNITCHES
July 26–31

Map of Maple Street as of July 26, 2027
*116 Wilde Family
*118 Schroeder Family

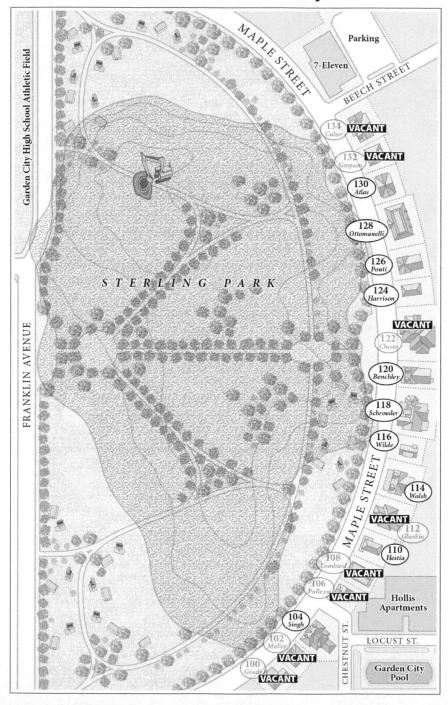

Index of Maple Street's permanent residents as of July 26, 2027

128 The Ottomanellis — Dominick (44), Linda (44), Mark (12), Michael (12)
130 The Atlases — Bethany (37), Fred (30)
132 VACANT
134 VACANT

TOTAL: 39 PEOPLE

A Garden City woman was rushed to NYU Winthrop Hospital early this morning when a brick crashed through the window of her residence, 116 Maple Street. The woman, Gertie Wilde, remains in critical condition. She is twenty-seven weeks pregnant.

Because of satellite interference, an ambulance was not immediately available. An investigation of the incident is ongoing. Detective Don Bianchi asks that anyone with information contact the Garden City Police Department.

FROM *BELIEVING WHAT YOU SEE: UNTANGLING THE MAPLE STREET MURDERS*, BY ELLIS HAVERICK, HOFSTRA UNIVERSITY PRESS, © 2043

With the brick, all of Maple Street became complicit. We know now that nearly every family was represented. These families have been framed as a mob. Angry and intemperate, striking without evidentiary foundation. In the years since, many of them have voiced public contrition.

But many others have not, and it is these in whom I'm interested. A decade later, Linda Ottomanelli has only grown more adamant. "Arlo hurt that girl. Gertie covered for him. We knew that. I mean, the guy ran stark-naked through Sterling Park. Somebody even said he had a boner, and he was chasing Shelly so hard she wound up falling down a sinkhole. Can you imagine how frightened she must have been? I mean, before that, he'd hurt her so badly that she'd bled all over our trampoline. What more proof do you need?" Linda told me in an interview at her apartment in Floral Park, Queens, where she and Dominick have downsized to in order to pay outstanding medical expenses.

"Can you imagine, my having to see that horror? To talk my kids through it? Their best friend was murdered right in front of them! The monsters who'd done it were living a hundred feet away, off scot-free. No wonder Mark had a nervous breakdown. No wonder he hung himself, God rest his soul! And Michael, who's to say his multiple sclerosis isn't from stress? . . . I could never get them to admit it — it's so shameful when it happens to boys — but I'm convinced Arlo hurt them, too. They didn't turn out normal . . . Something messed them up."

Jane Harrison agrees. "What I learned from Maple Street is that you can do your best, try your hardest, prep your children for the brightest possible future, and then a monster buys the house next door and ruins everything. The day he moved in, I knew. I could see it in his eyes. Honestly, I know he's long gone, but those eyes haunt me still."

"We weren't crazy," says Marco Ponti. "We were protecting our own. I only wish we'd done more, sooner."

Indeed, many of the Maple Street children have failed to thrive. The Ponti boys are in jail. Sarah Kaur ran away from home at twelve. Her older brother Sam Singh dropped out of soccer upon returning to school that fall, though he was expected to join the varsity team. He's one of many children on the block who never went to college — a rarity for Garden City during that time. Finally, it's been well publicized that FJ Schroeder's best friend, Adam Harrison, became a heroin addict. What's less widely known is that his drug use started that summer.

Given these outcomes, it's no great leap to theorize that the children were traumatized. My contemporaries posit that the Maple Street murders caused irreparable damage. The children blame themselves for spreading a false narrative about the Wilde family, kindling Rhea's madness.

But does this theory hold water? The evidence of Arlo's innocence has never been conclusive. It's entirely possible that his actions are what haunt the survivors of the Maple Street Massacre. They're traumatized because, even more than a decade later, they're too ashamed to reveal what he did to them.

It's time we reexamine, giving credit where it's due. In putting a stop to the Wildes, the people of Maple Street were heroes.

120 Maple Street

Monday, July 26

Peter Benchley was out of practice placing calls. He fumbled a few times, therapy mirrors reflecting his movements like silent ghosts.

"Hello? Something's happening on my block!"

Outside, neighbors with anonymous faces assembled in front of the Wilde house. The moonlight played against their makeshift disguises; a luminescence that was both absorptive and reflective, emitting hues in blue and red. It wasn't the craziest thing he'd ever seen. In Iraq, a kid with an IED had taken out his commanding officer while civilians watched through broken windows. Some of them had cheered. So yeah, he'd seen some crazy shit, which was how he knew what crazy shit looked like.

"Can you hear me? Send a car to Maple Street." A bad connection. Too much static. Peter hung up and tried again.

Outside, the moonlight stretched the neighbors' silhouettes. A slender man with broad shoulders took the lead. A small woman walking slowly, as if in pain, came up beside him. The man wound his arm. Released something heavy in a high arc —

Clink!

Glass broke.

Someone inside the house cried out.

"Help!" Peter panted into the phone.

Crackle.

Crossed signals. All he could hear was Arlo's static-riddled song: *You nod. It doesn't mean "come in."* He hung up. Tried again.

The woman — it had to be Rhea Schroeder — handed the tall man another piece of ammunition. He wound his arm.

"They're trying to kill someone!" Peter shouted into his phone, but there wasn't any connection. He hoisted himself and leaned out. Even as he shouted, he wondered if this was real, or if he'd finally lost the plot. Fifteen years living in his parents' house, stapled to an Oxy habit that rendered the waking and the sleeping into the same dreamlike chimera.

"I see you, FJ! I see you and I called the cops!" he screamed.

The kid had already released the second brick. Another crash, another cry from inside the house. A pain cry.

In eerie near-unison, the neighbors turned. Their faces reflected the earth and the sky and the houses ahead of them, and he knew that if he got close he would see his distorted self, too. "I see you! I see every one of you!" he bellowed.

Like the night the sinkhole appeared, the people of Maple Street disbursed. Some jogged for their houses, some hid behind hedges. Some, like Rhea Schroeder (who limped just slightly), walked slowly and steadily back toward home. A leisurely pace. Infuriatingly fearless.

Lights went on in the Wilde house.

Then came another panicked yelp, this time from a child in there.

Peter rushed past his therapy mirrors and rolled out to the hall. Considered waking his parents, who slept deep, but they got confused at night. Taking the time to explain would only slow him down. He hoisted himself and went down, down, down the chairlift.

His all-terrain chair waited at the bottom of the stairs. The one he'd saved up his disability for. He hurried. Got in, reached to unlock the front door. Then out and down the ramp to the sidewalk.

As he rolled, he felt eyes. They watched from houses. The gape out there, surrounded by reflective orange cones, seemed also to watch. It felt like being in-country. Like Iraq.

He got to the Wildes' house, only they had no ramp. He hoisted himself down, his stumps on footrests, then rolled to the ground. Dragged himself by the arms, his belly against black, sticky mud. Pulled himself up the first set of steps, panting from unaccustomed exertion, wondering if he'd imagined all this. If he was about to arrive at the Wildes' door in the middle of the night, and they'd think he was psychotic.

He wrapped his stumps under him. They hurt — fire where his knees ought to have been. Not enough mirror therapy today. He banged on the wood just below the doorknob.

Knock! Knock!

The air was still and hot. It reminded him of the bad place. An oil field, on fire. A kid offering a nail bomb to his CO like an apple, changing all their lives forever.

Knock! Knock!

The boy who answered wore a dingy tank top and no shoes, and for a moment, he was sure this was a trick. He was back in-country. The past had folded over. Followed him six thousand miles and fifteen years.

The boy stood with his hands in his pants.

He shook with shock. *Larry.* That's right, this was the neighbor child. Larry Wilde.

"S'okay," Peter panted. "You're okay. Your mom and dad home?"

The girl with the bandage on her hand appeared beside him. Julia. "My mom's hurt," she said. "We can't get an ambulance and we're scared to move her 'cause of the baby."

It took Peter another beat. So this was real after all. How strange, that it should be a relief to him.

"I love the New Yorker magazine, but that article and the book that came after aren't true to life. I don't think like a computer, in binaries. I didn't pick a side. Hate one family, love the other. It's not how rational people engage with their surroundings.

"We were bystanders that summer, watching something bad unfold. Those searchers out there were a constant reminder. Some of the newspeople came to us for comments. We didn't have any. What could we say that they didn't already know? . . . People who'd never lived in our town, who'd never met anybody involved, they kept writing about it online. They had all these theories about how Shelly had escaped and run away, or was faking it. The global warming occultists were worse. Who gets possessed by a hole? Everywhere we went, people at work and the grocery store and our extended families asked us about it. Especially, they asked about Arlo. We knew that we had to do something, take it back from them, because if anyone had earned an opinion, it was us . . .

"Look at it the other way. What if we'd done nothing? Acted like it was Rhea's problem. The press and all those blogs would have come down on us just as hard. You can't get away with being a bystander anymore. There's too much information. You have to take a stand or people think you're guilty, too . . . We didn't mean anything by the brick. If they were innocent, no harm done. And if they were guilty, well, we'd put them on notice." — Margie Walsh

"People talk a lot about health effects, but I'm fine and it's been years. No cancer or what have you. None of my buddies have it, either . . . What I noticed about those people — the ones you call the people of Maple Street — is that they didn't have respect. They shoved their way all over like they thought looking busy meant they were helping. They kept asking all these questions. They made us nervous. They made that woman, Rhea Schroeder, nervous, too." — Alex Figuera, Garden City Fire Department search supervisor on Shelly's case

"We moved to a short-term rental as soon as Sterling Park caved in. My eldest had asthma. I didn't want to take any chances.

"I wasn't as friendly with the people who

stayed. They had their own clique. Their children all played together. Rhea was their Top Dog. I never got a bad feeling about her. She was always polite. Some people say that now, that she'd seemed dangerous. But I never saw that side [of her] and that's not why I left . . .

"Would it have happened if the rest of us had stayed? I'll bet they'd have felt more self-conscious. The brick thing wouldn't have happened . . . And I suppose all the worse things after that wouldn't have happened, either.

"They acted like good neighbors, but they weren't. They've all written blogs and gone on chat shows and cashed in and I don't judge that. Everyone's doing their best in this economy. But there's not a single account by any of them that they went over to Rhea's house and asked how she was doing. Not a single mention that they offered to take care of Ella or drive FJ to lacrosse practice. Nobody ever invited Fritz for a beer. Even Linda Ottomanelli, who claimed to be Rhea's best friend, never set foot inside that house. Not for the entire four weeks. Honestly, were any of them really friends?" — Anna Gluskin

Maple Street

Monday, July 26

In the hangover-like aftermath of the brick, the people of Maple Street turned inward. They went to work and cleaned their floors and paid their bills and neatly arranged the things that, over the long search for Shelly, had gone untended.

Those who'd watched Peter Benchley roll to 7-Eleven, presumably to call the police, and then return with an ambulance and three cop cars, had been surprised. Who would have guessed that Peter was so capable? And why would the Wildes need an ambulance?

They'd been appalled when thrashing and pregnant Gertie Wilde got wheeled out on a stretcher. What were the odds, throwing blind, that FJ would have struck anyone at all?

They'd watched the Wilde house after it emptied, too. Its lights stayed on and its front door open, though the family was gone. Peter Benchley got out from his motorized chair and crawled up the Wildes' front steps, stumps shimmying, until he was at the top. He looked back at the crescent. House to house. Could he see them, watching him? They stepped back, out of the light. He reached high, got his hand on the knob, and closed the Wildes' front door.

This small act of decency proved unnerving. An accusation, boomeranged back at its accusers.

More detectives — people named Hudson and Gennet — appeared early that next Monday morning before many left for work. They went door to door. *We saw nothing,* they said. *We heard nothing.*

We know nothing.

The children of Maple Street were not so sanguine as their parents. Their testimony had hurt the Wildes and they knew it. They thought about the things they'd said. The conversations they'd repeated. They'd used the word *rape,* hadn't they? But was that a word Shelly had ever used?

Or had they invented it, to cure their boredom, engineering a summertime fantasy that they'd never imagined responsible adults would believe?

Through eavesdropped whispers, they

246

heard about their parents' greased faces, and Gertie Wilde's hysterical shrieks inside an ambulance, and poor Julia and Larry, riding after in tank tops, shorts, and sleep-caked eyes.

The brick was a double insult, too soon on the heels of the first — Shelly's fall. They had not yet caught their breaths. They wanted to mourn their missing friend. To digest that unless she'd perpetrated a great hoax, she really wasn't coming back.

"Could we pretend I never told you?" Sam Singh asked his mom on the morning after the brick.

"It's not your concern," Nikita answered while her four other children buzzed, each tossing glasses and spoons and bowls into the sink. Even though the house had a "no shoes" rule, the floors were caked with bitumen.

"But it wasn't true. Shelly lied. I only told you because you asked."

Nikita was a busy woman, and this American culture was still new to her. It always would be. She hadn't the tools to measure nuance here. That was someone else's job. "Just be lucky he's never been alone in a room with you, Sam Singh! . . . . He hasn't ever been alone with you, has he?"

"I don't think so?" Sam asked.

Nikita visibly began to shake.

247

Charlie Walsh had an even harder time.

"Mom, you've got it wrong. Shelly was the one who went after Julia. Her family's nice. She's the nicest girl on the block. I like her. I've been over their house a hundred times," he told Margie. She was sitting at the polished kitchen table, scrolling through a grant proposal for Habitat for Humanity.

"Can I tell you something?" Margie asked. "This is for grown-ups. It's a grown-up matter. I know you think they're good people. Maybe they are good people. But good people do bad things. That's why it's so awful." Her tears had welled, as if from personal experience. "Look at what they come from. That song about heroin and cartoons. That's a true story Julia's dad sang, about his own life. That kind of history leaves scars, Charlie. It damages a person. Victims turn into predators . . . I know this from experience . . . Tell me the truth," she asked, earnestly and for the ninth time, "has he touched your penis?"

"No, Mom." Charlie backed away, one foot after the other, until he was out of the well-lit study, and in the dark hall.

He approached Sally Mom after that. "We

have to stand up for them. They're inno-cent," he said.

Sally looked up from her papers, the model of practicality. She was shut up in her home office, her printer singing as it pooped out another land-use proposal. She did property law and he saw her for maybe a half hour a day. But he liked her. If they were strangers, he'd seek her out, and he had a feeling she felt the same. This wasn't love, necessarily. It was that lucky thing you have when two people understand each other utterly.

"This isn't our problem. If they didn't do it, no one'll file charges. We'll all for-get about it in six months. Not even Rhea Schroeder can hold a grudge that long when she's in the wrong."

"But someone threw a brick at them!"

"And the police have been hunting them down all morning. Let Margie Mom have her way on this. Trust me. This kind of ac-cusation isn't something people like us can fight."

Dave Harrison sucked it up and approached both his mom and his dad. This wasn't a pleasant endeavor. They really had divided the house with a black Sharpie marker.

He started with his dad, Tim, who hadn't worked in years. Some days he was dizzy, other days he ached. There were fevers and chills. He'd been sick for so long that everything scared him. He was scared of public places and too hot days and anyone with a cough or head cold. He was especially scared of the hole — afraid it was radiating cancer. The doctors and Dave's mom called it hypochondria. Long ago, they'd stopped believing his complaints, so he'd turned to hypnotists and aura readers and scammers who'd promised cures and never delivered. Dave didn't think it was hypochondria. The old man really was sick. But after more than a decade of sharing his body with an enemy he couldn't evict, he'd lost faith.

"It's gone too far," Dave said. They were in the den with the old, Scotchgard-covered couches made of chemicals that were now banned in forty states. His dad's shoes had tracked bitumen everywhere. The floor was sticky goo. This whole crescent was seeped with it.

Tim blew a lazy raspberry, eyes closed, as he lay on the couch. The only channel that got reception was local news. The static-riddled story was about a potential pedophile on Maple Street, implicated in Shelly's death, whom sources claimed was the ex-rocker Arlo Wilde. The camera showed footage of the Wilde house, and of the hole, too.

Nobody except Rhea Schroeder was available for comment. *I can't tell you anything for certain,* she exclaimed, her eyes bright and fanatic. *But there's no way Shelly went out into that park, unless she was running from something.*

"FJ Schroeder threw that brick, didn't he?" Dave asked. "Were you there?"

Tim's face was puffy from the Chinese herbs his holistic healer had given him. He smelled like plum flower.

"God, Dad. I told you it was all a lie. What's wrong with you?"

Tim finally opened his eyes: creepy green lights, focused on nothing, clots of luminescent sand oil in their crevices. "You don't understand the kind of evil a person can do," he answered. "I'm protecting you."

"Dad, were you out there last night? Did you help them throw that brick?"

"You don't want to tattle. Imagine what would happen if they took me away."

Dave imagined. His life would be a lot easier with one of them gone. He'd have a whole house again.

Tim read his mind. "You'd have the house, but you and Adam would be all alone with her. No buffer."

Dave approached his mom after that. Jane was his practical parent, who paid bills and

251

got groceries and set boundaries. When Tim first got sick, she'd been really upset. Cried herself to sleep and all that. But she cried herself dry. All her sympathy ran out. And not just her sympathy for Tim.

Jane wore her hair in a loose bun and dressed in pretty floral outfits and spoke softly because she was the headmaster of the Hillcock Preschool. She read lots of child rearing books and had a PhD in early childhood education, too. You never got the real Jane when you talked to her; just this textbook automaton semblance of sweet compassion.

He found Jane in his parents' bedroom. The fucked-up part? They'd even split the bed. Some nights, neither giving an inch, they both slept in it. Her side was made and she was sitting, papers neatly stacked all around. She kept her things clean, in order. No bitumen. No crumbs.

"We should go to the police before anyone else gets hurt."

Ringlets of hair streamed down from her loose bun. She was going through a roster for next year's class. "You think we should go to the police?"

"Yeah. Because it's not true. That story about Mr. Wilde. It's not true. But everybody's acting like it is true. We don't even

252

know for sure that Shelly's dead. You went to a service for her and we don't even know for sure."

"You think Mr. Wilde is innocent?"

"I told you that. I've always been telling you that."

Same calm voice. Except she wasn't a calm person, not really. Because she'd been the one to divide the house with a Sharpie. It went all the way into the kitchen, bisecting it so they each used different cupboards. He got the microwave; she got the stove. They'd been to court only once. The lawyers said it would last for years unless she signed a paper allowing him half of everything, including her huge inheritance, because he was too sick to work. But she wouldn't do that. She just kept redrawing the lines every time the Sharpie smudged. She used an online ruler app to make them perfect.

"You're scared that unless you help him, he might hurt you?"

"No, Mom. You're not listening."

"You've said that twice, honey, that I'm not listening. But I am. What makes you think I'm not listening?"

Tears of frustration ran down Dave's face. She had the power to do this to him. No one else. Which was why he only ever talked to her when it was house-on-fire-absolutely-necessary. "Mom. Please. Dad's sick and Adam can't say shit unless FJ Schroeder tells him to. It's just us and you know that. Please, Mom. Listen to me. The Rat Pack are lemmings and so are their parents and because of them Mrs. Wilde is in the hospital. What do we do?"

She turned a page. He noticed that there was sand oil underneath her fingernails. Which meant she'd been out with the mob last night, too. For once, his parents had agreed on something. A terrible something.

"So you think worse things will happen. That must be scary. Is that scary for you?"

"You're a piece of shit," he told her.

Her expression was dumbfounded.

The mean Markles took the incident with the brick hardest of all.

Crash!

Mark whaled his pillow into a Tiffany lamp that shattered against his father, Dominick Ottomanelli's, bare, swollen feet. Pieces of painted glass specked the floor and his miraculously uncut skin. "Jesus! What's wrong with you?" Dominick asked.

Mark dropped his pillow and started laughing. Michael followed. It wasn't good-humored laughing. It was hysterical, Shelly Schroeder–brand laughing, because they'd sneaked out last night and followed the adults. They'd thought it would be funny. An adventure. Life-and-death, but not really. Life-and-death in *Deathcraft,* when the creepy things crawl out and you have to hide until morning.

And then the bricks, and Arlo Wilde's horrible, low-pitched moan as he'd helped Gertie into the ambulance while she held her fragile baby belly, and the knowledge that it was their fault. They'd known, even when confessing, throwing out the word *rape* like it meant nothing, that their mother would tell everyone. They'd known this and done it anyway, for a free PlayStation.

They'd done this. They'd hurt sweet Mrs. Wilde. Maybe they'd murdered her baby, too.

They'd run back to their house last night before the rest. In the dark of their adjoining rooms, pretending to sleep, Mark had dry-heaved. Michael had put the heel of his hand into his mouth and bitten hard enough to leave a mark that was still angry eighteen hours later. A swollen semicircle of teeth.

Today they'd traded bedrooms. An old game from preschool that they hadn't played in years. They'd been answering to the wrong names. It was an effort to be someone else. To run from their very skins, except it didn't work. As brothers, the new skin they assumed wasn't much different.

They directed outward, too. They flung their dirty laundry from closet bins. They took gardening shears to the trampoline and punctured it in six places. They tore up all their mother's green beans and mint. And now, tracking bitumen through the house, they jammed pillows deep inside their cases and let fly against lamps and books and each other.

"Clean this up. Money doesn't grow on trees," said Dominick, a man of medium build with a giant belly. Bitumen oil crammed the crevices of his ears. The Tiffany lamp lay dead at his feet.

"Mom cleans," Mark said.

"Don't be gay," the other said. Michael.

Together, almost of one mind, they hit their dad too hard with double pillows.

"You're such a fat slob," Mark said, his expression a pained and furious grimace.

Dominick stepped on blue stained glass; the bulbed eye of a dragonfly. Blood ran along the floor. His eyes watered. Real tears from their giant hulk of a father, with fists like boxing gloves. This wasn't what they wanted. They wanted to be yelled at. Punished for what they'd done. Set straight and exonerated. They wanted a capable person to take charge of this house, and reverse the terrible thing that had happened first to Shelly, then to Mrs. Wilde, and now to all of them.

"Come on, Dad! Grab a pillow!" Michael cried. He swung again, this time with his fist, straight at Dominick's groin.

They expected him to yell.

Daintily, he walked backward, feet trailing blood. His voice stayed soft. "Boys. I know it sucks being cooped up, but you're being too loud. Do something quiet. Play the video game your mother bought you."

The Markles smiled sidelong. Finally. It would happen. Finally, this would bring order. Mark pointed at the PlayStation. The thing they'd been bought, for selling out the Wildes. "Too much static. There's no point," he said.

The PlayStation was smashed to wires and plastic. Tiny pieces caught the hard sunlight.

"Why do you do these things?" Dominick hissed, cheeks wet with tears. Then he shut Mark's door, leaving them quite alone.

Dominick found his wife, Linda, in the kitchen. She was a round woman who wore overalls and soft, comfortable shoes with open toes.

"I can't take them," he said. "They're monsters."

257

Normally, she defended them. Talked about the nanny on TV, who claimed it was super important to be your kid's advocate and best friend. This time, she burst into tears. "They've been so bad today!"

He made his way to her slowly, like if he took long enough, he'd figure out what to say. Behind, he left a trail of blood. Linda patted the seat beside her. Without air-conditioning, the heat was thick and miserable. She took one foot at a time, running her fingers along them, scouting for three tiny shards, which she pulled.

"Remember their Penguins teacher? She always talked about how well behaved they were. She called them her *angels* . . . ," Linda said. "She said Mark was a leader. She said Michael was an artist. Special, she called them."

"I don't remember. Which preschool?"

"Cathedral . . . I got a call from their camp last week. The director used the word *cruel*. She said they're *cruel* to other children. How is this happening? Who's teaching them this?"

"We give them so much. They can't even say thank you," Dominick answered. She dabbed his feet. The cuts were shallow but his muscles ached. Though he didn't do the heavy lifting anymore, he still worked long hours managing construction sites. She squeezed his arches and at first it hurt more. But then the pain ran out like juice from a lemon.

"They won't even help me in the garden."

He looked around. This house had been a mess for a long time. Nice things, teak tables, antique chairs. But because of its child inhabitants, it was falling apart. He felt ashamed to admit that. A personal failure.

"The video games?" he asked.

She kept rubbing. "I used to think it was Dave Harrison. I mean, really. A house divided. That child's a mess. Or Charlie. Say what you want; two moms isn't normal. But I don't know. This stuff about Arlo."

"What are you saying?"

"There's been so many clues. The fad diets, those cheap Parliaments. I don't think those boobs of Gertie's are real and she flaunts them so shamelessly. Even when he's happy, Arlo yells. They have no boundaries. We thought it ended there. We gave them credit they didn't earn. But now it's clear Arlo hurt Shelly. We know that. Rhea would never lie about something this important. She's too precise a person."

"I can see that."

"What we did last night was the right thing."

"I know."

"I'll bet my mint that she's not even hurt. It's impossible those bricks actually hit her."

"I hadn't thought of that. You're right. She probably wasn't hit at all."

"We had to, Dom. Arlo did a terrible thing right under our noses."

"Yeah. I hate thinking it."

"That's how it happens, because we fail to imagine the worst."

Upstairs, the kids hooted. Something smashed. The guttural shouts they made didn't quite seem human, but like the kids from *Pinocchio* who stay too long on Pleasure Island.

"You think he interfered with them," Dominick said at last. "In our house. During some dinner." It was the fear he'd had from the start — from the first time he'd heard this story. No, even before then. From the first day they'd moved in, all tattooed and cheap, bringing their misery through the barricades of suburbia, infecting everyone. It was why he hadn't screamed at the twins just now, even though they'd earned it. Because they might be the victims. Because he'd let them down, and this behavior they were exhibiting came from pain. Something terrible the Wildes had done.

"Yes," she answered. "I believe he did."

And just like that, Dominick believed it, too.

A PARTICIPANT OF THE INTERACTIVE BROADWAY SHOW *THE WILDES VS. MAPLE STREET*, REGARDING HIS CHOICE TO PLAY RHEA SCHROEDER, THE MOST POPULAR CHARACTER

"Rhea's my hero. She's like Iago [from *Othello*], the poison whisperer. If you read that play, you can totally tell Desdemona never cheated. The scarf was planted evidence. Othello knew that. He wasn't a meathead; he was a tactical military commander. Besides, why murder a woman just for cheating? He murdered Desdemona because he could. She threatened him in some way he couldn't stand to confront. That's Maple Street. They were scared of the Wildes . . . The Maple Street shootings happened about three years before the Great Collapse. I remember those days. You could feel it coming. You kind of knew the banks and farms and pretty much everything were about to fail. It's a perfect metaphor — a hole that keeps getting wider, and you can try to ignore it, but one day you're going to get swallowed. Those people were about to lose their jobs and their homes. They were about to *become* the Wildes.

"I don't blame Rhea. I mean, Maple Street

could have ignored her — told her to go take a nap or pop a Prozac or whatever. But they didn't. They whispered the poison right back.

"Did you read her dissertation? It's like Freud meets Frankenstein. She was totally delusional. So, no. I don't blame her for what she did. I blame the people who knew better. I blame the people of Maple Street." — Evan Kaufmann, Menlo Park, California

118 Maple Street

Monday, July 26

Ding-Dong!

Rhea Schroeder put down the brush she'd been using to clean the sticky crevices of her fingernails.

Ding-Dong!

"Don't come out of your rooms," she warned as she rushed on one good knee, one aching knee, out of the bathroom and down the steps to the hall. She scanned the floors for oil. Clean of evidence. No trace left. She swung open the door.

"Detective Bianchi, hi!" she said. A smile, under the circumstances, would be overkill. "Did they find my Shelly?"

"I'm sorry, no."

This was the second police visit today. The first had come just after dawn, and she'd met them on the porch. Told them everybody else was asleep and played the *my kid's missing and probably dead so show some respect card*. Now she leaned, so Bianchi couldn't see inside.

"Is it something about Arlo Wilde?" she asked. "I thought after I made that complaint that something would happen. But nothing's happened!"

"I'm on it," Bianchi answered. "He's under full investigation."

Rhea pointed at the house next door — the torn Slip 'N Slide, the broken window. Their car was parked but the Wildes weren't home. Seeing all that, she felt real pity. Look at the mess they'd brought upon themselves with their bad choices. "I hate to think people can do such things. Arlo . . . I trusted that man. I trusted Gertie, too."

"May I come in?" Bianchi asked. "I know your family was sleeping this morning, but I really do need to talk."

She'd been through this before. Back at U-Dub, they'd investigated. The police first, then the university, then her department. She knew she had to answer *yes*. Anything else brings them back with a search warrant.

"Of course!" She backed up and showed him into the dining room with its missing drapes. It smelled in 118 Maple Street of heat and wine. Fermented and human. The maid had stopped coming after having to clean the wrecked house last week — to bleach the sink and sweep all the broken

265

shards. She'd quit via text: *Sorry Missus! I move to Peru. God Bless you!!!*

"Have a seat!" she said, pointing at the chair, which she just then realized was still stained with a ribbon of Shelly's menstrual blood.

She led the detective around to the other side so he didn't notice.

"Please excuse the mess." Her voice and diction were more demure than usual. More housewifely. She located this persona easily — it was the same one she used with the PTA and Linda Ottomanelli. Invoking it made explaining herself to stupid people more tolerable.

"Your house is very nice."

Bianchi was of medium build, average height, with a middle-aged paunch, and he was invisible in the way all middle-aged people with unlucky genes are invisible. He had a gentle manner, too, shrinking deeper into his mid-priced suit to set her at ease.

But he was looking everywhere, at everything.

"What happened there?" he asked, nodding at her knee, which she'd wrapped in an Ace bandage for the first time in years.

"Oh, I had an accident a long time ago. With all the stress, it's been acting up. I just need a cortisone shot. So, coffee? Tea? It's almost five . . . Shall we be intrepid? How 'bout a beer!"

"Just your son," Bianchi answered. His hair was so fair you couldn't discern whether it was gray or simply blond. "I'd like to speak to you together."

"Oh. FJ's too broken up. He just can't. But I'm happy to clear up whatever."

He smiled. Even his smile was bland. "If not here, I'll need you and FJ at the police station first thing tomorrow morning."

"Tomorrow? Oh, sure," Rhea answered. "He can drive himself over . . . So, what is it?" she asked, feeling an alive kind of nervous, like the time she'd defended her dissertation. She'd mattered back then. They'd clung to her every word.

"Where were you last night?" he asked.

"How do you mean?"

"A felony assault occurred on your block. Someone threw two bricks through the Wildes' window. Where were you and the rest of your family last night?"

"Goodness! We were home!" Rhea cried. "Snug as bugs. In rugs!"

Bianchi didn't take his eyes away. Just waited to see if she'd say more. The room got distant like when you stand up too fast, and she knew that he didn't believe her. She also knew that because of her circumstances, she had his sympathy. Sometimes, that's enough.

"Is it possible that any of you left the house while the rest were sleeping?"

She pretended to think. "No? It's an old house. It creaks. I'm a light sleeper."

"Did you hear anything? Music playing? Or a window breaking?"

"No."

Bianchi pointed at the naked windows — she'd torn down the toile drapes and now they were landfill. "I see you're suffering from a brownout like the rest of the block. No air-conditioning. Your windows are open. How did you sleep, though?"

"Was it noisy? I have no idea! Will she be okay?"

"Who?"

"Gertie Wilde." Just saying her name made Rhea's heart beat faster.

Bianchi didn't answer, and she had the feeling he thought he'd caught her out. Which he hadn't.

"That's right, isn't it? That's what they said this morning. Gertie was hurt?" He kept looking at her, fixated. A thrill built up inside Rhea, scary and good. And it wasn't because she wanted Gertie or her baby dead. She didn't even want Arlo jailed. She just wanted them to understand what they'd done. She wanted them to feel so bad about hurting poor Shelly that they couldn't stand to live. That they killed themselves. Julia, too. And even Larry. Their heavy deaths would pull a pocket out of time. This pocket would gather all the murk and bead into oblivion, washing clean all that remained.

"Yes, it was Mrs. Wilde."

"Is the baby going to live?"

"I have a witness. He says a man of your son Fritz's build threw the bricks."

Terror. A delicious candy bath of it. "FJ? You mean my son, FJ? Or my husband, Fritz?"

"Your son."

"I don't think that's likely. I mean, he's got a ride to Hofstra! He wouldn't blow it for something like that . . . It's just not possible! And I certainly wasn't up in the middle of the night, playing with bricks. We don't even have bricks! Our house is a Tudor!"

"Why do you think my witness believes he saw you and your son?"

Rhea let out breath, affected sorrow. Whisper-talked. "Do you know he's a drug addict?"

"I'm aware he has a medical condition."

"You might check with the pharmacy on that. Most people's legs don't still hurt a decade after the amputation . . . . It can't have

269

been easy to see the rest of Maple Street grow up and move away while he's been stuck. His poor parents have gotten frail. Has it occurred to you that what he saw wasn't what he thinks? I mean, it's strange Arlo's song was played. What was it? 'Achy Breaky Heart'?"

"'Wasted.'" He had that same expression, like he'd caught her in a lie. But he wasn't smart enough for that. No one was.

"Oh, I don't know that one. Well, it's strange, isn't it? It makes me wonder if it was his fans. You know how people get about celebrity."

"How do they get?"

Rhea shrugged as if to say: *Look what happened to my poor child. I should know best of all: this world's a crazy place!*

Bianchi grinned a tiny grin. "I'll leave you. Thanks for your time."

"That's it? You sure I can't help with anything else?"

"You and FJ can come by tomorrow."

"We most certainly will! We feel very badly about the Wildes. Really — an awful thing. But I have to admit, we're filled up right now. We're just so sad about Shelly it's hard to think about anything else. If it's all right by you, could you respect that? Give us peace unless you have news of her?"

He looked at her. In her eyes. Calm and piercing. "We'll find her."

"What do you mean? Do you have a lead?"

"Peter Benchley," he said.

"Hm?"

"I never named him, but you knew he was the witness who spoke out against your son."

Rhea shrugged. Their eyes stayed locked. Tense. She was afraid she'd look guilty if she looked away. "People talk on this block. Good or ill, we're all in one another's business. I hear everything."

Bianchi's eyes moved at last. They scanned the hall, which she'd neglected, she now realized. Her own bitumen shoeprints marked the edge of the carpet. He looked toward the dining room, too. Shelly's bloody cushion in plain sight. He looked right at it and a crazy urge filled her, to bludgeon him. With a chair or the metal base of a lamp. Right there, right then. Wait till dark and dump his body down the hole. And if anybody else saw, she'd kill them, too.

"She should be well preserved in that cold water. There are people whose job is to examine every detail. We'll know exactly who's to blame," he said.

He looked back at her. Locked eyes. In her mind, she saw a girl, slumped against the bathroom floor, unconscious.

Quite against her will, Rhea Schroeder gagged.

He saw that, too. Then he was walking slowly down the steps, so unassuming as to seem invisible.

Obstetrics, NYU Winthrop Hospital, Mineola, New York

Monday, July 26
Early Morning

Gertie remembered everything. The sounds. The smells. Her children's terrified expressions. The flashing ambulance she'd had to ride alone in, that had tinted everything a worrisome red. She remembered the many bedrooms she'd grown up in as a girl. Doors knocked down. Fists in walls. One time, there'd been a man making soft noises she hadn't been able to locate until hours later, in the dark, when she'd finally opened her own closet door. She'd remembered these things, and then everything had gone red.

In the emergency room, sonogram pictures had shown a little girl. Head and eyes and spindly limbs. A baby sea creature.

Gertie'd cried and screamed. She'd carried on, knowing it was scaring the kids and Arlo, but unable to stop herself.

The doctor had been shaking her. Then a nurse. More screaming. So red. How could she have a baby inside her? Had a bad man put it there? She was still a baby! And then a shot in her arm, and the slow, cold rush of weightlessness.

"Calm down," the doctor had said. "The baby's fine. Look." And there, on the sonogram, little Guppy averted her face from the camera. "It's a surface wound nowhere near your womb. Some resulting pressure on the spine."

Gertie heard that her family was healthy. She understood it. But she didn't feel safe. She felt like the whole earth was made of sharp things. She couldn't stop shaking, wailing, shouting foul words in baby talk. This had happened before, during her years with Cheerie, and then again, very briefly, when she'd been hospitalized with post-Julia baby blues.

"Fuck that cunt Schroeder bitch," she heard some crazy woman say, in a freakish baby voice. And it was her. She was that woman.

The kids hid behind the next hospital bed's curtain, peeking out with wide eyes. Arlo stood a few feet back, hunched and making himself small. She knew that they would not remember the brick from this night. They'd remember the heart of their family going mad.

"Bee bee boo," she said. "Shitty neighbors down the hole."

The doctor got in her face. Whispered hard and urgent, in the way that women do to each other, when important things happen and children are involved. "Stop it! Right now!"

Wide-eyed and terrified, pleading for help as best she knew how, Gertie opened her mouth. "The hunters are coming. They take the children first!"

Another prick, and everything faded.

Creedmoor Psychiatric Center

Tuesday, July 27
Day

She woke up in a different hospital, in a room with a locked door. The guy who interviewed her was the chief psychiatric resident at Creedmoor, Queens's version of a public madhouse.

She lucked out. The resident was better than the social workers from when she'd been growing up, or even the shrink who'd helped her process her baby blues. He asked her about her childhood and whether she ever hit her kids. If she'd lately considered hurting the baby in her belly. If she'd stayed on the medication her records showed she was supposed to be taking, which she had. Whether she and Arlo loved each other, or if she needed a referral to a family shelter for battered women. He asked her why she'd reacted that way, gotten so hysterical. She'd told him maybe his neighbors should get together and hit his pregnant belly with a brick in the middle of the night, and then he could call her hysterical.

Because she had a history of mental illness, and also because she was responsible for young children, he placed her on a thirty-six-hour hold. He'd check in again. If she was still rational, he'd release her.

Arlo came that night. She wanted to be strong; show him that she wasn't crazy or damaged or any of those things. But as soon as he sat down in the chair beside her, she was weeping from the shame of it, the brick entirely forgotten.

He didn't comfort her like she'd expected. Didn't seem to have his usual sixth sense, to know that this time, she wanted to be held. "I'm so ashamed," she said.

"I'm tired of shame. We didn't do anything wrong," he answered. Then he stretched out his arms. You had to look closely. They'd healed after all these years. But she'd seen him naked. He had track marks in other places, too.

"I feel like *I* did something wrong. I always feel that way."

"I know that feeling."

"Can the kids come? Are they here?" she asked. "I need to hold them."

"Cafeteria."

"They don't want to see me?"

"Don't take it personal."

She cried more. Took a while to get hold

of herself. He didn't comfort her and she saw that he was exhausted. Body aching, not sleeping, marrow-deep exhausted. "Sit down next to me," she said.

He shook his head. He was trying not to cry. "I'm afraid I won't be able to stand back up."

"Did I upset the children very much?"

"They'll get over it," he said. They both knew from experience that this wasn't true.

Tuesday, July 27

It took a while, but she returned to herself. Her thoughts stopped spinning so very hard, and she stopped feeling so horribly frightened. When that happened, alone in that hospital with distance from the neighbors, she had time to think about the brick.

Arlo hadn't just spotted a single psycho out on Maple Street. If that were the case, what happened might have made some sense. No, he'd spotted at least ten neighbors out there, all smeared with sticky oil to appear anonymous.

What kind of people commit such acts?

Did Maple Street truly believe that Arlo had raped Shelly? They could not. Physical evidence placed him elsewhere.

So what was going on?

She knew these people. Not just Rhea, but the rest of them. She'd seen them stay up all night to finish their kids' science projects. She'd seen them get weepy over news reports about teen drug addicts and pediatric cancer and lead-contaminated water. They had date nights and took salsa lessons. They read popular fiction about the women's movement, even the men. They'd gone to real colleges — the kind with ivy and real dorm rooms — and they aspired to send their kids to even better colleges. So how could people like that turn on her and Arlo, and by proxy, Julia and Larry?

She regretted moving to Maple Street. She'd been the one to push for it. Arlo'd wanted to buy an apartment in their old building. Stick with the kind of people they already knew. Nice people, but people so strapped they didn't have the time or interest to self-improve unless you counted dieting and trying to quit smoking. She'd been the one to insist on Long Island. She'd had this idea that they'd be like undercover agents, learning the life secrets of the suburban middle class. They'd develop habits like them, and wind up with better jobs like them. She'd reasoned that even if she and Arlo weren't comfortable with Maple Street, their kids would learn to be. Upward mobility was what counted.

But when they got here, it hadn't been like that. Nobody except Rhea had shown any interest. She'd felt distance when she talked to the neighbors, like everything she'd said had been stupid, but they'd never explained to her why. Never explained the *right* things to say. They'd never referred clients, even though Gertie had kept handing out her business cards. They'd never suggested Arlo stop by their offices and talk to their office managers about new copiers, even though he'd told them he was available, anytime. Aside from Rhea, they'd changed the subject whenever Larry's name came up, like she ought to be embarrassed. Like, if your life isn't perfect, you keep your mouth shut and don't talk about it until it *is* perfect, and then you brag.

Rhea'd proven she was a terrible person. Rhea was a hunter worse than Cheerie, whom, God help her, Gertie wished dead. But she'd had more time than she wanted in this hospital, most of it alone with her thoughts. At first she'd reviewed everything that had transpired between herself and Rhea, searching for indications of treachery. But she searched so thoroughly that she'd inevitably reviewed her own behavior, too.

If she was honest, there had been trouble in paradise long before the Fourth of July. Unanswered texts, half-smiles and waves instead of stopping to chat, the withdrawal of Shelly from sleepovers — these all should have been obvious to anyone paying attention. Even at the Memorial Day barbeque a month before, Rhea'd barely stopped to say more than a *How are you?* before moving on.

If the friendship really had been important to Gertie, why hadn't she done anything about it? Why hadn't she rung Rhea's bell, a red wine bottle bribe in hand if necessary, and asked to sit down with her and have a frank talk? *Is this about the night on my porch?* a poised, normal person like the kind you see on TV would have asked. *Whatever's going on, you know I'm here for you, because you're important to me. And you were right. I won't judge, this normal woman would have said.* And the truth was, Rhea really had been important to her. She wouldn't have judged.

After Shelly's fall, a regular person would have baked a ziti for Rhea's family, then stood next to her while she'd kept vigil at the sinkhole. She'd have said: *I love(d) your daughter. Her absence is a physical pain. So I can't imagine what you're going through. What can I do to ease your burden?*

Why hadn't she done these things? Why hadn't they even occurred to her until now? Why, for that matter, had she left Julia alone with crazed Shelly Schroeder that morning, when any sane mother would have stopped her car?

What was wrong with her? How could she have been so blind?

Gertie once read that when people start to lose their sight, they don't know it. Their minds fill in the missing parts. So, when they're driving, maybe they're passing a field of cows, but what they see is just green. Their minds make an assumption based on past experience. It occurred to her that people's personalities were like that. Full of holes. We think we're complete but we're not, and usually that's just fine. It's typical. But sometimes the holes line up. You get hit with a brick and you lose your shit like a psycho. Your kid falls down a sinkhole and you turn into the Wicked Witch of the West.

And maybe, between her and Rhea, something electric had happened. Their blind spots had lined up.

Tuesday, July 27

Arlo, Julia, and Larry arrived as soon as visiting hours started. The TV shouted infotainment in the corner of the ceiling and Gertie tried to turn it off, but her drugged-up roommate had the remote.

Gertie smiled wide. As calming as she knew how. But her voice broke. "Oh, my babies. It's so good to see you."

The kids made their slow way to Gertie's bed. She patted the side of it, but neither of them climbed up. "That's okay," she told them as they elected to share the floor while Arlo took the chair.

Everybody looked tired and on edge. They waited for her to explain what had happened, what that baby talk was all about.

"I'm better now," she said. "I got hit on the head. It made me loopy."

"Really?" Larry asked. "You're better? Can you come home? I need you home."

"This is a psychiatric hospital," Julia said.

284

"We had to prove we're family just to get allowed in."

On a good day, Arlo would have cracked jokes to lighten the mood: *What's red and green and blue all over? Who's buried in Grant's Tomb? What do you get when you cross a skeleton and a chicken?* Now he crumpled in the armchair like a trench coat without an owner.

"Julia, she's all better!" Larry said.

"I am. I'm all better," Gertie promised.

Normally, Julia would have confronted. She'd have persisted until Gertie admitted that no, she hadn't been hit in the head. Yes, this was a loony bin. Mom's a little bonkers. But something had shifted in her. A loss of innocence. Instead, she stood. Slowly, so as not to cause surprise, she put her hand over Gertie's hand. Held it. "Okay," she said.

After that, they tried to talk like things were normal. The kids told her about the heat on the crescent, and the fact that the sand oil had surfaced as far as the town pool. Arlo said that they'd been cleaning the house in her absence, getting it ready for her homecoming.

"Are they giving you a hard time about not coming to work?" Gertie asked.

"No," Arlo said. "Josh Fishkin told me to take as long as I need."

"Are they still gonna pay you?"

Arlo looked at his fingernails, which were clean and filed. She noticed that the kids' hair was brushed, too; their faces clean. Even under this stress, he'd kept things up. But that was his nature. He was a caretaker. "My name got leaked to the press, so . . ."

"Leaked how?"

"Just that I'm the guy who wrote that song, and the cops questioned me about what happened to a missing girl. No specifics yet. I was worried paparazzi'd show up at our door, but they're just using the stuff they find online, plus a picture of our house from the sales records."

"You're fired?" she whispered.

"Temporary leave. Half pay."

"Oh, Arlo."

"Yeah. It's not as personal as it feels. On the down low, they told me the division's closing. It's a bad time for office products. Nobody really works in offices anymore."

News played at low volume. On-screen, a picture of the sinkhole flashed, and then Shelly's seventh-grade class picture. That long, black hair, gossamer as angel wings. Rhea's voice followed: *I just don't understand it . . .*

"She makes me want to upchuck," Gertie said.

"The worst. I feel like any second all of Maple Street is gonna drag me out. Dip me in tar 'n' feathers."

The kids were listening. This wasn't for them. Julia stood. Took Larry by the hand. "Can we have some money for Cokes?" she asked. Arlo handed her five dollars, told her to take her time.

Once they were gone, Arlo said, "I don't think we should go back to Maple Street."

"Where else is there?"

"Cheerie's still got that two-bedroom, doesn't she?"

"Not while I'm alive. Not while I'm dead, either."

"'Kay. I called my mom but she took a turn."

"I'm sorry."

"Yeah. The Medicare has her covered but she's in no position . . . I hate the idea of bringing you back to Maple Street. They got it out for us. The signs are in neon. And the way it affected you . . ."

She blushed, remembering it from a dense and murky place. "I don't do well with things in the night. In my bedroom. It's just a thing with me. I'm not crazy."

"I know." Arlo didn't reach out to her. And that was probably right. Maybe he knew her better than she knew herself. Because she wanted to be touched and consoled by him, her husband, but she wasn't ready for it yet. The shock of what had happened with the brick was still too fresh. Her nervous system was still in panic mode. "It's understandable, what with the stuff you've been through . . ."

"Yeah," Gertie said. "If it hadn't happened in our bedroom. At night . . ."

"I know . . . I talked to Bianchi. He assigned a beat cop to the crescent. But it's only an eight-hour shift. We're alone the other sixteen. I'm worried something'll happen again."

Gertie took deep breaths to keep from losing control again. "Why are they doing this to us?"

"I don't know."

Gertie pressed her hands to her wet eyes. "If they're so scared of us, why don't *they* go? They're the ones with the money."

"I think they feel like they're taking a stand."

Arlo reached out for her. She flinched. They stayed like that: a hand on a bed, a body inches away. The distance between them felt hot.

"I hate them. I wish they were dead. Every one of them," she said.

"Yeah."

The kids came back.

The TV returned from commercial with a new clip. This one was live and in front of the hole, where rescue workers were making a last-effort search. They'd widened the tunnel as much as they'd been able and were now flying in a special diver, just five feet tall, to wriggle through. *I trust the truth to come out, Rhea said. My daughter was running from a predator when she fell. I happen to know the police questioned him.*

All four of them watched. Thin and shadow-riddled, Rhea looked so haunted by grief that it could have been cancer. Her story was so compelling that even the Wildes almost believed that there was a stranger on Maple Street. A threat.

"It can't be coincidence. This was her plan since Shelly fell. She's been laying the track. To blame you," Gertie whispered.

On-screen, the picture now showed Arlo, standing in front of 116 Maple Street beside Gertie and the kids. Rhea had taken that one, when they'd first moved in. A circle got drawn in red around his neck.

Arlo and the kids looked for the remote in Gertie's drooling roommate's bed, but they couldn't find it. They couldn't make it stop.

118 Maple Street

Tuesday, July 27

Rhea saw herself on the nighttime news. Static made the image ribbon. It didn't look like her. Didn't sound like her. Her face was wrong.

Just like that girl from the Hungarian Pastry Shop.

The hackles along the back of her neck stood on end. She turned, and there was FJ, in the doorway. She had the feeling Ella was there, too, hiding just behind.

They'd spent the afternoon at the police department. It had gone well. They'd stuck to the proper story. FJ'd been so nervous the whole time that he'd bounced his legs under the table until Bianchi asked him to stop.

"What?" she now asked.

He lurched into the room. Eyes red. Unsteady.

"Are you drunk?"

"Is Mrs. Wilde's baby okay?" he asked.

"You worry too much," she answered.

"Mom. It's all over the news. Why isn't she home yet? Why's she still at a hospital?"

"*EF-JAY,*" she singsonged.

His breath was foul. His brown hair napped. "It was supposed to be a warning. Nobody was supposed to get hurt!"

"Ella! Upstairs! Now!"

Silence.

"Ella. I know you're listening."

A small shadow in bare feet squeaked like a mouse from behind the door, then ran. FJ started to talk again. Rhea held up her hand until she heard footsteps above and out of earshot.

"She'll tell everyone," she said.

"Sorry. I'm sorry. Is it murder?" FJ asked. "Am I a murderer?"

"Of course not."

"The baby's okay? Mrs. Wilde's okay?"

Rhea frowned. Her face was still rippling under static lines on the news, and like a public beheading, it felt all wrong. She wasn't that strange, angry woman with wrinkles. That woman looked scary! She was the mother of four, a professional, married to a professional. She wore Eileen Fisher. She'd spent seven years as head of the Garden City PTA. She was not a crank, an accuser, an hysteric. She certainly didn't have the spare time to spearhead a witch hunt like some miserable stay-at-home loser. This was real. She was sounding a very serious alarm.

Her daughter, her most precious thing, was gone.

"Why are you worried about Gertie? She *hit* me! It hurts so much! That woman's an ox. Do you know what she's probably doing right now? She's eating ice cream with her feet propped while everybody hugs her and tells her she's pretty. The baby's just fine or that cop would have said something, believe me. He would have called it a possible homicide but he didn't. Honey, I don't even think she got hurt. Did you hear all that screaming and carrying on? A woman about to miscarry doesn't move like that. The EMTs practically had to restrain her to the gurney. She just got histrionic. She's like that."

FJ leaned against the counter. Wracking sobs contracted and expanded in his chest but made no sounds outside. "Oh, they're all right. They're all right. They're all right. They're all right," he whispered.

She walked in his direction. Because of his maleness, she'd always felt a distance from him. Fritz had not filled that space. As a result, FJ had spent most of his childhood alone. It resulted in a romantic streak. He was always chasing girls, breaking his heart against them, imagining this was love.

"You're upsetting me," she said.

He tucked his chiseled face into giant man hands. He smelled like vodka and he needed a shave. She realized, suddenly, that he'd been missing practice. But he'd still been going out to all those parties.

"It's just, what if we're wrong? What if she just fell? What if it was all an accident?" he asked.

Rhea's cheeks turned red. She pounded her bandaged knee with her fist. Sparks overloaded her vision — a slurry of color. She cried out from the pain.

"Mom!"

"Well, who do you think did it? Me?"

"Of course not," he answered, but there was a flash, a pause. Something hidden.

"You're trying to hurt me when I'm already down. You know I'm under all this stress!"

"No, Mom. Please."

She didn't look at him. The words wouldn't come out right if she looked at him. "You loved Shelly, didn't you?"

"Ah, mom. I was never around. Even when she was little and wanted to play, I was such a jerk. I just wish I'd been —"

"So many children have come forward with testimony. This is only the beginning. The police won't help. I know that now. It's up to us. You and me."

FJ placed his hands on the counter and began to sob. The sound filled the room, jarring and baritone.

"Stop. It hurts me to see you cry like that."

"Sorry. I'm sorry."

She reached over the refrigerator. Pulled down a bottle of red and got a pint glass. Filled it halfway. "Here," she said.

He was too far gone. Didn't seem to see it.

She forced it into his hands. "I've never done wrong by you. You're on varsity. You've got a full ride. What more could you want?"

He gulped it down. His lips and teeth went as red as his eyes.

"Go to bed. You're overstressed. In another week, when you're rested, you can start back at practice. I'll call the coach. I'll explain. You know how I'm good with that. It'll be fine. Back to normal in no time."

He made this pain grimace that she wasn't used to seeing on him. Only on Shelly.

"There's no fingerprints. You wore gloves. There's no witnesses except Peter Benchley, and that junkie never saw your face. Trust me, I've been through this. They've got nothing. They were just trying to scare you today. That Bianchi's a toad."

"Yeah," he said, soft.

He needed something from her. She tried to imagine what she'd want to hear right now, if she were in his place. "She adored you. You were so special to her. She thought the sun rose and set by you."

"Why? I wasn't nice to her."

"She understood," Rhea said, and she didn't know why, but her voice was shaking. "Shelly loved you despite the things you did, and she knew you loved her. She was a very understanding child."

FJ started crying again. At last, Rhea came to him. Held him by the waist and he folded over into his smaller mother. He'd been hungry for this. Starved for it. She could tell, and it seemed sad that it had taken tragedy to draw them together. She wished she'd known sooner. They both might have felt less alone.

"There's so many ways to make it up to her," Rhea soothed. "Peter Benchley, to start." She gave him another squeeze, then disentangled from him, even as he clutched.

Starbucks

Tuesday, July 27

With shoddy reception out on Maple Street, Arlo and the kids stopped off at Starbucks on the way home from the hospital. He bought everybody a mini maple scone, then called that old friend with the house in the Hollywood Hills. Danny Lasson with the Hohner 64. Turned out the number was the same more than fifteen years later.

Danny picked up on the second ring like no time had passed. "Arlo!" he hooted. "You shiner, how the hell are ya?"

"Well . . ." Arlo's cheeks flushed. Standing by the cream dispensary, he whispered so the kids didn't hear, though a man pouring about a pound of sugar into his nonfat latte craned his neck. "I'm not a junkie anymore."

"Yeah? I heard that. I follow your wife on Facebook. Your children are adorable! When I speak about them I call them the adorables."

"What?"

"I talk about you all the time, man. We were *Fred Savage's Revenge!*"

Arlo shoved an entire scone into his mouth. Then he couldn't talk. Because it was super dry. The fiftysomething man was listening and pretending not to listen. He put down the sugar and traded it for cinnamon. *Shake-shake.*

"What's happening?" Danny asked, all happy and Hollywood. "What can I do you for?"

Still chewing, his voice muffled, he blurted, "I thought I'd sell the Grammy. But I figured I should call you first. Out of respect."

The man started stirring his latte, which had to be semisolid by now. He was looking at Arlo, trying to place him.

"Whoa!" Danny cried. "You can't do that!"

Arlo walked away from the latte guy, and from his kids, too. He headed for the corner. Stayed there, talked to the wall like the bad kid from *Blair Witch.* "I know it's not cool. But I'm in a bind. I thought you should know before it goes on the market."

"Did AA put you up to this?"

"No. There's all different kinds of addicts. I never had a problem with alcohol. I don't like it enough to have a problem with it. So the Grammy. So I'm sorry, obviously."

"Oh, I forgot! It's NA, not AA. Are you in NA? Did Narcotics Anonymous put you up to this?" Danny asked, polite and concerned, his lockjawed accent from a tax bracket Arlo had only seen on PBS. Had he always enunciated this much? Where was that inner-city drawl they'd all shared?

"This is stupid. I'm sorry to interrupt your life. Can I sell the Grammy or what?"

"You can sell it. I don't think it's worth much."

Tears burned. He pressed his head against the corner, and he could feel the eyes of the people in Starbucks, including his kids. "Thanks. I appreciate that."

"Hold on. I'm at a recording studio. Let me take this outside," Danny said.

Arlo waited, forehead against cool plaster. Looked back once, to see that in fact the kids weren't watching. They were playing slap hands, at which Larry was a master. The latte guy had taken a seat. Was on his phone, but also looking at Arlo, which maybe meant he was looking him up.

"Okay." Danny got back on. "That's better. How are you?"

"You know. Been better. Been worse." Arlo's voice was shaky. Since sobriety, everything felt raw and new and scary, because it was.

"Want to tell me about it?" Danny asked, the voice of supreme confidence. Arlo remembered now, how they'd gotten that record deal in the first place. Danny had hounded this agent at UTA for months. Written e-mails and even tracked down his cell phone and texted him. It wasn't an accident when the guy showed up at their first gig at the Music Hall of Williamsburg, and it was no coincidence he'd brought his friend from Virgin Records. Danny, whose parents had owned a restaurant on the Upper West Side, and who'd gone to this private school called Regis (and who Arlo only now realized had exaggerated his street accent to put scrappy Arlo and Chet at ease), had been a self-promotion machine.

"It's not drugs. Just real life. I don't think this is the time to talk about it. It's been years. It'd be a dick move to call you out of the blue, just to unload."

Nobody talked. Arlo felt choked up in all kinds of directions.

"You're right. Don't tell me. But here's the thing. I don't mind your selling that Grammy, so don't think this is about that. The problem is, the Grammy people. If you win an award from them, it's not legal to sell it. They could fine you."

"Oh . . . Do you want it? Like, a private sale?"

Another long pause. The latte guy seemed to have found what he was looking for on his phone, because he started playing *"Kennedys in the River."* You'd think this was a rare event in Arlo's life, but it wasn't. Everybody loved doing that, once they found out. It wasn't always in a nice way. A lot of middle-aged white men used to play lead guitar in high school bands. A lot of them thought they'd been screwed out of fame.

"I don't want to buy it. It's nothing personal."

Arlo nodded into the phone and it occurred to him that when people say it's not personal, what they mean is: *It's 100 percent personal.* "I should say I'm sorry. I messed it up for you guys. I think about it every day. I can live with what I did to myself. But I hate that it broke up the band. I know you made a lot of that professional stuff happen. I never thanked you for getting us signed."

Arlo could hear somebody else on Danny's side of the phone. Some fellow musician, probably. "I don't think about it," Danny said.

"Oh."

"What I'm saying is, how often do bands ever stick? We had a great ride. We made some good money. I got my life out here because of '*Kennedys in the River*.' I'd never have gotten work writing music without that Grammy with our names on it."

"That's really great."

"I wish I'd said something. You were so high. I knew it was your dad. But I couldn't believe somebody would get their own kid hooked, just to steal everything. He was the worst manager. I look back and I wish I'd said something."

"Naw."

"Yeah. I should have said something."

"It's my fault. I blew it."

"I don't think so. Me and Chet are fine. We're working the business now. You're the one who wrote the music."

"So, you don't hate me?"

"I did. But not anymore. Listen, my sound guy's giving me the stink eye. I should go."

They promised to talk again, which maybe would happen and maybe wouldn't. Then they got off the line. Arlo was shaking when it was over. Relief and something else. He'd felt enormous shame for a long time, to the point where hearing his own music had been like needles under his skin. But after apologizing to Danny, some of that subsided now.

Baby, run away with me.
We'll shake these blues . . .

301

The song finished playing, and Arlo remembered why it had resonated with so many people. *It's nostalgic for something that isn't real, and it's sad about that. Everybody's nostalgic for glory days that never happened.*

"*Kennedys in the River*" ended. The latte guy was looking at him with recognition. Arlo nodded as if to say: *Yeah. I'm that guy.*

The latte guy's face scrunched in anger. He pointed the phone at Arlo. "I know you," he said.

Like always happened when threatened, Arlo's hands turned to fists. The latte guy stood from his table and walked backward, phone held higher, like a weapon. Now the barista, the other patrons, and Julia and Larry were looking, too.

"I know what you did to that little girl!" Latte guy screamed.

302

Creedmoor Psychiatric Center

Wednesday, July 28

Another day at the hospital. Julia's parents were angry but not saying why they were angry, which made Julia think they were mad at her. If she'd been faster, grabbed Shelly by the arm or taken the fall instead, this wouldn't be happening. People wouldn't be saying bad things. Strange men at Starbucks wouldn't be yelling. Their house and pictures of their family wouldn't be on the TV.

A lot of this was happening because Shelly's body was missing. Everybody knew, for her dad to prove his innocence, they needed the body.

After visiting hours, they didn't go back to Starbucks, because people in Starbucks are crazy and yell crazy things. They did get ice cream at Baskin-Robbins. In cups not cones, even though Julia preferred cones. But her dad did the ordering, and he looked tense as a rubber band about to snap. She'd decided to go with the flow, take the cup.

Julia got plain vanilla with chocolate sprinkles. Larry got pistachio for the green. Their dad got three scoops of chocolate plus syrup. He acted pretend happy. She hated when he did that. He said all the right, reasonable things, and underneath, you could tell he was boiling.

"You're gonna get fat," Larry told him, deadpan. "Mom says keep the ice cream, spare the syrup, or it's jelly belly city."

Julia leaned forward, just in case she needed to get between her brother and her dad. Just in case he really did snap.

Arlo threw the ice cream in the garbage, hard, so it passed all the random pink plastic and stuff and sank straight to the bottom. Then he stood in the doorway, waiting for Julia and Larry to follow. So Julia got up and threw away her ice cream, too. She stood next to her dad. Didn't say anything. Tried not to cry. She'd wanted that ice cream. That ice cream had been the only good thing to happen in weeks.

Larry took another bite like nothing was happening. The more nervous he got, the weirder and more obstinate he acted.

"Get up. Now. We're leaving," Arlo said.

Julia went over to him because right now, Larry was especially her job. If she could take care of him, at least she was doing one thing right. Even if she'd failed Shelly. There wasn't time to nice-talk him. So she took a chance, grabbed him by the arm and pulled, which worked 90 percent of the time. The other 10 percent, he tweaked. She used too much force. He got taken by surprise and shoved her. Little brothers. She reacted instead of thinking and shoved him back. He fell, landing upright, his ice cream intact.

The Baskin-Robbins was crowded. Everybody was looking at them, even the people in uniform who worked there. This was bad. They weren't allowed to fight, especially now that Julia was twelve years old. But the golden rule was Never in Public.

Larry scrambled to get up. He used Julia's leg for support and Julia yelped. It looked like more tussling.

"Let go of each other! NOW!" Arlo shouted.

Still holding Julia's leg, Larry froze, too scared to do anything else. Julia tried to shrink inside herself without actually moving her body or looking away or attracting attention.

Arlo rushed at them in two lanky strides, then jerked Larry up by the arm. He made this grunt that wasn't pain, but probably sounded like it to strangers. Everybody in the shop got quiet. Somebody took out their phone and pointed. Larry's pistachio ice cream dropped, and it slimed their clean floor.

Arlo's voice went low and rasping. It carried the way lead singers' voices fill any room, no matter the volume. "Why can't either of you ever do as told?"

"Sorry," Julia whispered.

"You know you can't act like this. Not now! What the fuck are you thinking?"

"I'm so sorry," Julia said. She could feel the people in the store watching. The green ice cream had smeared. Was all under Larry's flip-flops, and on his toes, too.

Arlo ran his hands through his hair, hard, the skin of his forehead pulling back, making stark his receded salt-and-pepper hairline. His Wolf Man tattoo looked like it was scowling.

"I want more ice cream and Julia, too," Larry said.

It was maybe the worst thing he could have said.

Arlo bent low, looked just to Larry now. "They blame me for what happened. If your mom's in the loony bin and I'm in jail, do you have any idea what's going to happen to you, you little freak?"

Larry started shaking. He didn't cry. He just did that thing, and went far away. Julia started crying, though.

"Goddamn," Arlo whispered as he backed away from his kids. Then, the worst thing. A thing she'd never seen before. He was wiping his eyes. Her super tough rock star dad was crying. His voice was scrapyard gravel. "Meet you outside," he said. Then he left the store.

The people in the Baskin-Robbins were still staring, and Julia couldn't tell what they were thinking. She just wished they'd stop looking. Larry was wiggling his ice cream–covered toes. "Come on," she said.

He didn't follow, so she took him really gently this time. They found Arlo in the Passat, engine turned. They both climbed into the back, not wanting to sit next to him. He didn't look back at them. She couldn't tell if it was because he was mad or because he'd been crying. When they got home, he went down to the basement. Julia was glad. Hoped he'd stay there. Except, he was the only grown-up left.

She took Larry by the hand and brought him to his room. He was still far away. The room looked even more perfect than usual. Clean and Spartan as a robot's. His bed was far from the window now. They'd moved all their beds far from windows.

She made him wash his feet, brush his teeth, put on his pajamas, then pulled back his covers and had him climb into bed. She handed him the Robot Boy replacement doll she'd made for him: two dishrags rubber-banded together in a cruciform shape, with nuts and bolts glued down for face, hands, and feet.

"He wasn't gonna get us more ice cream. It was a bad time to ask," she said.

Larry just shrugged.

"Why did you hide in that truck? It makes us look bad. Like we planned to get her alone and hurt her," she said, and part of her question was curiosity, but mostly she asked because she wanted to jolt him awake. Hurt him into it, like she was hurting, so she wouldn't be so alone with these feelings in this house.

"I was scared to leave the park without you. But Shelly didn't want me there." He was shaking still, and now that he was under his sheets, he'd wormed his hands down his pants.

"Gross," she said. "You're so weird and gross. The whole block's talking about us. They're gonna take Daddy away, and it's all your fault!"

Consider the panopticon. When Foucault, the father of semiotics, originally imagined it, he'd intended the guard to stand center, watching a periphery of prisoners. The tool was effective for surveillance because none knew when they were being watched, but they knew that it would happen eventually. They couldn't escape it. And so they behaved their best. But we can all agree that Foucault was drunk on his own ideas, responding not to real-world social surveillance, but to his own personal scars from having been raised by totalitarian parents.

Modern culture is an inverse panopticon. Not a drunk father, but a vigilant mother. The masses elect a single person to the hot seat for their five minutes of fame. We, the periphery, are the judges and jury. Because we're separated (like prisoners, we can't connect to each other through these impossible walls), we've no option but to connect via the sacrificial lamb we've placed dead center. Even when we privately dispute the censure or praise we heap upon them, publicly, we echo popular sentiment.

To avoid loneliness, we become a single, unthinking mass.

And yet, the mother and father both reveal their very limited ability to connect. The proverbial child cannot attach. We participate in this mass identity, but it does not serve us. Our language is reduced to a series of agreed-upon signs reflecting not nuance, but binaries: like/dislike; good/bad; yes/no. We are even more lonely for the failure of it . . .

118 Maple Street

Wednesday, July 28

Night. Far past time to sleep. A knock came. Rhea Schroeder did not say, *Come in.*

"Are you there?" Fritz called through the old, thin wood. All this time in America, and he still had an accent.

Rhea was in her office, unmarked papers heaped in piles. She turned the volume down on *The Black Hole,* playing off an old VCR in the corner. The one from college, that she'd brought with her to every place she'd ever lived.

"Rhea?" *Rhee-a,* he said, had always said, making that first syllable especially long. But he so rarely spoke her name that it shocked her.

The room was dark, lit only by the TV light. He wasn't often home, and when he was here, he never came to this place. She fiddled with Shelly's Pain Box, which she'd been trying to pick with an unbent paper clip for hours on her lap. So late in the day, her fingers had lost their dexterity.

She crossed the room. Put her hand on the door, turned the lock inside the handle, so he couldn't get in. She felt panicked, though she couldn't explain why. Would he care that she'd gone through two bottles of wine tonight? Was this about the brick? Or Shelly? She didn't want to talk to him about those things. He had no business offering an opinion, knocking on her secret place.

She could see the shadow of his feet beneath the sill of the door. He ran his hand, skin on wood, so specific and so similar to the sound of night rain. "Yes. I understand," he said at last. "I'll leave you." And then footsteps; his thick leather loafers, walking away.

In the dark, she returned to her chair, her lockbox, to her *Black Hole*. The paper clip caught, then lost the catch. On-screen, it was at the part in the movie where the good guys discover that the captain of the spaceship has lobotomized his own crew and turned them into slaves. They're not robots after all. She wished her dad were here to watch with her. Imagined him in the chair beside her. Willed it.

She'd been having fun that day at the Hungarian Pastry Shop, the café all the smart kids frequented. Close enough to graduate-student age that she could have passed for one.

All nine of them had been talking about the panopticon when this second-year PhD, Aileen Bloom, had started babbling about Bertrand Russell. There's a troublemaker in every class. They can't abide authority figures, or they care so much about the subject matter that they self-destruct, or they simply have bad personalities. Aileen Bloom was all three.

Aileen had this idea that no educated person could believe in God. Politely, Rhea had offered the counterargument: intolerance works both ways. When that hadn't worked, she'd shut her down, which had been easy, because Rhea knew her Bertrand Russell.

The rest of them left to get the fresh babka that had just come out of the oven. She'd thought the argument was over. But then, red-eyed with fury, Aileen had scooted her chair close to Rhea, like they hadn't been teacher-student at all. Like this was the schoolyard, and Rhea was still that awkward, scrawny kid who hid in hallways to avoid recess. Who called home from the office every chance she got. Once in a while, she'd caught her dad when he wasn't at work but had stayed home sick. He always came when that happened. He'd drive her back home, car swerving. They'd always napped together on the couch the rest of the afternoon, watching old sci-fi.

"This is about your father," Aileen had said, fast, so no one else would hear.

Rhea had stared down at her beer. The noise in the café had been so loud that she'd wondered if she'd misheard. "What do you know about my dad?"

"Everybody who clings to this fairy tale of an all-supreme being — it's always daddy issues."

Rhea had looked away, trying to hide her full eyes.

"I don't care that you're my teacher. I'm older than you anyway. Just be honest and admit that there is no God. He's dead."

"My father was perfect," Rhea had answered.

Aileen had looked at Rhea askance, like there was something wrong with her. She'd unmasked something broken in her teacher that she'd craved to see.

The students getting their babka returned. Aileen excused herself, and then Rhea did, too. And then, somehow, she'd kicked in a door. Sprained her knee against it. The face on the other side hadn't looked right.

Rhea's knee burst with pain now, just remembering. Or perhaps she'd been hitting it with the Pain Box, that was why. Somehow, more than an hour had passed since Fritz had come knocking. *The Black Hole* had ended and started anew. It was at the opening credits, the John Barry overture wild and foreboding and even cheerful. After *Star Wars* and *2001,* America had been so excited about things like gravity boots and rotating hallways, a future of space stations and galaxy exploration. They'd expected such great things.

She put Shelly's box in her desk. Pain shooting through her bad knee, she got up and she shut the door behind her. Let *The Black Hole* keep playing in there, by itself. A loop upon a loop upon a loop.

Dishes had piled up in the kitchen. She'd cooked pasta with butter tonight, left it on the table for them, and retreated into her office, like she'd done most nights since Shelly. The house was quiet, the heat oppressive. Circulars and newspapers, letters of condolence, had all fallen to the tribal Persian rug. She'd bought it for the authentic indigo, so much more subtle than the typical methylene.

She climbed the stairs, where another tribal Persian rug ran the length. She listened first at Ella's door, heard soft breathing. Next at FJ's, heard the same. Last at

Shelly's. She listened for a long time. Imagined the breathing there. Willed it.

Time passed. More than should have passed. Fritz Sr. had to be asleep. It had to be safe, by now, to go to bed. She limped all the way down the hall, to her room. Opened the door. He was awake, even though it had to be after three. He sat on the edge of the bed, his face in his hands, his shoes perfectly neat and facing out the way he liked. Beside him was a wet washcloth, which he'd used to clean his ears.

She sat a few feet from him, on the other side of their enormous bed. He smelled like tea rose, her favorite of his scents, and she thought that perhaps now was the time. In the dark, at night, with a man who'd been so invisible to her for so long that it would be like telling no one. She would confess about the Hungarian Pastry Shop, and about all those doubts she'd had, which she'd never voiced when she'd agreed to marry him. How she'd found herself so very alone on Maple Street. How she'd turned inward. How she'd used a brush. Most of all, she would tell him about the murk that had weighed her down ever since *The Black Hole*. The murk she couldn't wash clean of, that had assumed a personality all its own. The murk that had committed unspeakable acts.

She'd tell him these things, and in doing

316

so, unmake them. It would be as if going back in time, back before Shelly, back before the Hungarian Pastry Shop, washed clean to the better life she should have lived. She willed this so very much.

"I have to tell you something," she began.

He looked up at her, and she saw that he was crying. She couldn't remember the last time she'd seen him do that. If he'd done it before now, he'd done it alone.

"I miss her so much," he said.

"She's not gone. Not to me."

The floodlights in the faraway park shined a human-made moonglow through their windows.

"How do people live with this?" he asked.

"With what? Do you think I should feel guilty?"

"No. I mean, how do they live with losing a child?"

He'd grown a prickly mustache in the years they'd been together. And his hair was gray. He still dressed in khakis and polo shirts with chemical stains. Still worked long hours. She tried to think of a time he'd taken Shelly on a fishing trip. A time he'd played Uno or catch with her.

"You didn't raise her. I don't understand why you're the one who gets to cry when you never did anything."

317

"I'm overwhelmed," he answered. "This isn't my area of expertise. But I have the capacity. You've always known that about me. You and the children are the only people I've ever loved."

She thought about the way the police had questioned him, and how he hadn't backed her up. Had only said he wasn't around enough to know about bricks or sinkholes or sleepovers. Whatever Rhea had told them was probably right. She thought about all the times she'd wanted to come to him over the last twenty-plus years, crying and begging for help. For affection. Approval. Validation. A single kind goddamned word.

She'd assumed that he'd come knocking on her study door because he'd been concerned. Perhaps even suspicious. But no. He'd just felt lost, like always, and had wanted her to tell him what to do.

"I hate you so much," she said. "I wish you were dead."

116 Maple Street

Wednesday, July 28

It was crazy late, but Julia couldn't sleep. She tiptoed into Larry's room. She didn't know what she planned to say. *Sorry* didn't seem to cover it. And anyway, *sorry* didn't mean anything to somebody like Larry. He didn't believe in words. Just actions. She planned to crawl into his bed and cuddle him. But he was sleeping. The new Robot Boy she'd made him was in the garbage by the door, blue dish towel arm curved over the edge, bolt hand resting outside the plastic bin.

She took it out, put it beside him. His cheeks were splotchy from crying. It was too hot for covers, so he was splayed, his hair wet with sweat.

"Larry," she whispered.

He flopped in his sleep, turned over.

"You were right. I did want more ice cream."

She went back to her room, to her window. Charlie Walsh was looking out his window, too. For most of the time she'd lived on this crescent, she'd kept the blinds closed. So had Charlie. They were a year apart; boy and girl, to boot. It wasn't cool to live so close. Downright awkward, given Charlie'd told the whole Rat Pack he had a crush on her. But then Shelly fell, and she'd been tempted. Just to explain herself. To show him her dog-bit hand, her half-dissolved stitches, and say, "I got hurt, too. So, do you hate me? Do you blame me? Does everyone?"

Even then, neither had pulled back their curtains. It had taken the brick.

Curtains pulled, shade lifted, he'd acted as emissary for the whole Rat Pack the night after she came home from taking her mom to the hospital. *Is your mom okay? The baby?* he'd asked. *It's so bad,* she'd answered. *She went so crazy. I didn't recognize her.* Then she'd broken down and cried. He'd just watched until she was done. She'd hoped he would tell her that everything would be okay. He knew such things, because he was logical Charlie. But he'd just stayed with her instead, and that had felt scarier and more honest.

"How's your mom?" Charlie now called across the divide.

"Better."

Julia came out, sat perched on the sill, her

legs dangling in arcs. It was dangerous, a deadly drop. She braced her hands against the inside walls in case she started to fall. A gesture of wildness, of what was happening inside her heart, made just for him.

"Is that safe?"

"I dunno."

Charlie came out, too. Mimicked her. It surprised her, that he'd take the risk. Now they were closer. It felt personal. Like on a playdate, when the mom leaves and you're alone in the house together and you could do anything.

"I hate this block," Julia said.

Charlie knocked the glass from the inside. Looked sad and angry both. "I like your hair."

Short. She combed it behind her ears with her fingers. "Shelly was wrong back at the hole . . . I do like you, Charlie. I'm glad you're my neighbor."

He clicked his Tevas together. "I like you, too."

"Good."

"Do you like me more than friends? More than Dave?"

"I dunno. Don't ask me that."

"Sorry," Charlie said.

"S'okay. It just feels wrong to think about right now."

"Yeah."

"Charlie? Remember when you said you told Dave and Sam and Shelly that you liked me, when I first moved in?"

Charlie nodded. His bowl cut was just long enough that it curled up at the ends. It was girly by Brooklyn standards, but she decided that girly was okay. It's fine for boys to be pretty.

"Why? What's good about me?" she asked.

Charlie swung his Tevas. Looked at them, and at her bare, dirty feet, too. She wished she'd washed.

"You don't have to say. It's a weird question."

"I like that you're nice," he said, all fast, so it was hard to understand.

"Oh," Julia answered, because everybody's nice.

Then he added, just as fast: "You're funny and you notice people when they talk. You pretend you're low-rent but you're not. I like that you're a good sister."

Julia let go of the edges of the sill. Her body rocked, the fall thirty feet, and she wondered what it had felt like for Shelly, when she'd fallen. Had she snapped out of that trance, and realized what was happening? Alone down there, did she think that Julia had forgotten her?

"I was mean to him tonight. I told him he was weird and gross."

Charlie made a sad face.

"I'm supposed to take care of him, but I was mean. I do wrong things all the time. Did you know that Shelly told me something? She said a person, not my dad, was hurting her. And I said we should go to the police. And when her mom started chasing us, that's why we ran. We didn't want to get caught and stopped. I made it this urgent emergency. It got her worked up. That's why she wasn't paying attention. That was my bad advice."

Charlie got out of the window and stood. She thought he didn't believe her. Or maybe he was just disgusted. He was going to close his curtains. But then he said, "Go to your back door. I'll meet you."

"Really?"

"Yes." He waited across the way like a mirror image until she climbed back in and started walking, then he did, too.

She went down on tiptoe. Knew the house well enough that she didn't need light. She got to her back door, and he was there. He didn't usually break rules. He liked his parents too much. It made her feel special, just like that morning in Sterling Park, when he'd taken her hand.

He waved through the glass. He looked more grown than she was used to. She'd never noticed before, that he had nice skin. It wasn't pimpled like hers, but clear.

She opened the door. Was scared to look at him, but happy to have him. Happier than she'd have been with Dave, she realized, because Dave had something hard in him. Even when you were joking around, you couldn't really let down your guard, because he might tease in a bad way.

They walked through the kitchen. He was at her side instead of behind, and he stayed quiet. They went up together, to the only place that made sense — her bedroom. She closed the door behind them, turned on just the reading light. The bed was made because her dad had made everybody keep up their chores. She was glad for this. But she also didn't want to sit on it, because then he would sit on it. They'd be sitting on a bed together.

She sat on her windowsill. He came next to her, peered through, to his own house. Studied the new vantage.

"I've wanted to know what that looked like for a long time," he said.

"What does it look like?" she asked.

He shrugged. Smiled just slightly with lips that were more pink than red. Looked around her room, at the Billie Eilish and Ruby Bridges posters, at her pile of manga. He lingered on the floor, on her purple cotton underpants, which she hadn't put away. She wished they were fancy days-of-the-week, like Shelly's.

"You were going to the cops?" he asked.

Julia nodded. "She was getting hit. It was my idea, but she wanted to. We decided together."

"Who was doing it?"

"Her mom." She'd been worried that telling too many people would betray Shelly's trust, but once Julia said it, she felt a weight lift. That meant it was the right thing.

Charlie breathed out. She expected him to ask lots of Charlie questions. When was she hit? How often? Had Shelly considered telling a school counselor instead? Was Julia even sure it was true, because Shelly was kind of a liar. But all he said was, "That's awful. It makes sense, but it's awful . . . I wondered what you guys were doing out there for so long. I was afraid she was being mean."

"She wasn't. I think she wanted to get me alone. But she was so turned around she didn't know how to make it happen, except by doing what she did."

"Yeah," Charlie said. He was still standing

in front of her. She scooted so they could share the sill. The window was still open, their backs precariously exposed. Jostling, he lifted his arm, circled it around her waist. His hand cupped her stomach, then reconsidered and went loose. She liked the smell of him: expensive detergent and pretzels.

"Is that okay?"

She nodded. "I was lonely in this house before. It's nice that you're here."

Charlie looked at her in a way that she felt all through her chest. "What else happened with Shelly?"

"It was going on for a while. I don't know how often. It wasn't the hitting that bothered her. Kids I knew in Brooklyn used to get spanked and they'd laugh it off. It was the secret. That's what was messing her up. She thought she was going crazy," Julia said. "She thought we all knew the secret. She thought we knew but weren't helping."

Charlie took this in. Didn't seem surprised by it. Julia remembered how he'd talked about 118, and its perfection. "Did you know?" she asked.

"I wondered," he said. "But it's not something you ask somebody. Not Shelly, at least. And like Dave said, everybody's got problems."

She leaned into him. His hand flopped

around, and then decided. He rested it on her hip. She leaned into his chest and started crying again. He was wearing a Giants T-shirt and shorts, warm and damp with sweat.

"I keep wishing I'd done or said something different. Then she wouldn't have fallen," she said between sobs. "My family wouldn't be in trouble."

"It's okay."

"Is it?"

"I don't know, but it's not your fault."

She sat up. His eyes were wet, too.

"What is it?"

He sniffed. Breathed until he had control. "I keep thinking the worst of this has happened, and then another worse thing happens . . . Your dad got blamed and that was bad. The whole block went after him, even my parents, and that was worse. It turns out Mrs. Schroeder was hurting her and we never even knew. She must have been so sad. That's bad, too. But you know the worst part?"

Julia shook her head.

"She's down there, Julia. Shelly's down there. She fell and she's probably dead and I knew her since we were five. I shared Chap-Stick with her and I took swim lessons with her and I shared my Pirate's Booty every day of third grade with her and she's gone.

People in your life can just go away and you never had the chance to say good-bye. I'm sad now but I won't be forever. I'll forget her. That's the worst thing. We all just move on, until we're dead, and then everyone else moves on."

He was crying now, trying to hide it. Gentle, she took his hands away from his face. "You won't forget her," she said. "I send her messages with my mind. I push them out and down the hole. I tell her I love her. I tell her to stay strong."

He smiled through his tears. "I like you, Julia."

She didn't have an answer for that, and she didn't want to think about it, because they were talking about Shelly, and Shelly was more important. Still, he made her feel safe. She liked being close to him. This was a stolen thing in the night. A remedy to the trouble with her mom and dad, and to the mean thing she'd said to Larry. A good kind of secret in the midst of so very many bad ones. She turned her face. Closed her eyes and leaned in.

It took a second. And then she felt his lips. They were warm and soft and wet from tears and spit.

It was a quick kiss. Her first. A good one, too.

"Was that okay?" he asked.

"I liked it."

He squeezed her waist. Kissed her again. She opened her mouth. He opened his, too. This one lasted longer, and she felt it in the rest of her body, not just her lips. She wasn't as scared anymore, or as lonely.

After, she leaned into him. "If that new diver doesn't find her this week, they'll fill the hole. They'll bury her down there. She'll be trapped. Nobody'll know what happened or that my dad's innocent. He'll go to jail, and she'll be buried with a lie."

"I know," Charlie said. "It's not right."

"We could do it," Julia said.

Charlie didn't immediately say this was a bad idea. Dangerous and crazy. He was full of surprises tonight.

"I'm smaller than any diver. I could go down there before they fill it. You could stay above and make sure I'm okay. We could save her."

"When?" Charlie asked.

124 Maple Street

Thursday, July 29

Shit's tough all around, Dave Harrison had once told his favorite members of the Rat Pack. This was particularly true under his own roof.

Dave's mom, Jane Harrison, was standing under the small hall chandelier next to Rhea Schroeder. Dave was at the top of the stairs, his view partially obstructed. He could only see his mom's floral skirt, Rhea's loose linen. He had the bizarre impulse to chuck an ax at the chandelier. It would fall, pinning them both to the floor like old-school criminals.

"Did you hear about the twins and Lainee Hestia? He got to them, too!" Jane exclaimed. She kept her voice low, like gossiping about the neighbors was a secret best kept from fourteen-year-old boys.

The worst part was, nobody talked about Shelly anymore. Nobody wondered whether she was still alive down there, a frightened and lonely miracle.

"Sam Singh, too," Rhea said. "Maybe all of Nikita's children. It just came out."

"Dominoes. My God, Rhea, you must be going crazy. Jail's not good enough. He ought to be castrated," Jane said. She was standing on the left side of the Sharpie line that bisected the hall. Like she didn't care, a super alpha dog, Rhea stood astride. It cut her right in half.

His parents used to hide the Sharpie line from the neighbors, but since the hole and then Shelly, they'd stopped bothering.

"The detective — what's his name, Bianchi?" Rhea asked. "He was drunk. Is that bad to say? I don't want to besmirch his character. He's definitely trying very hard. Maybe just Parkinson's? Parkinson's or whiskey. Let's leave it at that."

"He swayed?"

"He had to hold on to the door. And he told me there wasn't enough evidence."

"How much more evidence do they need?" Jane asked. "Can you imagine the therapy these children will require? The damage? It's years. As a preschool teacher, I'll tell you: they'll never recover. It's going to hurt through entire generations. I get sick just thinking about it."

"I'm learning so much about the justice system," Rhea said. "You hear it's corrupt.

331

You read it in the paper. But living it's a whole different thing."

Dave took a step down the stairs. Then another. Now both women could see him. He glared at Rhea Schroeder, and it was totally unreal, because even though she was a grown woman, she glared right back.

It felt like a bite. Like having your face clamped down on by a python.

His mom acted like it was normal. Like it was totally cool for this lady to be standing in his hall, visually skewering him. He figured it out right then. His mom was scared of Rhea. And the reason Rhea was glaring like she hated him was because she really did hate him. He was the only Rat Pack member not to come out against Arlo Wilde. He hadn't toed her line.

Dave looked away. Rhea relaxed, victorious.

"A neighborhood watch is a marvelous idea," Jane said.

"Oh, I'm so relieved you agree. I hate to seem overboard," answered Rhea.

"I think you're calm."

"Oh, good. I'm glad. We'll take turns. One house at a time. I've spoken with everyone but the Benchleys — they're leaving for Florida. And the Atlases. She's too sick. Plus, they don't have children. I don't think they really understand any of this. Did you know Fred tried to find Arlo a lawyer? Can you believe that?"

"We're the last?" Jane interrupted. "You should have come sooner! I'm very good at organizing."

"I came this morning but you weren't home. You would have been third."

"Third's good. That's part of the club." She said this like she was making a joke, but she absolutely wasn't.

"Great. Either Linda, Marco, or FJ will drop off the schedule. We've all got two-hour shifts. It's very important. You can't shirk or who knows where that pervert'll strike."

Jane nodded.

"I've been very clear with the Pontis and it bears repeating. Violence is the last option. This watch is to keep that from happening," Rhea said.

"Don't you worry, sweetheart. Whatever happens, I'm on your side."

Rhea smiled. "That means so much . . . But there are no sides. Arlo's in pain, or he wouldn't have done the things he's done."

Jane made this funny barking sound. A cry. Voice cracking, she said, "I don't know how you can be so understanding."

Dave came halfway down the stairs, alarmed by the sound of his mother's pain.

"I hope you never have to understand," Rhea answered. "Take care of your mother, Dave. Bye-bye, Tim," she called, and then was gone.

Tim?

Stomach tight, Dave looked behind. There was his dad in a ratty bathrobe, unshaven. Bitumen still caked the creases of his eyes. Three days since he'd been part of that brick-throwing mob, and he still hadn't washed it off.

His mom, down below, looked up. Direct eye contact. Not with Dave. She took a baby step over the Sharpie line. You never knew when this kind of thing would blow up. When they'd start yelling horrible things at each other. In his mind, Dave psychically blew her back into the safe zone. Then he blew her out of the house. Then he blew the whole house away and was free.

For a sick man, his dad took the stairs fast. They met like that, each facing the other. Standing close, his dad spoke directly to his mom for the first time in recent memory. "I'll help with the neighborhood watch."

Silence. Then, "Are you well enough?"

"Yeah. It doesn't ache today. The little fibers. Thank you for asking."

They started for the kitchen, shoulders so close they nearly touched, Sharpie line between them, like that coyote and sheep dog from those old cartoons, relaxing at the end of a long day.

Soon after, Dave broke the house arrest that the Maple Street parents had quietly agreed upon. Charlie Walsh opened on the first knock, like all he did was sit around, praying for visitors. He'd planned to suggest that they sneak out and drink the oilcan of Foster's that he'd nabbed from his big brother. But the inside of Charlie's house (pretty furniture, books organized by subject, happy family photos on the walls) looked so inviting. "You got any food?" he asked.

"I'm making a turkey sandwich. Want one?"

As they ate, Charlie said, "I've been talking to Julia. We're gonna find Shelly."

116 Maple Street

Thursday, July 29

At dinner that evening, the Wildes were interrupted by a bang on the door. It sounded like a rock. Arlo's first instinct was to flip the table and use it like a shield.

Another rock: *Bam!*

"Hey! Hello?" a man's deep voice called from outside. "It's me! Peter Benchley!"

"Stay here," Arlo called to the kids, gruff. Then he checked the window. There was Peter, right at the edge of the stoop. He'd been tossing pebbles because his chair couldn't traverse the steps. "It's okay. Everything's okay. Just stay where you are," Arlo told Julia and Larry, then went out, shut the door behind him, and met Peter at the landing.

The guy wore a plain white T-shirt and khakis pinned back. He was carrying a leather case on his lap. He'd shaved, but there was a pallor to his complexion. His eyes were pinpricks. More than a decade sober, Arlo still felt a twinge at the back of his neck. A pull and release pleasure-memory.

He crouched and extended his hand to Peter. "You vouched for me with the cops. I never thanked you. Thank you."

Peter nodded.

"I'm sorry I didn't say it sooner. It meant something to me and Gert that you helped us and you stood up. Can I do anything for you?"

Peter let go. He had a loose grip and baby-soft skin, like maybe he only rolled that chair once a week. "I need to tell you something," he said. His voice was distant, like he was only half living in this world. Arlo remembered that feeling with fondness and alarm. It's different from drinking. It's different from anything you can imagine.

"What?" Arlo asked. Though he didn't want that hot shot of white gold, he could hear the pant of desire in his voice.

"They're after you."

"Who? Did you happen to see which one threw the brick?"

"Do you know for how many years I've been looking out my window?"

Arlo shook his head.

"I grew up here. But all my friends moved away. I'm like Peter Pan," Peter said with a smile.

"Sure."

"I know these people like the ridges of my stumps."

"Yeah?"

"They've always been predictable. Sleep and eat and work, it's always the same. And then this thing happened." He nodded his head in the direction of the hole. "And it's all different. They're different."

Arlo stayed crouching in front of Peter. His knees wobbled, off-balance, and he steadied himself by lowering his hands to the bitumen-sticky ground. "What's different about them?"

"Did you know I was in Iraq?" Peter asked.

"I figured."

"A kid set off a homemade bomb. He was holding it. His parents made him do that, I guess. Or whoever." Peter's eyes stayed far away. "The boy died instantly. So did my CO. I wasn't hurt that bad. His bones turned to shrapnel inside my legs. The problem was that pieces of his marrow got mixed. The boy's immune system grew inside me. That's why the amputation. That's why the mirror therapy. My whole room's covered in mirrors. People think it's made up. I'm a junkie. But it's real. Did you know that?" He didn't wait or look to Arlo for acknowledgment. "It hurts so much that I can't even wear the prosthetics — they're just for the mirror therapy. I wear them to see my reflection as a whole person. So my brain gets confused and thinks I'm healed. Anyway, when it happened, when that boy did that to me and my CO, I heard these cheers. The people in hiding. Civilians. Neighbors. They cheered."

Arlo pictured that. Tried to.

"There was this energy to the place. It wasn't happy cheering."

Arlo gave up crouching and balanced himself by holding on to the sides of Peter's chair. Up close he saw that Peter wasn't as old as he looked. It was just his sunken eyes.

"Maple Street has that same electricity."

"What is it?"

"It's hysteria. And I don't even know why. I don't know if it's about you. You're just the target."

Peter nodded behind him, at a handicap-accessible airport shuttle van. A man was loading luggage while a couple in their seventies, the senior Benchleys, waited at the curb. "It's too hot for them. They're making me leave for Florida."

"Bet you could use a change of scenery."

Peter nodded.

Dark had settled over Maple Street. You could see movement through the open, lit-up windows of half the houses. There weren't any night sounds, though. No crickets or cicadas or hooting birds. It made their own voices carry that much farther.

"I wanted to tell you about my therapy mirrors," Peter whispered.

"Yeah?"

"When I use them, I don't hurt," Peter whispered. "I mean, it's agony if I don't do my hour or two. Every day. But it's getting better. Every year, it's a little better."

"Sure."

Peter held Arlo's eyes. "People around here don't know about my mirrors. They don't come over. They think we're weird. We stayed too long. I'm grown. Not a little kid. We don't fit in. But Rhea Schroeder's nosy. She got my mom to give her a tour. You see what I mean?"

"She's nosy," Arlo said. "She's a lotta things."

"But I wasn't home yesterday. I was at the VA for my checkup. So were my parents. When we got back, we saw FJ Schroeder and Adam Harrison running out from around our backyard. The Harrison kid was crying."

"Yeah?"

"And when I got inside, all my mirrors were broken."

340

Arlo felt his scalp tighten, because yeah, now he did see the point of this conversation.

"Maybe I'm crazy," Peter said, looking around, still whispering. "I have a hard time, knowing what's real and what's not."

"You seem to be doing okay."

"But somebody wrote a word across the shards. I didn't tell my parents. They don't need this. The word? It was *snitch*."

"Shit. I'm sorry you got mixed up in this," Arlo said.

Peter kept talking, not hearing Arlo at all. "I used to have to clean latrines once in a blue moon — that's just the deal, it wasn't a punishment. I was a good soldier. I got a Purple Heart and I deserved it. But I had to clean latrines. You see?"

Arlo waited, still crouched, his thighs burning. Peter kept looking with intensity, like Arlo should have guessed by now.

"The word. *Snitch*. I'd know. It was written in shit."

Arlo lost his balance and fell back.

"But maybe I'm crazy. Because people don't do that on Maple Street. It's not like Iraq."

"You're not crazy," Arlo said.

Peter sighed out with great relief. "They threw bricks at your house and one of them hit your wife."

"They threw them."

"They did it because they blame you for the Schroeder girl falling into the sinkhole. They think she was running away from you because you'd raped her, even though I saw you come home that night. I saw Shelly come out that morning. It never happened. It wasn't possible. If she was running from anyone, it was her mother. But the neighbors believed her story and they think you raped all the kids on the block, don't they?"

"Aw, God. I guess they do think that."

"And then they broke into my house because I defended you. They broke my mirrors and smeared their shit. That's what happened."

"Yes," Arlo said. Even with his hindbrain clawing with old desire, Peter made the junk seem like a nonoption. Like suicide. "You're not crazy, Peter. You're sharp. But you're on too much junk."

Peter winced. It was the first thing Arlo said that the kid had actually heard. Then he smiled, and it was clear to Arlo that he still wasn't sure this conversation was happening. Wasn't sure of anything. "Yeah. I know." Then he lifted the case from his lap. "So here. Take it."

Ass on ground, Arlo took the case. Something heavy. "I don't like these," he said once he looked inside.

342

"It's loaded," Peter said. "Only use it if you have to. Because they really are. After you."

Arlo closed the case. Peter didn't say goodbye. He wheeled around and rolled fast for his parents, who were waiting in front of the service van to load up his chair.

It was eight at night. Still as an echo chamber.

Arlo stood to follow. To hand it back. But something prevented him. Mostly, it was awkwardness — did Peter's aged parents really need to worry about all this? Didn't Arlo owe the kid something, if only his silence?

The safety of his children, who were back inside that house, prevented him. The neighbors prevented him, too. Because he noticed, then, that all of them were watching. The Pontis and Hestias and Singhs-Kaurs. The Harrisons and Walshes, too. Rhea Schroeder was standing in the middle of her dark dining room, under the misapprehension that he would not see her if she stood very, very still.

What stopped him was *snitch*, smeared in shit.

Friday, July 30

Arlo would have carried Gertie over the threshold of 116 Maple Street, but the kids were buzzing around, so nervous and excited to have her back home that he was afraid they'd get underfoot and topple him. So he wrapped his arm around her and they walked in together, arm in arm.

Her temporary bed was the ground-floor couch. She'd been ordered by the doctor to stay in it, feet propped, until her next checkup, when they could be sure the swelling was gone. No stairs. It was still morning and the mercury would take hours to reach its summit. Right now, it was ninety-six degrees.

Once the kids went to their rooms, Arlo showed Gertie the gun. It surprised him when she held the thing with skill. "It's a .42 revolver. Safety wasn't on," she said, clicking it into place. "See this? Red means dead. You have to pull hard." She pulled a metal piece and the red disappeared.

Then she emptied the chamber. Reloaded. Six bullets, no extra. "Do you know how to use one of these?"

"Do you?"

"Gun shows and beauty pageants. They go together like peas and carrots."

While their kids stayed in their separate bedrooms, unusually quiet, she showed him how to aim, how to hold, how to carry.

"Did Julia mention where that Pain Box evidence was hidden?" Gertie asked, nonchalant.

Arlo loaded the chamber. Bullets landed with metallic clicks. "She doesn't know. I asked her."

"It's in that house, though," Gertie said.

Arlo put the safety on, pointed. "Should we break in?" he joked.

Gertie waited a beat. "Maybe."

They decided to keep the gun in their bedroom, closer to him. While she knew better how to use it, her behavior in the hospital did not marry well with a gun.

Friday morning passed into afternoon. They learned that the special diver had given up, unable to traverse the underground tunnel. It was too small. The rescue workers packed up and went home. Trucks pulled out. Neighbors went inside their houses.

Reporters disappeared. After the weekend, the hole would be filled.

No body recovered.

The Wildes waited for police to arrive. An arrest, or another inquiry. Someone at the police station had to be making a decision right now. Choosing whether to proceed with the case against Arlo Wilde.

But hours passed into late afternoon and nothing happened. No police came. Due to the excavation, the hole and surrounding broken ground had grown to an improbable sixty square feet, the entire park and streets and pavement slick with tar. It looked like a terrible massacre had happened, and the Wildes began to wonder if Maple Street's madness, having gone too far and frightened even itself, had died down.

It was disappointing, then, when a new set of authority figures arrived at their front door. These introduced themselves as representatives of Child Protective Services. They'd been alerted by the police of potential child endangerment. Could they talk to Arlo alone, at their office?

"I thought this got settled already," Arlo said as he stood at the front door. "Call the Garden City Station and check for yourselves. Detective Bianchi."

"This is a separate investigation. The

346

Garden City Police are obliged to forward all child endangerment reports. They only alerted us this morning."

"They didn't tell us they'd do that!" Arlo said. His voice, like sometimes happened, got louder than he'd intended. The authority figures cringed, then came back more ferocious.

"They're not obligated to tell you. We'll need to clear this up. Today. Now."

Arlo looked behind the door, back at Gert in the den, who was listening. At least the kids were still upstairs. "I'm tired of this. It's not right. I need to take care of my family."

The man in front put his hand on Arlo's shoulder, and normally, he'd have acted cool. He'd have suffered through. He shoved the guy hard enough to knock out his breath.

"Sir, we have the power to remove your children from your home!" the other guy shouted.

"Sorry. I'm so sorry," Arlo said, hands lifted in the air. "I didn't mean it. I take it back."

"He didn't mean it. He's so sorry!" Gertie said in her fake light voice that was too close to baby talk. "Better go with them, hon. Sooner you get it done, sooner it's over and we can have dinner."

Arlo walked back to Gertie. The

investigators from CPS followed though they had not been invited inside.

"Sir? Do we need to call the police?" one of them asked.

Arlo fake smiled. The rage underneath was palpable. "You take care of yourself," he said to Gert.

She held his eyes. "Stay calm."

It hurt the middle of Gertie's back to get up but she did it anyway. She went to the stoop and watched the car take Arlo away. It was late afternoon now. The sun had crested and was now dropping back down behind the tree line but the damage was done. The whole block was hot enough to melt. You could see tar sand all over. Since she'd been gone, it had risen. The park, the lawns, the street, all oil smeared and leading, like a spider's web, to that enormous hole.

The cop car stationed for the day was parked in front of the Atlas house. Gennet was inside. Most people were at work or picking their kids up from camp or summer tutors. But Rhea was out there. She waved to Gertie like everything was great. Smiled wide and happy. Maybe the happiest Gertie had ever seen her.

An hour later, Detective Bianchi stopped by. He said he wanted to see how she was feeling, and also to relay a message from Arlo, given she probably didn't have reception. CPS had taken him into custody. He'd be staying overnight.

"Four more families stepped forward. They're saying Arlo may have interfered with their children, too. We're keeping it out of the papers as best we can."

Gertie winced, bit her lip to stay the tears. "Arlo's not a hunter. He's not that guy. You met him. You must know that."

"Time will tell."

"Fuck you. Why didn't you search Rhea's house? Why didn't you look for that evidence? That's the real crime here, that Rhea got away with hurting her own child. And now she's getting away with framing my husband for it, just in case a body turns up and they find it scarred or God knows what, they'll blame him and not her. Why are you helping her do this? What's wrong with you? Is it that you can't stand the scandal she's making? Everybody's rooting for poor victim Rhea, and you're afraid to stand up? It'll get in the news that you're defending a pedophile?"

She hit a nerve. Or maybe he just didn't like getting yelled at by a pregnant lady. He left. Told her that the cop driving by every hour would also relay messages between her and Arlo. She followed him to the door, wincing with pain as she moved one foot after the next. Watched him get into his car, her fury leaking away, leaving just sadness.

Rhea was still on her porch. She smiled at Gertie again. Big and cheerful.

Gertie thought about what Julia had told her, about a Pain Box hidden someplace in Rhea Schroeder's house. She thought about how tomorrow, Rhea would be at work, and so would Fritz.

Slowly, Gertie smiled back.

Saturday, July 31

Gertie watched as Rhea drove her Honda out from the crescent and to Nassau Community College — her usual Saturday-morning routine. Then Fritz took his Mercedes and headed for BeachCo Laboratories in Suffolk County. The kids were still inside. FJ and Ella. She knew that. But she also knew this was as empty as that house was going to get.

Julia and Larry were eating cereal. As a reward for their general hardship, Arlo had selected Lucky Charms. Julia was giving Larry all her green clovers. In return, she was getting the purple horseshoes. The milk was swirled brown rainbow.

"You're not gross," Gertie heard her whisper. "But you're still weird."

"I know," Larry answered. "You're not as funny as you think."

Julia chuckled, looked at him with surprise. "That was good! Good for you!"

Gertie tousled Larry's short hair, then

Julia's blond little mop, too. "I'll be right back," she told them.

Her back hurt less if she walked very slowly. She wore a tank top and stretch pants, her hair in a ponytail. Because she was Gertie, she also had on hoop earrings, a long chain necklace to distinguish her cleavage, and silver eye shadow. She walked around the back of her house so the cop parked out front wouldn't see.

Her lawn was small and caked with littered things: a Wiffle ball, a deflated basketball, some boxing gloves. The Slip 'N Slide had ruined anything resembling grass. What remained was a top layer of sand oil. She walked past all this, and cut her way through the naked privets that divided the plots.

Into the Schroeders' property. The grass here had a green hue. Despite the drought, they hadn't shut off their underground sprinklers. There was more oil back here, too. It pooled. Her eyes followed to the thickest center, where some birds were trapped. It was like a bath they couldn't escape. What startled her wasn't the sight, but the realization that these were the first birds she'd seen in weeks.

Gertie came to the back of the Schroeders' huge Tudor. The kind little girls dream about, if they're taught to have those kinds of dreams. The windows were all open. Everyone's windows were open. The heat.

Slowly, she tried to twist the back doorknob. It didn't turn. Locked. She lifted the straw WELCOME mat. Underneath was a copper-colored key.

She pushed it into the lock. It wouldn't turn. Not a fit. Not a fit?

A few strides to the side, surrounded by hedges, gutter stairs led down. She walked them, slow and unsteady. The steps were caked in years-old grime. She got to the bottom. The cellar door.

The key fit. She turned it, ever so softly. A *click!*

She opened the basement door to the Schroeders' house.

Inside, the soft floor had cracked. Shining bitumen pushed through. It webbed and then pooled in the middle of the room and when Gertie stood over it, she could see her own reflection. It came back distorted, her face a bluish tint, her eyes reddish black. A couple of mice squeaked, trapped in its morass. Her shoes got filthy and she couldn't help but make tracks as she walked into the next room.

She'd never been down here. Hadn't known this basement was finished. There was a dry bar, unused. She looked behind. Instead of bottles, a stack of bricks. Bright red.

She snapped a photo with her phone.

She opened a closet door. Empty red wine bottles were stacked. Maybe fifty. Maybe one hundred. It was hard to count. The dark walls inside seemed to glimmer. She flashed her phone light and saw that this glimmer was the gossamer wings of small fruit flies, trapped in oil on the walls and floor and even the ceiling. She covered her mouth with her shirt, afraid the stench might contaminate the baby.

She opened the next closet. Here was the same. Bottles. Empty but not properly washed, so they smelled fermented and sweet. Glimmering with trapped flies. Rhea must have been hiding them here ever since the sinkhole. The garbage men couldn't get through. She must not have wanted to use the community bin by the 7-Eleven, worried neighbors might discover how many bottles she went through every week. Gertie'd known that Rhea could knock them back. But she'd never guessed it was this bad.

Where was Fritz in all of this? Did he see what was happening in his home? Did he care?

To keep from tracking oil, she took off her shoes and tucked them behind the landing,

354

then started up the stairs. Opened up. This door led to the open kitchen, which stretched along marble counters and nooks and stainless steel appliances, all the way to the dining room in the front of the house.

It smelled clean in here. Like bleach. And vaguely, like something burnt.

Her heart beat fast at the wide-openness of this first floor. Here, there was no place to hide. She could get in trouble if she got caught. Jail. With Arlo gone, the kids could wind up in foster care.

Her heart was pounding. Guppy kicked, too.

She walked slow. Through the open room. Past the Schroeder family Christmas photos neatly magnetized to the refrigerator, marking every year for the last twenty-plus. Red sweaters, blue sweaters, green sweaters — they always matched. Past the strangely blackened sink. Past the oak dining table that was Rhea's prize. There were plates scattered across it and stuck-on crumbs. What looked like spilled milk that hadn't been sponged, too. It had ruined the wood.

Gertie walked out and through the hall. She could see the front yard from here. Her own small house with chipped paint and random, rusted toys strewn all over. It was dumpy. They hadn't taken care. She'd never seen it from this vantage before and it left her so embarrassed she stopped looking.

She started up the stairs. Creaking, creaking. She could hear sounds coming from the bedrooms. Ella and FJ. Where were they? Would they catch her?

Creak, creak, creak.

At the summit. Down the long hall was the master bedroom. A smaller bedroom, too. One door was open. She peered. Ella Schroeder sat on the floor with a pillow hugged to her knees. She watched *Buffy the Vampire Slayer* with intensity, even though the picture was mostly snow.

Gertie tried the next door. Opened. Awkward and man-sized, FJ lay on top of his sheets in just loose, light-blue boxers, sleeping deep. He seemed so smug, this brick thrower. This would-be baby killer. She noticed something before walking away. There was a circle of dark stain. In his sleep, he'd soiled his bed.

She got to the small bedroom off the master. Shelly's room. The door wouldn't open. Something blocked it. She bent down, belly pressed against her knees, and reached through the crack to ease a bright-pink item of clothing out of the way. She opened the door.

Covered her mouth to silence the gasp.

The walnut dresser had been overturned and lay on its side. The mirror yanked down and broken atop a pile of days-of-the-week underpants and bathing suits and terry cloth cover-ups. Small fists had punched the walls, leaving knuckle indentations. Rhea? Shelly? FJ? Fritz? Who had done this?

Jesus, God: Had all of them done this?

She opened the desk drawers. Empty, their contents spilled out. Looked under the bed and then under the mattress. Nothing but clothes and old schoolwork, an occasional key chain or snow globe or piece of art drawn in charcoal or pastel. She looked in the closet, in the very way back. Nothing there, either.

She headed for the master bedroom. Rhea's room. Fritz's room. Turned the knob. Though she'd seen Rhea and Fritz leave, she was still afraid they'd be here, waiting. Punching walls and guzzling red wine while their children wallowed in hot rooms.

In the center was a king-sized bed. Either side was sunken from years of weight. She could make out their individual shapes, the duvet covering the mattress. Rhea on the right, Fritz on the left, two full feet of space between them. Their furniture was spare.

She walked inside. The air was stagnant and human. It smelled like sweat.

Her bare feet crossed the blue Persian rug. It felt frightening in here. In this whole house. And it always looked so nice on the outside. She opened Rhea's nightstand. Nothing but old books. No small letters written by children, swearing eternal love. No jewelry or antihistamines. Not even a vibrator. She opened Fritz's nightstand. Just a rosary in its case that smelled like cheap perfume. At the foot of the nightstand, slippers pointing straight out.

She opened their dresser drawers. Nothing unusual. Nothing, even, of interest.

She started for their shared bathroom and as she walked, the bedroom door opened wider. Someone turned on the light.

FROM *INTERVIEWS FROM THE EDGE: A MAPLE STREET STORY,* BY MAGGIE FITZSIMMONS, SOMA INSTITUTE PRESS, © 2036

"I remember hearing about a girl down a sink-hole, but it was just a blip [on my radar]. I didn't know they were talking about my sister . . . I get all this flack for not coming home, but my mom didn't even tell me Shelly'd gone missing until a few days after the memorial service. She didn't want me home. I was in the summer program. She wanted me to ace my courses so I could graduate early like she'd done. That was my job. Nothing else mattered . . . My mom was a decent person. She never hit. It was always hugs . . . She raised us alone. My dad wasn't around. She was always a little more intense when it came to Shelly and you could probably make the argument that she invented problems with her so she could fix them, though I never saw it that way at the time. It just seemed like she cared. I guess things changed after I left. Even now, it's hard to hear this stuff about her. To me, all it proves is how sick she was, and how hard she tried to protect us from ever seeing it." — Gretchen Schroeder

Nassau Community College

Saturday, July 31

The English Department. Summer school midterm grades were due, plus there was some kind of faculty meeting about the new staff starting in the fall. Through everything, Rhea had kept working. It kept her sane. Work was the only place where the murk didn't unfurl.

But even that was changing, because she didn't remember what had happened over the last hour she'd been sitting here, thinking about a girl on a bathroom floor, and the final, confusing scenes of *The Black Hole* (Did the bright center of that singularity lead to time travel? Heaven? Hell?), and how much she wished Gertie and her whole family dead.

A knock at her door. The chair of her department arrived, looking chagrined. Which was strange. Usually, he looked like Sneezy or Dopey.

"Hi, Allen!" she said. Allen was forty-two and a graduate of some crappy southern school that everyone was always calling the Harvard of the South.

"May I speak with you?" Allen asked.

She winced as she moved her legs out of the way. Her knee was really swollen. She'd been picking at it, moving the cap around, and now the scarring inside had torn. She gestured at the extra chair's emptiness. "My desk is your oyster."

He nodded, flustered and breathing too fast. "Funny. Listen. I've got a problem." He opened a file folder over her desk and pulled out something that looked familiar. She blushed before she even saw it, remembering somehow, even though she no longer remembered the act itself.

"This is Miguel Santos's paper. He came to me yesterday . . ."

"He malingered, then. He missed class. He told me he was sick," Rhea said.

"Did you nickname him Speedy Gonzales?"

Rhea's face went red. Last week, she'd done this. He'd laughed. So had the whole class. "What kind of jerk do I look like?"

"Okay. That's a no. I'm glad. And this red. All this red." He lifted the paper. Panted harder. "What is this?"

"I got carried away, Allen. I'm sorry. I'll go talk to him." In the moment she said it, she meant it. She really did.

361

"I think it's better you step out. I can have someone cover your classes until the fall. You're back too soon." He said this in a rush, and she understood that these were the exact words he'd planned to say upon entering. He was set in them, the way people tend to get set and stuck in the positions they take.

Rhea pursed her lips. Chewed on the flesh of them, then spoke. "I need this job. I have to put on pants and brush my hair like a person to come here. I'm the best teacher you have! Don't take this away from me!"

"It's not my choice."

Rhea's eyes watered. "One kid. I messed up with one kid."

"No."

"Who else?"

Allen fanned out two more papers behind the first, both more red with corrections than white. It was as if she'd spilled wine on them. The names were Debra Lucano and Tom Mijares, which meant nothing to her. "If they have a problem, they should come to me," she said. "They shouldn't be rewarded for going behind my back."

Allen tapped Debra's paper. "This is good. You gave it a D."

"Oh, you're an expert?"

"She's shown all the indicators for the

point system. Subject is thesis, backed up with annotated text evidence."

"And content means nothing? She quoted Bertrand Russell! Who does that? We're America. We have Noam Chomsky. It's my class, Allen! Why can't you back me up? I work so hard here. But the first kid to go crying and making up stories, you take their side?"

Allen squeezed the bridge of his nose. Looked honestly saddened. "I've never understood you."

"We have coffee every semester. You've had plenty of time for million-dollar questions. Yes, my dad died of cirrhosis and I never knew until after the funeral that he drank. It was a secret. In his orange juice. In his milk. In his Coke can. In his coffee thermos that never left his side. Nobody knew. He never even kept beer in the fridge. No liquor cabinet. He was so sly. He raised me. We spent all our time together. I know every piece of science fiction in the canon by heart, especially *The Black Hole*. I have something called an attachment disorder. Read a book once in a while and you'd have figured that out."

Rhea stopped talking. The room seemed to ripple, like barbeque heat rushing through summer wind. Had she just spoken such terrible things out loud? Her mouth felt as if it had done so. But she couldn't have! There was no way. She braced herself, blinked the ripple away, and looked to Allen for a reaction.

His expression showed surprise. An insight into Rhea he hadn't expected. It reminded her of Aileen Bloom's smugness, all those years ago. And of Gertie, that day she'd tried to confess. And of Shelly, always watching the things no one else saw. Aside from her dad, Shelly was the only person she'd ever watched *The Black Hole* with. The only person to whom she'd ever explained, tears in her eyes, why the movie was so important.

Allen blushed because he was one of those polite, southern guys who were especially deferential to women. A pussy, in other words. "I'm so sorry you're going through all this. I had no idea."

"Oh, please. You think you got out unscathed? Look at you. Never played a sport in your life, which can't have made your Big Southern Daddy happy. Oldest brother and Mommy's hero, right? She probably filled out your college applications. Would have followed you around for the rest of your life if you hadn't married MaryJane. Except MaryJane's a lot of work. Gotta rub her feet

every time she gets her period. One kid between you and it's too much for her."

Allen's eyes watered as if she'd struck him.
"That's out of line."

His voice expressed true pain. She could
hear it, and it brought her back to a saner
place. "Oh, God, Allen —" she started. "I'm
sorry. I didn't mean it."

"You don't belong here," he interrupted.
"You hate it. You act like you're smarter
than the rest of us. You probably are. It's not
a fit."

"I'm upset. You have to know that. Please
don't fire me. There's no place else."

"This conversation is at a close."

Rhea started crying for real. Genuine
tears, not fake ones to rile up the neighbors.
She wiped her eyes and her hands came
back small, like Shelly's hands. With wide
nail beds, like Shelly's nails, and the reminder made her so sad she could have cut
them right off.

"Don't do this," Rhea said. "I need this
place."

"Rhea . . . I feel for you. My heart goes
out to you. You and your family have been
in all of our thoughts and prayers. But even
outside these circumstances, you're teaching
semiotics to remedial teenagers when they
haven't nailed down *subject is thesis*."

"I'll do better. I'll be better," she said, and now she pressed her hands together, begging him. "This is the only thing I have left. I can't stay on Maple Street. It's a tomb. She haunts me. She's everywhere."

"You need to leave," he said.

Allen remained and she understood that he meant *leave right now.* She packed up her tiny cubicle-sized office. Eyes red, she started out. By rights, she ought to be this man's boss. The whole school ought to be bowing. Begging her for nuggets of brilliant wisdom. She turned back. Limped to the desk on that useless, betraying knee. She spit. It landed on the top red paper. Speedy's.

"Rhea!" Allen cried out, prissy and shocked.

The spit spread and turned red. Such a crazy thing to do. Obscene and uncivilized. She meant to say: *Sorry. Forgive me. We'll talk in the fall and I'll be ready, Allen.* But that wasn't what came out. "Look what you made me do," she said.

The rest was a blank. She skidded out of the parking lot, flooring it, to the only place left. To Maple Street.

118 Maple Street

Saturday, July 31

Amidst the chaos of 118 Maple Street was the oasis of Rhea and Fritz's strangely perfect bedroom that smelled of cheap perfume. Everything in order. Not a coffee ring on a nightstand; not a bra hanging from a doorknob. It felt like looking into the clean and wealthy adult life she was supposed to be living. Or the imagined Martha Stewart pretense of what adult life looked like.

No sign of Shelly's evidence.

The door creaked open. An overhead light turned on. Gertie had no place to hide. She was caught.

"Ella?" she asked. The girl walked slowly into the room. She had to be nine years old by now. Not so little. That wonder age, where stuffed animals and sexy hip-hop strutting coexist. Where Santa is real but the tooth fairy isn't. She looked nothing like her big sister. She was round and broad-chested. Small brown eyes and mousy brown hair.

She wore a pretty green dress with cut-out shoulders that cinched at the waist.

"Could you help me?" Ella asked.

Gertie held her belly. "How?"

Ella walked out. Gertie waited in the bright light, then followed. She stayed on tiptoe as they passed naked FJ's room, then crept back down the stairs. Gertie in bare feet, the child in cute water sandals. Gertie followed her into the open kitchen, and then to the tiny room off that kitchen. It had a door, and was not much bigger than a closet.

Ella waited outside. Gertie looked in. It was a wreck. Shredded papers were stacked by inches on the floor. The walls were painted with red Sharpie. *Fuck You!* someone had carved (With a letter opener? A knife?) into the small wooden desk. There were no windows here.

Rhea's office.

"What are we doing?" Gertie asked.

Ella just stood there. She had a plain face, phlegmatic. And Gertie understood that this expression concealed a very real rage. This house was like that. It concealed. And then in corners, things burst out.

"Are you going to tell your mother you saw me?"

Ella picked a key from her dress pocket

and held it out. "There's a box in the bottom drawer. It's Shelly's. I want you to show me what's inside. I'm the only one with the key. I took it to make Shelly mad. I used to take things from her."

Gertie walked over. Her belly was too big to sit at the desk to check, so she pushed the chair aside. Opened the bottom drawer. A lockbox. On it was written: *Pain Box.*

Gertie felt a rush of relief.

She pulled it out, noticed the papers underneath. Printed-up newspaper articles. The one on top read, "In Aftermath of Hungarian Pastry Shop Accident, Little Jessica Suffers Aneurysm." The picture was of a girl who looked just like Shelly. Long, black hair. Fair skin and eyes. High cheekbones. About the same age, too. But the paper was dated 2005.

Gertie pointed. "Do you know who this is?"

Ella shook her head. "Shelly?"

Gertie shut the drawer. "Looks like her, doesn't it?"

Ella placed the key on the desk. "Will you show me what's inside?"

"You're sure?" Gertie asked.

The girl's eyes watered. "Please show me."

Gertie opened. It took a while because it was bent at the top, the lock inside it twisted.

She had to jiggle it to unclench the spring. It popped open. It was empty except for a set of blue silk hair ribbons and a phone.

"What is it?" Ella asked.

"I don't know," Gertie answered. "We have to charge it to find out. Do you think I can take it home with me?"

"Shelly's my sister. Did you know that? Lots of people don't know because we don't look the same."

"Yeah, honey. I know."

"Will you show me what's in it if I let you have it?"

"I will, sweetheart."

"Promise?"

"Yes." Gertie closed the box, put the phone in her pocket. Then she bent down to eye level. "Are you okay, honey? Why aren't you at camp?"

"I need to be close for when she climbs out. I watched all the *Buffys*. Even season six. So we can play like she used to want. I'll be Dawn and she can be Buffy. Because I'm her sister. Her real sister, not like Julia. Julia's not her real sister."

"That sounds so nice, honey. Was there anything else Shelly was keeping? Secrets?"

"There was only that. Know why she called it her Pain Box?" Ella asked. "Because she was always hurting. I hurt her by telling on her. I won't tell on her anymore. When she climbs out."

"No. You'll be a wonderful sister. Are you going to tell that I was here?"

Ella shook her head. So calm. So odd. Like a miniature adult. "Shelly wouldn't like it. Did you know she wanted to live with you?"

Gertie squeezed the lockbox to her chest, her voice rough. "That would have been nice," she said, as a car rushed past the kitchen window. Rhea's car.

Hempstead Turnpike

Saturday, July 31

Rhea's vision turned spotty. Her heart pounded so hard that she could feel her pulse in her eyes. Everything flashed, just like the ending of the movie *The Black Hole*. She was going to faint. She pulled to the side of the road.

She'd done something. A bad thing.

She'd spit. So ugly. So base. But something else. She'd talked about her dad. Allen had no business knowing anything about her saint of a dad! She'd said that because of her dad, she had something wrong with her. That she was damaged. She wasn't damaged! She was the perfect outcome of a perfect family!

Cars passed around her, slow, even though she'd left them plenty of room.

Why was her heart beating so hard?

Attachment disorder? It was true that she'd never been close to other people. Not after her dad, and even then, that closeness had been a kind of lie (the orange juice, the milk, the swerving car, *The Black Hole*). In all the years she'd been raised by him, lived in his house, she'd never once had a friend over, or laughed like the people on TV. She'd only laughed later, with Gertie. She'd always assumed the media lied. That no one was really close to anyone. And they weren't, were they?

This myth of love was manufactured. People pretend to have things in common because they're afraid of being alone. She wasn't like that. She'd always been honest. Brave. It's lonely that way, but at least she'd been true to herself.

Another car passed. Another too-wide berth with quick, polite honking. So passive-aggressive. It occurred to her that normal people don't kick down bathroom doors. They don't spit in rage. They don't hit their children with brushes. They don't frame their best friends' husbands for rape.

. . . But maybe they did.

Her heart wouldn't slow down. The weight of this was unbearable. An impossibly heavy murk, accumulated for so many years that everything behind her, every memory, was contaminated. It unfurled now, sucking her into its infinitely dense mouth, reaching into her future and dissolving her there, too. Forever unclean.

Rhea began to pant. Her heart convulsed in her chest. She'd done so many bad things. Knowing this was a physical pain. Car lights flashed all around her, disorienting. The blind spots in her vision got bigger.

Cars passed and she hated them for noticing. Hated the drivers for peering out, to see if something was wrong.

Puzzle pieces. She thought about her dad, weaving in the road. The candy apple–sweet smell of his breath and the way he always went down to his workroom at night. Went away. Just like Fritz. She thought she'd liked being alone, but maybe that was only because she didn't know how to accept company.

She thought about Aileen, that piece of shit.

She thought about kicking down a bathroom door. The too-young face on the other side.

She thought about Shelly, goading her. Too sensitive and too needy.

She thought about cruel Gertie, who'd only pretended to care.

She thought about all the world, filled with stupid people.

She honked her horn at the next asshole who passed. Long and hard. All the blind spots came together. They smeared into a too-dense point, and became nothing. Oblivion. Erasure. The murk overtook her.

Rhea went blank. This was not new. This happened all the time.

There was nothing wrong with her. It was them. They'd forced her hand with their stupidity. Their ignorance and their incompetence. No thinking person quotes Bertrand Russell or grades on a point system. They don't allow sinkholes to form in their neighborhoods, school lunches to be composed of grade B meat. The moronic masses were steering this country into ruin. She was the only person who could see through the lies, the social convention, the politeness. She was the only person who could will it all away, into a new and better direction.

She pulled back onto the road.

118 Maple Street

Saturday, July 31

Rhea sped into the driveway. Gertie watched her stride from her car to the back door in a frenzy.

"We're gonna die!" Ella hissed in blind panic.

Gertie didn't have time to replace the lockbox. Still holding it, barefoot, she rushed out of Rhea's office just as Rhea yanked open the back door. It rammed the opposite wall, shivering.

"What are you doing in my office?" she shouted.

Heavy-bellied, Gertie stood as still as she knew how in the archway between the dining room and hall. Clearly visible, if Rhea looked.

"You know you're not allowed in there!"

"I'm sorry. I'm sorry," Ella's soft voice answered. "I thought I heard Hammy."

"Who?"

"Hammy. He got out?"

"I don't want a hamster in my office!"

Gertie was on tiptoe. In the hall. So slow. She made it to the front door in plain sight.

"I'm sorry," Ella said.

"Sorry doesn't cover it. Now come here!"

" 'Kay."

Gertie opened the front door. Stayed in the threshold. Down the long hall, Rhea was in the kitchen, her back to Gertie. Ella was on the other side, facing them both.

Rhea raised her hand high.

She slapped herself: *wholp!*

Gertie gasped.

Rhea didn't hear, because Ella yelped at the same time.

Gertie took a step back inside the hall. Her adrenaline rushed so fast that even Guppy had noticed and was swimming.

Rhea took Ella's hands in hers. "Calm down," she said. "You're not the one who's hurt."

Ella nodded.

"I'm not going to hurt you," Rhea said. "I'm just sad about what the Wildes did to Shelly. I bet you're sad, too. I bet you could just kill them."

"Yes."

Rhea pulled the girl in and squeezed until she stopped fighting. Until she went along with the hug. Until, finally, she returned it, and stroked Rhea's back with her tense little fingers. "Don't be sad, Momma."

They rested like that. A wisteria and oak, intertwined. The one strangling the other, in order to survive. Ella watched Gertie all the while. But she wasn't like Shelly. She didn't plead for help.

Gertie backed out of the house. Shut the door softly. Maybe the cop stationed there saw her. Maybe he didn't. Holding the lockbox, she jogged with bouncing belly down the walk, past the naked topiary, to her house. Her run-down house, which didn't smell like cheap perfume.

118 Maple Street

Saturday, July 31

Back in the Schroeder house, Rhea poured herself a nooner of wine. Glugged, hoping to find some relief for this excruciating pain in her knee. Red and rage-eyed, she searched with her daughter for Hammy, who really was missing. They checked all the usual places, and when that didn't work they checked the basement, where bitumen had gathered and someone had left footprints all over the tile. They found Hammy there, trapped in oil that had seeped up.

Ella cried.

Rhea intuited that Ella could not tolerate one more indignity. She needed this animal. So she waded through the muck. She lifted Hammy and rinsed him gently with detergent. Got into the car and drove with Ella and Hammy to the East Williston Veterinary Clinic, where he was declared healthy. Or she? Who knew. Who cared. It was a rodent.

"You see?" she asked. "We found him and he's fine."

Ella began to cry uncontrollably at that, but she was in the back seat, and Rhea up front. There was too much traffic to pull over.

When they got home from the veterinarian's office, Rhea limped back down to the basement. Something had bothered her that she couldn't place. A scratch carved into her memory; something not quite right.

She returned to the footprints. They were bigger than hers, but narrow. Feminine. For the briefest of moments, she turned flush, thinking it was Shelly, come home at last.

But then, beside the stairs, tucked neatly in a shadow, were Gertie Wilde's cute and practical Payless walkers.

116 Maple Street

Saturday, July 31

Shelly's phone. It had no signal. Wasn't on network. Gertie charged it. Went through all the applications. Only one of them had files — the photo app. She flicked through the dozens of images she found there. Some showed shoulders. Others a side, or a stomach, or a bottom. But most showed a back. All were fresh, taken soon after whatever blow had been issued. Viewing the pictures felt pornographic, as if the simple act of seeing made her guilty, too.

Gertie remembered Rhea's words from that night months ago: *Shelly can't keep her hair neat. It goads me. I'd like to talk about it with you, because I know you like Shelly. I know you like me. I know you won't judge.*

It came to her that the oval-clustered bruises in these photos were from a brush.

In the quiet of that den, where she'd pinned so many hopes for a better life, Gertie curled up on herself and cried.

She might have gone to the police. But to get this evidence, Gertie had broken the law. The bruises, all inside Shelly's bathing suit line, did not have an obvious author. None were more than a year old. In other words, none preexisted the Wildes.

What if she handed this to Bianchi, and it only made Arlo look guiltier?

She returned the phone to the Pain Box. Locked it, so the kids didn't stumble across those awful photos. Put it beside her makeshift bed in the den.

Lunch and then dinner came. She tried to pretend to the children that everything was normal. Explained that they had no reason to worry. They knew something was wrong, or else they were absorbed in their own emotions. They didn't ask questions.

That night, Bianchi stopped by to tell Gertie that CPS was keeping Arlo for another night. She lingered in the doorway, thinking she should hand over the evidence. But for all she knew, Rhea had planted the brush that had made those bruises in the glove compartment of the Passat. Or Arlo's nightstand. Anyplace at all.

"Is something wrong?" he asked.

She looked at him for a while.

"Point taken. Have a good night."

She couldn't climb the stairs, so the

children put themselves to bed. They called good night from far away, their voices uncertain.

On the couch, in the dark, without the protection of her husband, Gertie's mind roamed: *Shelly can't keep her hair neat. It goads me. I'd like to talk about it with you, because I know you like Shelly. I know you like me. I know you won't judge.*

But Rhea hadn't just vented about Shelly that night. Boozy, she'd talked about how trapped she'd felt, and her unhappiness. These were all the things that Gertie also felt, but had always been too scared to say out loud. Sometimes having a family and people who depend on you is too much. But you can't leave them. They need you. So you resent them just a little.

She'd been grateful to Rhea, for her honesty. Relieved by it, that someone as special and smart as Rhea'd had these same feelings. It's lonely, being a grown-up. It feels like walking through life in a mask.

Looking back, she hadn't shown that gratitude. Making close friends is scary. Gertie was better at fake smiles and keeping people at a distance. She didn't like them to know that at home, her family had a foul mouth. That she was messy, had never learned anything domestic until Arlo. She didn't read

383

novels like the rest of the people on this block; just self-help. She was easy to sneak up on. The kids knew this and made lots of noise when they walked into a room to keep from startling her. She could have confessed all this to Rhea, but she'd confessed so much already. When you let people know things about you, sometimes they use it against you, to hurt you. That's what Cheerie had always done. Rhea hadn't been the only one to avoid their friendship after that; Gertie had avoided it, too. Not because she didn't like her. Because it had all felt too momentous.

In hindsight, Rhea had been asking for help.

If Gertie had asked questions, been as open as Rhea had been, things might have turned out different. It didn't change her opinion: Rhea was horrible. A hunter. Just this evening, she'd slapped herself in front of her own child.

But it did give clarity to something that before had been opaque.

Late that night, Larry couldn't sleep. He cried out. Julia scampered to his room to soothe him. Gertie heard, too. She'd had enough of sitting around, of calling up. Gertie went to him. She climbed into the bed with both of them and held them. They snuggled. It was good and necessary. But after a time, they were all too hot, the bed too small.

Gertie was snoring and no one wanted to disturb her. So Julia and Larry left that room, playing musical beds. Everyone slept in someplace new.

The night turned to early morning. Rhea didn't send her son to do this job. She used the spare key. The one Gertie had given her months ago. She wore bitumen over her clothing. Painted her face with it so that she appeared even to herself as something obliterated. Her gait was crooked, her knee undone.

She crept through Gertie's dark living room. Beheld the slumbering figure huddled beneath pillows and blankets on the couch. So small, all curled up. Almost childlike. She knelt on her good knee, leaving the other straight and sideways. Matched her breath to blanket-covered Gertie's; deep and slow.

Almost a quarter of a century ago, she'd chased Aileen Bloom into a bathroom. She'd kicked open a door with her knee. *Whock!* It had hit a girl in the head. The girl had slumped, her forehead streaming blood while Rhea had lain beside her, wanting to cry out in pain but afraid to attract attention. The face had been wrong. It hadn't belonged to Aileen Bloom.

"It was an accident," Rhea had explained once people filled the women's restroom at the Hungarian Pastry Shop. "I slipped." Except for Aileen Bloom, they'd all believed. Because what kind of maniac would knock a thirteen-year-old child unconscious?

The slumberer in the Wilde house woke. Struggled to sit up; pinned by all those blankets and pillows. The grunting reminded Rhea of an old slapstick movie. Funny and unreal.

The blanket came down. Everything was smeared, her vision just spots. Rhea saw a reflection in this opposite person's eyes, but it didn't belong to her. Shining oil and snarling lips, it belonged to the angry murk.

She'd learned from the movie *The Black Hole* that it's not magical thinking. It's not a cancer born of shame. It really is possible to travel through time, and correct your past. Jettison the murk, and come out cleanly on the other side.

I didn't do it, she thought. *Someone else.*

Like making a wish, she took the lockbox that bitch had stolen. Slammed it against the side of Larry Wilde's head.

THE MONSTERS ARRIVE ON MAPLE STREET

August 1–2

Map of Maple Street as of August 1, 2027
*116 Wilde Family
*118 Schroeder Family

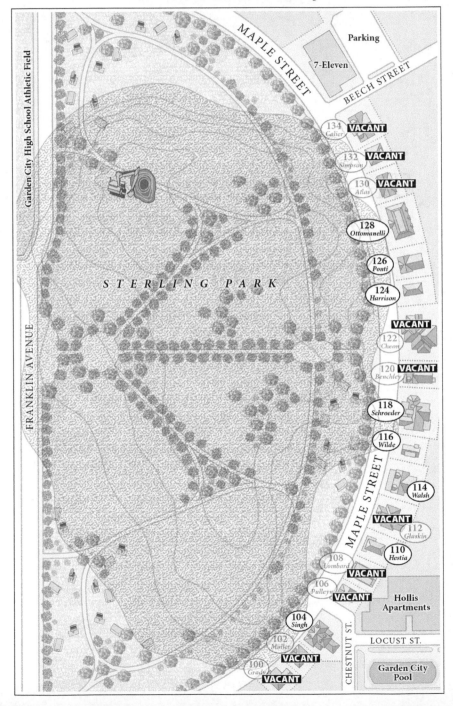

Index Of Maple Street's Permanent Residents As Of August 1, 2027

100 VACANT

102 VACANT

104 The Singhs-Kaurs — Sai (47), Nikita (36), Pranav (16), Michelle (14), Sam (13), Sarah (9), John (7)

106 VACANT

108 VACANT

110 The Hestias — Rich (51), Cat (48), Helen (17), Lainee (14)

112 VACANT

114 The Walshes — Sally (49), Margie (46), Charlie (13)

116 The Wildes — Arlo (39), Gertie (31), Julia (12), Larry (8)

118 The Schroeders — Fritz (62), Rhea (53), FJ (19), Ella (9)

120 VACANT

122 VACANT

124 The Harrisons — Timothy (46), Jane (45), Adam (16), Dave (14)

126 The Pontis — Steven (52), Jill (48), Marco (20), Richard (16)

128 The Ottomanellis — Dominick (44), Linda (44), Mark (12), Michael (12)

130 VACANT
132 VACANT
134 VACANT

TOTAL: 34 PEOPLE

FROM *INTERVIEWS FROM THE EDGE: A MAPLE STREET STORY,* BY MAGGIE FITZSIMMONS, SOMA INSTITUTE PRESS, © 2036

"Charlie was never the same. None of those kids was ever the same. They stopped trusting us. They stopped being kids. Margie and I got divorced. I was mad at her for making the whole Arlo thing about her own childhood. I felt too bad to challenge her so I went along even though I knew it was wrong.

"It was awful, the way they beat him senseless in the middle of the street. I've heard them all say in the years since that he had it coming. He didn't. Everything he said about us was right. It haunts me. Sometimes I feel like that's what being an adult is all about. Being haunted."
— Sally Walsh, former resident of Maple Street

Discovered among Ms. Schroeder's belongings was a scrapbook she'd apparently kept on Jessica Sherman, the thirteen-year-old girl she'd knocked unconscious at a café in Seattle. Little Jessica woke from the incident within minutes, but family members later connected that kick to the brain aneurysm from which she suffered six months later.

According to her family, Jessica's aneurysm rendered her permanently disabled. In Facebook posts, her mother, Skylar, announced that she would be the family's forever child, needing extra care and staying close to home. She was both a blessing and a cross to bear. Her mother reported that while she'd formerly been a calm child, she now suffered wild mood swings and rages.

Rhea Schroeder's scrapbook ended after two years, when Jessica turned fifteen years old. There's no evidence that she continued to monitor the child's progress. Jessica, now forty years old, lives in a group home in Seattle.

The Sherman family sued the University of

Washington, Rhea, and the Hungarian Pastry Shop, but because Jessica never went to a doctor after her initial injury, experts couldn't prove a causal link between the violent incident in the café and her subsequent disability.

As seen in these photos, the likeness between Jessica and Shelly Schroeder is uncanny. They could have been twins. It's hard not to wonder if Rhea was thinking of little Jessica . . .

116 Maple Street

Sunday, August 1

"It's been a while. I haven't seen you take the train. How are you?" the guy at 7-Eleven asked. His name tag read OSCAR.

"It's a steaming garbage kind of day," Arlo answered.

Oscar took an especially long time to make change, counting and recounting the dollars and then the cents, and Arlo understood that he had seen the news. Knew about the accusation. "Happens."

The ride service that had picked him up from CPS hadn't been able to stop right on the crescent. The road was still closed. So he'd had it drop him here, where he'd picked up a six-pack of ginger ale for Gertie, an avocado for Larry, a fresh pack of Parliaments for himself, and more milk and cereal — Frosted Flakes — for Julia.

"Huh?" Arlo asked.

"Sometimes you have bad days."

"Yeah. You have a good one for both of us."

"I can try."

Carrying his bag, he walked across the park. It was afternoon on a Sunday. The park was empty. No crickets or cicadas. No chirping birds. Just orange cones, a slab covering the hole, and a lot of bitumen. It mucked his shoes and he walked fast, never pressing down too hard, to keep the suction from stealing them.

The accusations at CPS hadn't made sense. Three out of the four kids wouldn't talk to the cops; only their parents had done that. The one who would go on record claimed only that Arlo had repeatedly put his hand on the kid's knee, which the CPS people had decided was "grooming." None of these kids' names was given to Arlo and there was not enough evidence for an arrest or any kind of action at all.

While stuck there, Arlo had called Fred again at his office — water from a dry well. Fred called back from the Mount Sinai Hospital in Manhattan. Turned out Bethany's fancy new immunotherapy cancer drug wasn't going to work. They were out of options. "What's the trouble?" Fred had asked.

"Nothing. Just wanted to let you know we're thinking about you," he'd said. "We want to visit as soon as possible."

Fred's voice had caught. He'd taken a

while and Arlo had waited, hand pressed on MUTE so the guy didn't hear the CPS workers calling to each other, loud and oblivious. "When she got sick. It's been years. You have no idea how many people have scattered. At this point, I'm the only one."

Arlo let go of MUTE. "I'm here. Gert's here."

"That means more than I can say," Fred said.

For the second night in a row, the CPS people asked if he could stay overnight in the GCPD jail as a courtesy. He should have said, *No, thanks.* But they'd made it clear that if he tried to leave, they'd have taken Gertie in for questioning.

So he'd agreed.

This morning, Bianchi showed up for the second time, his suit rumpled like he'd been up all night. He'd reassured Arlo that he'd sent a cop car over twice and had visited Gertie in person as well. "Have you considered moving away from that block?" he'd asked Arlo.

"We have to get our ducks in a row. It's . . . not easy. Nothing's easy."

Bianchi reached through the bars and patted him on the shoulder, and for the first time, Arlo realized the guy was on his side. "These people are the kind you leave behind. Take the high road."

A few hours later, CPS asked him all the same questions. After answering them, Arlo finally stood. "We're not done, sir."

"Are you charging me?"

Nobody answered. Arlo didn't ask permission; just walked out.

He took the Uber to 7-Eleven. Carrying his groceries, he now saw Linda Ottomanelli on her stoop. Saw Margie and her wife, Sally, hosing their front walk of tar sand. The Ponti men were on their stoop, too. As he got closer, he noticed that they were looking at him. All eyes.

He had a bad feeling. Worse than usual. First the Pontis went inside, which he wouldn't have expected. Those mooks should have been itching for a fight. Then the Walshes. Last, Linda and Rhea. They moved quickly, practically running.

He noticed that the door to 116 Maple Street, his house, was open.

Garden City Police Department

Sunday, August 1

"I didn't do it," Rhea Schroeder said. "Some-one else." She was sitting in Detective Bian-chi's office. Fritz Sr. was beside her. He'd in-sisted on coming along, which had surprised her.

"Who?" Bianchi asked.

Rhea shook her head in slow shock. She was so overtired that she was having a hard time seeing straight. Everything was bright spots of emptiness. And the weight of it. She felt heavy as an astronaut on Jupiter. "Honestly. It wouldn't be beyond me to hurt Gertie. I can't stand her. But Larry? I'd never do something like that. It's not in me."

Bianchi nodded. "I'm told there was a lockbox that's now missing. It was origi-nally taken from your home, by Mrs. Wilde. Someone broke into the Wilde house and took it back last night. Do you know any-thing about that?"

Rhea blew a deep breath out. "A lockbox?"

she asked. "What do you mean, taken from my house? Was Gertie in my house?"

Bianchi waited.

"I have no idea what you're talking about," she said. "Can you explain it to me?"

"Did you hear anything last night? See anything?"

She shook her head. Then whispered. She meant this as she said it. She really did. Because she had a dim memory of visiting the Wilde house that night, but only to get back what had been stolen. To teach Gertie a lesson. She would never have hurt a child. Someone else, possibly, but not her. "Could Gertie have done it?"

"Why would she do something like that?"

"Why would anyone? She's not right in the head. I was getting aspirin in her bathroom once. She takes Klonopin. That's not a light medication. She's had a history. A really bad one." Rhea's eyes began to water, because this was just so awful. All of it. So unthinkable. "She's been talking in baby talk. I heard her. This Arlo pedophilia thing put her over the edge."

Bianchi looked at her for a long while. "When did you hear her talking in baby talk? Was it the night of the brick? I thought you were sleeping that night. You didn't hear anything."

Rhea turned red. "Another time. She did it a lot."

There was more silence. Bianchi kept looking at her.

But something new. Fritz was looking at her, too.

"I'd like to go home now," she said, though there wasn't a rush. Even if he searched her house, he'd find nothing. She'd hidden the hair-gristled Pain Box in a safe place. The Benchleys' mailbox. Not even her property. "Can I go home?"

"Yeah."

116 Maple Street

Sunday, August 1

Julia was the one to find him. Everybody slept in late, or as late as you can sleep in summertime heat. She went downstairs. The figure on the couch hadn't looked right. The house still quiet, she'd wondered if she was having a nightmare. Or if the world had cracked open and changed, its rules all different. The blanket had been caked to Larry's cheek by dark blood.

She'd stood, afraid to go closer. Afraid to tell her mom, too. Afraid the person who'd done it was still in the house. She should have gone to him. Touched him. But she'd been so scared. She'd left. Walked in bare feet and grimy old sleep clothes down the crescent. She could have knocked on doors. But whose? Which one of them wasn't an enemy? She'd gone through Sterling Park, past the hole.

The tiny diver hadn't been able to get through. Her hips had been too wide. The

401

hole was covered now, about to be filled. Shelly lost inside.

She called 911 using the 7-Eleven clerk's landline. They tried to get her to stay on the line but she hung up. She needed to wake her mom before they arrived. Keep her calm so she didn't wind up in a psychiatric ward again.

Back home. Through the park and back to her house, this time passing Rhea Schroeder, who was standing on her porch. She seemed completely normal. Calm and well dressed. "Hello, Julia," she said.

Julia felt something like terror, only deeper. Something in her bones that screamed. "Hi, Mrs. Schroeder."

She got inside. Her mom was up now. Bent over Larry. Julia backed up, afraid. "Is he?" she whispered. And then she was sliding down the side of the wall, the atmosphere on this strange planet too heavy.

"He's breathing," her mom answered. She was shaking with manic energy as she lifted him, put a pillow beneath his head. Larry wasn't Larry right then. He was a doll that she moved, pale and inanimate. "Everything's going to be okay. I'm the adult and I have this under control," she said, but there wasn't meaning attached to it. Julia understood then, that her mom was quoting some

402

mantra she'd read in one of her child rearing books. She was winging it. She had no idea what she was doing.

"I called for an ambulance," Julia said.

Gertie's eyes were especially bright in the dark. They pierced. "Oh, thank God. You always do what needs to be done," she answered.

The ambulance came. The neighbors watched from inside and from out. Only one person was allowed to ride along. So Julia told her mom to go ahead; she'd figure it out. She'd planned to ask Charlie's moms for a ride, but lost courage when she got to their door. Didn't ring the bell. Because maybe they'd call Child Protective Services. Accuse her mom of abandonment.

She went back inside her house. Threw away the bloody blanket. Showered. Changed. Packed a bag for Larry and her mom. Left a note for her dad in case he came home. It occurred to her that now might be a good time to stop and cry. But she didn't want to do that. It was easier to keep moving. She started the three-mile walk to the hospital on her own.

116 Maple Street

Sunday, August 1

Arlo got Julia's note. He tried to reach the hospital and Gertie by phone, but reception wasn't clear. So he jogged back out onto the crescent. All the house doors in both directions were shut, the people inside. He could feel them watching him. They must have known what had happened. They couldn't all have been ignorant of his son's attack. The ambulance had probably been very loud.

He stuck up his middle finger. Waved it. Then got into the Passat.

Halfway there, he saw a kid by the side of the road. Awkward-looking, her short hair a wild mess, she lugged a canvas bag, straps looped around both shoulders in a makeshift backpack like a runaway. His first thought was of his own childhood. The world's full of loveless urchins. But then he saw that the kid was Julia.

He pulled over. Leaned across and opened

the door. Julia climbed in. He didn't start driving right away. Just sat. He was reluctant to reach out to her. Maybe she'd heard all the bad things people were saying about him. And she looked so grown, all of a sudden. So adult. So they breathed, looking ahead.

"I feel very heavy. Lately, it hurts to walk. I'm afraid to go to the hospital. I'm afraid this moment is the last one where we're still a family," he said, though he knew he shouldn't have. But sometimes you can't hold things in. Because you've done that your whole life, and it builds up so much you think you might die.

"I don't know if I told you this," he said. "But when I met your mom I had nothing. For the life of me, I'll never understand what she saw. She was so nice. The nicest person I ever met. I know it doesn't always seem like it. I make mistakes. But you and Larry and your mom are the most important people, the most important everything to me."

She eased to his side of the car and cried in his arms. He ran his hands down her short, wet hair, her pimple-picked neck and back. She was substantial in his arms. Grown. He'd been chipping by the time he'd been her age. Fighting a nascent addiction. When he'd looked at other kids back then, they'd

405

seemed like a different species. He'd never imagined they had anything in common with him. He saw now that wasn't true. All kids are fighting their own kind of war.

"You'll hear some things about me. Maybe you have already," he said.

"You didn't rape my best friend. I know that," she said.

"No. I didn't."

As he held her, cars passing, his head over hers, he cried, too. She couldn't see his tears, but she was Julia, so surely she felt them.

NYU Winthrop Hospital

Sunday, August 1

Larry had suffered a concussion. This accounted for his lethargy. The Wildes were told they would have to wait for the swelling to go down to know whether the damage was permanent.

Gertie spoke with the police as soon as she'd arrived at the hospital. They returned a second time. In the waiting room, among strangers, she repeated the events of the previous day and left nothing out. They asked Arlo questions. He had a good alibi. After that, they asked if they could speak with the psychiatrist at Creedmoor who'd attended Gertie after the brick. She agreed to this.

When all that was done, they were told that they could see Larry, but no more than two people at a time. The Wilde family heard this. They were in so much trouble already that they didn't care. The hospital was busy. No one noticed. They sneaked Julia in between them.

They gathered in his room. He'd been struck with something sharp and hard. It had cut a flap of his skin open along his forehead and upper brow. He had an intravenous tube to keep fluid moving through his system so his brain stem didn't swell.

Gertie was glad to see that his eyes could focus. When he'd first woken, they'd goggled.

They didn't say much. Just showed him all the green clothing that Julia had packed, and talked about how lucky he was to get an unlimited supply of lime Jell-O. Then they sat on the bed, careful not to disturb him. They breathed in and out in time. As if matching him, trying to be him, and carry his pain. This didn't last. They were too different.

For a long time, Gertie had blamed herself for Larry. Worried that she'd eaten the wrong things while pregnant with him, or been too stressed out. She'd yelled too often and tweaked his nervous system in the wrong direction when he'd been little, or she'd not been affectionate enough and because of that he couldn't connect with others. After the accusation, she'd even worried that Arlo had done something to him.

But now, Julia's homemade Robot Boy in his arms, vigilant and cheerful despite his heavy eyelids, she saw that he was the perfect incarnation of all of them. A misfit, who never stops trying.

They talked quietly in the car on the ride home. Julia was in back, but these things couldn't wait until she was someplace else.

Gertie told Arlo her story about the photos of brush bruises, about the bricks and the state of Rhea's house. She told about leaving her shoes behind. That the evidence she'd worked so hard to get was now gone, though she hadn't been sure it would have proven his innocence anyway.

It might have been Rhea who'd sneaked in during the night. But was Rhea strong enough to cause such damage? It might also have been Fritz or FJ, or anyone else from Maple Street. Why they'd picked Larry to retaliate against was anyone's guess. Perhaps, on the ground floor, he'd just been closest and most convenient.

They kept driving. The closer they got to Maple Street, the less they talked. From her slinked-down position in the car, Julia could only just see blue sky and green trees and an airplane flying too close to the ground, its engine rumbling.

At 116 Maple Street, they packed their belongings. Enough for a couple of days.

They'd decided to go to that Motor Inn in Hempstead. They closed their windows. They passed under the crystal chandelier that Gertie loved so much because it reminded her of the convention center in Atlantic City, all rainbows and light. They took their favorite things from the small bedrooms and the bathrooms with real tile, and they passed the squeaking stairs they'd loved so much because they'd never had stairs before. Never had a house before.

They looted the fridge, grabbing the stuff they could microwave at the extended-stay, plus apples and frozen cherries. They took the gun. They locked the door behind them. Julia took the back seat again. She slunk down again, too, so that all she could see was sky.

Arlo and Gertie packed the trunk. It hurt her back to move but she did it anyway. As they packed these things up, the patrolman left the block. After that, the neighbors began to appear. They didn't come out of their houses. They were too cowardly for that now. They brushed aside curtains and peered through windows, no breeze on that unbearably hot Sunday afternoon.

Arlo glared from one house to the next, trying to catch a single eye. The Walshes, the Harrisons, Pontis, Schroeders, Singhs-Kaurs,

Hestias, and the Ottomanellis. Unabashed, they met his gaze. The people of Maple Street. They'd won. He and his family would never come back to this place they'd dreamed about. This place that was supposed to be their golden ticket. Maple Street had deemed them not good enough. And now they were gloating about it.

You reach a certain point, and there's no going back. It's a place so hot that logic breaks down.

"I could kill them," Gertie said, and that was all he needed.

The safety was on. That was the important thing to keep in mind. He hadn't wanted to hurt anybody; he'd just wanted to scare them. Because he'd finally understood what they wanted. This wasn't about Shelly. It wasn't about rape. It was about his tattoos. It was about Gertie's accent. It was about Julia, stealing those Parliaments, and Larry's Robot Boy. It was about their crappy lawn, and their Slip 'N Slide, and the ludicrous music of a has-been.

He and Gertie had dared try to become one of the All-Americans. They'd had the audacity to move to Garden City, and for that all of Maple Street had wanted to punish them. To tear up their family. To erase them. They'd won that. Arlo was ready to surrender. If that was all they wanted, he might have left quietly. Sold 116 at a loss, taken the family, and never come back.

But now that they had their hooks in, they wanted more than erasure. In order to prove themselves right, to soothe their own guilty consciences, they wanted the Wilde family's total evisceration. They wanted Julia in foster care and Larry dead. Gertie in a mental institution, the baby wrenched from her belly and delivered to strangers. Arlo back in jail and on the needle, because nothing else was left.

That's what they wanted, and they couldn't have it. He couldn't let them win.

At first, the people of Maple Street probably didn't see what he was holding. He didn't carry it like a cop, but like a first-time fisherman loosely gripping slimy bait.

He veered from the Passat and in their direction, walking through oil so thick now that grass and pavement were no longer visible. Faces looked out. He hadn't planned to do anything. Had just wanted them to know that he was carrying. That if they tried to burn down his house tonight, or come after Larry at the hospital, or call the cops on Gertie, bearing false witness that

412

she'd attacked Larry in the night, he'd be ready.

He started with the Walshes. Stood at the edge of their walk. No trespassing with a firearm involved. Sally peered out from her den. He smiled in a friendly way while holding the thing daintily, safety on. "Hey!" he cried. "Thanks for breaking my kid's skull last night. You've been great neighbors."

Kept walking.

Next the Hestias. The parents both took marijuana for their anxiety, which they baked into cookies and offered for dessert at dinner parties, like they thought they were the first people on earth to turn addiction into social convention. They treated their daughters like their best friends, confiding frustrations and work problems, and the frequency with which they had sex. They considered themselves hip. Cutting edge. They listened to Eminem. They didn't tell people what they did for a living, and sometimes lied about it, claiming to be doctors. That was because they worked for the insurance company that managed the greatest number of World Trade Center victims in New York. The company was famous now, for denying dust as causation. Trade Center dust, they'd argued in court, with science backed by people like the Hestias, might be no worse than regular dust. They'd tied the money up for years while the sick had died and continued to die of heart failure, emphysema, and cancer. The world was falling apart. They were making it worse. There was a hole in the middle of the park that kept puking black bile. But the Hestias had this idea that Arlo and his family were the real threats. Fucking Brooklyn accents were the problem.

The drapes in their living room ruffled in the bitumen-stinking breeze. "I saw you fuckers the night of the brick. Nobody else walks that slow."

He walked next to the Singh-Kaurs. They owned the Baskin-Robbins–Dunkin' Donuts chain on Garden City's main drag, plus two more in Rockville Centre and Mineola. Arlo stood just in front of their Honda Pilot, in which Julia and Larry had carpooled to countless Little League games. They had a big TV in there. Watched crappy Netflix teenage rom-coms on it. Shit like *The Kissing Booth 2,* which they mistook for the essence of Americana. He knocked on the car. Just a tap with his knuckles.

Next, the Harrisons, those crazy assholes with the divided house. The only people who'd never hosted dinner parties because it would have been too much of a shit show. "Hypocrites!" he shouted. And then the

Pontis, that house of craven men with giant biceps. "Hypocrites!" And then the Ottomanelli house, where Linda and Dominick didn't have the sense of a bird between them, and their mean-spirited twins ran their roost. "All of you, hypocrites!"

A door opened. The Pontis started toward him. Dominick Ottomanelli came out from his house, too.

"Arlo, come on. Let's go," Gertie called.

Arlo saved the Schroeder house for last. Fritz's car wasn't in the drive, which was too bad. It felt more comfortable to threaten when the man of the house was home. He stood for a five-count, then raised his gun and pointed. Aimed at the front porch.

"Arlo!" Gertie cried.

"Daddy!" Julia screamed.

Something hard slammed against the back of his head. He was on the ground, eating gravel and sand oil. The gun skittered away from him. And then somebody kicked him. A vivid sense memory flashed. His dad. He got up on all fours.

It was Steven, Marco, and Richard Ponti. It was Dominick Ottomanelli and Sai Singh. He tried to stand. Steven was holding a baseball bat.

Another swing. His legs went out from under him. He tried to get up again, because

Julia and Gertie were watching. A scream — deep, masculine, and primal — emanated from Dominick Ottomanelli as he kicked Arlo in the chest with a heavy work boot. The blow lifted him from his knees and back down. He tasted salt. Adrenaline didn't let him feel his broken ribs, one of which now poked his left lung.

Wearily, Arlo noticed as Rhea Schroeder bent down. Lifted something from the ground . . . The gun?

He saw a leg and held on to it. Pulled himself up by it. Gertie and Julia had pushed through the men. They were at his side. There was shouting but it wasn't coming from them. It came from the rest of Maple Street. Some came out to their porches. Others hollered through their windows. The sound came from Nikita, Pranav, and Michelle Kaur and Sam Singh. It came from Rich, Cat, Helen, and Lainee Hestia. It came from Sally and Margie Walsh. It came from Rhea, FJ, and Ella Schroeder. It came from Tim, Jane, and Adam Harrison. It came from Jill Ponti. It came from Linda Ottomanelli and her weird twins. They were screaming and smiling and pumping fists. Jesus God, they were cheering.

Gertie shoved Steven Ponti and his bloody bat. He had the good sense not to fight back.

Then she was on the ground next to Arlo, her hands on his ribs as if trying to hold the falling-apart pieces of him together. Julia was next to her.

Arlo realized that it was Dominick's leg he was climbing. The man's expression was animalistic and ugly. A sweaty-sex face on the verge of completion. Still that cheering. Dominick stomped him down, then cranked his foot. The treads dripped bitumen. Arlo had the time to roll. But would that cause collateral damage to Gertie and Julia, beside him? Would his unborn daughter accidentally take the brunt?

He didn't swerve. Cheering, cheering, like Romans at the Colosseum, the people of Maple Street rejoiced as Arlo Wilde received his punishment. A direct hit: work boot to face.

From *Interviews from the Edge: A Maple Street Story,*
by Maggie Fitzsimmons,
Soma Institute Press, © 2036

"Yes. I recall that. I recall the cheering."
— Sally Walsh

"I don't remember. You tell me witnesses saw me laughing and clapping. But I don't remember that." — Rich Hestia

"There's times in your life that you regret. I watched what was happening and I knew I should go out there and try to stop it. It wasn't like you think. My moms weren't happy when it happened. Almost nobody looked happy. I don't know why they cheered, but they weren't happy."
— Charlie Walsh

"He was a pervert with a gun. We took him out. You do what you have to do." — Steven Ponti

"We had a problem on the block and the cops wouldn't solve it. So we solved our own problem." — Dominick Ottomanelli

"Don't be ridiculous. Nobody cheered." — Nikita Kaur

Hempstead Motor Inn

Monday, August 2

They didn't get back to the motel until late. Gertie felt tired inside. In her bones and her blood. She paid for the room but didn't take the bags from the car. Just walked with Julia to the room and turned all the locks. At times, she cried. She was too tired to try to hide it.

They sat in their beds of the first hotel room Julia had ever stayed in. Gertie noticed that she didn't touch anything unless she had to. Probably afraid she'd break the mini fridge or the water glasses and they'd have to pay for them.

"He's alive. That's what's important," Gertie said. "We all are."

Julia looked straight ahead. They hadn't brushed their teeth and wouldn't. They hadn't changed into pajamas, and wouldn't do that, either. These were the kinds of things Arlo kept up. The maintenance things.

There'd been more police at the hospital. She'd told them what had happened. The

420

men — the Pontis and Dominick Otto-manelli and Sai Singh — had already been arraigned and released on bail. They'd doubled down on their accusations against Arlo, now more convinced than ever that he'd sexually harmed every child on Maple Street. Child Protective Services would be back. With the hole getting filled in the morning, they'd lose their last chance at clearing his name. Probably, Arlo would go to jail. Just as likely, Gertie would get charged with attacking Larry. Linda Ottomanelli claimed to have been watching through her window. She told the police that she'd seen Gertie strike her own son and then start screaming about it, as if shocked.

Arlo had suffered a broken cheekbone and jaw. It would have to be wired shut. A liquid diet for the next three months. Also, three broken ribs and a punctured lung. But he'd live, and that was something. After seeing him, they'd visited Larry, who was still sedated.

While Gertie'd been at the hospital, Bianchi had gotten a search warrant for both the Schroeder and the Wilde houses. They'd searched everything, but neither the gun nor the lockbox with the phone in it were found. In the morning, she was

421

expected at Bianchi's office to talk more. He would probably take her side. He was a reasonable person. But that might not be enough.

For now, she sat in the bed, too tired to move. She'd slept in crappy hotels a lot growing up. Had always hated them. The air-conditioning spewed dry air, and the carpet smelled like cats, and the bedcover was coarse. She'd come full circle. All these years she'd spent, trying to break free from her old life, and here she was again, in a hotel room with a twelve-year-old girl. Hardly a penny to her name.

She got up with a grunt. Walked slow. Pulled back Julia's sheets. "Move over," she said. Then she spooned Julia, and Julia clutched back, sighing out the deepest of sighs.

Late night. Julia waited beside her softly snoring mother. The air-conditioning whined its strange sound. She got up ever so slowly.

She sneaked out. There wasn't anybody to follow. No annoying little brother, asking what she was doing, holding his Robot Boy. Just the dark, and the street outside, where the only passersby were the kinds of people you see in East New York. White-mouthed junkies and streetwalking women.

She wore her good shoes. It was two miles to Maple Street.

It got quieter once she returned to the residential neighborhood. Cars didn't screech as much when they turned. There were more trees. She kept walking, and it got even quieter. You couldn't hear the insect night song, and you didn't see possums in the streets or raccoons raiding garbage cans. You didn't hear squirrels and no tree branches shook overhead.

By the time she got to Maple Street, it was nearly dawn. Because of the brownouts, the grudging streetlamps surrounding the park shone soft yellow. It seemed normal until you got to Sterling Park, where light both absorbed into and reflected against the tar sands, making the whole area glow.

No one was out here, even though they'd agreed to meet. But that was fine. Better, even. She preferred to do this on her own.

She passed her empty house. It looked foreign, like it had never belonged to her. She kept walking, averted her eyes. It felt too haunted. And maybe there'd still be her dad's blood on the driveway out front.

She crossed the pudding stone periphery of the park. At first it was sticky grass, and then it was just oil. The closer she got, the more she felt that something was out there. Not a person. A thing. The listening thing.

When she got halfway, something bright flew, blinding her. The light swung away. "It's me," Charlie loud-whispered. Then he cupped the flashlight under his chin. It made him look scary.

A lump expanded in Julia's throat. His presence made this real. He came over, stood close. Offered his hand. She took it. Then he swung the light to his left, illuminating Dave Harrison and the sinkhole behind. Dave looked like always, only more so: angry and frustrated and vibrant. He'd been a good match for Shelly.

They were closer to the hole than she'd thought. It had grown too gaping for a giant wood cover, and parts were exposed. She could see bright things atop the pitch. These were tools for the excavation, but in the glow they looked like bones.

In the quiet, more human sounds. Charlie shined his light on four more kids standing along the half-lit dark: Mark and Michael Ottomanelli, Lainee Hestia, Sam Singh, and even little Ella Schroeder. Pinched face and light brown hair, she wore all black like a widow.

"You told them?" Julia asked, letting go of his hand.

"They want to help," Charlie said.

"They can't help. They suck!" Julia hissed.

"Your dad had a gun!" Lainee Hestia cried. Lainee was in pajamas that said MAY THE FORCE BE WITH YOU, and the shirt and shorts were raining pink stormtrooper heads.

"Fuck you! You stup—"

"We took it back. We said it's not true," Michael Ottomanelli, the mean twin who'd once said she had food line feet, interrupted. "We all did. We took it back."

"You took it back? Your dad was beating on my dad! He broke his jaw. My brother's got a concussion!"

"It's not our fault," Lainee said. "You can't blame us for stuff we got tricked into saying."

"Let us help, Julia," Sam said.

"Go home," Julia answered.

"I'm sorry," Mark Ottomanelli said. He was crying. "I tried to tell my parents. They didn't listen."

"Go home," Julia said.

Then everybody was talking over everybody else. Lots of words Julia didn't care to hear. Words of regret and conviction and justification. Words of wounded pride and childish words. Words and words. At last, she covered her ears until they stopped.

"This doesn't belong to you. I'm going down there to prove my dad didn't do it. When I bring her back, you'll be the ones who go to jail because you lied and I'll be the one who laughs."

Pinched, tattletale Ella Schroeder spoke for the first time. "It doesn't belong to you, either."

Julia had no answer to that.

Mark cried harder. Sobbing and slurping. Then Michael started in.

"They're sorry," Charlie said. "Let them help."

Julia looked away, so she didn't change her mind and feel sorry for them.

"She's my sister," Ella said.

"Yeah," Julia let out.

"Was," Ella added.

"We don't know that." Even as Julia whispered it, she knew it was wishful thinking.

"We were all friends with her. Even before you came, Julia," Lainee said.

Julia tried to keep it together, but now she was crying, too. "If somebody gets hurt you'll blame me. You're just here to get me in trouble. Then your parents'll stomp on *my* face, too."

"I don't tell anymore," Ella said. "I'm here for my sister."

Mark was still blubbering. Everybody stood

close. By flashlights and cell phone lights, she could see their intense faces, assembled in a semicircle. She wanted to hate them.

"We're not our parents," Dave said. "Neither was Shelly. We need to do this together. The Rat Pack."

She looked from one kid to the next. She didn't forgive them. She didn't think she could trust them. But how could she stop them? "Fine," she said.

They went to the edge, the place from which they'd seen the rescue crew descend. Dave bent down first. Then the rest. Somber as pallbearers, they lifted the slab's edges and wrenched up stakes. Chemical candy apple wafted as they eased the giant thing to the side, leaving a small opening through which to squeeze. Inside the deep hole, the ladder rungs disappeared into nothing. They'd heard and read that hydraulic shoring went down to the bottom. Beyond that was the small, metal tunnel that narrowed into something impassable, at least for an adult.

Julia looked each of them over: Charlie, Dave, Ella, Lainee, Mark, Michael, and Sam. All earnest. All here to right a thing that had gone so very wrong. None of them remotely resembling their parents.

She climbed inside the hungry hole.

One by one — Charlie, Dave, Mark, Michael, Lainee, Sam, and Ella — followed.
Down.
Down.
Down.
Into the murk.

118 Maple Street

Monday, August 2

The police searched Rhea's house, leaving no bottle unturned. They found nothing.

Instead of leaving for his office or hiding out in his basement once it was all over, Fritz stuck around. He watched out the dining room window, and he made phone calls, his voice hushed. He knocked on Ella's door. Then, in muffles she couldn't hear, was afraid to listen for, he spoke to FJ. At some point, FJ broke down. Rhea heard him crying. Heard Fritz whisper, "I'll take care of it."

She understood then, that Fritz was plotting. That's why he'd followed her to the police department. He was setting the grounds for their divorce.

She retreated to her office with her wine. Locked the door. With nothing else to do, she went over all the stored things. The dissertation she'd wanted to turn into a book about the panopticon. In her memory it had been brilliant, but upon inspection this was not the case. She'd written it before her father's death, though it was evident a part of her had known, even before the final, grand mal seizure, that he was a drunk.

She looked up what had happened to Aileen Bloom. She'd become a professor, just like Rhea. She'd taught first at the University of Washington, but they didn't give her tenure, so she'd moved to smaller school upon smaller school, and now she was an adjunct at an online university. She mocked her students' stupidity in online posts, which a large portion of her following thought was funny. Her teaching reviews were mostly negative. She graded too hard, and kept trying to teach Bertrand Russell to remedial teenagers.

This was the loser who'd ruined her life.

She looked up Jessica, but then stopped, afraid to learn that the child had died. So instead, she looked up Larry Wilde. Saw pictures of him from various feeds. A newborn. A toddler. A Little Leaguer who never got off the bench. An uncomfortable feeling rushed over her, similar to the feeling of prey when it's watched by a predator. She thought about how strange it was, that Gertie had done such a horrible thing to him in the night.

Who would hurt a child like that? Why?

She remembered her dad driving her home from school in a swerving car, feeling so safe. She remembered watching the sci-fi channel with him, each drinking from separate Coke cans. She remembered the first time he'd shaken, his arm going tight to his chest in a palsy, eyes open but unseeing. They'd been watching *The Black Hole*. She'd been four or five years old. They'd been talking about time travel, pushing through one side, becoming infinitely dense, and then coming out the other side, clean and new. *If you think about it like cellular teleportation, it's purifying. Time and distance are the same,* he'd told her. *The farther away you get from an event, the easier it is to fold it back on itself, to change it.*

And then her dad's body had seized. She'd tried to wake him. He'd been rigid, his arm fastened to his chest, fingers locked in bent positions like claws. His skin frozen in a grimace. It had gone on long enough that she'd had time to look back at the TV. A spaceship was riding through the hole. Bright flashing lights smeared all together into infinite, rainbow density, and then darkness. Meaningless and murk. The sins of the world. And then it transgressed, through heaven and hell and then back again, to before it

431

had all begun. The ship survived. Pristine now. New.

When her dad woke, he didn't remember. He acted as if it had never happened. He smiled at her, and she'd seen a godlike glow all around him. So bright. And she'd known that she'd harnessed time. She'd pulled away from the earth and traveled through a black hole. When she'd come through the other side, she'd entered them both into a new reality. She'd saved his life. His seizure had taught her that she was special.

Years passed. She remembered the school nurse noticing her wrinkled clothes that she didn't know how to wash, her knotty hair, and asking, *Is something wrong at home?* and thinking, *Of course. Why else would I be here every day?* But instead asking, *What could be wrong?* She'd meant this question seriously. Because she hadn't lived anyplace but with her father, so how could she know? *Seriously,* she'd wanted to ask. *Explain to me. What could be wrong?*

She grew up and forgot, the way all adults forget about magic. And then her dad died. She should have been there with him on that couch when it happened. She should never have moved away. She knew it was magical thinking, the illusions of a child; and yet magical thinking imprints. It leaves a mark, a binary of real and unreal that never goes away. On one hand, her dad was a drunk who raised her in a vacuum of neglect. On the other, he was the hero she'd abandoned and could have saved.

She remembered Aileen at the Hungarian Pastry Shop that day, smug. Aileen with her perfect future and her perfect family from Connecticut and her fancy Tory Burch cashmere sweaters. Aileen, catching Rhea out as broken in ways Rhea herself had never guessed. The way she'd look at her, so smug, Rhea wondered if the murk around her was visible. If people who looked closely, who hated her enough, could see it.

She'd wanted to travel again. Expunge herself. But it had been so long that she didn't remember how. With a woman as special as Rhea, the murk built up, a force all its own.

She remembered going blank after entering that bathroom. When she woke, she'd been sitting on the floor with a sprained knee, across from a bleeding young girl.

She remembered sitting with Gertie, confessing so much. Her words, every one, a gasp for breath from a drowning woman. And then Gertie'd seen her for what she was. She'd seen the dirty murk monster inside her. She'd pushed Rhea back down into it.

Tried to drown her. Rhea'd had no other option but to fight back.

She remembered the way Shelly had always watched her, as if seeing what she could not. What she would never see. The holes. The missing things that made her incomplete, and the murky things that made her disgusting. The wrong things in a house of wrong. She remembered a brush, a thrumping into the quiet, to contain those revelations. To hold them still.

She remembered smashing her daughter's Pain Box against the wrong person's head.

These memories came at her like gunshots and she saw clearly, what she was and what she had done. She saw herself as something knotted and too large. A raging thing. She and the murk were the same. It was time to unburden. If she could not do it the one way, through time, she would do it the other way. She must confess.

She considered doing this. Today. She imagined Bianchi in his midpriced suit, hiding his grin. She imagined Gertie, at last given permission to retaliate, screaming at Rhea, the veins in her graceful neck taut as a barking dog's. She pictured all of Maple Street, pointing and whispering. Her house would be like a prison. She'd sit center, the object of all that opprobrium.

Your fault, they would say.

But it wasn't true. It wasn't her fault. Someone else had done this.

A wave of terror bathed her. This was too much. She preferred the nothing. The murk unfurled then, heavy and glistening. It swallowed her.

She blinked, wet-eyed, over the papers and photos before her. Did not recognize them, or remember having brought them out. Put them away and stood. Left her office and turned out the light.

116 Maple Street

Monday, August 2

Gertie woke to a strange, empty room. She oriented quickly. Found the note on the nightstand. It read:

Gone to get Shelly.

She put on her shoes, brushed her hair, put it in a ponytail, and washed her face. Invented these ablutions as a means of keeping calm. Of taking a breath and staving off panic. She didn't want to collapse again.

She got her keys and her wallet. Her phone. She called Detective Bianchi even though the sun had only started to rise. "Julia sneaked out. She's at the hole looking for Shelly, I think. I'm going there now."

Then she got on the road, back to Maple Street.

Sterling Park

Monday, August 2

Those with lights shined Julia's path. It reminded her of those movies they showed in woodshop class — archaeological digs in faraway places, exposed to modern air for the first time in thousands of years. The smell thickened with acid sweetness. The walls were vast, stretching far wider than the hole's mouth, and honey-combed by the wear of composite metals. To prevent collapse, hydraulic steel barriers shored the hole's wide sides. These appeared sturdy, mechanical, and clean, even though bitumen seeped over the steel and red-painted pistons that ran the length between them and held them in place. The ladder ran down along the middle.

She was wearing her dad's Hawaiian shirt again. It felt like a kind of synchronicity. Like going back in time. Her Toms sneakers went *squish-squish*. She got to the bottom where the ladder ended on a ledge, made room. The rest came down. They shined their phones. The water was ice cold and ankle deep.

Just a single path led downslope and they followed it, leaving the dawn behind. They went deeper, beyond the safety of the hydraulic barriers that prevented cave-in. Like bats, they could feel the hollow up ahead before they saw it: an absence. Their lights shined the path — a black, scaffolded shoring tunnel, made just for people to walk single file. They knew intuitively that it wasn't big enough to prevent cave-in, but if the walls gave way, it might protect them long enough until someone found and rescued them. The tunnel was about two feet deep with springwater because the dredge they'd used to keep it clear was gone, the hole slated for fill later today. Straight ahead through the tunnel was the only direction to go.

"Here," Charlie said, pointing. "It's a current."

"So, let's follow," Dave said, serious and awed.

Julia walked atop the tunnel's steel girding that led to cool water. Girding was above, too — narrow steel beams like an animal cage. She grazed a top bar with her shoulder and it was ice cold.

Squish-splash. She went down for maybe five hundred feet. She could hear only the single-file splashing behind her, and the rushing of water. At last, the girding beams ended. Nothing was shored. All that was left was an unsupported tunnel of dirt and sand that weaved beneath Sterling Park. They shined their lights into the last section, where the water was higher and the tunnel much smaller. The current pulled them toward it.

If there was a cave-in here, nothing would save them.

She braced herself, holding to the last of the steel girding. Her thighs and toes were numb. Her heart pounded hard. She kept hoping her body would get tired, forced into calmness by exhaustion. For how long can a person stay so *wired*?

"This could cave in," she said. "People should only keep going if they want to." She looked back at them, let the light blind her, so they could see her face. So they could know that she forgave them whatever they'd said or done. They didn't have to prove anything.

She forged ahead. They followed.

Deep water. The current dragged her and she ran-swam. So cold. Rushing sounds, and also a distant hum she couldn't place

— like the rhythmic shaking of trees in a heavy wind.

She felt the others splashing nearby. They arrived at a crevasse, through which all the water rushed. On a ledge, something reflected the flashlight. She picked up a depth gauge — that last, specially small diver must have left it. This must have been where the diver had stopped and given up. The crevasse was narrow and long and submerged under freezing water. Virgin territory, it was made for people with small hips and shoulders. People not yet fully grown. A part of the earth no human but Shelly had ever known.

The depth gauge read something impossible: *1,000 feet.*

She'd read and heard that the deepest parts of the lowest Lloyd Aquifer went down 1,800 feet. Could Shelly be that far down? If the trained, professional adults hadn't found her, how could they possibly do it?

Even as she reached her hands through the tight gap and held her breath, she understood that this was insane. Foolish and in some ways, selfish. But she couldn't go back. She'd either surface with a body, or not at all.

She took the deepest of breaths, silently whispered the briefest of prayers (*Please*).

Then underwater. Her arms went through first, catching purchase of soft rock. She tried to squeeze her head and shoulders through but had the angle wrong. She pulled back out. Breathed again. Submerged. Pushed through again. This time her head went first, tender and vulnerable to whatever waited on the other side.

Breath held, she wriggled. Everything felt tight, the surrounding walls of sand and tar and dirt unstable like they might crash down. Still holding her breath, still underwater, she pushed her shoulders. Easier. Then the rest. Small, child hips. She shimmied, bound tight as a worm, her shoulders doing the work. Sound took a long time to echo through water. She could feel life behind her — her friends. They felt so far away.

She burst through. Out! Her lungs still full of air, she went buoyant, carried by water to the top. She burst up, gasping into a wide-open space.

A current ferried her. She worked not to panic. Not to struggle and drown. Just to stay on her back, breathing, and let herself be carried, as surely Shelly must have been carried. She could see only with her hands and her breath, and the hairs on her arms.

The current brought her to an enclosed shallows where she was able to stand. The water rushed past her, knee deep. This was a kind of chamber. She could feel but not see the walls, the center where the water rushed and seemed to drain. There was a flapping; that tree sound in wind only much louder. The room oscillated, and in the dark, it was hard to tell what was happening.

One by one, the rest appeared. Phones recovered and wiped clean, they shined their lights, illuminating the enclosed crescent where everything above seemed to have dragged down. The shallow current rushed past the ledge and down, gathering depth as it pooled in the middle of the high-ceilinged room, a pile that moved. The water drained down.

She placed the rhythmic tree-shaking sound, at last. It was the sound from which the crescent had been bereft all summer. The sound that defined East Coast summer: cicadas. They'd swarmed down here, instead of above.

The movement, yes, the movement. This room was alive.

Ella shined her phone on a bird beside Julia's sneaker, flapping its wings, trapped in tar. And then more phone lights. They lit up this closed, dead-end chamber and Julia could see hundreds of flapping things beneath the shallow stream, all trapped in dense tar: birds and squirrels and possums. Cicadas, too. Seventeen-year and thirteen-year broods and annuals. Every size and breed. They were stuck to the center pile and to the walls and even the ceiling by tar, their bodies glimmering.

Their death made a vibrating hum.

"Is she here?" Dave whispered. Julia turned and Dave Harrison, toughest kid in the Rat Pack, was wiping away tears. "Julia, we have to find her. I *hate* this place. She can't stay here."

Julia started wading, following the water to its deep unknown. She held her Hawaiian shirt and tried not to trample. Pretended these birds and squirrels and household pets were something else. Butterflies in cocoons, about to take flight on a great adventure. It was a field of them, beautiful and terrible.

The sound got louder. A living friction. The current drew her to its inevitable end where it drained, leaving just the living pile, as massive as a killer whale. Shivering and shaking and sick, she scanned the monstrosity. The rest shined their lights. They circled the pile, and yes, even climbed it, despite its wailing pain-song of flapping, mewing struggle.

Shelly.

It was Ella who discovered her on the

opposite side of the pile, halfway up. She recognized her Free People skort. The Wildes' funeral box lay open at her side, a harmonica and a necklace and a Robot Boy and blond hair spilled over her knees.

They had known, of course. There was no way she could have survived. But until now, they had not believed. Shelly Schroeder was dead.

Julia was the first to touch her and she was as cold as the water. The rest followed. They touched her, too, as if to warm her. They wiped away the oil and dirt. They cleaned her arms and legs and face — a thing they could never have done alone, and yet a natural thing to do together. She was cold and still and perfectly preserved. As haunted as she'd been on the morning of the fall.

Shelly Schroeder
Shelly Schroeder.
Shelly Schroeder.
I know what happened to you.

A challenging girl. Smart and kind and fragile and sensitive and wonderful in the ways of wonder. A hero and a villain and a bitch and a savior. Shelly Schroeder, their friend.

They tried to lift her, but the murky pile held her tight. Like cement, it had hardened. But it was Julia and Ella and Charlie and

Dave and Mark and Michael and Lainee and Sam, all pulling. Some were scared to touch her, weeping and mewing along with the trapped animals as they did it, but none-theless doing it.

The muck held tight.

Julia thought about the listening thing that she'd *felt* all summer. The thing she'd no-ticed from the very first time she'd come out to the sinkhole. Not a dog. The thing that lived in absence. The lonely thing. It was here now. This was its terrible home, where it trapped the weak and the broken. Because this was Shelly, she lost her fear of it. All that remained was her fury against it.

"You can't have her!" she shouted.

They pulled again but Shelly did not come free. And then they all shouted it, so loud it echoed through the entire chamber. It pushed out the tunnel and up the hole. It reverber-ated through Sterling Park. It entered base-ments and blasted through windows. It went everywhere, each young Rat Pack voice rec-ognizable and distinct and clarion as nothing had been before or ever would be after.

"YOU CAN'T HAVE HER!"

The sound loosened the pile. It shook the chamber and rattled the crevasse. It sent the metal ladder and shoring apparatus singing. It moved even the hole.

Shelly came free.

They plucked her from the murk as if from a watery womb. They carried her out, all hands lifting, even as the secret chamber began to cave. It shriveled upon itself, collapsing in animal screams. As they sped, the crevasse opened for them, liked wilted tulip petals off a bloom, and they were not afraid.

Later, authorities would insist that the children's collective weight had broken the tunnel's soft ground, or that their shouting had resculpted the sensitive architecture of the chamber. The children would agree to this, without promoting their own interpretation, that the sinkhole submitted to them, because they had won.

They ferried her back to the opening, as gently as they'd have carried their own bare hearts.

118 Maple Street

Monday, August 2

"You can't have her!"

Rhea Schroeder woke to those words, and *knew*. It wasn't a psychic connection. It wasn't a mother's love, though these things did exist. It was simply that she'd known all along that Shelly would be found. Just like that girl, on the floor of the bathroom, her scalp running red.

She'd meant only to hurt herself in the women's room of the Hungarian Pastry Shop. To kick hard enough to split herself in two. To frighten Aileen, who'd have stayed safe inside her locked stall. She'd have left after that. Returned to her seat and pretended to have been there all along.

In another world, that happened. In another world, she got over her dad's death. His betrayal, too. She moved on and dated one of those passionate grad students from her class. Her life was clean and perfect in that other world.

But Rhea slammed too hard against the cheap stall door with its sharp metal corners. The lock broke. The small person sitting inside must have been leaning down, head parallel to her hips.

Rhea had yelped in pain as she'd fallen, and then she'd been on the floor, her knee too tender to bend. So she'd scooted against the wall. She'd closed her eyes against the thing inside the half-open stall. The girl's ebony hair, immobile as a wig. Not Aileen Bloom. An accident. The wrong girl. Bright red ran out, adhering to grout around the baby-blue tiles.

People crammed the women's room. The mother came first. And then more, including Aileen and the rest of the class. They'd seen Rhea, some running straight for her, to tend to her. Her kneecap had floated just off center. And then they'd seen the blood.

Jessica Sherman.
Who did that to you?

Gertie Wilde was just parking her car in front of her house when she heard Julia's voice: "You can't have her!" More young voices followed, all saying the same thing: *You can't have her!*

The sound resonated. It roused Dominick and Linda Ottomanelli, who hadn't been

448

sleeping anyway. They'd decided that Arlo wasn't really hurt. Just like Gertie and the brick, he was being hysterical. They'd decided they'd done the right thing in defense of their twins. And yet, they couldn't sleep.

It woke Sai Singh, Nikita Kaur, and their children who were seriously considering moving to Jackson Heights, where it wasn't nearly so upwardly mobile but at least you weren't the only South Indians on the block. And these Americans were fucking drama queens.

It woke Cat, Rich, and Helen Hestia, who'd stayed inside during the beating, and now felt they'd shirked their moral responsibilities. So Rich and Cat had drafted a letter to the *New York Times* about the mistreatment their daughters had likely received at Arlo Wilde's hands.

It woke Sally and Margie Walsh, who'd begun to wonder if they'd gotten carried away by all this child abuse talk.

It woke Tim and Jane Harrison, who forgot about the Sharpie line when they exited their divided house, smearing it as they walked.

It woke Adam Harrison, whose best friend, FJ, had cowed him into breaking into a veteran's painkillers. What FJ did after that, smashing the mirrors and smearing them

449

with his own waste, hadn't been part of the plan. Adam had been disgusted by it, and by his drunken friend, too. Ever since, he'd popped Oxy at night, just to sleep.

It woke Steven, Jill, Marco, and Richard Ponti. Bolstered by their apparent heroism (they'd taken down a shooter!), they sped out from their house, hell-bent on protecting all of Maple Street from the monsters outside.

It woke FJ and Fritz, who each walked alone and at a different pace toward the hole.

But it did not wake or even startle Rhea, who brought up the rear. She'd been expecting it all along.

On her way, she opened the Benchley mailbox, took out the gun she'd hidden there. As she unlatched the safety, she followed the shouts and the vision in her mind of Shelly's open, knowing eyes.

Sterling Park

Monday, August 2

Julia Wilde. Ella Schroeder. Charlie Walsh. Dave Harrison. Mark and Michael Ottomanelli. Lainee Hestia. Sam Singh. These were the remaining members of the 2027 Maple Street Rat Pack.

The ground filled behind them, the hole narrowing ever smaller. Shelly had to be carried up the ladder. Between the rest of them, this was possible. They made sure not to lower or drop her until they were all out, and when they set her down, they did so carefully.

When they reached the summit, they were no longer alone. Julia was not the last to let go of her dead friend. It was Ella who held tight, her face pressed deep into what remained of her sister's soft, black hair. The Rat Pack surrounded Ella, keeping the adults out, as they knew Shelly would have wanted.

The adults only watched, impotent in this

as they had been in all things before. Ella curled up inside her sister, pulling the dead girl's arms so they wrapped around her. The Rat Pack let this happen for a long time. Long enough that their own sorrow subsided, and they could be of use.

And then they cleaned her, smearing away the last remnants of oil. With hands and grass and their own shirts, they excavated her features while they themselves remained painted and nearly indistinguishable. Slowly, Shelly appeared. Her face, so grown up with strong cheekbones and hollow under-eyes. Her bitten fingernails and long limbs.

They continued to do this until every part of Shelly was revealed.

In the stark presence of a body, everything changed.

The adults saw the care with which Shelly was exhumed by their children. They witnessed the bravery of which their children were capable, and they were awestruck.

They made a second circle around Shelly Schroeder. Mesmerized, Dominick, Sai, and the Ponti men forgot they were supposed to shield Maple Street and in particular, the Schroeders. Or perhaps they simply abandoned that silly plan, faced now with its reality.

Hands in pockets, Rhea limped forward. Once she came closer, the rest did, too. They saw Shelly's sides and back, pristine yet mottled with tiny bruises. They saw, too, that her skort was stained with blood.

"Let me have her," Rhea said, but the Rat Pack would not. Dave and Charlie joined hands, to prevent her from pushing through the child-made link. Ella stayed wrapped inside Shelly. Rhea limped, circling to the weakest of them. She pushed through Mike and Mark Ottomanelli. Shelly's shirt was lifted, her skort hiked up. Visible: horsehair brush bruises and pricks, still scabbed and never, ever healed.

Ella extricated herself at last. Her expression was agony. "You did this."

Rhea fell, her knees buckling just like that time years ago.

"You hit her with the brush. I was with her that morning. She was too sad to stay in the house. That's why she ran out so early. It had nothing to do with Mr. Wilde and you know it."

Rhea tried to stand. She pressed her hands to the earth, grunting. The Rat Pack watched her. The grown-ups watched her. Fritz and FJ and all the rest. All eyes. Slowly, she stood. She gazed upon Shelly. Not sleeping. Not trapped in time.

She screamed, as she had screamed last time. Howling and awful. The sound reverberated down the hole. It pounded against the earth and sky, shattering and augmenting in a hungry loop.

The people of Maple Street heard, and this time they knew the answer to the question they had been asking all summer: *Shelly Schroeder. Shelly Schroeder. What happened to you?*

They understood the scream for what it was.

They made a wide path for Rhea as she staggered away from her daughter's body, beseeching once again. No one wanted to be near her. To touch her. Way in the back, some were startled to see Fritz taking hold of FJ, as if to shield him. But mostly, they saw Rhea. Her mouth opened wide, an intolerable pain-wail emitting from and through her.

She walked through the crowd that parted for her.

At last, she came to the back. To Gertie Wilde, who did not budge.

"Rhea," Gertie said.

Rhea's stark and terrified expression went still. She stopped screaming, and at last there was quiet.

"This is the worst thing," Gertie said.

"You and Arlo did this," Rhea said, loud, for all to hear.

"I'm so sorry, honey. I feel so bad for you," Gertie answered. And the people of Maple Street at last understood what Gertie had meant when she'd said she was sorry.

Rhea fidgeted inside that heavy pocket and took a closer step.

Gertie didn't know what Rhea carried. Her instincts warned her to protect Guppy and shrink away. But that old conversation had been playing in her mind: *I'd like to talk about it with you, because I know you like Shelly. I know you like me. I know you won't judge . . . God, aren't I a monster?* She'd been thinking, too, about the way she'd shirked in a moment just like this, with Ralph the dog: a body found, over the hole.

Still, these thoughts were not what moved her. What moved her was Julia, who'd gone to such reckless lengths to produce her best friend.

Gertie opened her arms.

Bewildered, Rhea froze, hand in pocket. "It was Arlo," she said, still loud enough for all to hear. "He raped her at sleepovers. You all can see the blood."

"Your daughter is dead," Gertie answered. "There was an accident and now she's dead."

Rhea's breath gulped and gasped as if she were drowning. "She's not dead. She's in the murk. I have to find a way to the other side," she said. And then she heard herself, recognized all the eyes on her, and looked ashamed. "It was Fritz," she said. "He did it. He hit her. He raped her. And Dom Ottomanelli, too."

"Rhea, she's dead. Your daughter is dead."

Panting, Rhea clutched her throat as if some living thing were caught inside it. "She's not dead. She doesn't know I'm sorry so it's not permitted."

Gertie was crying, too. It wasn't just for Rhea, but for Shelly, and for her own children. "Of course she knew," Gertie said. "They always know."

Rhea took her hand out of her pocket, holding on to nothing. Gently, careful of Guppy, she pressed herself inside Gertie's arms. Gertie held her. The women remembered that they'd once been friends.

"I'm so sorry," Rhea cried, tears falling.

"Shhh," Gertie whispered back. "Don't think about that. Don't think about anything but Shelly."

"My baby. I'd die to have her back," Rhea said.

"I know," Gertie said.

"Oh, Gertie," Rhea wailed, clutching

tighter now, hanging off of tall Gertie Wilde. "It hurts so much."

"I know," Gertie said.

At last, Rhea felt this thing she'd been too afraid to confront. She cried not for herself, or for her secrets, but for Shelly. The people of Maple Street witnessed this, and understood why they'd been watching all this time. They'd needed to be here for this moment. Not to tear down, but to support. They crowded closer, a different and better kind of circle.

And the lonely thing listened. The lonely thing stayed alone.

For Rhea, it was unexpectedly cathartic. Real friendship. A true connection. The unburdening she'd coveted for so long. It felt so wonderful, for the briefest of moments, to be known. To be seen for the monster she was, and nonetheless accepted. It was the truest moment of her life.

But there are some people whose greatest fear is to be known.

FROM *BELIEVING WHAT YOU SEE: UNTANGLING THE MAPLE STREET MURDERS,* BY ELLIS HAVERICK, HOFSTRA UNIVERSITY PRESS, © 2043

For years, the press has participated in widespread scapegoating against the people of Maple Street. They're blamed for their part in both the victimization of the Wildes and for the death of the Schroeder family. Authors like Donovan and Carr use the neighbors' contrition in the aftermath of Shelly's discovery as evidence of guilt. But the people of Maple Street might easily have pitied all parties, regardless of their guilt or innocence. It's a testament to them and to Rhea that they embraced Gertie Wilde rather than ostracizing her.

As Linda Ottomanelli states, "I know that lockbox was found in the Benchley mailbox. And I know the police think Rhea used it against Larry. But I was awake that night. It was my turn for the neighborhood watch. I know what I saw. Gertie hit her own kid."

Steven Ponti agrees. "For a second, I almost changed my mind. I felt really terrible. It almost worked. But then I thought about it. There's no way all of us could have made it up. Sure, Rhea might have hit Shelly once in a while, but what Arlo did to every kid on Maple Street was so much worse. There is no doubt in my mind that I did the right thing. He was guilty!"

Sterling Park

Monday, August 2

All life-changing hugs eventually end. Like a one-night stand between mutually damaged parties, these endings are often awkward. Their authors tend to retreat, giving each some space. So it was with Gertie and Rhea. They let each other go.

After, Nikita Kaur brought a fresh white sheet out from her house and draped it over Shelly's body. This, she fussed with, unsure of whether to wholly cover the child or leave her face exposed. And then again, was it wrong to whitewash her bruises? Conceal, after the children had gone to such efforts to raise her up?

It was Marco Ponti who lifted the sheet over her forehead, leaving just tufts of glossy black hair. It was Sally Walsh who pulled it back, revealing Shelly's high cheekbones and V-shaped chin. "Let her breathe," Sally announced.

There, the sheet remained.

460

The police arrived with the dawn. Detective Bianchi lifted the sheet and peered under. His expression didn't change, though surely he noticed the bruising. Surely it had to have come from the horsehair brush from Paris that her mother had bragged so often about. The nightly sessions the girl had endured, for cornrows and plaits. For long, soft hair as silky as gossamer wings.

Shelly. She'd once flipped lithely on a trampoline.

A blue-striped coroner's van pulled softly into the crescent, wheels rolling over bitumen and pebbles. Doors opened. Shelly was packed into its hold. The doors shut softly. Rhea covered her ears with her palms. Others held their chests or wiped their eyes or bowed.

It was at this point that Fritz approached Rhea. She would not have him. Her ears stayed covered. And so he whispered something inaudible to his son, then drove his Mercedes out of the crescent.

Rhea watched him go, her eyes dull.

Bianchi asked the rest of Maple Street to remain. He took statements from witnesses, including the children. Rhea was seen nearby, pacing large circles around the hole, her body hunched, her gait uneven. The children answered questions with soft

461

voices, parents holding them by their shoulders. Occasionally, they pointed at Rhea.

Last, Bianchi approached Rhea. He stopped her pacing by standing in her path. She bumped into him. They didn't hear the question he asked, only her answer, which she called out loudly. "I think . . . I think someone did that by accident. It wasn't anyone's fault," she said, pointing at the empty ground where Shelly's body had been.

They sat on the bumper of the John Deere out there. The interaction was not climactic. He smiled sometimes, and so did she. He walked her back to her house. She leaned on him. He shut the door. Saw her safely home.

The mystery of Shelly Schroeder was over.

One by one, the people of Maple Street went home. This long, hot summer had caught up to them. A terrible poison had seeped inside their hearts. Expunged at last, the muscle was that much wearier.

118 Maple Street

Alone in the house, Rhea staggered to her bedroom. Flung off worn clothing and stood in the hot shower. Remembered her dad. They used to share this red afghan blanket, her head tucked into the crook of him, feet kicked up and piled next to each other on the old coffee table. She remembered the candy apple smell of him. The safety of a dark room, the TV playing.

She dressed. Saw her reflection. Wild, silver-black hair, complexion greenish from exhaustion and a diet composed mostly of red wine. She winced at the sight, frightening herself. Who was that woman?

She put the gun back into her sweater pocket. It wasn't safe anyplace else. The children might find it. She came down her stairs, each step a white shock of excruciating pain. Her kneecap floated now, removed from its joint.

The children hadn't returned to her. The

house was empty. Where were they?

She looked out from her dining room window. Like birds after a storm, Maple Street chirped softly. She saw FJ out there with the older Harrison boy. They huddled conspiratorially and she knew that he was telling secrets. Badmouthing her. He had a right, of course. Everyone has a right to speak. She tapped her fingers against the glass. He stiffened and looked in the direction of 118, first through her bedroom window and then through the dining room window. Maybe he saw her. Maybe he didn't. He backed up, waving for the Harrison boy to join him.

Julia was out on her stoop. Ella was with her, smiling softly as Julia taught her a hand game:

ABC, My Momma Takes Care of Me
My Papa Drinks Black Coffee
Ohh, Ah, I Wanna Piece of Pie
Pie Too Sweet, I Wanna
Piece of Meat . . .

She would have to collect them soon. Bring them inside and make them eat like any other day. If she wanted, perhaps it could be like any other day. She could come back from this after all. Jail time wasn't likely.

464

Not with a good lawyer. Child Protective Services might come calling, but she'd keep up appearances.

The things she'd done — those bad things — she'd never do them again.

Fritz could be a problem, but she knew how to work him. He needed her, after all. So did the kids. If it made them happy, she'd offer to see a therapist or whatever. Clean out the rotten parts. Become the mom she'd pretended to be — wanted so much to be. She'd do this right. She'd become clean in this best way. Not a magical way. This was her last chance.

She would start today. Right now.

She opened the door. Heat slammed down, along with the scent of sweet bitumen. She started for Ella, knee screaming. Holding a suitcase, Gertie opened her own front door. She didn't smile like she used to, all needy and hopeful. She hardly even nodded.

It occurred to Rhea then that despite their hug, Gertie would not stand by her. Of course she would not. Her husband and son were in a hospital. Rhea had put them there. She and her daughter were living in a motel. As soon as they were able, Gertie Wilde and her family would sell their house and move away. They'd find a new block and new

465

neighbors. Gertie would never speak to her again. Too much ugliness had passed between them. It wasn't possible.

Tomorrow or the next day, Bianchi would return, knocking on doors, taking second statements from the judging people of Maple Street. She would sit center to that judgment. She changed direction and started for Gertie now, to say good-bye. Her knee screamed, and the pain felt so familiar. Like that other time, when she'd knocked down a bathroom door.

Dizzy. It felt like time overlapping.

Gertie set down her suitcase. Whatever she saw in Rhea, she didn't like.

Rhea kept coming, because she had to explain.

She wasn't insane, she would tell Gertie. She knew it was magical thinking, like people who talk about their spirit guides or the power of turmeric. But that day of her dad's convulsion, when the lights had blinked in the dark through a beautiful and infinitely dense space, it had felt so real. It had felt like a promise she'd made to four-year-old Rhea, to never forget. To always believe, even when logic and adulthood told her otherwise. She was special. She'd gone back in time and saved her father. She was not vulnerable. She was not in danger of losing everything because the sole person charged with her welfare was damaged. Her powers would repair him, keep them in this perfect place under a warm blanket, forever.

So many times, when the indignities had mounted — unkind kids teasing her for her hair, which she'd never combed because there'd been no combs in her house; fellow teachers at U-Dub who'd gossiped, calling her weird behind her back; Aileen Bloom, with her Tory Burch sweaters and perfectly coiffed blond hair, whose family had paved for her a perfect future. Her dad, especially her dad, who'd died because she hadn't been around. He'd had no one to pretend for. She'd gone back to that house to clean it out and found it covered in bottles and vomit.

So many times, she'd felt the murk of it accumulate. In her dorm rooms, her studio apartment, her small office nook, she'd tried to go back in time, knowing it wasn't possible, but hoping so very much. She'd wanted to loop through to the past and do it right that second time. She'd brush her stupid, wiry hair that she hated so much. She'd say all the right things when she got teased, turning it around so that everyone loved her. She'd laugh at bitter Aileen Bloom, knowing the woman was beneath her. She'd never enter that bathroom stall. She'd go back in time and save her dad. Make him better, and in doing so, save herself.

She'd come through clean and new.

Hand in her pocket, making sure that gun stayed safe, she limped. Sweating hard. Seeing almost nothing, except for Gertie's terrified expression.

"Hey!" she shouted, and her voice sounded so angry. She tried again, "Gertie! Hey, girl!" she screamed.

A car pulled into the crescent. Fritz's Mercedes. He stopped right in front of her and opened the door. His expression was all wrong, too. He wasn't happy to see her, like he should have been after all she'd done for him. His expression was grim.

"Rhea," he said. *Rhee-a.* "I need to talk to you."

By now, she saw that Maple Street was watching. They came out in doorways or looked through windows. They looked at her like Gertie looked at her. Like Ella looked at her. Like FJ looked at her. Like Fritz looked at her. Like she was not a good person. She had done awful things.

She was disgusting.

Maple Street witnessed what happened next.

Fritz Schroeder got out of his car. He looked irritated and tired. Put upon. Later, they would learn that he'd spent the time away hiring a criminal lawyer, in case either the police department or the Wildes charged Rhea with perverting the course of justice. They'd learn that he'd intended to stand by his wife's side, as he'd done in his limited way since the day he'd met her. But they didn't know that yet. All they saw right then was his apparent disdain.

Perhaps Rhea'd been thinking about it, planning it. Gertie liked to think not. She liked to think it was a fluke. A toss of coin that could have ended in a much better way. Hand in pocket, Rhea veered. Before she ever pulled her hand back out, Gertie knew beyond a doubt.

The distance was close.

Rhea pointed, just like all those years ago with her dad at the Calverton Shooting Range. Fritz saw. Despite that, he kept coming. They met in front of their house. 118 Maple Street. Close enough to touch. Fritz didn't try to stop her.

She was thinking about the divorce. How he'd take the kids. But they needed her. They needed someone who cared about playdates and whether their clothes were stained. They needed someone who cheered

469

at soccer and lacrosse and who went over their spelling tests. They wouldn't have any of that. He'd ruin them.

She pushed the barrel of the gun up against his chest. Those watching would imagine meaning in what Fritz did next. They would define it as perfect trust, or as disbelief, or even as true love. This man had placed his life in her hands since the day he'd met her.

"Rhee-a," Fritz said. He moved the butt of the gun just left, so it was over his heart.

She pulled the trigger.

He fell back. Went down. It happened so fast that it didn't feel real. Her ears rang. There was blood. Or water. Or perhaps the dense splatter from a black hole. She knew then that she had control over this. These people, her children and husband and everyone she'd ever loved, they belonged to her. With her mind, she kept them safe.

The sound still ringing, her hands hot, she heard her son, FJ, scream, "Mom! No!"

The boy was in the middle of the street, his eyes bloodshot. An autopsy would show his blood alcohol content at .3 percent, with lesions in his brain from chronic abuse. Like Rhea's father, he'd been born with alcohol-induced epilepsy.

Rhea pointed. He wobbled too much to run. Before he was able to get inside 118 Maple Street, she fired. A miss. He lurched, unable, somehow, to go inside. He headed for another house (which house?), but couldn't decide. She fired again. It lodged in his neck and he went down, too.

The next one. For this to work, she needed them all. Ella was frozen on the Wildes' stoop next to Julia. Rhea pointed and shot. A miss. The second was perfect. Straight through Julia's protective hand, to Ella's head.

Belly heavy and with a sore back, Gertie ran, placing her body between Julia and Rhea. Rhea charged to intercept her, loping and running on one good leg and one useless one. Panting, like two embattled animals, they deadlocked.

For the first time, Rhea saw Gertie for what she was. She was a woman and a mother and a wife and a mediocre Realtor. She was nervous and damaged and she dressed trashy. She was an ordinary slob, who had never offered salvation. She was a friend. Like the ocean before a tsunami hits, the murk receded and everything became clear.

The Black Hole was just a movie, and a crappy one, at that. Her thesis was slightly above average. Her father had been a drunk, not a saint. The sinkhole in the ground was just a hole. The kind that were happening more and more, all over the country. It was not magic. She was not so special, so extraordinary, as to have birthed it from the weight of her own feelings. Those feelings had not stolen the person she loved most, the only person who had ever seen her and still loved her. The person she'd wanted so much to protect and keep close that she'd crippled her: Shelly Schroeder.

She'd made mistakes and then repeated those mistakes. She'd carried them, imagining that they accrued, an infinitely dense stain on her person. But there was no murk. There was no monster. There was only Rhea Schroeder. The woman who'd murdered almost her entire family.

She'd seen patterns where they didn't exist and forced their reiteration. Jessica. Shelly. FJ. Ella. Fritz. Arlo. Gertie. Larry. Maple Street. Any one of her actions against these people was unforgivable, and she'd committed all of them.

"Please," Gertie begged, a sentry in front of her own front stoop.

"Help!" Rhea cried. But there was no changing course now. No possibility for redemption. She'd transgressed a very real event horizon. It engulfed her then. Thick and impossibly heavy, the unbearable wave of murk. It dragged her down and she gave up struggling.

She cocked the trigger. Gertie gasped, her hands protecting her belly while Julia cringed behind her.

Those watching would think that this decision was rooted in mercy, or because she only had one bullet left. She did it because she'd finally figured out how to go back in time and right all the wrongs. How to come out the other side, clean and new and as the loved, and adored, and perfectly special person she'd always wanted to be.

In her mind, Rhea Schroeder was about to enter one of those perfect family photos people send out on Christmas. There was Gretchen, tall and bright. A laser of ambition. There was FJ, cheerful and sweet and searching so hard for some girl to raise on a pedestal and treat like gold. There was Shelly, a smart, pretty pistol who kept them on their toes. There was Ella, Rhea's Mini-Me; serious and snappy and a little bit mean. There was goofy, successful Fritz, so grateful for this life she'd given him. There was a ghost girl from the Hungarian Pastry Shop, small and innocent, caught half in the picture, moving on with her life. There was her father, white-haired and jolly as Santa, always free to babysit. And in the center was Professor Rhea, devoted to all of them, the loves of her life. These were the Schroeders.

Rhea put the gun in her mouth and pulled the trigger.

Maple Street will host a memorial service to-morrow for the Schroeder family at the Dunn and Nally Funeral Home from 9–noon. Those who'd like to send flowers are asked to donate instead to the Maple Street Recovery Fund.

Fritz Henrich Schroeder (62) died yesterday from a gunshot wound outside his home in Garden City. A pillar of the community and longtime resident, he was the vice president of development at BeachCo Laboratories. He was known throughout the neighborhood as a committed father and husband who doted on his children and took them to visit his family in Germany every year. He was also a eucharistic minister at Saint Anne's Church.

Fritz Henrich Schroeder Jr., "FJ," (19) also died from a gunshot wound. A popular student and "One of the best attackers the Garden City lacrosse team has ever known," according to Coach Nolan, FJ was scheduled to attend Hofstra University in the fall on an athletic scholarship. The high school has decided to name the annual lacrosse MVP award after him.

Ella Elizabeth Schroeder (9) also died from a

gunshot wound. Ella attended Stewart School, where she excelled at reading and mathematics.

Shelly Wyatt Schroeder (13) was discovered dead at the bottom of the Maple Street sinkhole. Authorities had been searching for her for weeks.

Rhea Munsen Schroeder (53) died yesterday by suicide after shooting her husband, daughter, and son.

They are survived by Gretchen Schroeder (20).

Coverage of the Maple Street tragedy can be found on pages 1–5, 7, 11, 14, 16.

Filling of the Maple Street sinkhole was completed today. The task took less time than anticipated, as much of the hole and excavation tunnels used in the search for Shelly Schroeder, whose body was found on Monday morning, collapsed. Likewise, cleanup crews will conduct less tar sand remediation than anticipated, as once those tunnels closed, much of the surrounding bitumen resorbed. Says sinkhole expert from Hofstra University Tom Brymer, "Climate change is happening so fast that it's beyond our science. Right now, we can only witness what's happening. We don't yet understand it."

For more on the new preponderance of sinkholes, see page 18. For more on the Maple Street tragedy, see pages 2, 3, 6, 8, and 11.

From *Believing What You See: Untangling the Maple Street Murders,* by Ellis Haverick, Hofstra University Press, © 2043

Finally, we can look for evidence in the Wildes.

Gertie Wilde seemingly suffered no ill effects. She carried her third child to term and delivered without complications. Professionally, she continued in real estate, recently earning a Women of the San Fernando Valley Award in 2040.

Arlo's career was revived by all the attention, particularly after the police department issued a statement in support of his character. He sold a final album, *Blood Arrow,* and went on to teach songwriting at UCLA. He died of hepatitis in December 2037, an infection he contracted from intravenous drug use.

Gertie continues to live in the house they shared in Van Nuys, California. I visited her there. The house is a split-level ranch. There's a white picket fence, but the lawn is untended. Squatters occupy many of the surrounding houses, now that temperatures regularly reach 120 degrees.

Gertie sat across from me on an old couch

478

and spoke between her grandchild's squawks. The child is a two-year-old boy, belonging to Julia Wilde, who lives in nearby Sherman Oaks. Julia works as a social worker for foster children. Larry Wilde dropped out of college to found a video game company in Montreal. Both children declined my requests for an interview, but Larry sent this email:

Dear Sir,
Thank you for your interest in my story. It is not mine to tell. It belongs only to a girl who fell a long time ago.

Sincerely,
Larry Wilde

Gertie wore a low-cut shirt and chunky silver necklace with silver eye shadow that matched. Despite all this time on the West Coast, her Brooklyn accent remained thick. I asked her if she believed Arlo had harmed the Maple Street children and she denied it. I asked her how she could be sure.

"You're the only reporter still schlepping this story of Arlo's guilt. Nobody else who's investigated the case agrees with you. But you're so loud about it that people believe you," she answered. "You kind of remind me of Rhea."

I asked her to clarify.

"You know what's scary? It's not outside."

Gertie pointed at her heart. "It's in here. That's what scared Rhea.

"When I think about Rhea, sometimes I remember this old woman who lived in the apartment next door. She could hardly walk and she was alone most days. One time, I was just too tired. I wasn't myself and I hadn't recovered from my breakdown. But Larry didn't care about that. He was just little. Less than three months. He had spells. And there'd been a snowstorm, so Julia couldn't get to daycare. We were stuck for the second or third day in a row. Sometimes it's just like that. A messy scream of a day. And the thing about Julia was that she was always so worried about me, trying to help and scared I'd fall apart. But then, that made her anxious and difficult, too. It's hard coming from the other side of that, when you're the mom but you don't have such great tools to reassure. You feel bad, and that makes you feel ungenerous.

"I got so frazzled I frightened myself. I went next door to Mrs. Cotton, and I knocked and as soon as she answered I started crying. I looked a mess. She followed me back and she sat and watched while I tried to calm the kids. Entertain them, at least. I wasn't any good at it. I had no experience with it except what I'd made up or read in books. Mrs. Cotton was too old to do anything. She just sat. She hardly even talked. I probably should have fed her. But then it got late and Larry cried himself tired and Julia finally relaxed. I made her some tea and we sat. She hadn't done anything. Just been a body in the room, same thing she'd have done at home, but it helped. I had a witness, I told her that day, that I'd been scared I was going to do something bad to them. I acted like it was the most shameful confession in the world. I was sobbing. And she looked at me like I was crazy. *We all have those days,* she told me.

"After that, she came for every storm. I loved her. And then she moved to a nursing home in Poughkeepsie.

"I think about that lady sometimes, when I think about what happened on Maple Street. I won't pretend to be as smart as her, but Rhea and I were alike in a lot of ways. The difference was, I wasn't as scared to show people my mess."

Gertie broke here, to feed her grandson. She then cranked the generator and turned on a static-riddled screen. Reception on the West Coast is better than most other parts of North America. The child watched, transfixed.

I asked her whether Larry had moved to Canada for a reason.

"The thing is," she said, leaning forward. "Everything's falling apart. The heat's so bad I can't walk in my own neighborhood. Long Island's pretty much underwater, so I guess nobody over there's worried about white trash like me and Arlo lowering property values anymore. Everybody smart moves to Canada. I wish Julia would go, but she's loyal. She won't leave those foster kids. And I won't leave her . . . People talk about how the children of Maple Street suffered after what happened, like it's evidence of what Arlo did. But except for those poor twins, the Rat Pack turned out [okay]. They get together every year. They have a ball. Sam's family keeps complaining about how he stopped playing sports. Who cares? He was the youngest kid to start an LGBTQ club at Garden City Middle School. Dave turned out okay, too. He's a family therapist. Charlie followed Julia out to LA and makes vegan desserts. They're gross but he makes Julia happy, so what does my opinion matter? Lainee manages offices. Larry's earning coin in Montreal . . . The kid could buy all of Garden City if he wanted. What's left of it.

"The thing is, the world's breaking up. Fifteen years ago, we all saw it coming. We still do. Maybe there's even something we can do about it. But it's so much easier to invent boogeymen. That's all we were to Maple Street: boogeymen."

I asked her how she could be sure, 100 percent beyond a shadow of a doubt, that Arlo Wilde had not molested the children of Maple Street, many of whom were now suffering significantly.

"The question is: What evidence would prove to you that he didn't?" she asked.

I left soon after. I think we can clearly read this evasion as an admission of guilt.

FROM *INTERVIEWS FROM THE EDGE: A MAPLE STREET STORY*, BY MAGGIE FITZSIMMONS, SOMA INSTITUTE PRESS, © 2036

"I remember being scared that my parents were going to be taken away. I thought it was my fault. I don't remember the murders. I don't even remember getting hit or being in the hospital. I guess it traumatized me. But I'm not haunted. I don't have flashbacks. The only thing is that I'd never set foot back on Long Island. I can't even say the name of that street out loud . . . Okay, I'm traumatized." — Larry Wilde

"Your first real best friend is almost like a romance. I still miss her. Every day." — Julia Wilde

FROM "THE LOST CHILDREN OF MAPLE STREET," BY MARK REALMUTO, *THE NEW YORKER,* OCTOBER 19, 2037

It's apparent that the Maple Street murders captured the American imagination, but the reason has nothing to do with the spectacle. It's got nothing to do with the parents, who acted predictably, if horrendously. Nothing they did was remarkable.

We remember this story because of the children of Maple Street, who did the unexpected.

In our national discourse, we assume that we've taken wrong turns in our lives, and it is these forks that define us. There is Rhea, and her Jessica Sherman. There is Maple Street, and its brick. There are the Wildes, and their flight from Brooklyn to a hostile land. There is our national chaos, each election worse than the last.

But what if these forks represent nothing? What if there are no patterns, except those we invent? What if we can reach through our own murky histories, and come out cleanly on the other side?

What if, like the Rat Pack of Maple Street, we can break the cycle?

I'll close on this quotation from Grace Paley:

The kids! The kids! Though terrible troubles hang over them, such as the absolute end of the known world quickly by detonation or slowly through the easygoing destruction of natural resources, they are still, even now, optimistic, humorous, and brave. In fact, they intend enormous changes at the last minute.

ACKNOWLEDGMENTS

It's been a while, so I have a lot of people to thank. First to JT Petty, because nobody else would ever do. Thanks to my girls, Clem and Frances, for inspiring what I do. Thanks to all the people who took such good care of my girls over the years: Carole Langan, Susan Knisely, Kate Petty, the folks at Union Temple Preschool, The Co-op School, Wonderland Avenue Elementary, and of course, Marlene Winston.

Thanks to my dad, for holding down the fort, to my brother, Chris, for helping him, and to my uncle Michael, for keeping me in the loop. Thanks to my mom. I wish she was here.

Thanks to Stacia Decker, the smartest, steadiest hand I know. Thanks to Loan Le. I am so lucky. You know what I'm doing better than I know what I'm doing.

Thanks also to the team: Sarah Self (always), Hilary Zaitz Michael, and Circle of

Confusion. Antonio D'Intino, your enthusiasm is contagious, and you time it exactly when I need it. Lawrence Mattis, it's warming to have the first person to visit after Clem was born also steer my career.

Thanks also to the Atria Team: Libby McGuire, Lindsay Sagnette, Suzanne Donahue, David Brown, Megan Rudloff, Maudee Genao, James Iacobelli, Min Choi, Paige Lytle, Jessie McNiel, Liz Byer, Joshua Cohen, and Erika Genova. Wow, are you great.

I've been fortunate to have great friends who are also great writers: the past, present, and future members of the writing group Who Wants Cake, which will forever claim a piece of my heart. Lunch club! Nicholas Kaufmann and David Wellington, for everything. My Los Angeles writing group (Meg Howrey, J. Ryan Stradal, Chris Terry, Sarah Tomlinson), the Directors of the Shirley Jackson Awards (F. Brett Cox, JoAnn Cox, Jack Haringa, John Langan, and of course, Paul Tremblay). Jon Evans. Victor LaValle. Liz Hand. For help when I needed it, Kelly Link, Andrew Pyper, agent and mom extraordinaire Jennifer Carlson, and new LA friends, Kirsten Roeters and David Eilenberg.

Thanks finally to my hometown of Garden City, which hopefully has a good sense of humor.

ABOUT THE AUTHOR

Sarah Langan is a Long Island native, now living with her husband, two daughters, and pet rabbit in Los Angeles.

The employees of Thorndike Press hope you have enjoyed this Large Print book. All our Thorndike, Wheeler, and Kennebec Large Print titles are designed for easy reading, and all our books are made to last. Other Thorndike Press Large Print books are available at your library, through selected bookstores, or directly from us.

For information about titles, please call:

(800) 223-1244

or visit our website at:

http://gale.cengage.com/thorndike

To share your comments, please write:
Publisher
Thorndike Press
10 Water St., Suite 310
Waterville, ME 04901